...pen on...
...he perfect job
...e well as taking art to...
...e is a painter.

Regency Scandals

Regency Scandal:

Scandals of the Past

SOPHIA JAMES

MILLS & BOON

First Published in Great Britain 2021
by Mills & Boon, an imprint of HarperCollins*Publishers* Ltd,
1 London Bridge Street, London, SE1 9GF

www.harpercollins.co.uk

HarperCollins*Publishers*
1st Floor, Watermarque Building,
Ringsend Road, Dublin 4, Ireland

SCANDALS OF THE PAST © 2021 Harlequin Books S.A.

Ruined by the Reckless Viscount © 2017 Sophia James
The Dissolute Duke © 2013 Sophia James

ISBN: 978-0-263-29945-8

MIX
Paper from
responsible sources
FSC™ C007454

This book is produced from independently certified FSC™ paper to ensure responsible forest management.

For more information visit: www.harpercollins.co.uk/green

Printed and bound in Spain
by CPI, Barcelona

RUINED BY THE RECKLESS VISCOUNT

Chapter One

⁓⁓⁓⁓⁓⁓

London—1810

The door of the approaching carriage opened as it stopped beside her in a sudden and unexpected haste.

'Get in now.'

'I beg your pardon.' Lady Florentia Hale-Burton could not quite believe what she had heard even as the stranger standing above her on the top step of the un-liveried coach repeated it again more loudly.

'I said get in now.'

The man frowned when she did not move and leaned forward so that his face was not far from her own. A beautiful face, like an angel, she thought, though his voice held no notes of the celestial at all.

'Look, unlike your long-suffering paramour, I am not up to playing this silly game of yours, madam. If you don't get in this minute I will drag you inside and be done with it. Do you understand?'

'I will do no such thing, sir. Of course I will not.' Finding her voice, Florentia looked about wildly for some help from her maid, Milly, but the girl had dropped back, her mouth wide open in alarm as she turned to run. It was like some dream, Flora thought, the horror of it appalling, like a nightmare where no matter how much you wanted to escape you could not. Fright held her simply rigid. The sky was grey and the day was windy. She could smell cut grass and hear birds calling from the park across the road. An ordinary Wednesday on a walk she had done a hundred times before and now this...

As the stranger stepped down from the carriage and took her arm she finally found resistance, swinging her heavy reticule at his face and connecting with a thump. The two books inside the bag were weighty tomes on the history of art, leather bound and substantial. The edge of one cut into the skin above his right eye and blood gushed down his cheek, though instead of looking furious, which might have been expected, he only began to laugh.

'Hell,' he said, 'Thomas damned well owes me for this though he did warn me you might not come easily if he was not present. But enough now. We are beginning to attract some attention and if I am going to be of any help to you we have to leave immediately.'

Grabbing at her, he pulled her hard against his body and she bit into his hand. Swearing, he brought one arm down across her breast when she screamed as loud as she could manage. Then he simply clamped his fingers on the top of her right shoulder and all she knew was darkness.

James Waverley, Viscount Winterton, couldn't believe he was doing this, kidnapping his cousin's whore before Hyde Park and rendering her unconscious. But

Tom had insisted, pleaded, cajoled and finally called in any favour James had ever promised. So he had.

'She's a feisty one, you will find,' his second cousin had insisted, 'and if I was in any position at all to go and get her myself I would, but...' He'd looked down at his leg cast from the ankle to the thigh. 'She needs to be out of London, Winter, needs to be safe from those who might hurt her.' And because one of his own unruly horses was responsible for his cousin's broken leg, James had consented.

'What does she look like?'

'Blonde and sensual. She will be wearing red, no doubt, as she always does and will be waiting on the corner of Mount Street opposite Hyde Park at five o'clock precisely.'

Lord help me, James thought. Tom hadn't mentioned that she would be the type to scream her head off in fury or whack him with a heavy bag full of books.

She didn't have the appearance of a whore either, with her demurely cut pink and red day dress and old-fashioned hat, but then what was the look of one? He'd never required the services of a lady of the night before, though he had seen them around Covent Garden and the Haymarket and many of them had appeared... quite ordinary. Perhaps Acacia Kensington was one of those girls, thrown into the game by dire circumstance and the need to survive.

She certainly had good teeth. The bite mark on his hand stung badly having cut the skin to leave it swollen and throbbing.

Laying her down on the seat opposite, he took off his jacket and placed it under her head as a pillow. She'd wake up soon and there would be all hell to pay, the journey north taking a good few hours to complete. With a frown he looked away.

Is this who he was now? A man who would hurt a woman? A man who might take the path of least resistance when quite plainly it was the wrong thing to do?

Swearing, he sat back and glanced out the window. A young maid was running along the pathway and shouting at the top of her lungs, another couple joining her. When the man raised his hand in a fist the first shudder of things not being quite as they ought to be went through him and he was glad when the carriage turned into the main road north, its speed increasing.

The blood from the cut above his right eye had begun to blur his vision and he swiped at it with the sleeve of his jacket, blotting the redness against dark linen.

Thomas could do his own courting next time, broken leg or not, he thought, and if the girl came to as angry as she had been he didn't quite know what he would do next. Put her out, he imagined, and let her make her own way from London, or not. In truth he didn't care any longer.

She had a damn expensive ring on the third finger of her right hand, the diamonds winking in the light. No false gold or cut glass either, the patina and shape of the piece telling him this was the real thing. Perhaps a paramour had gifted it to her. Tommy had the funds to procure such a bauble, should he have wished it, so maybe this was his doing. He was a man inclined to the grand gesture.

The anger that had been his constant companion threatened to choke him and he pushed back the familiar fury. Once he would have told his cousin exactly where to go with his hare-brained schemes of procuring women, but now…

The war had knocked the stuffing out of him and he had returned from Europe and the first Peninsular Campaign unsettled. He did not fit in here any more, having neither property nor much in the way of family, save a father who had taken more and more to the drink. He wanted to be away from the London set and its expectations, but most of all he needed to be away from the brutality of war. It had settled into him the aftermath of violence, making him jumpy and uncertain, the ghosts of memory entwined even in the ordinariness of his life here.

He swore again twenty moments later as sky-blue eyes opened and simply looked at him, the paleness of her cheeks alarming.

'I think… I am going…to be…sick.'

And she was, all over his boots and on her dress, heaving into the space between them time after time and shaking dreadfully. Her eyes watered, her nose ran and the stench of a tossed-up lunch hung in the air as she simply began to cry. Not quietly either.

Banging his cane against the roof, James was glad as the conveyance drew to a halt, the countryside all around wide and green, the road empty before them and behind. He didn't stop her hurried exit as he threw water he carried for the journey on to the carriage floor, drying what he could with great bunches of wild grasses pulled from the side of the road.

She was gone when he had finished, disappeared into a tract of bushes behind a stone fence. He caught the hue of her red gown at some distance dashing between the trees of a small grove.

Part of him wanted to simply leave her there and go on, but it was getting late and dusk would soon be upon the land. If she fell into a ditch or in with the company of someone who might really hurt her...

Cursing again, he bade Thomas's driver to wait for him and went in after her.

Florentia ran from tree to tree, her breath ragged as the asthma she had had since childhood came upon her with this unexpected exertion.

She was crying and running and trying to draw in breath, sharp branches tearing at her gown and at the exposed skin on her arms and legs.

Would her kidnapper follow? Would he kill her? Would he chase her and trap her here in the woods and the oncoming darkness and so very far from London?

She tripped and went down hard, then got herself up again, the pathway more difficult to discover now, the sound of a stream further on and dogs.

Dogs? Her heart leapt in her throat. Big dogs? The horror of it kept her still, the sound of crashing feet drawing nearer as two enormous black and brown hounds padded out from a break in the undergrowth and came towards her, lips bared and teeth showing.

'Keep very still.' His voice. The man from the carriage. Raw. Brutal. Furious. He sounded as though he would like to kill her along with the canines though the hackles of each dog were raised along bony spines, ready to spring.

He'd stooped to pick up a few of the bigger stones around his feet and threw one hard and fast. A direct hit to the flanks had the lead dog crouching down and slinking backwards. Two long scars at the back of her abductor's head were easily visible in the fading light. She wondered how anyone could have survived such wounds as that.

'Get back, damn it.' His words seemed to be having some effect as the second dog followed the other.

'Walk slowly towards me.' This was directed at her now. 'Don't run. They are hunting dogs trained to protect and defend. Any quick movement will have them upon you and my pistols are still in the carriage.'

'You…would…shoot them?'

He laughed at that, a harsh and savage sound. 'In an instant, were I armed and they were attacking. Now do as I say.'

She did because just at that moment the slobbering teeth of the hunting pair were infinitely more worrying than the possibility of this stranger hurting her. Again. She was pleased when he stood before her shielding her from the threat. 'Now, walk backwards, keeping my body in a direct line with the dogs. Don't make eye contact with them. Don't trip. Look as if you are in charge until you get through the green shelter at the edge of the clearing and then turn and run for the carriage as fast as you can go and get straight in. Do you understand me?'

'And…what…of…you?'

'I will be fine.'

He picked up another of the big rocks with one hand and a dead branch from the ground as a weapon and planted it before him. One of the dogs growled loudly in response and the noise had her moving back past the shelter of the bushes and away. As she scampered through the scrub at the edge of the clearing she simply turned and ran for the carriage, screaming at the driver about the dogs and the danger and slamming the door shut behind her.

It was wet inside and smelt like hay, though the dress she wore bore the stronger stench of vomit. Taking a flask of water from a shelf at the back of the conveyance, she poured it across the skirts of her gown, the cold seeping through the red-sprigged muslin and making her shiver.

Her breathing was worse. She could barely take in air now and the panic that she knew would not aid her was building. Placing her head back against the seat, she closed her eyes. This sometimes helped, but she needed the expectorant and the anti-spasmodics that her mother procured from Dr Bracewell in Harley Street. She needed calm and peace and serenity.

Would she die here on the side of a country road and alone? Would her family even know what had happened to her? Would her body be left to the dogs to devour after strangers had stolen her jewellery and books and her dress?

Not to mention her virginity.

The dreadful terror of it all had her sweaty and clammy and she began to feel strange and distant from things. It was the air…she couldn't get enough of it.

Finally, and with only the slightest whimper, she fell again into the gentler folds of darkness.

Hell, this whole journey was turning into a fiasco, James thought as he rejoined Thomas's mistress in the carriage. She was on the floor now in a puddle of water, the cold liquid seeping into the red dress and darkening the fabric to scarlet. She was breathing strangely, too, the skin at her throat taut and hollow and a blue tinge around her lips.

Finding his blade, he leaned forward and slit the tight fabric of her gown from bodice to hem, peeling it away from her. Without hesitation he threw the stinking wet dress straight out of the window and tucked his jacket about her before lifting her to sit up on the seat opposite. An erect position would make breathing easier, he thought, for he'd seen a soldier once with the same ailment on the icy roads between Lugos and Betanzos, and the man had insisted his head should be above his lungs or otherwise he would perish.

Reaching over to a net shelf at the back of the carriage, he searched for the tin of peppermint grease he'd bought at an inn from a medicine man on the way down to London. His cousin was prone to a weakness of chest and the vendor had been so insistent on the healing properties of the treatment James had found coin and purchased it.

Now he fingered a large translucent blob into his palm and rubbed at the skin around the girl's throat, though the fumes of the ointment were strong and his eyes began to water. Surely such potency must have some effect on allowing breath. He wished she would speak to him so that he could see how she fared, but she simply sat there, a tight and angry presence. He knew she was now conscious—years of hard soldiering had taught him that difference—but he did not wish to harry her with the malady of her condition and the skimpiness of her clothing so he left her to herself and willed the miles gone.

Her legs were badly scratched beneath the skirts,

he'd seen that as he had lifted her and the shoes she wore were nothing more than thin leather and silk. A woman used to the boudoir and an inside life. Her hair in the fading light was the colour of honey and gold. He had imagined whores to be cheap and brassy somehow, an artificial enhancement on show for the customers they would be trying to attract. Acacia Kensington's locks looked natural and unfussy.

Forty minutes later as the carriage slowed to rest the horses at an inn, her eyes opened. When she moved his jacket pulled away from her neck and her cheeks paled again as she registered her extreme lack of outer wear.

Such false theatrics irked him. 'I am sure in your profession you must have some days in less than your petticoats, Miss Kensington.'

'Miss…Kensington?' Her voice sounded rusty, the fright evident in every single syllable for she trembled as she took in breath. 'I think…you are indeed… mistaken.'

'Acacia Kensington?' He heard the horror in his tone. 'You are Miss Acacia Kensington, the paramour of my cousin Thomas, are you not?'

She shook her head hard, the long blonde hair falling loose now in a swathe across her shoulders and down over her chest.

'I am not, sir. I am… Lady Florentia Hale-B-Burton…youngest daughter…of the Earl of Albany.' Each breath was raw with the effort of talking.

'Hell.' He could not believe it. 'Hell,' he repeated and like the tumblers in a safe all the clues fell into place. The servant running down the road before the park screaming. The ring. The priggish dress. Her voice.

He'd kidnapped the wrong woman, rendered her unconscious, stripped her almost naked and subjected her to the sort of danger and terror she'd probably never ever manage to recover from.

For the first time in his life he was almost speechless.

'How old are you?'

'Eighteen. This…was my…first…Season.'

Young. Unprotected. Defenceless.

'Are you married?'

His eyes searched the fingers on her left hand and saw them bare.

'I am…not, sir…but I soon…may be. I…have a… suitor…who…likes me and I am…sure that we… will….'

She didn't finish for shouts filled the courtyard of the inn as another conveyance reeled wildly into view. Several men alighted and came towards them and as the door was snatched open all James felt was pain as a firearm exploded into his face, the smell of gunpowder one of his last and abiding memories.

He was dead.

Her father had killed him, the blood oozing from his neck and his mouth in a slow dribble of frothed red.

The sound of the shot had deafened her so that all she could see were people with open lips and corded throats and wildly gesticulating hands.

She felt him fall and she went with him, the green-eyed stranger who had taken her. She saw the spurt of his blood and the quick steps of the horses as they danced against the movement. She saw the rough broken face of her father above her, too.

Crying.

That single thing shocked her more than anything else had, his tears against her face as he tried to pull her up.

Everything smelt wrong.

The blood. The gunpowder. The fear of the horses. Her sweat. The last tinge of vomit in the air.

It smelt like the end. For him and for her. A quick and final punishment for something so terrible she could hardly contemplate just what might happen next.

He lay on the ground beneath her, her abductor, young and vulnerable, one arm twisted under himself, a bone sticking out through the linen shirt and blood blooming. She wanted to hold on to him, to feel the lack of pulse, to understand his death, to allow him absolution, but her father was dragging her away, away from the people who had gathered, away from the driver who was shouting and screaming, away from the light of a rising moon.

The smell of peppermint followed her, ingrained and absolute, the heat of it sitting atop her heart which was beating so very fast.

He had rubbed the ointment there. She remembered that. He had lifted her on to the seat and placed his jacket around her shoulders to cover her lack of clothing, to keep her hidden. He had removed her dress so that she might breathe, protecting her as he done against the threat of the dogs.

The wrong person.

He had said so himself.

The wrong punishment, too. She began to shake violently as her father discarded the jacket she'd clung to before calling to his driver and footman. Then the horses jolted forward as they left the country inn and raced for the safety of Mayfair and London.

A warm woollen blanket was tucked carefully about her and she heard the soft sound of her father praying. Outside it had begun to rain.

'Is she ruined, John?' Her mother's voice. Tear filled and hesitant.

'I don't know, Esther. I swear I don't.'

'Did he…?' Her mama's voice came to a stop, the words too hard to say out loud.

'I do not think so, but her petticoats were dishevelled and her dress was disposed of altogether.'

'And the cuts all over her legs and arms?'

'She fought him, I think. She fought him until the breathing sickness came and perhaps it saved her. Even a monster must have his limits of depravity.'

'But he's dead?'

'Yes.'

'Who was he?'

'God knows. Florentia could hardly draw breath and so we left. I don't want to send anyone back either to the inn to make enquiries in case…'

'In case our name is recognised?'

'Milly said the Urquharts saw Florentia in the park a moment before the abduction and that she had spoken to them. They are not people who would keep a secret easily. I doubt Milly is a girl of much discretion, either. But they did not see our daughter as I did.

They did not see her so underdressed in the company of a stranger, her gown gone and her hair down. There might be some hope in that.'

Her mother's sob was muffled and then there were whispered words of worry, the rustle of silk, the blown-out candle, the door shutting behind them and then silence.

She was in her room in Mayfair, back in her bed, the same bunch of tightly budded pink roses bought yesterday from the markets on the small table beside her. It was dark and late and a fire had been set in the hearth. For heat, she supposed, because all she could feel was a deathly cold. She wiggled her toes and her hands came beneath the sheets to run along the lines of her body. Everything was in place though she could feel the scratches incurred during her flight through the woods.

She breathed in, glad she could now gather more air than she had been able to in the carriage. Her neck throbbed and she swallowed. There was a thick bandage wrapped across her right thumb and tied off at her wrist.

He was dead. All that beauty dead and gone. She remembered the blood on the cobblestones and on her petticoats and in the lighter shades of his hair.

The beat of her heart sounded loud in a room with the quiet slice of moonlight on the bedcovers. A falling moon now, faded and low.

Was she ruined because of him? Ruined for ever?

She could not believe that she wouldn't be. Her sister had not come to seek her out and extract the story. She imagined Maria had been told to stay away. Her maid, Milly, had gone too, on an extended holiday back to her family in Kent. To recover from the dreadful shock, her father had explained when he first saw her awake, but she could see so very much more in his eyes.

The howls of the dogs came to mind. Her abductor's voice, too, raw but certain. She remembered his laughter as she'd hit him hard with her books. There was a dimple in his chin.

Where would he be buried? She'd looked back and seen the servant lift him from the ground, carefully, gently, none of the violence of her father, only protection and concern.

She was glad for it. She was. She was also glad that she was here safe and that there was nothing left between them save memory. His pale clear green eyes. The shaved shortness of his hair. The two parallel scars evident on his scalp. The smell of wool and unscented soap in his jacket. She shook away such thoughts. He had ruined her. He had taken her life and changed it into something different. He had taken her from the light and discharged her into shadow.

The deep lacerations on her arms from the trees in the glade stung and she could still smell the peppermint even after her long soak in a hot bath scented with oil of lavender.

The scent clung to her and she recalled his fingers upon her as he had rubbed it in. Gently. Without any threat whatsoever.

He was dead because of his own foolishness. He was gone to face the judgements of the Lord. A deserved punishment. A fitting end. And yet all she could feel was the dreadful waste.

A tap on the door had her turning and her sister was there in her nightgown, face pale.

'Can I come in, Flora? Papa said you were sleeping and that you were not to be disturbed till the morning. But Milly has been sent home and she was so full of the horror of your abduction it began to seem as if you might never be back again. What a fright you have given us.'

Florentia found her sister's deluge of words comforting.

'Mama says that there is the chance we might have to leave London for a while and retire to Albany. Did he hurt you, the one who took you from Mount Street, I mean? It is being whispered that Papa shot him dead somewhere to the north?'

Flora's stomach turned and she sat up quickly, thinking she might be sick, glad when the nausea settled back into a more far off place.

Warm fingers curled in close as Maria positioned herself next to her and took her hand, tracing the scratches upon each finger and being careful not to bump her thumb. 'You are safe now and that man will never be able to hurt you again, Papa promised it would be so. At least we can leave London and go home for it's exhausting here and difficult to fit in.'

The out-of-step sisters, Flora suddenly thought. She had overheard that remark at their first soirée. One of a group of the *ton*'s beautiful girls had said it and the others had laughed.

They were an oddness perhaps here in London, the two daughters of an impoverished earl who held no true knowledge of society and its expectations.

Heartbreak had honed them and sharpened the

edges of trust. But she would not think about that now because she was perilously close to tears.

'I heard Mama crying and Papa talking with her and she asked if we were cursed?'

'What did Father say?' Flora stilled at Maria's words.

'He said that only the weak-willed can be so stricken and that the true curse would have been to never find you. He also said while there is life there is hope.'

Life. Breath. Warmth. No hope for him though, the stranger with his blood running across the cobbles.

'Papa also said that perhaps we should not have come to London in the first place, but Mama asked how are we to be married off otherwise. Father replied there was an unkindness here that he found disappointing and I think he's right for people laugh at us sometimes. Perhaps we are not as fashionable as we should be or as interesting as the others are? Papa's title is something that holds sway here, but I suppose they also realise there is not much more than that behind our name.'

Flora pulled herself together and spoke up. 'We are who we are, Maria. We are enough.'

'Enough,' her sister repeated and brought her fingers up into a fist.

This was an old tradition between them, joining hands and making a chain. Pulling them together. Keeping them strong. Maria was only a year above her in age and they had always been close. But even as she tried to gather strength Florentia felt that something had been irrevocably broken inside her, wrenched apart and plundered. She wondered truly if she would ever recover from a sadness she could not quite understand.

* * *

Her father called her to his library the next morning and he looked as tired as she was, the night past having been a long and fitful one to get through.

'I thought we should try to remember something of yesterday between us, my dear. To keep it in memory so to speak, in case we have to think about it again in the future.'

'In the future?'

'If he has left you with child—?'

She didn't let him finish. 'It was not like that, Papa. He did not…' She stopped. 'I think he thought I was someone else entirely. Some woman who needed to be escorted north because she was in trouble. He did not touch me in that way.'

Relief lay in the lines of his face and in the lift of his eyes. 'But your dress and the scratches?'

'I had been sick and used water to try to make my gown clean again and he took it off me because it was wet and I was shaking and breathless. I also ran through a forest to try to get away and the branches snagged at my skin.'

'He is a monster to do what he did.'

'Is? I thought the man was dead. Are you saying he could still be alive?'

Her father's hands came up. 'I am certain he is not, but we shan't stay in London to find out. I have ordered the town house to be closed and have put in motion the means to remove us once again back to Kent. We shall leave on Friday.'

Albany Manor. Two days away. The bloom of thankfulness made Flora dizzy.

'There is something else that I think you should know.'

The tone of his words was gentle.

'The story of your abduction is all over London this morning. There were people near Mount Street who spoke when they should not have and Milly was not… careful with her own words either.'

'I see.'

'Well, perhaps you do not see it all. There will not be a gentleman here in London who would now offer his hand in marriage. Quiet ruination is a completely different thing from this utterly public condemnation and I doubt that we can recover from such a spectacle. If I had more capital behind me or the title was not an entailed one…' He stopped and took another tack. 'For the moment I think withdrawal might be our best defence. Your mother has the same thought. The Honourable Timothy Calderwood has sent a message to say he shall not be able to call upon you again, but he is sorry for your trials.'

Sadness welled. She had enjoyed Timothy's company with his laughter and his conversation. When she had danced with him a few days ago at the Rushton ball he'd intimated that he would like to know her much better and she had smiled back at him as if all her world was right. A kind man. A man of integrity. The first man who had made her feel special.

Her father's eyebrows raised up.

'Did your abductor say anything at all about who he was?'

'He didn't.' Florentia wondered if she should mention the name of Acacia Kensington and a man called Thomas. She decided against it, though, reasoning if her kidnapper was identified and still alive he'd be badly hurt and unable to fight off any further recriminations against him. 'I am sure he imagined I was another and had just realised his mistake when you came and shot him.'

'And mark my words I would do exactly the same again for I am not sure how you might recover from this travesty.'

'With fortitude, Papa.'

Her reply made him laugh though there was no humour in it. 'I wish Bryson was here…' he said and stopped, realising what he had just uttered.

Her brother stood in the empty space between them. Beautiful funny Bryson with his golden hair and blue eyes and his cleverness. The glue in a family that had come unstuck ever since his passing.

The son. The heir to an entailed property. Florentia's twin.

She sat down on the nearest seat, trying to find breath. It had been so long since his name had been mentioned out loud even though he was silently present in every moment of every day.

'I no longer think the fault lay with you, Flora, and am sorry that I once implied it such.' These were words she had heard before and foolish apologies that she had long since ceased to refute. 'We will get through this. All of it. There will be an ending to the pain, I promise.'

But there wasn't. There hadn't been. There never would be.

The nausea she had felt in the carriage returned and she forced it down. She hadn't been able to eat anything and although she felt hungry she just could not swallow even the smallest morsel of food. A new symptom that.

Perhaps she was going mad in truth. The completion of a process that had started as she had sat there with her brother dying in her arms and both their clothes splashed in red.

Her fault. Her dare. Her imprudence. She began to shake in earnest.

'Shall I fetch Mama, Flora?'

'No.' She shook her head hard and the memory shattered.

The ache was lessened now, the burn and throbbing of it where his neck met the collar bone. Tommy was beside him.

'Here, take this. It will help.'

Bitter like almonds. James screwed his face up at the taste, but after a few moments he started to feel as if he was floating, as if the land was somehow below him and he was flying through the clouds on a murmur.

He liked the sensation. He liked the freedom though his head still throbbed with each beat of his heart, leaving him squinting his eyes against the light.

'What happened?'

'You were shot.' His cousin lent closer, eyes shadowed. 'It was the wrong woman, Winter. You got the wrong damn woman.'

The red dress. The dogs. The breathlessness. It all came back in a fractured whirl.

'Is she safe? The girl I took?'

A curse and the shifting of light was his response, quiet between them until his cousin spoke again. 'She's fine. It's you we are worried about.'

'I…won't…die.' He managed to get the words out one by one.

'Why the hell do you think you won't, when you've lost so much blood?'

'Because…need…to say…sorry.'

'Her father shot you by all accounts, for God's sake. Point blank and without dialogue.'

'Deserved…it.'

Then the dark came and he slipped away from the hurting light.

Chapter Two

Albany Manor, Kent—April 1816

'Come to London with me, Flora. I am tired of you never being there and that ridiculous scandal from years ago is old news now. No one will remember it, I promise. There are far worse wrongdoings in society catching people's imaginations. Your downfall is barely recalled.'

Her sister, Maria, had always been difficult to say no to, Florentia thought, as she finished the final touches of a painting depicting the faces of three men caught in dark light at a dinner table.

'Roy will be there, too, and his mother. We will have a number of people all about us at every important social occasion. It won't be like the last time at all, I promise.'

The last time.

Three years ago when Florentia had finally decided to step again into society the whole thing had been a disaster. No one had wanted to talk to her, though Timothy Calderwood to his credit had made an effort to

try and converse before his new wife had pulled him
away. The memory of it stung. She had felt like an
outcast and even Maria's marriage to one of the *ton*'s
favourite sons, Lord Warrenden, had not softened her
dislike of social occasions.

Shaking away the memories, Flora stood and took
off her smock before hanging it across the back of her
easel.

'If I did decide to come, I'd need your promise that
I can leave as soon as I want and return to Albany
without argument.'

Maria smiled. 'I'd just like the chance for you to see
the worries you harbour are totally unfounded. You
cannot possibly let the unlawful actions of one un-
hinged individual ruin your life for ever. A stranger.
A man who has never been apprehended for the heinous deed and one who in all probability is long dead.
It's finished and over. You need to live again and find
someone like I have. Roy has been a blessing and a joy
to me. He has made me happy again.'

That certain look came across Maria's face as she
spoke about her husband of eighteen months with the
true contentment of a woman in love and knowing it.

Placing the paint back in their glass containers,
Flora wiped her easel with turpentine. She could not
work in a mess and she hated waste. The yellow ochre
had dribbled into the cobalt blue to make a dirty brown-
green, the swirl of the mix blobbing on the cloth.

For over a year now she had been sending a new
portrait every second week to London and to an agent
she had acquired through word of mouth from Roy.
Mr Albert Ward had been hounding her to come and
visit him in the city to meet some of his private cli-

ents, many who had expressly asked for her by name to draw their portrait.

By name…? Well, not precisely, she thought, frowning at the mistake.

Mr Frederick Rutherford was making a splash in the realms of the art world with his dark and moody portraits, and his reputation was growing as fast as his list of prospective clients. A young man with a great future before him, if only he would show up at the events planned around his unique style of painting.

A sensation. A mystery. A talent that had burst on to the London scene unexpectedly and with a vivid impression of genius and worth.

The letters from Mr Ward were getting more and more insistent on a meeting face-to-face. The agent needed to understand what sort of a man he was, what had fashioned his sense of design, what had shaped him into a muse who could seemingly interpret the feelings of those he chose as his subject in each painting so brilliantly. Hopelessness. Loss. Grief. Love. Passion. Deceit. All the shades of human emotion scrawled across a canvas and living in the application of pigment.

Ward's letter had been full of exaggerated prose and superlatives. The agent had seen in her paintings many of the themes that she herself had no knowledge of and yet her silence had seemed to propel him into a fiercer and more loyal promise.

It was worrying this temperament of his and Florentia often doubted if the ruse was even worth going on with, but as a woman bound by her past to never marry she had been somewhat forced into finding a vocation that did not include family and children. And she loved painting. If her life was not to follow the direction she once had thought it might have, she did not wish to be derailed into another that she hated.

It could be worse, for the money she garnered was supplementing her father's lack of it and as Albany Manor was entailed the promise of a longevity of tenure was gone without a male heir. After her father's death the Manor and title would pass to her deceased uncle's oldest son, a fact that Christopher, the heir, reminded them of every time he came to visit.

She'd thought to send her youngest cousin Steven in her place to see Mr Ward in person, instructing him on his conduct and in what to say, but she knew for all his good points he was a tattlemouth. The fact that she had duped one of the prominent art critics in London in her role as Mr Frederick Rutherford would be gossip too salubrious to simply keep quiet about was another consideration altogether and she did not think her parents would be up to a further scandal.

So she was essentially bound to the charade she had thought up. Besides, a new idea had begun to form at the back of her head. She could go herself to London. A young artist who was slight and effeminate would not be much remarked upon and if she gifted him with a cough and a propensity for bad headaches and poor health she might not have to stay around anywhere for very long.

A quick visit might suffice to keep her hand in the game, so to speak, and with her father's bouts of despondency that took him to bed often and her mother's insistence in looking after him, she would have much freedom to move around.

Her sister could help her, too, for she had been in on the deception from the very start.

'If I agreed to come to London, I would not wish to attend any major social events, Maria. If I went anywhere it would have to be something small and select.'

'An afternoon tea then would be the thing to begin with. A quiet cultural affair at Lady Tessa Goodridge's, perhaps, and afterwards a play in the Haymarket.'

Flora unbundled her hair and shook it free. She always placed it up when she painted in a messy and oversized bun fastened with two ceramic clips that she had been given by her sister.

Her good-luck charms, she called them, because after receiving them things had improved and she had survived. She smiled to herself. Perhaps that was putting too good an interpretation on it, she ruminated, for in truth she had become the sort of woman who was decidedly eccentric and superstitious. She'd been enclosed in the Hale-Burton country seat of Albany Manor for the last six years and had seldom ventured out, apart from her one sojourn to London, the small world she called her own allowing her much time completely alone.

She used to like people. Once. Now they simply frightened her. She could not understand them or interpret their true meaning. The inspiration for every portrait she had completed and sent to Mr Ward by mail had come from the pages of books of drawings in the extensive library at Albany. Fictional, altered or copied.

Save one, she amended, but then she did not think about that.

So many topics now that were out of bounds to her sense of peace. She wished she were different, but she did not know where to begin to become so.

'We will go to the dressmaker in Bromley, Flora.

She will fashion you some clothes and she is as talented as the expensive modistes in Paris. One of her patrons is a friend of mine and every person who ever orders a gown from her is more than delighted with it.'

Listening to Maria's plans for their sojourn made the enormity of what she had agreed on to become real. Appearance was so important in the city and the old feelings of being not quite good enough resurfaced with a dread.

'I don't want anything fancy, Maria, and I shan't be wearing bright colours at all.' Last time their mother had insisted on gowns that were so dreadfully noticeable and so very wrong for their colouring. Since her abduction she'd never worn that shade of red again.

'Roy prefers me in pastel,' her sister was saying and even that sent a chill of horror down Florentia's neck. Women in society had so little say in anything. They were mute beautiful things, needy and powerless. Well, the paintings had given her back her power and she knew that she would never willingly relinquish it.

'I also need to visit Mr Ward in South London.'

Maria was silent, her brows knitted together. 'He thinks you are a man, Florentia. How can you see him at all?'

'It will just be quickly and I shall be dressed as Frederick Rutherford.'

'I hardly think you could do that for it would be… scandalous.'

Flora laughed. 'Well, I am an expert in that field by all accounts, so I should manage it effortlessly. I'll wear Bryson's clothes and his boots. They would fit me well.'

'What of your hair? Mr Ward would not think that to belong to a boy.'

'A wig and a hat would be an easy disguise. I can procure a moustache, too, and stuff paper in my cheeks to change the shape of my face. That should make me speak differently.'

'My God, Florentia.' Maria simply stared at her. 'You have been thinking of this for a while? This dupe?'

'The art of pretence lies in painting just as truly as it ever would in the world of acting. It just requires sure-mindedness, I think.'

'And you truly imagine you could pull off such a character?'

'I do.' She smiled because her sister's face was stiff with disbelief. 'I've been practising, Maria. The walking. The talking. The sitting. I am sure I could be more than convincing.'

'And what of the serving staff at the London town house of the Warrendens? I am certain they should notice if one moment you are a girl and the next a boy and goodness knows who they might tell. Your true identity would be all over London before we ever got to our next appointment if the stories of the gossip-mongering between the big houses is to be believed.'

'Then perhaps I should simply go as Mr Frederick Rutherford right from the beginning. The Warrendens' staff in London does not know me and it would completely do away with the need for new gowns and shoes. I shan't have to even take a maid with me. I shall simply arrive as Mr Frederick Rutherford and leave as him with no questions asked.'

'I don't believe I am having this conversation with you, Florentia. You cannot possibly be serious.'

'Oh, but I am, Maria. I have no wish to be out and

about in society again, but I do have a need to continue selling my paintings. I could, of course, simply go up to the city alone and in disguise, but…'

'No. If you are going to do this ridiculous thing I want to be there to help you, to make certain that you are safe.'

'Thank you.'

'You have forced my hand, dreadfully, but I do want to state quite forcefully that this is a terrible and dangerous idea.'

'I know I can do it, Maria. Remember the plays we used to put on as children. You always said I was marvellous at acting my parts.'

'That was make believe.'

'As this is, too. It's exactly the same.'

'If you get caught—'

Florentia cut her off. 'But I won't. I promise.'

'My God, I can't believe I should even be considering this. I can't believe you might talk me into it.'

'Try, Maria. Try for my sake.'

'All right. I'll visit the wigmakers if you fashion a drawing of your wants and I can simply say it is for a play we are putting on at Albany for Christmas. Did you have a preference for a colour?'

'Black.' Flora was astonished to hear such certainty coming from her mouth. She could mimic Bryson because she had known him so very well, his habits, his stance, the way he walked and watched. His hair had been golden just like hers, so she needed something distinctly different.

'And I would require some height inbuilt in the boots. I have seen that done so it should not be difficult.'

Maria groaned. 'I cannot believe that we could even be contemplating this farce, Florentia. God, if we are discovered.'

'It will never happen.'

'Well, Roy needs to know at least. I will not lie to him.'

Flora walked to the stream late that afternoon through the small bushes and the flowering shrubs, through the birdsong and the rustle of the wind, through air filled with the smell of spring on its edge and the promise of renewed warmth.

She had always come here to think ever since the time she had returned in disgrace from London.

The glade reminded her slightly of the woods she had run through besides the North Road as she had tried to escape the carriage of the man who had abducted her.

Her kidnapper.

That was how she named him now and here she allowed him to come into her thoughts just as surely as she had banished him from everywhere else.

His smile was what she remembered most, slightly lopsided and very real. He had a dimple in his chin, too, a detail that she had forgotten about until, when painting from memory, she had rediscovered the small truths of him.

Beautiful. She had thought him such then and she still did now, his short hair marked in browns of all shades from russet to chestnut and threaded in lighter gold and wheat.

She wondered why she still recalled him with such a preciseness, but she knew the answer of course. He

had died for a mistake, his own admittedly, but still…
He was like a martyr perishing for a cause that was
unknown, his blood running on the forecourt of the
inn in runnels of red, the dust blending indistinctly at
the sides so that it was darker. She had used that colour when she had drawn him, that particular red on
the outlines when first she had formed his face and
body on canvas and now even when the painting was
finished the colour was a part of who he was, both his
strength and his weakness.

She'd bundled up the portrait with its power of grace
and covered it with a sheet before placing it at the very
back of her large wardrobe. Often, though, she looked
at him even as she meant not to. Often she lifted the
fabric and ran her finger across his cheek, along his
nose and around the line of his dimpled chin.

It made her feel better, this care of him, this gentle
caress, this attention that she had not allowed him in
life even after he saved her from the dogs and wrapped
his jacket around her shoulders to deter the chill of
spring.

Contrasts. That was the worst of it. The disparity
of caring or not.

Her kidnapper had made her into a woman of detail and fear. He had changed her from believing in the
hope of life to one who dreaded it. At times like this
sitting in her private grove she wondered if perhaps
this introspection was exactly the thing that made her
take up the brush, for she had never lifted one until
she had returned in shame to Albany Manor after her
fateful London ruin.

Seeing yellow paint on her nail, she scraped it off
with her thumb, the small flakes falling into drops of

water caught on a green waxy leaf and turning the colour yellow. With care she tipped it over and the hue ran into the mud and the soil, swallowed up until it ceased to exist at all.

Like him. Perhaps?

Sometimes she imagined he still lived, scarred and angry, as closeted away as she was, afraid to be seen and exposed. Did a wife live with him now? Had he found a woman who might listen with her whole heart to the story of his narrow escape and then stroke his cheek in comfort, just as she tended to the image in the painting? A mistake to forget about, or to laugh over.

Crossroads for them both.

Him in death and her in life. Everyone seemed to have moved on since for good or for bad. Her father to his penchant for sickness, her mother in her willingness to play his nursemaid, Maria in her love of a husband who suited her entirely.

Everybody but her, stuck as she was in this constant state of inertia.

That was the trouble, of course, the puzzling hopelessness of everything that had happened. The scandal she could have coped with easily. It was the grief of it all that had flattened her. Everything for nothing.

Picking up a stick, she began to draw lines in the earth. Six lines for the years. She wanted to add a seventh because this next one would be no different. Then she embellished the lines with twelve circles each representing the months. Seventy-two of them. A quarter of her lifetime.

She wanted to live again. She wanted to smile and laugh and dance. She wanted to wear pretty clothes and jewellery and have long dinners under candlelight. But she couldn't, couldn't make herself take that first little step out and about.

It had got worse, her lack of air. In winter now she gasped and wheezed when she walked further than she ought to.

Sometimes she wondered if she were indeed addled by it all. Pushing that thought away, she concentrated on another.

Mr Frederick Rutherford.

With care she raised herself up on to her heels and walked across the clearing with a swagger, her head held high, her shoulders stiff. Then she ambled back, this time with a stick in hand shaped from a branch that she had stripped from a tree.

The accoutrements of a gentleman. Better. It felt more…right. So many parts made up a man, though. Stride. Voice. Arrogance. Certainty. Disdain.

She walked faster as though she was important, as though in the wasting of even the tiniest of seconds there lay a travesty. Men about town knew where they were going. They did not falter. They acted as though everybody might wish to know of them and their opinions. There was a certain freedom in being such a one as that.

Lengthening her stride, she tried again and again, all the while adjusting things slightly so that it felt more real, this person whom she was becoming.

She could do it. With spectacles to hide her eyes and a moustache to disguise her lips. A neckcloth tied in the high manner would see to the rest. The cane her grandfather had owned sat unused in the attic, just another prop to draw the eye away from her with its silver dimpled ball and dark walnut wood.

Everything was beginning to fall into bands of colour. Her wig. The clothes she would sport. The heightened leather Hessians that would easily come to her knees.

Like a painting established layer by layer, of substance and structure. Drawing the eyes. Finding the essence. Creating the illusion.

Chapter Three

'I think you are a veritable tease, Lord Winterton, and if half the things that are said of you are true I should imagine you find us very dull.'

James glanced down at Miss Julia Heron, soft blonde ringlets falling around her face and smiling brown eyes. One of the beauties of the Season, it was said, though there was a wide ring of other young ladies around her who looked every bit as charming. He wished they would not look at him as if he was the answer to all their heartfelt dreams. He wished he could have simply crossed the floor and left, to feel the rain on his face and puddles beneath his feet, and smell the green of London in the spring.

How he had missed it.

His neck ached as it always did at about this time of the night and he breathed through the pain with a measured practice.

Lady Florentia Hale-Burton was not here, he was sure of it, and from what he had managed to find out about the family in the last few weeks he could well imagine why. His actions on the road across from Hyde

Park had ruined the youngest daughter of the Earl of Albany. For marriage. For the hope of a family. For life. For ever.

Her sister was present, though. He had met Lady Maria Warrenden, once Hale-Burton, on the arm of one of his oldest friends as he had alighted from his coach. Roy Warrenden had introduced his wife with pride, giving him her unmarried name to place her in a context and James prayed his surprise and shock had not been noticeable.

She'd showed no recognition of him or his name at all which was a comforting thing leaving him with a decided uncertainty as to what he wanted to do about the whole sordid affair. An apology to the Hale-Burtons would be a good start, but by all accounts the father had taken to bed with a broken spirit and he could well see that his very presence would be a nightmare for the entire family; a memory of a time they would have no want to recall or relive.

Lady Florentia Hale-Burton would be twenty-three now or twenty-four, he thought, and gossip had it she resided in Kent and only occasionally visited town.

James looked around, wishing he could simply leave and figure out his choices in peace, but as it had been only an hour since his arrival he thought any withdrawal would incite comment. Better to have not come at all, he thought, as he swallowed his drink.

Miss Heron before him was weaving her fan this way and that, a dance of wonder he found himself mesmerised with and repelled by, the female tool of flirtation and provocation holding no interest for him.

He had come home to England half the man who had left it, but with twenty times the fortune. There was a certain irony to be found in all he had lost when weighed against that which he had gained, here in a place where money mattered most.

'You promised me this dance, my lord.' There was a note of supplication in Julia Heron's eyes. He could not remember making such a promise and frowned slightly.

It was the way of the London set, he supposed, a world of chimera and delusion underpinned by a steely determination to marry well.

'I've written it in, Lord Winterton,' Miss Heron insisted, showing him the name placed in small and precise letters upon her dance card.

With a nod, he acquiesced. He'd never particularly liked dancing, but as the orchestra began into a quadrille he was at least grateful that it was not a waltz.

Moving on to the dance floor, James saw that many patrons watched them, smiling in that particular way of those who imagined an oncoming union. The jaded anger inside him rose with the thought and he pressed it down. A crowded ballroom was not the place for excessive introspection or regret.

As he fished about for a subject that might interest the young woman beside him came up with a topic of her own.

'Papa is having us all drawn by Mr Frederick Rutherford, the artist, my lord. He hopes the portraits will be begun as soon as possible.'

The words were filled with a delight tinged in trepidation.

'Have you seen anything at all of his work, Lord Winterton?'

James shook his head, the heady world of art a long

way from anything he'd ever been interested in. 'But I am sure he will capture your likeness with alacrity.'

The girl's face fell. 'Well, in truth he tends to embellish things with his own interpretation, though Papa says he cannot imagine the man wanting to do so with us.'

'Because perfection cannot be improved upon?' He heard the tone of irony quite plainly in his voice, but Julia Heron simply trilled and blushed, her hand tightening around his as her glance came fully upon him.

His heart sank further. He would need to be careful if he were to escape the gossip so often associated with these soirées and emanating from even the simplest of familiarities.

His fortune had singled him out now as highly sought after husband material and if beneath his clothes there lay deeper shades of tragedy no one else here knew of it.

The older Herons were watching them closely, another younger daughter of the same ilk beside them glowering at her sister. When the dance brought them together again Julia had a further question waiting.

'Are you here in London long, my lord?'

'Just for the next few weeks, I think, Miss Heron. I am hoping to move west.'

'To Atherton Abbey?'

'I see you have heard the rumour.'

'Who has not, Lord Winterton, for the Abbey is said to be one of the loveliest homes in all of Herefordshire as well as one of the most expensive.'

James gritted his teeth and smiled, glad as the complexity of the quadrille pushed them apart again, though the other woman on one point of the square was unexpected and he tensed as he saw her visage.

Lady Maria Hale-Burton, now the new Lady Warrenden, smiled at him politely. She was taller than her sister and much more rounded. Her hair was darker, too. He waited to see if in private she might mention the plight of her sibling in connection with him, but she did not, chancing instead on a mundane and social propriety.

'I hope you are enjoying your return to London after so long away, my lord.' Her voice was soft and carried a slight lisp.

'I am, thank you. It was good to see your husband again. We were at school together.'

She was about to answer, but the change in the figure took him back to Julia Heron who claimed his arm in the final flurry of the dance, her colour high and her smile wide with enjoyment.

Accompanying the girl back to her parents he gave her his thanks and went to find Roy Warrenden, grateful to see the Baron sitting at a table with a bottle of wine before him and a number of empty glasses, though he was in full conversation with another James had no knowledge of. Maria Warrenden now joined them, brought back to her husband on the arm of an older man whom she promptly thanked. As her dancing partner left she sat down and made her own observations.

'Roy said you led him astray more than once, Lord Winterton, but your presence here has made his night. He is usually desperate to get home early.' She laughed heartily, a joyous natural sound that was nothing at all like Julia Heron's practised society giggle.

'Are your parents here tonight, Lady Warrenden?' He'd looked around the room before just in case the visage of Florentia Hale-Burton's father should be peering back at him, his face full of violent memory, and had been relieved to see no sign of the man.

'No, I am afraid they seldom venture far from Albany Manor in Kent any more. Papa suffers from bad health, you see, and Mama feels it her duty to be there to wipe his brow.'

'A woman of responsibility, then?'

'Or one who enjoys playing the martyr?' Close up the resemblance between Maria Warrenden and her sister was more noticeable and he found himself observing her with interest even as Roy Warrenden stood and clapped him on the back.

'It's good to have you in England, Winter. I saw that my wife managed to find you in the quadrille. She said she was going to try.' His glance went further afield. 'I should probably warn you that the Misses Heron are fairly overwhelming and are not ones to take no for an answer lightly either.'

Glancing over, James was concerned to see them all looking his way, eyes full of the hope of more than he had offered them.

Maria laughed at their interest. 'The Heron girls are handsome, granted, but if I was a man I should not wish to wake up to only beauty each morning.'

Her husband concurred. 'No, indeed not, my love. Beauty and brains is what you are after, Winter, and the ability to be entertained for every moment of your life. Miss Heron looked particularly chatty in your company?'

'She was telling me of a portrait she is having done

by Mr Frederick Rutherford. Seems the artist holds a reputation here that is more than salutary and he has been commissioned to paint the three sisters.'

Lady Warrenden choked on the drink she had just taken a sip of, but it was the look of consternation in her eyes that was the most arresting.

'The man is indeed talented.' Roy had now taken up the conversation and James had the idea it was to give his wife time to recover her equilibrium. 'But I doubt the Herons will entice the fellow to London, for from my knowledge Rutherford does not do sittings in person.'

'No, he certainly does not.' Maria Warrenden was shaking. James could see the tremble of her hands as she placed the glass down on the table, though she immediately dropped them into the thick fabric of her skirt and out of sight. 'He would be appalled at such an idea, believe me, Viscount Winterton, and I cannot understand how they could think such a thing might happen.'

'You sound as though you know him well?'

The woman shook her head. 'Only a little,' she returned and changed the subject entirely. 'We will be walking in Hyde Park tomorrow, my lord. Perhaps you might wish to accompany us for the foliage of the trees there this spring is particularly beautiful.'

The past seemed to collide with the present and James shook his head. 'I am out of town tomorrow, I am afraid.'

'Of course.' Maria Warrenden looked uncertain. He would have liked to have asked her of the health of her sister, but could find no way to broach the subject. Perhaps if he met Roy alone one day he could bring her up in a roundabout sort of way. He had no mandate to be truly interested and besides Florentia Hale-Burton could have no wish ever to meet up with him again if the scale of the scandal that had ensued at their last meeting was anything to go by.

He wondered if the youngest Hale-Burton daughter was married and had a family now. He wondered if she was happy...

Her sister came to her room late that evening, having returned from the Allans' ball full of a bustling gossip.

'Lord Winterton graced the ball this evening, Florentia, and the Heron girls were all over him, though in truth I did not see him complaining. I think he had danced with each of them by the end of the evening.'

'Winterton is the Viscount newly home from the Americas?' Flora had heard of the man, of course. He was the newest and most interesting addition to the *ton*, a soldier who had made his fortune in the acquisition of timbers from the east coast and transported them back to London.

'That's the one and he is every bit as beautiful as they all say him to be. It's his eyes, I think, a true clear and pale green. You would love to paint him, Flora, but that's not my only news. No, indeed, my greatest morsel is that the oldest Heron girl, Miss Julia, apparently told Winterton that Mr Frederick Rutherford would be painting all three daughters at their town house in Portland Square across the next few weeks.'

Florentia put down her book. *A true clear and pale green and every bit as beautiful as they say he is.* The world tilted slightly and went out of focus, so much so that one of her hands twisted around the base of the chair on which she sat in an attempt to keep herself anchored.

'Are you all right, Flora? You suddenly look awfully pale.' Her sister moved closer as Flora made an attempt to smile.

'I am tired, I suppose, for London is a busy and frantic place when you have been away from it as long as I have.' Her heart was racing, the clammy sheen of sweat sliding between her breasts. Could it be him? Could her kidnapper have survived? Was he here now in London, living somewhere only a handful of miles from the Warrenden town house? She made an effort to focus.

'Mr Alfred Ward did ask me to consider the Heron commission in a letter he sent after we met him on Monday, but I declined.'

'Well, it seems he has not relayed your answer to the prospective clients.' Maria removed her hat and shook out her hair. 'I knew something would go wrong with this scheme of yours, Flora. I knew that we could not trust Mr Ward with one meeting. He is a schemer and he wants more and more of you for I could tell from his demeanour and by all the words he did not say. Goodness, if he keeps this up you will be unmasked summarily and then what?'

'He is a greedy man, Maria, but also an astute one. I told him if I am pressured too much I am inclined to bouts of severe melancholy. I inferred I was…brittle, I suppose, a highly sensitive artist who is not of this world so to speak. The cough helped, I think, though it has left me with a sore throat and a hoarse voice from having to do it so much.'

Maria looked aghast. 'We should leave London then and just go home.'

Florentia frowned for suddenly she did not want to desert the city with such haste.

A true clear and pale green.

The words kept repeating over and over.

'Is Lord Winterton married?'

Her sister's mouth simply dropped open. 'No. At least I do not think so. He is an old friend of Roy's, so I could ask him of it. Why would you possibly be interested?'

Ignoring that query, she asked another of her own. 'But he will be staying here? In London, I mean.'

'He's rumoured to be acquiring a substantial home somewhere to the west. He is also rumoured to be dangerous.'

'In what ways?'

'In every possible way, I should imagine. He is neither for the faint hearted nor for the timid. He looks as though he could eat the whole world up should he want to and everyone there at the Allans' ball was a little afraid of him. It's his wealth, I suppose, and the fact that he is said to have a scar upon his neck that makes it appear as though his head was almost torn completely off from his shoulders at some point long ago. He wears his neckcloth high to hide it.'

'I see.' Florentia stood and turned towards the mirror on one wall of her room.

For she did see. Everything. Too much. All of it.

It was him. She knew it. Knew it from the bottom of her racing heart.

She could ruin him in an instant as surely as he had ruined her. She could give her truth out loud and watch him suffer as she had, this lord of the *ton* with all his wealth and his connections and his beautifulness.

She felt sick and scared and elated and horrified. Every emotion melded into shock and then shattered again into coldness and fear.

But she could not just go home and leave it. To fester and burn and hurt her. Not again. She could not weather another six years like the last ones. The drawing she'd done in the dust of her grove came into recall. Seventy-two months. So very many lines.

'Did you speak to him, Maria? To Lord Winterton?'

'Yes.'

'And he knew your name? Your unmarried one, I mean?'

'I suppose so. Yes, I remember Roy introduced me by using it. Why? Why should that matter, Florentia? What is it that you are not telling me?'

But Florentia had ceased to listen altogether, lost as she was in her own desperate worry. Did Lord Winterton remember her? Had he recognised the Hale-Burton name? Had the world already tilted in a way that could not be stopped or altered?

The smallness of the room here in the Warrenden town house on Grosvenor Square suddenly felt like a trap and she longed to be out of it, walking and thinking.

She wanted her grove of trees and the soil of Albany Manor, but she wanted the truth even more.

Six years of hiding. It was enough. She just could not do it any more. Not for a day or a moment or a second. She needed to see Winterton, to look upon his face and understand what it was that lay between them, what it was she needed to do.

She could confront him personally or amongst a selected company and yet even that thought made her blanch. Her protections were no longer in place. Her father was ill and Maria's husband was an old friend. If she told her sister Winterton was the one who had kidnapped her, Roy would imagine it his duty to issue him a challenge and gain a penance.

Winterton was a soldier and from all she had heard he was not timid. Roy wouldn't stand a chance against him and if he died Maria would be miserable for all the rest of her life. Her parents would suffer, too, and the news would kill her papa. Had not the doctor said he needed to be kept in a calm and safe state of mind if he was to ever have a hope of recovery? Lately he had seemed happier, more himself, and she did not want to compromise that. Everything for nothing, but how could she meet him without being completely exposed in the company of society?

The higgledy-piggledy of it all whirled in her brain around and around until finally one perfect solution presented itself. She turned to her sister and her voice was certain.

'I should like to draw him, this Lord Winterton. If he is as beautiful as they all say he would be the ideal subject for a sitting. It also sounds as though he could afford to pay. Well.'

Maria's mouth dropped wide open.

'You would draw him while you are dressed as a youth? Winterton is no milksop lord who would be easily duped, Florentia.'

'If he is so very beautiful, I am sure that he would be flattered by the chance to sit for the first and only portrait I am ever likely to do in person. There is also the added advantage that if I complete this commission Mr Ward may leave me alone for a while. Perhaps this portrait is the answer we have been looking for.'

'You sound strange, Flora, unlike yourself. You have never drawn anyone before in this way, right in front of you—'

Florentia interrupted her. 'Then perhaps it is well past time that I did, Maria. A new direction, so to speak, a different turning.'

'And the Herons?'

'I shall leave London for good after completing the portrait of Viscount Winterton. After that it will all be finished. I can do other paintings to augment our income, but the requirements of Mr Ward will no longer concern me. I will be free of it and you won't need to worry about anything at all going wrong.'

When her sister had left Flora stood at the window and looked out. There had been so many times in the past six years when she had thought to try to find out about her kidnapper's family, the cousin Thomas and the woman Acacia Kensington that he had mentioned. But where did she even start to look without attracting attention? Quietly she had trawled through the books of the peerage at Lackington's because the man she had met was obviously from the aristocracy, but she had never managed to identify anybody, the small information she had more frustrating than none at all. Besides, if she had managed to find out his name what could she have truly gained from it?

Catching her eye in the glass she saw her lips move in the reflection.

'Please God, just let me understand him.'

* * *

James upended the brandy Roy Warrenden had handed him at Whites and called to the waiter to bring them another.

The night was warm for this time of the year and the windows along the whole east side were open. It had been three days since the Allans' ball and the most surprising of correspondences had come to his home in St James's Square yesterday morning.

'The artist Mr Frederick Rutherford has sent word that he wants to draw me. His agent, a Mr Ward, came to see me late yesterday afternoon.'

For a moment James saw complicity on Roy's face but dismissed the idea as ludicrous. Maria Warrenden had said they barely knew the fellow and Winter could not see what an ailing reclusive country artist might have in common with a wealthy baron and his wife.

'The agent intimated this commission would be the first and the last painting done in this manner, the fellow being a very private soul.'

'I see.' Roy watched him carefully. 'And you are agreeable, Winter?'

'I am not altogether certain, though the fact that he has sought me out personally does interest me.'

'Perhaps he is intrigued by the way society flocks to your side in admiration, particularly the women?'

James shook his head. 'I think there is more to it than the fleeting consideration of appearance. Your wife said she knew him slightly. How slightly is that?'

'Mr Frederick Rutherford made our acquaintance most recently so I should not like to give you any advice as to his sincerity or otherwise based on my knowing his character well.'

'Your wife has a sister, does she not, a Lady Florentia Hale-Burton if I am not mistaken?'

Horror crossed Roy's face as he asked it, giving James the impression of something being awfully wrong with the girl. His heartbeat quickened because he did not want to be told her shortcomings were his fault or that her abduction on Mount Street had led to some sort of a mind disorder that had never been resolved.

'Why do you mention her in conjunction with Frederick Rutherford, Winter?'

'Pardon?' The conversation had seemed to have got away from him and he waited for the other to explain the query.

'Florentia, my sister-in-law, is somewhat timid. She does not enjoy London at all but prefers the quiet of her parents' home of Albany Manor in Kent. But as to the other matter of the portrait—perhaps it is not to me that you should be addressing your queries. The agent you spoke of would hold a far better understanding of these things.'

With care James swallowed his brandy, liking the way it brought warmth into the coldness.

Secrets and lies. His own and Roy Warrenden's. There was a sense of wrongness here that he could not quite put his finger on, something held back and concealed and the mystery had to do with the artist Frederick Rutherford, he thought.

'I think I shall agree to the commission of the portrait, though the price is extremely high.'

'Well, look at it as a painting for posterity, Winter. A foothold into history.'

'But I won't take up the offer of using the agent's gallery in South London as the place of sitting. I want it done at my place in St James's.'

'The lad may find it difficult to get there with all the accoutrements needed for such a task. I doubt any artist is all that flush.'

'Then I shall send a carriage to pick him up. Where does he reside in London? No one I ask seems to know.'

'Here, there and everywhere, I expect. Rutherford is like a gypsy in his constant changing of addresses. My wife accompanied him on the first visit to see Alfred Ward, actually, so he spent the night at our town house.'

'Yes, I had heard of that.'

Warrenden smiled. 'I thought perhaps that you might have. Rutherford is a chameleon, Winter. You might be wise to get the sittings completed as quickly as you are able and without asking the fellow too many questions.'

'You think he might abscond otherwise.'

'I sincerely hope not for I'd like to see him settle,' Roy replied, 'and you could be just the one to do it.'

'You think it might be the beginning of a more lucrative career for him? Already he is a painter with many admirers. Does he wish for more?'

Roy's laugh was harsh as he stood. 'I leave you to make your own assessment of his ambition, Winter, when you meet him, but for now I'm off home. I am, however, more than interested in seeing exactly how this romp of yours turns out.' He stopped for a second as if debating if he should say more. 'Frank Reading intimated you had returned to England to try and understand something of your father's untimely demise.'

'He's right. I never believed William committed suicide and am looking for the truth of it.' The words came out with a strained anger that he could no longer bother hiding. He liked Roy Warrenden as he was not a man inclined to gossip.

'Reading also said he had word you were asking around in the more unsavoury parts of town. Sometimes there are consequences in uncovering secrets, Winter.'

'And I should welcome them if they allow me to understand more about the nature of my father's death.'

Roy nodded. 'Well then, I hope you find some answers that might make more sense to you. If you need any help…?'

James was quick to shake his head. 'I am better alone, but thank you.'

He watched as Warrenden threaded his way through the last of the patrons of White's and lifted the bottle of brandy up to pour himself another glass when he could no longer see him.

Roy was not quite telling him the truth about Rutherford, that much was certain. There was some faulty connection, but he couldn't put his finger on it.

He knew the Warrendens were better acquainted with the artist than they let on. The lad had returned to their town house on Grosvenor Square for all the nights he'd been in London and once passing by late on an afternoon in his carriage James had noted Maria Warrenden holding the fellow's hand with more than a little delight.

God, was the sister cuckolding her husband right under his nose? And where the hell did the reclusive Lady Florentia Hale-Burton fit into any of this picture?

* * *

The blow came from behind as he was walking to the corner to hail a hackney cab, a sharp blinding pain that had him on his knees and clambering for consciousness, and all James could think of was that the danger Roy had spoken of had suddenly come to pass.

A boot came next to his face, the edge of the tread connecting with his lip, but the shock was kicking in now and with it came the strength.

Grabbing his assailant by the leg, James brought him down and within a moment he was on top of him, a punch to the side of the head having the effect of keeping the other still.

'Who the hell are you and what do you want of me?'

'Perkins sent me, from the Red Fox Inn at the docks. You have been prying around and he don't like it. It's him who sends us on to see who is asking too many questions.'

James realised this man was only a messenger boy, all brawn and muscle and no idea at all as to what this was all about. Letting him go, he stood back, watching the fellow collect his hat and move away.

'Can I speak with Mr Perkins? I'd pay well for a few moments of his time.'

The other nodded. 'If he wants to talk, you will hear from us.'

With that the stranger turned and disappeared into the night, leaving James to wipe the blood from his lip and find his own hat spilled into the gutter by the unexpected retribution.

His father's death had rocked him and he had been trying to track down some of William's gambling partners to get some answers. Suicide was a shameful thing and he could not believe that his father had killed himself. Two parents lost to suicide painted a worrying family weakness, though in his mother the failing was almost to be expected.

He swore again and looked up into the sky. A small rising moon tonight. It had been much the same sort of moon when he had kidnapped Florentia Hale-Burton. Clenching his fists, he lent back against a stone wall and felt in his pocket for both light and a cigar in order to steady himself. He wanted to see her again, to tell her that it had all been a mistake and that he was sorry for it. He wanted to take her hand in his own and let her know that he had not thought her abduction a small thing and that it had changed his life as much as it had ruined her own.

Like a pack of cards, one fell and then the next and the next until finally in the remains of what was left was the realisation that there was nothing at all of value or of honour.

His neck ached and he drew on the cigar, liking the way the red end of it flared in the night and his heartbeat slowed.

Florentia Hale-Burton had had asthma. He wondered if she still had it. She'd had a suitor, too, and a bag full of books. He'd heard her name mentioned in the card room at some ball. It was said that she had always been odd, but that if the Earl of Albany's girls had made a bit of effort with their appearances they would probably have outshone every other woman in the room.

Perhaps it might be true, though the girl in the carriage had been either unconscious, furious or sick so he had no honest picture by which to measure this.

He did remember her face after her father's gun had gone off, though, for she had reached out for him, her hands around his neck, trying to contain the damage, his blood between her fingers and her blue eyes sharp with pain.

They had both fallen then, out of the door on to the road, her body wound about his own, like a blanket or a cushion. He had felt the softness of her and the honesty, her hair falling around them in shelter until she had been torn away.

'God.' He spoke that out loud. 'God, help me,' he added as if in that second and under the darkness of a spring London night he had understood exactly what he should have always known.

Florentia Hale-Burton had tried to help him even after everything he had done to her. After all the hurt and the dogs and the chill and the fear. She had reached out and tried to stem the damage of the shot, placing her own body between him and his assailants and the promise of another assault.

The realisation was staggering.

Roy Warrenden had said she was timid and seldom left Kent so how could he meet her? To thank her. To make certain that she was…recovered?

His life seemed to be going into a vortex swirling around truth. The artist. Roy's wariness. His wife's fear. The sister banished to Kent after he had ruined her by his own stupidity.

But first he had to deal with Perkins from the inn at St Katharine Dock, for the ghost of his dead father demanded at least some attention.

Spitting out the pooling blood in his mouth, he stood, waiting for a moment as the dizziness lessened. He was on the right track at least if he was being threatened.

It was a start.

Chapter Four

Winterton had agreed to everything Florentia had stipulated save the place to meet.

His note was in her hand, the letter stamped in wax and delivered that very afternoon.

His writing looked as beautiful as he himself was purported to be—a long slanted hand with an air of arrogance in the words alongside a tinge of question.

Dear Mr Rutherford,
I was pleased to receive your letter and would be most interested in your offer. I hope that my visage will indeed do your style a justice.

I would, however, prefer to have the painting completed here at the town house I am renting for the Season in St James's Square. The light is good and I should enjoy it more than sitting for hours in the gallery of a stranger.

If you could give me by return post the time and day you would like to commence I shall have my carriage sent for you. Warrenden intimated

you have been staying with his family on and off.
Is this the location you would want to be met?
  I look forward to our association on this matter.
Yours sincerely,
James Waverley

He had used neither his title nor his crest. The wax was of a plain sort one could buy for a smaller coin than the scented kind in any of the market places of London.

Not a man inclined to waste, then? Not a man who might lay his cards on the table either, for all to admire.

You should be careful of Winterton, Florentia. Her sister's words came back. *He is not a milksop lord who would be easily duped.*

She swallowed. Well, she was not a milksop lady either. The shrieking sharpness inside her had been honed in anger for years and years and her kidnapper was a great part of that. To be thrown off into a netherworld and away from society made one more independent, more resourceful.

The commission of a portrait was a medium to understand Winterton, to weigh up her options, to evaluate which way her dice would roll and what pathway her vengeance might take.

Vengeance?

She had never imagined herself as a vengeful person, even the word made her slightly horrified, but if Lord Winterton was indeed her kidnapper then he had to understand the ramifications of what he had done to her, to her family, to her father in particular who had withdrawn to Albany Manor much changed after his flight north to save her.

Ruination came in a series of degrees, it came in sickness and sleeplessness and in fright. It came in the nights when she would wake in a sweat and wonder what else she could have done to make it different. It came in the mornings when she looked in the mirror to see the fear there lurking in her eyes and the dark sleep-deprived circles beneath them.

Maria had married and was talking of having children, but she herself had faltered, trapped in the horror of her history and hiding from all that it had exposed. She needed to see Winterton privately in order to understand what she might do from now on, what pathway to a better life she would follow.

Forgiveness might bring around absolution. She only hoped she could find such mercy within herself.

She'd dressed this morning carefully, in Frederick Rutherford's clothes. She had jammed cloth down into the edges of her cheeks and practised breathing through her mouth so that her voice was more hollow and stuffed up. When she looked at her reflection she could barely remember the frightened woman she had been when she had first donned her disguise before coming to London. She seemed to have grown into the role in every way that mattered and was heartened by such a fact.

Lord Winterton had not seen her for six years and even then in the brevity and tenseness of the whole situation he probably had not observed her closely. These clothes would maintain her anonymity, she was sure of it.

As an added insurance she had placed a small paper

knife in her left pocket wrapped in leather and within easy reach.

She knew she would not use it on him, but it was a protection to keep him at bay if all else failed. She would avoid confrontation if she could, but if it was impossible she at least wanted to have a weapon in order to escape.

Her sister knocked on the door and came in, her face set in an expression that told Florentia she was not pleased.

'I think you should reconsider this whole mad scheme of yours, Flora. This may be the last chance for you to do so for once you are in that carriage—'

Florentia interrupted her. 'I shall be fine. Winterton is hardly going to jump on a young and sickly artist. He is from society, for goodness sake, and a product of years of manners and propriety.'

This observation did not seem to alleviate her sister's worries whatsoever, nor her own, in fact, given what had already transpired between them.

'Manners and propriety are not words that come easily to my mind when I think of Winterton, Flora. I could come with you?'

'No.' They had had this conversation a number of times. 'I do not need you there and from what I have read of the workings of a private commission it would be very odd to take an onlooker.'

'But the whole thing is odd and you should not be risking the chance of discovery. There might be others there.'

'He has said there would not be.'

'He might be able to see through your disguise.'

'Can you?'

'Well, no. If I did not know any of this, I would barely recognise you myself.'

'The painting shall take at the most four mornings. Twelve hours. After that I'll have a good amount of money for Papa and Mama and me to live on. My reputation with Mr Ward will stay wholly intact as well and so hopefully more sales of work will follow.'

And I will know exactly what I am facing, for better or for worse.

'I have already said to Papa that I can help, but he won't accept it.'

'Because it would be Roy's money, Maria, and Papa is too proud a man to take it.'

'Proud and foolish and if any of this leads to a problem for you I shall berate him for ever. I do hope you are not late back and if you need me at any time…'

'I won't.'

'Roy said if Winterton hurts even one hair on your body he will kill him.'

Privately Flora wondered if her sister truly believed in this absurdity. Roy was slight and short whereas everything she remembered of the Viscount was the exact opposite. 'I will bear that in mind.'

There were tears in her sister's eyes.

'Trust me, Maria. Please.'

The brown curls jolted up and down as she nodded and then the butler was there with Florentia's coat and hat and she simply followed him out.

Winterton's town house on St James's Square was far grander than any she had ever seen before. Certainly the Viscount must be somewhere at the very top of the social tree and climbing higher by the moment if the tales Maria told were anything at all to go by.

Suddenly Flora felt less certain, the clothes she wore that had seemed like a shield at home were now only thin layers over the heart of her deceit. But it was too late to back out and when the man waiting at the bottom of the wide steps leading up to the house asked her to follow him in she did so.

Once at the front door a different and even sterner-looking servant indicated a chair just inside the reception hall and, taking her prepared canvas and the small satchel filled with paint and charcoal, Flora sat down to wait.

Thirty minutes later she was still there and the bravery garnered over years of hurt had dissipated into a much lesser force beneath the heavy ticking of a clock in the corner.

The same servant finally returned, his face as dismissive as before. A mere artist was not to be bothered with or coddled, she supposed. She was surprised she had not been dispatched around to the back door when first she had come, reasoning it would be the carriage, no doubt. Anyone who arrived in his lordship's own conveyance was probably to be treated with some amount of care.

The room she was now taken to was darkened, the curtains pulled and a single candle glowing on the desk behind which a figure sat quite still.

'Thank you for coming, Mr Rutherford.' A hand gestured to the seat in front of him but he did not come to his feet.

Florentia sat as carefully as she could and as her eyes became accustomed to the dimness she saw exactly what she had hoped...and feared.

James Waverley, Lord Winterton, was indeed her kidnapper.

Still undeniably beautiful, but dishevelled somewhat, one pale and clear green eye wholly shot with red and his bottom lip split at the corner.

Her heart began to thump rapidly and she hoped the movement did not show through her clothing. The cloth at her neck felt as if it might rob her of all breath with its tightness. Please God let the asthma stay at bay, she found herself thinking, the catch in her throat worrying.

'I have been indisposed, Mr Rutherford, and I apologise for keeping you waiting.' The Viscount said this quietly and the voice was nothing like the one she remembered. It was hoarse and scratchy and deep.

Tipping her head by way of response, Florentia sniffed without decorum. The lump in her throat was so large she thought suddenly that she might just begin to cry. In deliverance? In shock? In the solace of seeing that he was alive and that her father had not killed him after all.

Years of guilt and anger melded into this one moment of utter relief. She swallowed a number of times to try to find a balance, uncaring as to what the Viscount might think of her and glad for the dimness in the room.

Another clock above the mantel beat out the seconds. This house was full of clocks, she thought, the sound of time passing, life disappearing by the second. Or rediscovered, she mused, the stoppage of life between them now running on again with a different rhythm, another truth?

The hand nearest to her lying on the table held deep bruising, the fight echoed on his face. The violence of such lacerations made the room seem smaller. Last time she had met him there'd been blood, too. And force.

He'd spoken again and she made herself listen.

'I thought to set your easel up here in this room, Mr Rutherford. It's the one I feel the most comfortable in.'

'I would need much better light, my lord.' Lowering her voice, she liked the way her words sounded. She breathed through her mouth as an extra measure and made certain to cough. Four times.

'I promise that the curtains will be pulled back when next you come.'

He smiled as he said this and Florentia's whole world stopped. The memory of him was so strong that she lost her train of thought, fumbling with her glasses as she jammed the spectacles on tighter just because she needed a distraction.

His hair was longer now. Much longer. It touched his shoulders and fell down his back, a heavy swathe of light browns and gold. The scars that had once been visible would now be gone entirely. His skin was darker, too, as though the lands he had travelled had been warm ones, brushed with summer. The hue suited him, suited his pale eyes, suited the shades in his hair. The years had been much kinder to him than they had been to her, she thought, and frowned at such a notion. The dimple in his chin was deeper.

'I wondered if you were a figment of someone's imagination, Mr Rutherford, because so few have ever seen you. I also wanted to ask you some questions before we started.'

'Yes, of course, my lord.' Subservience was a further disguise, a way to lead Winterton away from her true identity and as all the pieces of her ruse seemed to come together Florentia forced herself to relax. His grim frown heartened her. Please don't smile again, she thought, and glowered back.

'How is it you know Lady Warrenden?'

A different question from the one she had thought he might ask. Very different entirely. The chills down her spine returned in abundance.

'The Warrendens live near me in the country, sir. In Kent.'

'So you know the family well?'

'They have a penchant for my work, my lord.'

'Who does not, Mr Rutherford? It seems as if you have many admirers here in society.'

'Not as many as you seem to have garnered, Lord Winterton.'

He looked at her directly and raised an eyebrow. 'I haven't seen you at any of the soirées of the Season across the past few weeks. Do you not enjoy the pleasures of society?'

Averting her eyes, Florentia coughed for a good twenty seconds. 'I am more interested in painting,' she managed when she had caught her breath. 'I fear it takes up most of my time.'

'A passion then, this craft of yours?' He lowered his voice and gave her a quote. *'Of all base passions fear is the most accursed.'*

'Shakespeare?'

'One of the Henry's, I think. I forget which.'

'*Henry the Sixth*, sir.' Her answer was quiet. She had not expected him to rattle off Shakespeare so easily, a soldier with blood on his hands and danger imprinted into every line of his body. A man who was still fighting for his place in the world by the looks of him. The bruise under one eye would be worse on the morrow.

'You are both a scholar and an artist, then, Mr Rutherford?' He sounded amused.

When she gave no reply he stood and poured her a brandy. At least she thought it was such by the colour.

My goodness, she had not thought of this trap. A man would drink with another man and, as a woman who seldom sipped at anything stronger than a punch with very little alcohol within it, she was more than unsure as to what she should do.

Be the character, she thought, and lifted the glass to her lips. The heat of the brew warmed the blood from her toes to her hairline and after a moment or two she started to feel decidedly light-headed.

This would not do at all. Another lapse in her concentration and he would begin to wonder. Already she could see a frown of puzzlement on his brow as he watched her.

She resorted to the coughing again, taking the large kerchief Maria had procured from her pocket and blowing into it, the sound hideous and fabricated.

The longer this went on the harder it became. She felt like an insect under a microscope, peered at and questioned, everything about her turned on its head. Did he suspect? Could he know? The horror of discovery made the effects of the alcohol seem more heightened than they actually were. How many sips did one need to take to become drunk? It was frightening to feel the control she'd always had loosening.

Mr Rutherford barely looked old enough to be out of the schoolroom with his smooth cheeks and his thinness. He also looked as though he should be in an infirmary somewhere laid out on a bed with camphor and peppermint.

Peppermint. The memory of the debacle in the carriage resurfaced and James swore under his breath. God, his head ached, his knuckles stung and the lucky strike the adversary had landed last evening had broken some blood vessel in his eye so that the whole thing was a violent showy red.

He had not wanted to meet Rutherford this morning for shafts of light hurt his vision, but Mr Ward's last words had prevented him from simply cancelling the appointment.

'The lad is brilliant, Lord Winterton, so brilliant that he does not know it, the brilliance that comes from inside and not from any formal education. This painting could be worth twenty times what you will pay for it within a few short months, you mark my words, but if you frighten him off he will not be back either.'

That warning now irritated him. So far everything he'd learnt about the lad was baffling and contradictory.

'Have you always worn spectacles, Mr Rutherford?' The thickness of the glass made it seem as though the fellow was only one step away from blindness.

He nodded. 'Since I was young, sir.'

James noticed that he had pushed the brandy aside as though it were a danger, knotting his fingers together on the desk before him. Small hands and very smooth. There was a good-sized scar across the top of the thumb. When Rutherford saw his interest he immediately dropped them out of sight.

'A strong tipple does not help you creatively?' he ventured, thinking of those artists he had met in the Americas who swore the contents of a bottle allowed them their best work. The moustache above full lips looked awfully out of place amidst the smooth skin of youth. He wondered if it could be false.

'How old are you?'

'Twenty, sir. Almost twenty-one.'

He'd been caught at that age by the French in the battle for Madeira and when he'd finally got free four days later he thought it would have been better if he had simply died.

'Do you have family?'

'I do, sir, they live in Kent.'

James saw hesitation and tension cross into what little he could see of the blue eyes. Was Rutherford afraid? Was he overwhelmed? Was the drink starting to make inroads?

He raised his own glass.

'To the painting, then.' He lent forward. 'Would you mind if we did not begin today, for I have an appointment in an hour that is unexpected and urgent.'

'Of course, my lord.'

'Perhaps in private you could call me Winter.'

The lad nodded, a vulnerability and uncertainty about him so touching James wanted to protect him. That thought had him sitting back again. Rutherford's black hair was scraggly and dull, but there was a beauty about the lad that was fragile and unexpected, a quiet oddness that made him interested in knowing more, a sort of tragic undertone that shouted his life had not been easy.

He would have liked to have reached out and laid a hand across his bony shoulders, just in reassurance. But of course he did not.

'Is there something special you would require me to wear for the sittings, Mr Rutherford?'

For the first time a true emotion ran across the lad's face.

'Wear anything that makes you feel the most comfortable. It is not a showpiece I shall make for you. It will be only who you are.'

'And you can see that as you paint? Who I truly am, I mean?'

'Would you want me to, Lord Winterton?'

The room stood still suddenly, so still that James felt his hand grasp the desk he sat at, a giddy feeling that told him all was not quite as it seemed. A sort of feeling that was so foreign he could not quite decide if he was sickening for something or if a lack of sleep had finally caught him up.

The darkness inside him spiralled out through the careful face he managed to portray to society. His wealth had protected him here somewhat, but the forces of change were looming, the danger he had always lived in creeping back through the cracks of manners and propriety. He wondered if he might have a sort of delayed concussion from the blow of his assailant last night and had an image of a painting with the scar at his neck emblazoned with broken hearts and betrayal.

Nothing was safe any more.

He should send Mr Frederick Rutherford away from

the house, pay him the money owed and tell him he had changed his mind. But he couldn't. Something held him connected to this lad, bound by a thought he could not quite decipher.

'It is not a showpiece I shall make for you. It will be only who you are.'

But who was he now? The truth of not knowing had him standing and bringing this first meeting to a close.

He obviously expected her to leave, but as Florentia gathered her canvas and leather satchel the door opened and a woman and a man came through, the female throwing herself fully against Lord Winterton to kiss him on the lips and not timidly either. Looking away Florentia waited until he broke away from the caress.

'Mr Rutherford, may I present Mr and Mrs Rafael and Arabella Carmichael.' He turned to the others and smiled. 'Mr Frederick Rutherford, the celebrated artist, is here to paint my portrait. For posterity and prosperity,' he added, 'in the words of his agent.'

'I doubt anyone could do a fine job with a likeness in such semi-darkness?' The woman stated this with humour in her tone. 'It would be a wonder if he can even see you.'

Arabella Carmichael looked her over carefully as she said this. She was simply the most beautiful female Flora had ever seen anywhere, each lady of society paling against her vivid colouring. The red in her hair was that of rust and rubies and dying autumn leaves and with her full lips and her flushed cheeks she was all fire and fertility, the colour of joy and summer and success. The sort of red Flora used only sparingly in her paintings, the hue that made every other colour fade into insignificance. Her husband was just as striking. He wore a ruby pin on the lapel of his frockcoat, a dozen diamonds embedded around the shape of a serpent.

Florentia felt like a dowdy pigeon beside them, swathed in grey and brown and hidden, the patina of her deceit unattractive and ordinary. With the sensuality in the room and an undercurrent of question she wanted to be away and gone quite desperately.

Of course she knew who Mrs Arabella Carmichael was, even sequestered as she had been in the depths of rural Kent. She was a famous courtesan, trained in the profession of serving men with her body and her mind. The man Rafael Carmichael looked as though he had stepped into the room from some old painting as well, all black hair and golden eyes. An engraved silver ring sat in his left ear.

The day felt suddenly flatter, the truth of all she was and wasn't dragging her into worry. Her ruse felt wrong somehow as she had stood and watched the kiss, the hope and grief in her heart changed to only a more honest understanding.

She had built her kidnapper up as both a martyr and a miscreant, as a man of too much principle and one of none at all, and now she was uncertain as to where the truth lay. The middle ground, the grey without the black and white, the place where Winterton had left her all those years before with so many questions and so many memories?

It was his smile, she thought. It confused her now as much as it had done the first time they had ever met. She wished she had not suggested this painting. She wished she could just leave London and go home. She wished Winterton had not been beautiful and that he did not have the look of a battered angel who needed saving.

She mostly wished she did not care at all.

'I shall see you out.' His words as he came over to her. 'Perhaps tomorrow we could begin earlier. Shall we say at ten o'clock?'

As the others gave their goodbyes the same servant as before came to the door, shepherding her down the corridor, past the chair and the grandfather clock and out into the cool London day.

The sumptuous interiors of the house and the people within it stayed with her on the carriage ride home, but another thought also surfaced.

The masculine gender saw a lot more than a woman was ever allowed to, it was a freer world for them and a much more interesting one. Drink. Sex. A lack of rules and the ability to flaunt them.

The worry of a few minutes ago began to subside and she laid her head back against the smooth leather of the seat.

Well, she had done it. She had survived the first foray. Winterton hadn't suspected her and she knew initial impressions always lingered. It would be a protection and the answers she was seeking were beginning to be understood.

She would not confront the Viscount yet because underneath the strangeness she felt a kinship and a vulnerability she had not expected in a man she barely knew. It was surprising and worrying, both vengeance and absolution tumbling into another feeling entirely.

She clenched her fists together until they shook before releasing the tension.

'Enough,' she whispered to herself. 'I am enough.'

* * *

'You look worse for wear, Winter, for your wounds are visible even in this dim room and God knows what fracas you have been in now.'

Moving forward, Arabella turned his cheek into the light and he winced as one finger brushed across the bone beneath the reddened eye. 'The artist is very beautiful. I think he should have been a girl. Do you know him well?' Raising the brandy he had poured for her, she drank a good third of it. Rafe wasn't drinking at all, a fact that surprised James.

'I have just met him, Bella. He has come to do my portrait.'

'A lovely job, then, to look at you for hours. Would you not agree, Rafe?' She laughed, the sound filling the room.

'I'd say you have not told Winter that you are pregnant, Arabella, and you are teasing him in that way you regret later.'

'A baby.' James snatched the brandy from her. 'I read an academic treatise in America that warned against consuming too much alcohol whilst with child. It was most adamant in its conclusion.'

'I've told her about that already.' Rafe spoke now. 'And I have stopped drinking to try to convince her to do the same.'

'He would put me in isolation and keep me there, Winter, and nine months is a long while to worry. Frederick Rutherford was trembling quite markedly. Did you notice?'

He was used to Arabella's penchant for changing the subject when it suited her and he smiled. 'I am the boy's first private commission. Perhaps it's nerves?'

'And you would scare anyone, James, especially with your blood-red eye, let alone an unprepossessing and effeminate artist.' When Bella stated this, the timid uncertainty of Rutherford came back, a young man caught in the expectation of others.

James had felt his tension and desperation. He had also understood that the lad was lying about everything. He had been in the game of deceit for too long to believe otherwise and he'd known many a man trying to hide his identity.

The cough was the first giveaway, of course, a means of diversion that was poorly executed. Rutherford had not coughed even once with Arabella and Rafael in the room. The glasses were also wrong for he doubted anyone so young needed all that magnification, especially one adept at building a detailed and intricate likeness of a stranger in the precise medium of charcoal and paint.

But what could Frederick Rutherford want of him that a hundred others had failed to discover?

'Well, I think that the little artist is intriguing.' Arabella said this as she pulled back the curtains.

'In what way?' He couldn't help taking the bait, as he squinted against the light.

'Frederick Rutherford looks at you as though you are a prize, but then everybody is inclined to admire you, if only you could see it. But you never stop in a place long enough to notice those who would lay down their lives for you and there are so damn many of them. Perhaps this artist, Rutherford, is just another you will not notice because you do not love yourself enough.' She shook her head as he went to speak. 'You are flawed in some way, Winter, that is incomprehensible, you with all your money and beauty and strength. You who can lead men anywhere you want them to go and they will follow.'

He could hear the blood hammering in his ears. 'You are spouting nonsense, Bella.' He looked across at Rafe for support, but Arabella was not yet finished, not by a long shot.

'We are all of us too good friends to lie to each other, James, and you have been my best friend since I was ten. Now it is my turn to help you. You will be thirty before you know it and for the past years, from what you say, you have not let a woman into your life. Not in any way that matters, at least. Oh, granted, you flirt with the possibility and allow your paramours to believe that there is a chance for everything, but you never take it further. A quick romp and then a parting, no true emotion in any of it. In Boston it was said you could have had your pick of any of the women and I have heard accounts of it being exactly the same in London. The Heron daughters, for example, have apparently spoken of nothing at all save of your allure since the Allans' ball. There is also talk of a stately home in Herefordshire.'

'How could you know this? You abhor society, Bella?'

'Rafe hears things in the same way as you do, Winter, because the channels of intelligence are never still and because once you are part of an underworld you never truly escape it. As for me, well, I was not born in such elevated circles as you both were, but in the worlds below that of the *ton* everyday life is most connected. The servants talk. The shopkeepers gossip. The man on the corner who sells herrings for a shilling has a story to tell for the right price and your name at the moment, Winter, is exchanged for the top currency. And I listen well to all of the gossip.'

'God help me.' He began to laugh. Arabella had always been beautiful, but few had understood the cleverness that ran along with it or the iron will that she had had to cultivate to survive.

Rafe finally pushed himself away from the wall and spoke.

'It is rumoured that the Rutherford chit is related to the Warrendens.'

'I'd heard that said. Do you know how?'

'Closely, by all accounts. Mr Rutherford has brought no servants with him from Kent, not even a valet, and those in Warrenden's employ are not allowed anywhere near the locked room that Rutherford uses at his town house. The most worrying thing is that the artist has also been asking questions about you, Winter, about your past. Quietly, I will give him that, but still...'

The shock of Rafael's revelation had James lifting his glass and drinking the last of his brandy.

'My past?'

'Your time in the Americas. Your family. That sort of thing. He will know that you are looking into buying Atherton Abbey and that you have returned to England wealthy. Was the portrait expensive?'

'Very.'

Rafe laughed. 'Well, then, perhaps there is method to his madness after all. Choose one wealthy mark and milk his vanity for all it is worth and then go on to the next. It could indeed work for a while.'

James shook his head. 'From what I have heard the man is prone to alter the appearance of his subjects.

At the Allans' ball the oldest Miss Heron told me she was worried that she might not be drawn with quite the fineness she would hope to be. I do not think an artist like that would pander to the shallow conceits of the very rich.'

'Interesting.' Arabella took hold of Rafe's hand and held it close. 'I'd like him to do my portrait then, for I am sick of all the wooden beautiful ones I seem to engender.'

'I doubt Rutherford will be tempted. I think this is his first and last effort at pleasing his agent. He told me as much.'

'It gets more and more fascinating. But why you, in particular, Winter? Do you know him? Have you met Mr Rutherford before?'

'No.'

'Could your father have?'

That thought had not occurred to James. William Waverley had gone bankrupt after a gambling spree that had lasted for ten years. Could the Rutherford family have been somehow involved in that scandal?

The artist did not look well off for a start with his old-fashioned clothing and scraggly hair. But in the lines of his body there was a fineness that was easily discernible and a watchfulness that hinted of other things.

He'd observe him more carefully tomorrow and try to ask his own questions. He'd make certain that no one was expected to visit either to allow him the hours of uninterrupted time he might need to persuade the lad to trust him.

He wished Rafe and Arabella had arrived when they were supposed to have, for he would have liked to speak with Rutherford longer. He'd seemed frightened and timid. James wondered how he had injured his hand for the scar upon it looked so very out of character.

Flora visited the church she'd found near Grosvenor Square because after her day she felt as if she needed to pray for guidance and help.

Her reactions to Lord Winterton made no sense. She should be loathing and blaming him for all the trouble that he had caused in her life and here she was wishing that he could look beneath the disguise and hurt to understand just exactly who she was. Ridiculous. Foolish. Imprudent.

The anger that had been building all afternoon under bewilderment and question bubbled over as she sat in the pew in the third row from the back of the empty church.

The candles were burning and she tried to concentrate on them, tried to inhale their scent and pull herself free from this fear she was consumed with. A statue of Jesus on the cross in marble looked down at her from the font. She wished the sculptor had made his eyes more believable. The lines of his arms were wrong, too. Foreshortened and thick.

Her sister had wanted to know everything that had happened with Lord Winterton, every nuance and word that had passed between them when she'd arrived home. Maria had been waiting in the front room, worry crossing her brow and darkening the blue in her eyes, but had then immediately taken her hand and shepherded her upstairs where their privacy was assured.

Flora had told her a little of her time at Lord Winterton's, but left out many of the more pertinent facts. She'd said nothing of the Viscount's unexpected visitors or of the offered brandy. She had not told her sister how she'd been made to wait either or of the darkness of the room she was finally ushered into or of the battered beauty of the man within it.

Shallow she knew to base so much of her opinion on simple appearance, but there it was.

By all accounts he was a womaniser. The kiss Arabella Carmichael had given him in front of her husband had been scandalous and it told her that the Earl ran in fast company and did not apologise for any of it.

She wondered what had happened when she left. Had they spoken of her? Had they laughed at her countenance, recalling her cough and her glasses and the dull colour of her wig? Or had she been a person of no consequence and very little thought? Dismissed completely the moment she had left the room.

Mocked or forgotten, both options had her bringing her hands together and praying…for what?

For his redemption. For her forgiveness. For her vengeance. For his atonement. For some resolution. For a hundred different things that could never be. For the life she'd been forced to live and for her papa who had slid into a depression fed by the worry of an entailed property and an unmarried ruined daughter.

She frowned and stood. The Lord above would not want to hear such complaints and whining from a woman who was hardly as desperate as a thousand others. Oh, granted, she had had her trials, but even those paled against the everyday life of many Londoners without enough food to eat or a warm and safe place to sleep.

No, she needed to deal with this effectively by herself. Tomorrow she would go to meet Lord Winterton again and begin the portrait. She knew his face. She could have closed her eyes and drawn him from memory. And she had done so for the painting in her wardrobe at Albany held a likeness she would never better, not even with him there right in front of her.

It was the essence of her subjects she loved the most to draw and his spirit was vivid and strong and clear. She couldn't show him any of it, though, this reality she knew, because he would understand who she was, where they had met, what had passed between them on the road north all those years before. She was not ready for that just yet.

It was a fine line she was treading between lies and the truth, the diverging pathways of exposure, scandal and ruin all a part of it, too.

The quiet of the church was comforting, the solace of a space to breathe and consider. The smell of candles and incense was embedded in the polished wooden benches and ornate hangings, the scent warm across the cool darkness. Light streamed in from all angles above, the smallest sound echoed back from the walls and the roof. As a woman she would never have been able to walk these streets alone or steal into the worshipping place with such an untroubled ease.

A man's life was a different life from the one that she had been brought up to. The boundaries were wider and there was a freedom that was exhilarating.

She wouldn't leave London just yet. She had accepted no money and she had signed no contract, but the strictures of her life were opening again, the dullness of the last years exposed in the running risk of what she was now a part of, an animation of stillness, an exuberance that made her breathe faster and more deeply.

She wanted the liberty and the emancipation that this charade allowed her. She wanted the independence to walk exactly where she desired to, a thought that was increasingly more fascinating and satisfying.

She wanted to draw what she could see here in the hidden parts of the world she had not been allowed to venture into before as a woman. The buildings. The river. The people who hurried across the parks in the wind who looked nothing at all like those who inhabited the *ton*.

Chapter Five

The next morning she was shown into the company of Lord Winterton without delay, past the wicker chair and the clock, down the corridor and into the library that was somewhat changed.

Today the curtains were drawn back and the light of springtime flooded into the room, making it look bigger and much more inviting.

Lord Winterton's appearance was different, too, his clothes this morning a reflection of his elevated station in life. He had shaved and pulled his hair back into a cue tied with leather. A severe style, but it suited him. His left eye did not look so reddened or his lip so broken. The purple bruise on his cheek, however, was much darker. It made him look rakish and dangerous.

'I hope the room and its brightness meets with your expectations, Mr Rutherford.'

'It does, my lord.'

Her glance was drawn to the books in long shelves on each side of the room. Milton. Edmund Burke. Swift. Shakespeare. The Viscount was a well-read man.

'Can I help you with the canvas? It looks heavy.'

He'd come closer now, much closer. It was the first time he'd been so near and she felt herself stiffen.

Don't touch me. Don't touch me for if you do...?

'No, it is fine, my lord, and most easy to handle.'

She thought she should cough, but yesterday's marathon had left her exhausted and her throat sore and so she decided to depend on the fact that he'd have her demeanour of sickness in his mind already.

'I have not sat for a portrait before.' He sounded uncertain now and a little shy and Florentia felt the tension inside her soften.

'It won't hurt, Lord Winterton, as long as you remain very still. Here.' She angled a small armchair in front of a window and invited him to sit, liking the way he crossed his legs in a long line and placed his arms on the chair rests.

No tightness in the gesture. No pretence. An easy subject and so very beautiful. Sliding the thick glasses down her nose so that she could see over the top, she began.

His eyebrows had risen as she watched him, arched in something akin to humour. She saw he almost went to say something, but did not as she raised the charcoal and squinted. Sliding her thumb up and down the length of the shaft, she tried to get down the proportions in a way she was happy with. His legs. His body and his head. The quick freedom of the medium began to fill the empty canvas, as it came alive with the essence of James Waverley, Viscount Winterton.

His hands came next, the line of the fingers and the shapes of each. His nails were square and short. There were many scars across the knuckles of his right hand and her glance inadvertently went to the one at the top of her own thumb. Hurts lingered in both skin and mind. She wondered if he had other marks beneath the linen and superfine apart from that which she knew would be on his neck. Some inner sense told her that there would be. He was a man who wore his history like an armour.

She moved on to his face next for the eyes were the strongest point of any portrait, though when his glance met hers straight on it was she who looked away first. There was laughter in the clear and pale green but also question. His cheekbones were high and angled, the play of light from the window drawing them up into sharpness.

The dimple on his chin she hurried over. She did not wish to remember the portrait she had already finished of him.

The Belvedere Torso sketched in red chalk by Michelangelo came to mind, the vitality and the beauty. But this Adonis was fully clothed and she was glad of it.

For the first time since meeting him Frederick Rutherford looked as if his fleeing was not imminent, his whole attention centred on the canvas and charcoal, his mouth pursed in focus.

'Can I talk? Or would that ruin the composition?'

He asked this carefully, fearing that even the slightest of movements might spoil things.

Rutherford looked up at the question, the surprised frown between his eyes giving the impression that he had just remembered the person he drew was alive after all.

'Drawing is not an exact science, sir. The interpretation of your face does not lie only within what is seen.'

'You try to look inside?'

'You quoted Shakespeare yesterday and I can see that your many books are well loved and used. Those things are a part of who you are and should be reflected in a portrait. But there is danger in you, too, and a contrast if you like. Stillness against energy. It must be hard to be so very noticeable when there is such a lot you want to keep hidden, Lord Winterton?'

He tried to keep his face clear of surprise. 'Are you a soothsayer, Mr Rutherford? A man who might think to read people's minds?'

'Bodies tell stories as succinctly as any words. The skin holds tales as surely as the eyes and face hold history. Even hands have a narrative to impart.'

He watched her straight on. 'Uncomfortable truths. Are you surprised when you are wrong?'

'Are you saying I am, my lord?'

'Age must be fairly definable, heartbreak less so. What if I told you my life has been a comfortable and joyous one thus far, without any trial or tribulation?'

'I might congratulate you out loud on your luck, but I doubt that I would believe you. Tragedy makes each of us stronger and I can see you are that, my lord. Strong, I mean. Perhaps you have had to be?'

He began to laugh because this was one of the most illuminating conversations that he'd had for a great deal of time.

'And what of you?' he asked after a moment. 'Has the loss of some great hope made you who you are? Has it boosted empathy?'

Winter saw the lad's eyes in full focus as he tipped his head, the pupils flaring over the top of heavy glass.

They were the blue of summer skies and gentle seas. But apprehension danced across the colour, striking shards of shock at the darker edges even as the contact was lost.

He felt his heart quicken in response as some far-off memory tried to reform and appear.

'Secrets define us, my lord, like small sharp pebbles caught in a shoe. You have yours and I have mine. To be rid of them is to tread a pathway differently.'

'Do I know you, Mr Rutherford?' He hated the way his voice sounded, foreign and tight.

'Know me as the artist or know me as the man?' There was no kindness in such a question. 'I do not imagine either would be possible for I rarely visit London, my lord.'

But Rutherford's hand shook as he clutched the charcoal and real anger crossed his brow.

'Of course.' James settled back into quietness, but something had changed between them and he could not quite work out what it was.

His eyes were no longer relaxed, she thought, no longer languid or threaded in humour. He'd remembered something, she was sure of it, the first finger on his left hand rapping out a rhythm against the wooden armrest on the chair.

She wanted to leave, to escape, to be far away from those probing pale eyes that saw everything, and nothing.

If she cried it would be over. If tears escaped from her eyes and ran unheeded beneath her glasses down to the skin at her cheek she would be exposed. So instead she gathered her courage and tried again whilst she still could.

'Do you think on the whole you are a good man, Lord Winterton?'

'As opposed to an evil one, Mr Rutherford?'

That small humour heartened her. 'Nothing quite so damning, I imagine. More of an overall summation of your character, if you like.'

'Then, yes.'

She relaxed, pleased for his answer. 'And do you believe in fate?'

'The concept of fate based on the belief that there is a fixed natural order to the universe that can never be changed, no matter how hard you try?'

When she nodded he went on.

'Oedipus struggled to escape his fate and couldn't.'

'Do you think that was because he was forewarned?' She asked the question lightly, but a lot rested on his answer.

'You are asking me, Mr Rutherford, if I believe man's character is his fate.'

'Perhaps I am.'

'A fatal flaw. Like Hamlet. Unchangeable. Constant. Set in stone?'

'The idea that no matter how much one endeavours one cannot change one's destiny?' She looked towards the books all lined up at one end of the room. 'You have shelves and shelves of Shakespeare and wasn't he the master of proving that fate, not will, pre-determines the order and course of events.'

'Anything you do is pointless and will not be made different, no matter how much you wish it?' He shook his head and the light caught the gold threaded through darker shades. 'No. I myself don't believe in that sort of fate.'

His fingers were alive now, as he spoke, not the quiet things that they had been before. Eloquence and intelligence had a certain line that whispered beneath the skin. Wiping out the charcoal, she began anew with her drawing, the energy within quickened, different marks appearing.

'In all of my reading in the subject, Mr Rutherford, characters aware of their fate inevitably try to escape it?' He finished that sentence in the cadence of a question and she could not help but to find an answer.

'Because *She* is a motif in folklore that draws people in and keeps them under her spell.'

'You see her as a woman? Fate, I mean?'

'I do.'

'Capricious? Often unfair?' His voice held laughter.

'Confident. Unfailing,' she returned, with the same sort of humour. 'A power applied by the truth of certainty.'

'A feminine muse who does not take kindly to her hand being forced?'

Florentia heard the regard in the words just as strongly as she felt the pull of his intellect, though his words cut close to the bone. Her hand had been forced by his on the road all those years before and it had brought her here to this moment, in disguise and hiding, the trust she had held in people shattered and torn.

'If you could begin your life again, Lord Winterton, would there be things you would do differently or change even a little bit?'

He shifted at that and uncrossed his legs, sitting

straighter, the fingers on one hand playing with the ring he wore on the other.

'Who would not admit to that, Mr Rutherford? Who would not relish the opportunity to have a second attempt in getting it right? There have been things…' He stopped and she saw a flat sadness in his eyes, the empty desolation of honesty. 'The Realms of the Lost Chances…?'

He said it like the title of a book or a song. He said it without any attempt to hide the sorrow in his voice. He also said it like a man who knew these things would never come to pass for him and something inside Florentia turned and changed.

Amazement. Wonder. The chance to speak with all her heart and soul and wit and to be answered back in the very same way. No limit in the opinions, no careful edging around truth. It astonished her this conversation, this discourse full of diverging thoughts, which echoed promise and honesty.

She wanted to know more about him, his place of birth and the people who had formed him, but did not quite know how to ask.

'What would you change if you could?' His question came through the growing silence.

'My brother's death.' She was astonished she had said that right out loud. She had never spoken to another beside her parents and sister about Bryson at all.

'How old was he when he died?'

'Sixteen.'

'And you? How old were you when this happened?'

She clenched her lips and teeth together so that she would not say. *Sixteen years, two months and nine-*

teen days. The exactness of it cut into her heart like a sharp honed blade.

'Were there other siblings?'

'There were, Lord Winterton.'

'And your parents?'

'My father is unwell. Mama nurses him. A martyr, if you will. A woman of duty.'

The words of Maria Warrenden rung out in memory. She had said almost the exact same thing of her parents at the Allans' ball when he had asked after them. A coincidence? He thought not.

Could Rutherford be some adopted son of the Hale-Burtons, a foster child or a bastard one? Every question he formed about the man demanded tenfold other questions and then more on top of those ones.

The sun was climbing now and the beams from the window fell across them both. Frederick Rutherford's cheeks were as bare as a baby's bottom, no stubble or fuzz upon them.

Perhaps he was even younger than he had said? Perhaps he was barely out of the schoolroom, but trying to make some coin for a family who were hurting?

The price tag on the painting was ridiculously high. High enough to keep the young man's parents in food, heat and lodging for at least a year if they were frugal?

The answers were beginning to line up in a way that worried James and he dearly wanted to see Roy Warrenden and his wife again to ask them some questions.

'I shan't begin the painting of your portrait today, my lord.' Rutherford said this just as James thought he might not speak again. 'I need to look at the lines of the work and know that they are the ones I want to continue with before I apply colour.'

'Can I see what you have done so far?'

Rutherford shook his head and brought out a cloth to drape around the canvas.

'It is bad luck to look at a work before it is finished.'

'Like a bride,' James said when he saw him frown. 'The groom should not see his bride before they are married,' he added, wondering why he should have used such an example when there were so many other better ones available. 'The last freedom. The final independence.'

Frederick Rutherford blushed, as red as a beetroot, from the throat to the hairline, a brilliant firelight red. 'You don't believe in marriage?'

'Well, I never married so presumably not.' He found himself saying this almost out of anger. Once he had believed he would marry. Once he had felt whole enough to become a half of someone else.

'The Warrendens are happy.' This statement surprised him.

'And you know them well?'

'Well enough to see that of them, at least,' Rutherford answered, bending to the bag he carried, the one of canvas and leather, buckled in silver. 'I cannot come tomorrow. The next morning suits me, though.'

'Then I shall see you on Thursday morning. Do I wear the same clothes that I am in now?'

'It does not matter about what you wear. I will change it anyway.'

'I see.'

'The room will look different, too. You will be somewhere else, I think, in another place entirely.'

James could not help but be amused. 'When would you like to be paid?'

'Not yet,' he returned quickly. 'If you pay me it will ruin everything. You will own what I make and I am not sure if…'

'You want to give it to me yet?' He finished the sentence and put out his hand. But it was not taken. Rutherford merely tipped his head once and then turned away from the windows and the light, the canvas clutched carefully under one arm and the oversized satchel under the other.

'Goodbye, my lord.'

Then he was gone, the door shut behind him, the lingering smell of linseed and lavender the only things left behind.

Rafe Carmichael turned up an hour later and he didn't look happy.

'London squeezes the life out of me, Winter. It's the air here, I think, and the lack of green. All I can say is thank God for the gardens Arabella planted at our house.'

'I'm hoping Atherton Abbey may bring me the same sort of refuge, Rafe. I signed the contracts yesterday.'

'Bella said you would do that, but I didn't believe her because you have never stayed anywhere for more than a few months in all the years I have known you.'

'I think it's largely to do with my unstable childhood.'

'I had heard your mother was…difficult?'

'So difficult she killed herself. It was a statement, I think, for her loathing of my father.'

'An effective one then. How old were you?'

'Fourteen. William was seldom sober afterwards but he was sometimes kind. For that I owe him at least an overdue reprieve of the soul.'

'The man who was mentioned the other night when you were attacked. Perkins? I have been doing some looking and it seems he is the son of a small northern lord. He drinks at the Red Fox Inn in St Katharine Dock usually on a Friday afternoon.'

'How much did that information cost you?'

'I will call it square after sharing a bottle of your finest brandy and giving you some advice.' He waited as the glasses were found and the tipple poured. 'Find a wife like I did. Find a woman who surprises you and who does not allow your soul the chance to fail. Bella said to tell you that she went to a soothsayer in Covent Garden yesterday and offered up your name and a drawing she had of you. The old gypsy, who can read the fate of even those who are absent, said you need to look into the places you least expect to find love and that the one you will marry has already come into your life, but you have not seen her yet.'

James laughed because he could not help it. 'You believe in this rubbish?'

'I found Arabella in a brothel. If a fortune teller had tried to tell me such a truth, I might have laughed, too. Harking back to the prophesy, Winter, who has surprised you and challenged you lately?'

'Frederick Rutherford.' James's answer came without thought and he swore beneath his breath.

His regard for the reclusive artist resurfaced. If he breathed in deeply he could still smell lavender and hear the strange cadence of his husky voice. Nothing felt safe any more. He felt as if Rutherford could see into the very shadows of his soul.

'Will you visit Perkins?' Rafe changed the subject of the conversation as sharply as his wife did and he was glad of it.

'I will.'

'Take a knife, then. It's a quieter bearer of death than a pistol and from all that I've heard of him the man is dangerous.'

'You're instructing me on battle, Rafe?'

'More like warning you, for I know you are far better at the art of violence than me. I do, however, want you settled at Atherton with the wife who you will be surprised by after you find her in a place you least expect to.'

James smiled and swallowed a good-sized sip of the smooth brandy.

Her sister met her as she came up the steps and followed her into her room, though she did not speak until the door to her chamber was locked and there would be no chance of any curious ears listening in.

'I thought you were never coming home.'

Florentia took off her hat and dragged the heavy wig from her head, spreading her own hair into the air in relief as she sat. 'A portrait is not an instant thing, Maria. It is made up of layers and every one of them is as important as the next. There is no hurrying of it. Today was the base layer, the beginning.' She flung the wig down on to the bed beside her.

'Was it difficult?'

'It kept changing, that was the trouble. Lord Winterton is one thing and then he is another. Like quicksilver.' Standing, she took off her boots and wriggled her toes before stretching out her feet. The height of the inlaid leather was uncomfortable and heavy and the back of her legs ached in a shared empathy with her insoles.

'You mean mercury?' Maria's voice was high. 'Isn't that a poison?'

Florentia laughed at her sister's horror. 'But it sits next to gold on the periodic chart. What does Roy think of him, Maria? Of Winterton?'

'He sees him as a friend. He says that he is to be trusted if he gives his word otherwise we should never have agreed to this charade of yours. Not for all the tea in China nor for all the money in his overflowing accounts.'

'Did he tell you anything of Winterton's history? It could be helpful. In my work...' she added lamely, because lying to her sister was not something she did well.

'He said that the Viscount had a difficult child-hood. From what wasn't said I think Winterton has been lonely for a very long time. He was also a soldier in the first Peninsular Campaign under Moore. A part of intelligence, Roy thinks.'

'Do you know a Mr Rafael Carmichael?'

'The steel baron? He is married to a woman who was a courtesan.'

'Arabella Carmichael. I met them yesterday at St James's Square.'

Maria began to frown. 'You didn't tell me that. My God, Florentia. They sound like fast people and people who might guess...'

'My secret?'

'There is more to it than that, isn't there? You would not keep this up if it were only for the production of a portrait. There is something you're not telling me.'

'Do you believe in Fate, Maria?'

'The sort of Fate that makes you sad for ever, you mean? The sort that takes you away from life because you have been dealt such a rum hand?'

Maria walked to the window. 'Your world is tiny, Florentia, and it has been for years, but everything is a risk, don't you see, every step you take, every place you go, every person you meet. It can either turn out well or it can turn out badly.' She shook her head. 'I asked Roy the same question about Fate once and he thought that perhaps it is really your own will bending everything that happens into what you think you deserve?'

The power of her sister's reply was unexpected. 'You were talking of me?'

Maria nodded.

'Well, now I think I deserve better.'

'Good.' Her sister's smile was disarming. 'And if it takes dangerous people to drag you out of obscurity who am I to complain about it, for you look happier and more vibrant by the minute. But remember, I will always be here for you when you do want to talk about what you are really up to and perhaps I can even be of help.'

'You already have been.'

'Then I am glad for it.'

Florentia met James Waverley unexpectedly as she walked from the chapel near Grosvenor Square later that afternoon. He was alone and dressed in clothes that were nothing at all like those of a well-born lord.

'Mr Rutherford? You are a religious man?' His glance took in the church behind her.

'I enjoy observing the paintings, sir, and the stained-glass windows.'

'A belief, then, in the finer aspects of the church?'

She laughed at that and forgot to disguise the sound. Caught unawares, she found her charade harder to effect, thrown out in timing for the careful preparation of forming the persona of another. The expression in his eyes also signalled danger.

Out in the open in the street he seemed taller and bigger and much more menacing than he had inside his town house in St James's. Out here the man he had become in the Americas, the powerful and compelling overlord, was so much more visible. The adornment necessary to exist in society detracted from his menace. Here the plainness of dress and the lack of any frippery left him intimidating and threatening and more beautiful than she had ever seen him.

That thought made her blush and she knew he had seen such a shyness for he looked away as if to give her time to recover. The colour of his eyes today was almost see through, the pale green translucent.

'You are a puzzle, Mr Rutherford,' he said finally. 'A man who might be everything or nothing?'

This was said as a question, the intonation lifting as he looked straight at her, the broken truths between them filled with hate and blame and betrayal.

She thought he might see it, all that was hidden underneath as he held her glance, the barrier of her spectacles counting for little.

'You are familiar to me, Mr Rutherford. Have we met before?'

***

Hell. This afternoon under a darker sky Rutherford seemed changed somehow, the lines of the lad's face softer, the colour of his eyes magnified.

Beautiful.

That word stung him with a shock.

For so long in his life he had stayed out of reach of others, giving little, expecting less. But here he felt a connection. He wanted to protect the boy, keep him safe from harm or hurt or sadness. He needed to understand the distance he wore like a cloak, that prickly layer of reserve so known because he had it, too, a fierce aloneness that drove everything he did.

'Do you have many friends here in London, Mr Rutherford? Do you go out much?'

'I don't, sir. By choice, that is. I am…busy.'

'With the paintings?'

'They take a while to finish properly, my lord. Often a long while.'

'Do you have a favourite?'

James could see that Rutherford did. It was written across his face in sudden shock, though he stayed silent.

'Where did you learn? To draw, I mean. Who was your tutor?'

'Books, sir. In my father's library. I was an ardent copyist before I tried anything at all on my own.'

'And your father is…?'

'Oh, you would not know of him, my lord. He is a simple country gentleman and seldom visits the town.'

'Because he is ill?'

'Pardon?' Fright now could be plainly seen.

'You told me he was a sickly man who has taken to his bed.'

At this the other breathed out, the sound shaking with a vulnerability that tugged at Winter's heart-strings. He felt every one of his twenty-nine years even as the artist began to speak again.

'I am ordinary, my lord, just as my father is and if it were not for the paintings the London *ton* would have tired of me years ago.'

'But that is exactly the point, Mr Rutherford. You were nowhere to be seen even a year ago. Nobody has heard of you in Kent and any lineage you may lay claim to here is indeed a mystery.'

The boy lifted his face to the sky and licked dry lips, the sensuality of the movement making James reel, a hot shaft of desire snaking through him. It was the smell of lavender, he decided later, and the slender pale shaft of his throat. It was the supplication of his hands, too, bent and small, paint on the edge of the thumbnail that held the scar across it.

He could discern a tang of incense from the church on his clothes and today a button on his shirt was undone, the cloth of some undergarment beneath fine.

There was danger here. The thought came with a violent swiftness, the same nausea he had felt in his recuperation after the skirmish in the northern inn, the same dislocation, too. If he had followed his desires he might have reached out there in the busy public street and brought the youth in against him, to try to understand just who and what he was. A pull of lust so fierce it almost undid him.

Instead he moved back and tipped his hat, pleased

for the growing distance between them and the poorness of the light.

'Goodbye, Mr Rutherford.' He did not wait for an answer as he left.

Chapter Six

After such a disconcerting encounter James had spent the evening at the docks in the darkness with the smell of the sea close and the knowledge that a thousand yards of Haitian mahogany was stacked in the hull of the *White Swan* clipper moored a hundred yards offshore. It was waiting for the tide to turn and the river to swell and the morning light to break across the dull silence of the Thames.

Those he had come to meet would arrive soon, he was sure of it, for the man he had waylaid last night near the Red Fox had been most emphatic his boss would meet him, doused as he was in badly cut liquor, the stench of it on his breath. The gold coins had probably helped as had the promise of more. James had always found that generosity was a far greater persuasive factor than any force in cajoling men of a dubious morality to do as he wanted them to.

Fifteen minutes later they arrived and he pocketed his silver whisky flask and stood away from the wall. If he thought this meeting too dangerous, he could simply escape by jumping into the river. He was a strong swimmer and the current here would take him across to the opposite bank.

The tall sandy-haired man he presumed to be Perkins spoke first.

'I had word that you wished to talk to me.'

Without hesitation James gave back an answer. 'My father was William Waverley and I've reason to believe he was drinking at the inn you own on the night of his death?'

'I beg to differ. The constabulary maintained he was not in my inn at all. The Viscount's death by all accounts was from misadventure further up the river.'

'His brandy flask and hat were found in a room at your establishment.'

'Says whom?'

'The man whom I bought them from a short while ago. He would be willing to go to the law with his information, but I hoped it would not have to come to that. I thought you might see the sense in establishing your own innocence in the matter before it went further, so to speak.'

'You are here to threaten me, then?'

'No, indeed I am not. All I am after is the truth of my father's demise.'

'Many say the old Viscount killed himself. A suicide?'

'I don't believe that to be true.'

'Sometimes what is hoped for and what is are not the same thing.'

'My father converted to Catholicism the year after my mother died. A penance, he thought.'

'A religion in which killing oneself is a dreaded mortal sin?'

James nodded. 'The preservation of life for the salvation of soul. He was not an angel, but he had a marked belief in the sacredness of the Fifth Commandment.'

For a moment there was a silence between them, the sound of the river close.

'It takes a brave man to come asking his questions here in the slums of the river and amongst men who would stick a knife in your back in an instant on a single wrong word.'

'I was a soldier, sir, and I promise at least some of you would die should you try to take me.'

The man opposite smiled, but he also relaxed, his fingers slipping from their place above his belt. He'd held a knife there no doubt and there was also the outline of a firearm under the right side of his coat. Left handed. So many clues to be gained by a careful observation.

'Did you know your father had a side business of transporting illegal brandy from the Continent? A way to try and makes ends meet, he told me once.'

James nodded. It was something he had only recently discovered.

'Two gentlemen came to visit him in his room, a room he often rented to be sure, and he left with them. Too quickly, I always thought, for the bottle of the best brandy in the house still sat on his bedside table barely touched. An unusual happening with the Viscount to waste any liquor of some worth…or of none.'

'You bought the contraband from him?'

'For a sum that was often more than I wanted to pay. But, yes, because he was honest in his promises and he always delivered. I recognised one of the men who came to see your father on the last night he was alive.'

'Who?'

'Mr Benjamin Heron.'

'You would swear on this?'

'To you I would.'

'Why would you give this name to me?'

'I liked your father. The drink blurred his lines, but under it all he was a good man and I think you are probably the same. The information I give you is in all confidence and I leave you to do with it as you will, but I shan't be involved further and there is nothing else I can tell you.'

Then he was gone, disappeared into the gloom of a night that held the promise of rain. James knew he would not see him again.

Heron. The name turned on his tongue. What had the connection been between his father and the man? Was Heron augmenting his own fortune by his involvement with an illicit trade in contraband brandy? The man's wealth was legendary, but he had never heard a whisper of anything untoward.

He would need to confront Heron in a way that did not send him into hiding. He'd need to become a confidant. His heart sank. The only way he could see of doing that was to make some sort of effort with his daughters.

The blonde giggliness of Julia Heron came to mind. A woman who would worry and fuss. The prophesy of the old gypsy Bella had given his name to also rankled.

The one you will marry has already come into your life. The *ton* and its rules had a way of tripping a man up and sending even those hell-bent on avoiding marriage straight into its arms and he did not wish to be the next Winterton driven to drink too much because of an unsuitable wife.

Chapter Seven

Ｊames watched from the upstairs window the next morning as his carriage drew up in front of the town house and Frederick Rutherford alighted. He had almost cancelled the appointment after their meeting yesterday and his own unease of it, but he hadn't because a delay would only increase his anxiety.

The fellow came down the steps carefully, his hand clutching the side of the carriage door as though he might fall. The slightness of his figure caught the first morning sun, a thin light today as if spring was still wrestling with the oncoming summer and had not quite let go its chill.

Rutherford looked uncertain as he turned to collect his canvas and leather satchel, the former still draped with thick fabric, and Winter wondered why the footman did not help him with it. Perhaps he had asked already and been refused. There was something about the young artist that was prickly and isolated, a reclusive spirit caught in a commission he so obviously did not want.

Why had he suggested it in the first place when the

labour of being in another's company was so clearly trying?

The boots he wore took James's attention because he noticed the soles were thickened in a way favoured by the London fops. Was Rutherford vain enough to want the extra height? His walk was mincing this morning though he lengthened his stride to avoid any cracks on the pavement or on the steps leading up to the house.

For luck? For superstition? To meet with a Fate he'd rallied against two days ago? An inescapable future?

As the lad passed the small tubs of miniature bay trees on each side of the front doorway he reached out and picked a handful of leaves, bringing the greenery to his nose and inhaling deeply, standing there completely still in the moment. His footman, a man of considerable gruffness and age, smiled at the action as he waited, the sheer enjoyment of the young man placing a spell over all who watched.

James stiffened. What must it be like to be so lost in all of the senses? A creative mind needed such inspiration, he supposed. He himself had passed those trees many times since coming to England and he had never thought once to lean down and smell the aroma. There was a certain honesty in such an act. When Rutherford opened his hands to let the leaves go he was careful to scatter them out of the harm of being trodden on.

A few moments later his man knocked on his chamber door. He had not moved from the window because all of a sudden he felt immeasurably tired, by Rutherford's mystery and innocence, by Perkin's revelations and by the Heron girls who seemed to be using each waking hour to try to find ways to inveigle him into their company. The shock of their father being named as one who might have killed his own parent was also a part of his fatigue, but although Benjamin Heron was a man of wealth he did not quite strike James as a murderer for he was too weak and nervous of life.

Then there was his reaction to the artist outside the church yesterday. That above all else was what kept him here unmoving and unsure, a feeling so unfamiliar he could not quite decipher what his next step should be.

'Mr Rutherford is come. He is in the library, my lord.'

'Offer him a drink, then, and I shall be down in a moment.'

He turned to the mirror as the servant left and observed himself. The bruise under his eye had lightened considerably and he could barely make out the wound on his lip. The shadow of uncertainty in his visage however was worrying for the lad made him nervous somehow. Rutherford's intellect had been surprising, his wit sharp and his opinions eloquently put.

He smelt good, too.

That thought had James frowning because it was such a personal observation, a notice one might give to a lover or a wife.

'Hell,' he swore out loud as the truth of such scrutiny settled. He hadn't been truly interested in a woman in years and here he was fighting off an attraction to a damned slip of a boy.

He should simply tell his man to send the artist home and pay the whole exorbitant sum of the portrait as a forfeiture. The cost would be nothing against the worry of his attraction.

And yet…?

He wanted to see how he might be perceived. He wanted to understand who Rutherford thought him to be, the real man and not the hidden one. He wanted to watch those slim fingers run along the shaft of the charcoal as he brought the stick up against his eyes and found the proportions, the small well-shaped nails, the heavy scar across his thumb.

Swearing again, he helped himself to a drink, hoping it would calm him down.

A further rap on the door had him turning.

'The young man downstairs asked me to give you a book, my lord. He said he would appreciate it returned after you have read it.'

James looked down. The volume of *Waverley* was in his hands. He had heard of this work, of course, but he had not yet purchased it. His interest was caught.

Five moments later he walked into his library to find the large canvas was not set upon the easel. Mr Rutherford himself was gazing out of the window, his timepiece in hand. Checking his client's tardiness, James thought, and tried not to smile.

'Thank you for the book, Mr Rutherford.' He met his eyes only briefly and the dark head opposite tipped in a tense acknowledgement.

Turning the cover over, James looked at the first page. 'Did you enjoy it?'

'I did, my lord. It is a tale of tolerance, I think, and of the belief that all people are basically decent.'

'It is set in Scotland, if I remember rightly, around the Jacobite Rebellion? Does the author portray the massacre with a sense of fairness?'

'All art is imagination, my lord. To stretch the mind

to describe the events leading up to such a point of breakage is illuminating.'

Rutherford's particular scent could be smelt from here, a quiet evocative note on the edge of furniture polish and the fresh bunch of white roses on the mantel. The bay laurels were there, too, a pungent heaviness almost like cinnamon. An undernote of sensuality.

Layers. Of truth and lies. He could feel it in the air around him and knew a quick moment of panic before he had it under control.

His eyes took in the canvas still wrapped in its shroud and he walked over to the same chair he had been in on both previous days and sat down.

'I think I might prefer you standing today, my lord, by the window with the light behind you, only this time I will begin in paint rather than charcoal. A freer style will serve my message better.'

'Your message?' he could not help but ask.

'The exposure of emotion is what I do best, Lord Winterton.' He coughed after saying this, a weak forced sound.

'I'm not sure if I should be pleased to hear that, Mr Rutherford.' Winter was tired of being placed on edge and tired of feeling off balance.

'Because you don't usually show your feelings?'

'To the world? No.'

'If you do not like the portrait, no one else ever needs to see it.'

'Apart from you and me?'

The frown on Rutherford's face was more than disquieting. 'Every subject gives away a little of themselves in the process of a portrait, my lord, it is a known fact. A literal likeness or a flattering representation with nothing else to it would, in my mind, be a failure.'

'I have not followed art much, Mr Rutherford. For years I was a soldier.'

'Is that where you got the scar on your neck?'

He felt his hand lift his collar before he could stop it, the raised flesh under his fingers near the corded veins of his throat. He knew the myths that had risen around him, the half-baked truths and lies that would seek to explain what people could see of such a mark.

'No.' He left it there and moved to stand at the window.

'Should I face you straight on?'

'I was thinking to do this more in profile against the light.'

Turning, he made sure it was his good side towards Rutherford. A small vanity. A useless conceit.

'Like this?'

'Not quite.' He could hear something in the words that was sorrowful and gritted his teeth. Pity was the last thing he needed this morning and as the youth came towards him he tensed.

'If you place your fingers on the back of this chair, Lord Winterton...' When Rutherford's hand lifted from his and their eyes met, a white heat of contact travelled down through his body.

He felt like he was in a dream with thickened air and no way out, a netherworld, the taste of memory sharp upon his tongue.

And the artist simply stood there, too, gazing at him, his own reflection shimmering in the thick-glassed dirty spectacles.

Two smears across the right-hand side, of paint perhaps. Red like blood. The accident. The carriage ride. The girl Florentia Hale-Burton bound beneath him in the aftermath of betrayal.

He had heard her screams and felt her pull at him, trying to stay close, to help, to staunch the wound that was driving life from his body.

The smell of gunsmoke, roses, hay, sweat and vomit. The sound mute and distant, the moon small and faint in a dark, dark sky. Her tears mixing with his blood, a gold cross on the end of the fragile chain that she wore around her neck.

God, please give me strength, he found himself imploring. Was he going mad? Why the hell should Florentia Hale-Burton be coming so forcibly to mind here in his London salon with the daylight outside?

Pulling away, he walked from the window, afraid to turn as the brittle silence bound them both. It was happening again just as it had yesterday, a mix of want and horror and shock.

Florentia knew he had felt something, too, when she had touched him, an echo perhaps of what had been or of what was to come.

She was playing with fire and violence and fear and fury. She could feel the vibrations in the air above the thick pretence of manners, barely concealed, naked, raw and ragged.

Winterton was all the colours of the rainbow. He was the darks and the lights and the quiet and the vivid. He was the rush of blood and the hush of shadow, the pure strength of a man whose history was drawn on his flesh with brutal and eternal strokes.

The paintbrush was in her hand before she knew

it, running across the canvas free and wild. She drew him from radiance and energy, from the bleak and from the empty. She found lines she had never placed in any painting before, soul lines, memory lines.

She drew him in red and gold and shades of brown. Scarlet was there, too, and a dark raw green. She did not stop even as she felt him watching her, she, who was always so private with her art and so very discreet.

She poured her heart into the painting and felt the shadows there lighten, felt the shifting of blame and vengeance and the welcoming luminosity of forgiveness. It was cathartic and redeeming, a liberation and a pardon, a way of moving forward and onwards. The repeal of guilt. Finally.

And after another two hours she laid her brush down and collected her satchel, leaving the painting where she had balanced it on the ledge against the window, the refracted light of the sun streaming in across the colour, burnishing it with a beauty that broke her heart.

It was over. The portrait was his. With only the briefest of goodbyes she tipped her head and left.

The painting was nothing at all as he had imagined Rutherford might draw him. It was not his outward appearance he had caught but the inner significance, his glance turned towards the sky and watching something that was out of view, stillness pervading strength.

He'd drawn him as a soldier, a uniform of scarlet and black adorning him, the mark on his neck vivid and unhidden, a human vulnerability against the anonymous and harsh force of the military.

For a moment he simply stared. For a moment the

war came back into him with a force that left him gasping, the battles, the pain, the loneliness. The lies.

On his finger there was an enormous ruby, a field of blood dripping from the intricate golden ring. Outside hanging from a branch sat a gilded cage with a sombre bird inside, its head lifted in agony. He felt that song in his heart, the melody pulling at all he tried to conceal. The hurt. The shame. The utter fury that he had lived with for so very, very long.

It was a masterpiece. Even he with only a limited understanding of art could tell that it was. It was the demons inside him translated into paint and howling to a world that would never understand.

Would Rutherford be back? Was it finished? He'd formed no plans to return tomorrow and had left no bill of purchase or payment.

He had not signed the painting either, not made it his.

'God, please help me.' The words fell into the emptiness of the room as he sat and tried to find a reason for everything that had happened.

Twenty minutes later he left the canvas exactly where it was and collected his hat and coat.

Outside he found the driver of his conveyance in a tither, the carriage still sitting in front of the town house.

'You did not take Mr Rutherford home?' He looked about to see if he could see the man, but he was nowhere in sight at all and he'd promised Warrenden he'd send Rutherford back to Grosvenor Square safely after each sitting.

'The Heron carriage collected him, my lord. Mr

Rutherford got into it on the arm of a young lady though he did not look too happy about it at all.'

'Did you hear where they were bound?'

'To the Heron town house, I think, sir.'

'Take me there now.'

Inside the moving carriage James laid his head back against the cushion and closed his eyes. Wild conjectures ran in circles around his head, but he dismissed every one of them and resolved to see what the truth was when he asked Rutherford to explain. The youth did not look like someone who would be good at lying.

His own connection with Heron also swirled in his head unchecked. Why the hell had the carriage been outside his house in the first place and why would Frederick Rutherford get inside on a whim?

Florentia was dread-stricken to find herself inside the Heron conveyance.

She had tried her very best to escape, but Miss Julia was both stronger and taller than she was and short of making a scene that would attract more attention to herself she was forced to sit down on the seat opposite and make the best of things.

'Thank you so much for agreeing to come, Mr Rutherford.' The young woman smiled though the lady's maid next to her did not look happy at all. 'Papa has been trying to find you for days and days in order to persuade you to draw our portraits, but you are most elusive. He will be so very pleased with today's visit.'

'I am leaving London tomorrow. There will be no time for more commissions—'

The girl shook her head and broke across her words. 'Papa is most persuasive and the money he will offer

will be substantial.' There was now a note of desperation in her voice so Flora said nothing. 'Besides, my
sisters are not without charm.' She tittered. 'At least
we have been told such by our many and most ardent
admirers. Winterton must have also made a lovely subject, Mr Rutherford?'

When Flora failed to reply she went on heedless.
'Did he tell you of the Abbey he is purchasing in Herefordshire?'

Florentia grated her teeth together and wondered
how quickly she could gain her release on arrival. Her
heart was beating fast and the thought crossed her mind
as to whether she was to be subjected to enforced rides
for ever because of the will of another.

'He is the man all the ladies would like to marry,
though of course there is talk of his dangerous past,
but that just makes him more…appealing, do you not
think?' The note of gossip was most pronounced in
Miss Heron's speech.

'Dangerous past?' Flora meant not to say anything,
but the temptation was too great.

'He was a spy with General Moore in Europe. An
occupation he continued on with in the Americas apparently. His father committed suicide last year. There
is a fatal flaw in the Waverley heritage, for his grandfather perished from excessive drinking. Many are wondering exactly what his inherited weakness will be.
Is that not…thrilling, Mr Rutherford, and romantic?'

'Perhaps the ladies of the *ton* should be aiming for
other lords who are less…damaged, Miss Heron?'

Laughter was the result of this advice. 'You do not
know women at all, Mr Rutherford, but then your youth
is probably a defence on that score. Mr Ward has prom-

ised Papa that any work you do for him would climb
in value very quickly so I suppose that is why Lord
Winterton employed you in the first place. He has the
golden touch, it is said, and with his wealth and looks
what lady would seek another if such a one should be
available to her?'

A short silence ensued after this. Miss Heron
seemed momentarily uncertain as to whether she had
said too much and the maid near her was craning her
head in her haste to be finally at home, her talkative
mistress and her unwise antics so obviously frowned
upon.

Florentia wondered what would happen when they
reached the Heron town house. She had seen the thin
and tall Mr Heron at a number of soirées years ago
and he hadn't looked like a man at ease with himself.
There was also the worry that the disguise she wore
might not measure up to the blatant and telling stares
of the fashionable Heron women.

Please do not let me feel breathless, she thought.
Please God just let me get through this and then be
able to go home. The painting of the portrait had exhausted her. It was always like that when she finished
a work and was parted from it. Just another piece of
herself left behind and lost. She wondered what Winterton had thought of it.

The carriage drew up to a town house a few moments later and a number of servants came forward.
Within a short time they were inside a substantial and
beautiful room, the other members of the family gathered around a table, the plates upon it all filled with
varying meats, breads and fruit.

'This is Mr Frederick Rutherford, Papa. I ran into

him on the street near the Winterton town house and asked if he might come back here with me in order for you to speak with him.'

At this everyone began to talk and, raising his hand, Mr Heron quelled the excitement.

'As you can see, Mr Rutherford, my daughters are most struck by the fact that you might fashion their likeness. I had had a conversation with your agent, but he was not very forthcoming and to find you here in our presence and so unexpectedly is indeed very heartening. Fate, I think, Ana...' he smiled at his wife '...and Julia's quick thinking.' His daughter looked more than pleased with the compliment. 'What is meant to be will always find a way. Is that your painting satchel, Mr Rutherford?'

'Yes, sir.'

He clicked his fingers and a servant came from nowhere.

'Please keep this piece of luggage safe at the front door, Sanders. Mr Rutherford will collect it when he goes.'

A drink was offered then and the chance to select something to eat from the overburdened table. With her mouth full of fear Flora asked for a cup of tea and was glad when it came to wet her dry lips.

The doorbell rang half an hour later and to the surprise and shock of everyone Lord Winterton himself stood beside the servant who had showed him in.

If Florentia's presence had created a furore here the Viscount's coming was a hundred times more astonishing and the young Herons rose as one from the table to greet him, eyelashes batting and hair and skirts smoothed down. Like a flock of birds preening.

'We were not expecting you, my lord.' Julia seemed the first recovered as she said this. 'Though indeed it is a most pleasant surprise.'

'I am here to escort Mr Rutherford back to Grosvenor Square, Mr Heron.'

All eyes turned back to Florentia and she blushed most horribly and stood, so relieved to be able to leave the company of people whom she could make no sense of.

'Mr Rutherford is here to go over the terms and conditions of a portrait I have commissioned him to do, Lord Winterton.'

'Such matters of business will have to be conducted at another time. The young lad has been in my employ and I have taken it on myself to make sure he arrives home on the hour he stated he would.'

His eyes came across hers for the first time since gaining the room, the shards of green cold and furious. He looked nothing at all like the man she had just drawn, every plane in his face raised into a sharp relief, the lines around his eyes far more noticeable in anger than they had ever been in repose. He looked menacing and intemperate and dark.

A chameleon? The words of the Miss Heron who had brought her here came to mind. A spy in both Europe and the Americas.

She rose, moving across beside him with gratitude. There was an undercurrent here she could not understand, a jeopardy that simmered just below the surface. She saw that Heron's hands were fisted at his sides, a vein on his forehead pulsating blue amongst the redness of his visage.

They did not like each other, these men. Winterton for all his expertise at masking his emotion was clearly furious and for the first time ever in the company of anyone she wondered if he were armed. He felt different, dangerous. He felt like a stranger whom she had never met before, a man who might do away with the other without a second's thought.

'We will see ourselves out.'

When she nodded the Viscount turned, the last vestige of social amiability lost in his retreat.

Then she was following him, on his heels and close. After she took her satchel from the surprised butler, they went through the front door and when they had gained the road she took the first real breath she'd been able to in the last good while.

He glanced at her quickly but he did not speak, not until the door to his conveyance closed behind them and the horses were moving out into the heavy traffic.

'If you wish to place yourself in the hands of a nest of vipers, Mr Rutherford, perhaps next time you will not do so on my watch.' Every knuckle on his hand was stretched into whiteness.

'I declined the commission right from the start, Lord Winterton, for I prefer to pick out my clients rather than allowing it to be the other way around.'

'The worth of one of your paintings negates the importance of your agreement for Heron, I should imagine. The man has not gained his fortune by way of soft words. You would be advised to stay well away from him.'

'And you are advising me?'

'I am, Mr Rutherford. Most strongly.'

'Why?'

'I think Heron had something to do with the death of my father.'

What the hell had made him simply blurt that out? Rutherford's surprise was about as great as his own for he seldom let another know the truth of his feelings.

'How?'

When he looked over he saw the lad stare at him across the top of his glasses as though he had forgotten to hide. The blue of quiet seas, he thought, and flushed anew. What the hell was happening to him that he should think this about a man? Moving apart to leave a wider space between them, he swore under his breath. He felt brittle and tired.

'My father imported contraband to pay for an escalating gambling habit and my guess is that his rivals decided he was making too much money.' There it was again, this strange trust he felt with Rutherford. Without it he would have stayed silent.

'Miss Heron told me your father's death was the result of suicide. She said you held many secrets and that was one of them.'

'People can say anything that they want, but it does not make it true.'

Rutherford laughed. 'I agree with you there entirely, Lord Winterton. The things that are said of me...' He stopped then and turned away, but not before James had seen consternation on his face.

What was said of the artist? He had never heard of anything apart from stories of his brilliance and his reclusiveness. Hardly derogatory or inflammatory. Another question on top of everything. A further puzzlement.

Surprisingly the lad kept on talking.

'I always thought that one should ignore what was said by the *ton*, the gossip and the unkindness. But now I am not so sure. Perhaps to rally and fight against lies is a better way of living.'

'As opposed to what?'

'Hiding. Disappearing. Forever being misplaced in life.'

'As you have been?'

'Yes.'

That word reverberated around the carriage, the truth of it and the loss.

'Can I help you?'

James thought there were tears welling in the young man's eyes at his offer, but then he turned away to look out of the window and he was no longer sure.

'You already have, Lord Winterton.'

That cryptic comment made him frown. 'The portrait, you mean?'

Rutherford shook his head, the dark hair catching the light. 'By rescuing me from the Herons.'

'They didn't hurt you...?' A sense of shock ran up his spine.

'No. But Heron is afraid of you, Lord Winterton. It was why he let me go and did not make a scene.'

'Do you often see things in people that others don't?'

'All the time, my lord. Ever since I was little.'

'Leave London then, Mr Rutherford. Go home to Kent and be safe.'

James wanted Rutherford gone, away from temptation and delivered from evil.

'Sometimes safety doesn't hold the allure it used to, my lord. There is a certain spice in the elements of risk.'

'Say those who have never lost to jeopardy and peril.'

'And you have?'

'I have killed men in the battlefields, Mr Rutherford, many times, and no man comes from the theatre of war untarnished. I think you drew that in the lines of my face in your painting?'

'Because I believe that the confrontation of such a truth might make it easier to absorb and accept.'

He laughed. 'You think it could help? Truly? You think men do not know what lies within them already? The agony of pain and the loss of compassion? If it were so easy…' He made himself stop because he did not trust what he might say next.

'"*No one saves us but ourselves. No one can and no one may.*"' The artist's voice was soft.

'Who said that?'

'Buddha.'

'You are well read, Mr Rutherford?'

'I have had lots of time to become so, Lord Winterton.'

The same shock that he had felt before returned with the words and he was astonished to see that the carriage had stopped as they had been speaking and his man was standing outside, waiting for the command to open the door.

Maria Warrenden was there, too, flying down the steps and towards them, her glance going to Frederick Rutherford as the door opened.

'You are very late…' James could see Roy's wife

was stopping herself from saying more, a smile plastered across her face that hardly appeared genuine.

Rutherford had ducked his head down and was looking at no one.

'Thank you, Lord Winterton, for bringing Mr Rutherford back personally. I could not think what had happened to make him so very late and imagined the worst and my husband is not at home at the moment...'

Lady Warrenden wanted him gone. That fact was scrawled plainly on her visage and in her stance.

'You are welcome, but now I shall bid you good day.'

She nodded at that, the frown across her forehead easing as he tipped his hat and left.

Maria was most agitated, but as usual with the servants within earshot she was also being careful.

'Roy would like to see you now in the library.'

'I thought you said he was not at home.'

'Now, Mr Rutherford,' was the only reply, the anger in her tone noticeable and worrying. The fiasco with the Herons had left Florentia agitated and on guard and she felt she might not weather another onslaught of her sister's concerns.

She wished Winterton had not left. She wished he was walking alongside her, protecting her.

Roy stood as they came into his library and he asked Maria to close the door.

'Your sister and I have been concerned about the days you are spending in the company of Lord Winterton and we both think it is well past time to call a halt to this deception and return home to Kent. My business here will be concluded in a few days.'

'And to be so very late today is more than concern-

ing, Flora. Where on earth have you been all that time?'
Her sister's voice was shrill.

'I finished the portrait and Miss Julia Heron happened to be going by as I left and insisted I accompany her home to talk about a further commission. Winterton finally rescued me from the Heron town house when he realised that was where I had gone.'

Maria rolled her eyes and looked furious. 'There is talk that your work is rising most quickly in favour and in worth and this is the result, don't you see? It is dangerous, this greed, and soon someone will dig around to try and find out things of you, personal things…'

Roy took over where his wife had left off. 'If your ruse is discovered, there will be a scandal of an even greater proportion than the last one and James Waverley has been trained as a spy.'

'Which is why hours in his company are such a poor idea, Flora.' Her sister's hand fastened on hers.

She knew they were right. She knew with the portrait finished and some of her questions answered they should now cut their losses and move away from town. But still…

'I want one more short session with the Viscount. I need to sign my work…'

'Very well. And after that?' Roy was standing by the window, watching over the street.

'After that I promise that I will accompany you back to Kent.'

Even as she gave them such a troth she felt the loss of it. The freedom. The power. The ability to go where she wanted to and whenever she wanted alone. A woman was tied to convention and propriety in a way a man was not and the knowledge of such a liberation had been life changing.

London allowed an anonymity that was impossible in the country and she knew bone deep that she could not simply turn her back on such emancipation. She still had Bryson's clothes and it should not be difficult to travel to London on her own accord.

The small hope of this made her smile.

Chapter Eight

Rafael Carmichael called on him later that evening, James's butler showing him through to the library.

'You look like hell, Winter. How is the portrait going?' His friend asked this after James had poured them each a drink.

'It is completed.'

'Do you like it?'

'Like might not be quite the right word. Frederick Rutherford is a talented artist, though he has left me with no bill.'

'I am sure you will receive the reckoning.'

'How? How are you sure?' James was tired of being thrown off centre.

'The lad needs the money, it is whispered.'

There was a tone in Rafael's voice suggesting he knew more. 'What else is whispered?'

'You tell me, Winter. It is more than out of character for you to be open to sitting for a portrait and so very protective of the artist doing it. I've also been listening to Heron's rant about you at White's this evening. Seems as though he was not happy when you went to rescue the fellow from his clutches today.'

'I'd promised Roy Warrenden I would keep him safe while in my company and Heron had carted Rutherford off to his house unbidden.'

'He's an adult, Winter, and it was only Portland Square he had been relocated to. Hardly hazardous. I doubt Heron would have harmed the lad in the presence of his family.'

'Heron might have had a part in harming my father.'

'You met with Perkins?' Rafael took a decent sip of the drink before him. 'What are you going to do about it?'

'Watch him. Try to understand just who he is or was.'

'And how is Rutherford involved in this? Why was the artist there at the town house?'

'The Heron daughters want their own portrait and they want it badly. I think it is only that innocent.'

'Will he do it?'

James shook his head. 'Rutherford isn't enamoured by London. I think he wishes to return to Kent. God knows why he wanted to fashion my likeness in the first place.'

'How closely is he related to the Warrenden family?'

'There is a link. Why do you ask?'

'Because Roy Warrenden and his wife seem overly concerned about a lad who by all accounts has gained his majority.'

'There is something you are not telling me, Rafe?'

'I had a search carried out after we met Rutherford at your place last week and it seems Mr Frederick Rutherford has never existed in Kent at all. All my sources tell me that there is a sister, Lady Florentia Hale-Burton, who paints, but…'

It was like being stung by a bee or burnt by a flame. At first James could not quite understand the implications of such a small shocking truth and then he did. The pain flicked in without warning, almost bringing him to his knees with the sheer and bloody strength of its force.

For he knew. He knew it all.

It was her, here, in London, standing there before him trying to make some sense of exactly who he was. The portrait with his scar and blood and the bird in a cage whose song was full of raging sorrow.

It was what he had done to her, all those years before, that random chance of Fate bringing Lady Florentia Hale-Burton with her sky-blue eyes and innocence into the orbit of his life.

He'd tried to hold on to her, then, through the pain and the fear, tried to keep her fingers in his own, the warmth of them and the gentleness amidst all that was agonising. The man who had shot him was shouting and he'd heard her cry out as she was pulled away, her guttural loss reverberating into the silence.

Ruined. Both of them. By chance and poor fortune and bloody dreadful luck.

'Are you ill, Winter? What the hell is wrong with you?' Rafael's voice pulled him out of the blackness, but still he had trouble processing what was to come next.

No one else had known the whole of what had happened save for Florentia Burton-Hale and he couldn't allow the truth of it to filter into a society that would not be forgiving. He had not protected her then, but perhaps he could now, here at this time. Perhaps he could try to remedy some of the hurt.

A deeper thought also ran through his mind in

threads of relief for the attraction he had felt for the lad was now explainable.

He wanted to see her. He wanted to say that he was sorry. He wanted to understand just what it was she needed from him. Money, perhaps? The fact that Warrenden or her father might want to wrap their hands about his throat and squeeze him to death in rightful retribution was also there, lingering in his conscience. A meeting at dawn, perhaps, pistols drawn or blades sharpened, in some final resolution of blame?

Rafael was speaking again and he made himself listen. 'I can help you with Heron if that's what is troubling you?' It wasn't the problem, but James decided to let him think so because it was easier that way.

'How?'

'He wants to invest in the things that I choose to place my money in here.'

'Your Midas touch? He plans to benefit from it?'

'Perhaps. But you can profit from it, too, for we will have him close, whenever we want him, and in an enemy that is always a good thing.'

'You are staying in England then, Rafe?'

'Well, with you around things are never dull.'

'And Arabella?'

'Is happy as long as I am.'

'You were lucky with her.'

'And don't I know it, Winter.'

Lucky enough to meet at the right time and the right place and in a way that would not alienate them from each other for ever.

Florentia Hale-Burton must have hated him even as she smiled, hiding behind her lad's disguise and lifting her brush to show him the truth of himself.

She had asked him if he was a good man. He remembered that. She had asked of Fate, too, and if he could do things over again would he have done anything differently?

And all the while she was garnering enough information about him. *A freer style will serve my message better.* Wasn't that what she had told him? *It is not a showpiece I shall make for you. It will be only who you are.*

Who am I?

God. He held his head in his hands and turned towards the window so that Rafael might not see the dreadful truth in his eyes. Florentia Hale-Burton had communicated her reality in so many ways, in paint, in words and in gesture and he had seen none of it.

Secrets define us, my lord, she had told him.

'I will return later, Winter. It seems that you have a lot on your mind.' James felt his friend's hand on his shoulder and was pleased for his going. He did not feel up to any questions or confessions. He felt numb and bewildered and paralysed.

And sad.

For him and for her. For life and for honour and for the lonely places they both had inhabited since last they had met.

Fate was a siren borne on the wings of force and duplicity. He could hear the deity laughing at him all the way from hell.

She arrived in the morning at the hour of eleven and James had been sitting in his library since well before nine.

To decide what to say, he thought, and shook his

head. That was not quite true for he had already made up his mind not to confront her with the truth directly.

He needed to understand more about her first, what her life had been like and what she now believed in. He had placed his portrait on the mantel so that it caught the morning light thrown across the room. It looked good there and solid. Like a talisman or a signpost. To the future. To what might come from the rubble of their past.

No one saves us but ourselves. He wasn't certain if Buddha had quite the right of it.

He saw her gaze catch the placement as soon as she came into the room, her boy's clothes this morning so patently a disguise he couldn't imagine how he had not known of the charade before. The black wig she wore was dull against the sunlight, the moustache oddly poignant over alabaster-smooth skin.

When she coughed he merely smiled and waited till she had stopped, reaching for a purse on his desk and pushing it over towards her.

'I hope this is the correct amount, Mr Rutherford.' He frowned when she did not reach out and pocket it and tried another avenue of thought. 'In your opinion is that the right position for the painting, there in the light?'

For the first time she smiled as she nodded and the dimples in her cheeks were like a punch in the flawed wisdom of his strategies. He had no defence against such beauty and he knew it.

'I wondered before you left if you might explain the work to me. I have not had much exposure to the art world before this.'

But instead of answering him directly she asked a

question of her own. 'What do you see, Lord Winterton? In the picture?'

'A man in need of salvation. A man who has lost his faith. A damaged man.'

She stood perfectly still, the sun catching her eyelashes through the glass as she blinked.

'Is that what I should see?'

She shrugged and coughed again, but he could tell shock lingered beneath the practised nonchalance. 'There are a hundred ways to read each of my paintings, my lord. Sometimes there is no true answer save for that of the soul.'

'And the bird?' He asked that quietly because he knew that it was she there, Lady Florentia Hale-Burton in a gilded cage of shame.

Anger flitted across her face and the quiet blush of it rose upon pale full cheeks.

'The bird is both fancy, sorrow and fate thrown into a palette of fury. Anyone can see her anger.'

'Because she is caught?'

'Chance can come creeping in ways wholly unexpected, my lord, and in a completely random manner.'

He should have told her then of all that he knew, should have simply confessed his mistake and his sorrow for it, but if he did? Would she leave? Would she walk out never to be seen again? Keep her with you, some voice shouted from deep within. Keep her safe.

'Could I show you something, here in London, something beautiful, Mr Rutherford? Would you come with me tomorrow to look? It would not take long at all.'

'Something beautiful?'

'A garden. The scented garden of a friend.'

Her brow furrowed as she watched him. 'How would you know I am interested in those particular sort of plants?'

'I saw you pick the bay tree leaves outside yesterday when first you came. I saw how you stood and smelt them. The garden is one of the best of its kind and it is not far.'

'I could not stay long.'

'We shall be quick then. If I collected you at eleven I could have you back by mid-afternoon. Would that suit?'

'There won't be a crowd?'

'I don't imagine so. If you wish for Lord and Lady Warrenden to come with us I would be agreeable.'

'No.' This was said quickly, without a scrap of thought. 'It is easier alone.'

She didn't want her sister there, that much was certain. James wondered what Maria Warrenden might think of her dressing as a boy. One thing he did know was that Roy and she had no whiff of his name and his part in the abduction six years ago or otherwise they'd have been on his doorstep like avenging angels. He was suddenly glad for at least that.

She stood then, her eyes fixed on his face, almost as if she was drawing him again in her mind.

He remembered the bag she had slung at him as he had tried to pull her into the carriage on Mount Street and the weighty tomes within it. The small scar above his eye was still visible there. He wondered if she had noticed the mark, but then the whole situation between them was fraught with layers.

He wished he were a better man. He wished all the demons on his shoulders would stop howling and allow him time to think. Other scars drawn into his skin in patterns smarted under the linen of his shirt and he took in a sharp breath of sadness.

Lord Winterton was different today, she thought, more unreadable. The coins that sat in the burgundy-velvet purse on his table also represented an ending that she did not quite want. The chance of visiting the scented garden with him had been an appealing one and yet she knew she shouldn't have accepted such an offer.

Every moment in his company was more dangerous than the last and there had been times when she had looked at him across the past few days when he had seemed to be waiting for something, expecting something, his jaw muscles grinding together in a way that was changed.

His hair was loose, too. She had not seen it thus before.

He suited it out, the formality of him lessened somehow and the roughness of a man who had been both a soldier and a spy more on show.

She couldn't ever remember seeing a more beautiful man anywhere. Even the images in her art books of heroes and statesmen had not held the sheer grace of line and strength.

No. Her head shook at such thoughts. She would absolve and forgive and forget. She would move on after this in her life in the knowledge that she had left behind blame and censure.

But there could be nothing else. Their past had seen to the impossibility of that and had not her father spent a great majority of the last years in bed because of Lord Winterton's ill-formed actions?

She suddenly felt in more of a tangled web than she had been a week ago before she had first met with the Viscount face-to-face. Before this she had concentrated on the disrepute, humiliation and scandal he had sent her into with his foolish and ill-considered kidnapping. She had not understood his goodness and his strength and the way that he spoke with his heart as well as his head. She had not watched him in the sunlight or spoken with him as an equal. She had not seen the secrets flit across his face even as a stronger force of will had banished them away. She had underestimated his truth.

Reaching down to her satchel, she extracted a brush and paint. Carefully she crouched before the canvas and signed her initials in the bottom left-hand corner, finishing with a flourish.

F.R.

Florentia Rowena Hale-Burton. At least such a signature held something of who she was. With another swirl she attached the year. *1816*. It had been the spring of 1810 when they had first met.

'Is it difficult to let your paintings go, Mr Rutherford?' He asked this softly.

'No.' She did not wish for him to know each time she left a piece of her work behind it broke her heart to do so.

With that she reached for the purse and felt its weight. A substantial sum. So many clients squabbled over the price of a work, but he had not. Being wealthy went some way in explaining his promptness, but often it was the richest clients who were the poorest payers.

She frowned as he extracted two glasses from a cabinet and brought forward a bottle of brandy.

'The world's finest,' he clarified and poured generous drinks. 'It seems only right that we should have a toast to the successful conclusion of your first private commission.'

Raising his glass towards her, he thought for a moment. 'To unexpected truths, Mr Rutherford, and to the future.' There was a tone in his words that she did not understand, but she drank anyway and the taste of the drink was astonishing.

'It's cognac. A Coutanseaux from 1767.'

'Old, then?'

He laughed. 'Not as old as some, but smoother than most.'

'I did not drink much before I came to London.' She offered this after a moment of silence as she savoured the taste. If this was to be the last time she was with him alone she wanted at least to enjoy it. 'Sometimes now I barely recognise myself,' she added as he looked at her.

'Is that so, Mr Rutherford? London allows a freedom, I suppose, which is different from that of rural Kent?'

'Very different, my lord.'

'And your art is admired by everyone I meet. There must be a certain victory in such praise though my next question must be one that asks is such fame to your liking?'

She shook her head before she could stop it. 'Once I had the more ordinary hope of living in a house in the country and enjoying a family.'

Once I thought to have children and a husband who

would cherish me and love me for ever. Once every-thing had seemed possible and probable and exciting. Until I met you.

Was it me who stopped you from realising all of those dreams? he wondered, and turned away, the co-gnac now only a bitter draft in his mouth and the truth of her hopes lying squarely at his feet.

He was so sick of fighting, so very tired of trying to find the best in each and every situation, the inter-pretation of which would not break his spirit.

With only a few words from Florentia Hale-Burton the Winterton title could be again dimmed and sul-lied and he did not think he had the strength to make it different.

The smell of lavender wafted close and he raised his head and reached for it, trying to find courage and tenure.

'Would you make a painting of the house I have just purchased, Mr Rutherford? I would leave the tim-ing largely to your discretion, but I am willing to pay three times more than I did for the portrait for such an endeavour.'

'"*A foole and his money be soon at debate*",' came her quick rejoinder and he had to smile.

'Your general knowledge is surprisingly wide, Mr Rutherford, and very eclectic.'

'You do not think such a truism might be of use to every man who has the need of thrift, Lord Winterton?'

'A man like you?'

At this Florentia Hale-Burton had the grace to blush and he was glad of it.

'Why would you offer me so much for a commission, my lord, when plainly the tariff should be less?'

'Perhaps because I am one who sees the true value in creativity.'

'Or…?' That word was filled with cynicism.

For the first time in a long while Winter laughed out loud.

'Or… I like you, Mr Rutherford.'

She blushed at that, vividly and satisfyingly. Her charade had kept him on edge for days and it was good to get something of his own back.

'How long were you there for in the Americas?'

'Three years. I'd been ill and it was a relief to get on a ship to somewhere else and feel the wind on my face and new possibilities in the air.'

He'd laid in that bed at Tommy's for nearly eighteen months after the fiasco at the inn, trying to regain his strength and get his body to move in the way it once had. He'd had to learn to speak again for his voice had been lost in the gunshot, ripped away in blood and flesh. It had never again been the same.

Taking a long swallow of the cognac, he liked the way it fortified resolve.

Was he telling her that it had been years until he had got back on his feet after her father had shot him?

Florentia thought that he confessed this in all he did not say and she moved closer, a feeling unlike any other encompassing her.

'They infer you are a man with secrets, Lord Winterton? Julia Heron said you were a spy.'

'A long time ago I was. With General Moore in Spain.'

'Lady Warrenden has heard you carried your particular trade to the Americas.'

'Then I was a poor intelligence officer if so much is known about me.'

'I do not believe you would be mediocre at anything you set your mind to.'

'Do you not?'

He leaned across her now, the green of his eyes bruised with caution and his mouth so near she could feel the whisper of his breath.

'Your painting was probably closer to the truth of my character than anyone has come in years, Mr Rutherford. As the artist of such a discerning work I am surprised you still allow me the chance of your company.'

A warning that was not quite as hidden as the others he had given her.

'Why should I not, Lord Winterton?' She had had enough of meanings under meanings in words, but it seemed he had, too, for he moved away, distance replacing the intimate.

'I shall pick you up at eleven tomorrow morning, Mr Rutherford.' He sounded irritated, the bruise under his eye making him look tired. She could see the last vestige of redness in the white.

'They are your friends? The people with the garden?'

'Yes. I've known them for many years and they have as little patience for the whims of society as I have. Which is a relief.'

Placing her half-empty glass on the table, she turned to go, glad to be departing for she felt uncertain somehow today, of him and of herself.

'I think you have forgotten something, Mr Rutherford.'

For a second her eyes fell to his lips, pulled by a force that was as strange as it was strong.

'Your money.'

The sense of those words brought her back and she bit down on regret.

'Good day, Lord Winterton.'

'Until tomorrow, Mr Rutherford.'

Maria had been furious at her refusal to cancel the invitation to the scented gardens, but on arrival at the house just on the outskirts of London Florentia was very glad that she had not done so.

The Viscount had been quiet today, his words few and far between. Even his greeting had been sedate, a fact that she forgot about completely as they alighted from the coach to be met with a myriad scents wafting all around them.

'The land as you see it was planted a few years ago. The plot was well irrigated and south facing and had been a garden even before they took it over.'

Winterton's explanation was quietly given and Florentia's hand fell to the wooden rail that was on one side of the pathway, the patina of it smooth and solid. There was thyme and basil and comfrey. Hyacinths and primrose filled the borders along with lavender and as Flora passed her boots touched the greenery and the scents lifted.

'It's beautiful.'

Bending, she reached into a thick planting of lamb's ear, all woolly and soft, before running her fingers over the pale blue Glory of the Snow. Feathergrass, witch-hazel, borage, evening primrose and pansies completed the tableau, each specimen tumbling across the other in a sensory delight of smell, touch and taste, the sound of wind chimes and a water feature further afield rounding out the senses.

'It's Arabella's masterpiece,' Lord Winterton explained and Florentia knew exactly whose garden they were now in.

'The Carmichaels live here?' She could not help the trepidation that coated her query or hide the worry when Winter nodded. Last time Mrs Carmichael had kissed him fully on the lips and her husband had barely glanced her way. Would they want her here? Would they wish that Lord Winterton had brought someone else who was far more interesting and colourful? As bright as they themselves were? As intriguing?

As the front door opened, however, the woman who stepped out looked nothing like the one she had met in London. Today Arabella Carmichael was buttoned up in a soft blue high-necked gown, a large apron with pockets tied across her modest dress and her hair in a simple chignon at her nape. The red of it was muted and tidy.

'Winter.' Even her voice seemed different. Today she kissed him once on either cheek. 'You have brought Mr Rutherford to see us? How wonderful. Rafe is inside in the library if you want to go through and I could show your artist the secret garden if he has the inclination for it.'

Winterton looked around at her, eyebrows raised.

'Thank you. I would enjoy that.'

When he turned Flora followed the woman down a path to one side of the house and entered a hidden garden with an entirely different atmosphere. Shaded by trees and planted in green foliage this place was cool, dark and peaceful. A small water feature that ran between the specimens gave an added sense of mystery, as if it were a glade in some far-off forgotten forest or a place devoid of people and their noises.

'You do this yourself?' Her eyes flicked to Arabella Carmichael's hands, gloveless today.

'Indeed, I do.' Her palms turned upwards for an inspection. 'A gardener cannot boast the fine hands of a lady,' she said and taking Florentia's fingers in her own proceeded to run her thumb over the skin. 'Or of an artist.

'But it is the place that I come to feel who I am, Mr Rutherford. A garden of truth, you might say. Perhaps one day I could ask you to draw it in the way that you see it?'

'A sanctuary.' The words slipped out before Florentia could stop them.

'I told Rafe that you would understand and you do. Winter has often used my gardens for his own refuge though I doubt he would admit to the fact.'

'You have known him for long.'

She laughed, the sound joyous and honest. 'My parents worked for the old Viscount on his family estate. His mother died when he was fourteen and mine died when I was ten so we had that in common, you understand. The grief of it and the futility. I always say it is the sad emotions that bind people together with a certainty. When I lost my way and went to London it was Winter who helped me find myself again. He introduced me to Rafael.' She stopped for a moment and then carried on. 'We came to London yesterday afternoon and I saw the portrait you did.'

'I hope I caught something that you recognised?'

'I think you know the answer to that one, Mr Rutherford. But my reply to you would be to ask what you left behind of yourself in the picture?'

'Pain,' she said before she knew she had and the other nodded.

'You were the bird trapped in the cage. The one who held no voice? Do you always do that, Mr Rutherford? Do pieces shear off you in every portrait?'

'Only in the ones that matter.'

'And this one did?'

'Yes.'

'Then I am glad for it. Winter has hung the painting in his library above the mantel for it is the room he most often uses.'

So it would not be hidden then. It would be seen.

They had left the grotto now and made their way around to the front of the house. Other small flowering plants grew by the steps and Arabella Carmichael took scissors from her pocket and clipped off some of the buds.

'Did you know flowers have a language all of their own, Mr Rutherford? Lily of the valley stands for purity and pansies are for thoughtfulness.' Both the white and the blue blooms were thrust into Florentia's hands before she knew it, their scent full and heady. 'They suit you. Entirely. A gift from my garden, but also from my heart.'

Then they were inside the darkness of the house, a room at the back opening into yet another vista and it was here that Lord Winterton and Mr Carmichael sat, a number of small carved tiles on a table before them.

'Are you familiar with the rune stones? Rafe collects them.' Lord Winterton asked this of her as he saw her, a certain challenge in his voice, and Mr Carmichael laughed at her silence.

'I do not use them for magical or divinatory purposes despite Winter's teasing, Mr Rutherford. An artist like you could surely understand that their intrinsic beauty, feel and age is what attracts me and if there is a shadow of the darkness to one side then it is all the better.'

Bryson had collected bones. Of birds and fish. Of larger animals, too, caught in death unexpectedly. In swamps and rivers. In the caves at Albany, the sandstone loose and heavy. They had been collecting the day that he had died… But Flora shook that away and looked instead at the rune stones, her heart beating too fast and the taste of iron on her tongue.

The strange angular inscriptions on the tiles were perplexing. Flora knew that they were usually cast in a certain direction and that if a question was asked the answer could be found in the way they fell as a pattern.

Am I ever going to be happy again?

For just a second she thought she might have said the query out loud and the fright of such a horror kept her still.

Collections held a safety zone, a way to organise, arrange and present the world just as you wanted it to be. A place where fears were managed and calmed.

Each bone that her brother had ever found was now carefully ordered and sorted in the wooden boxes she had made and painted in her room.

Sometimes when she was younger she had seen Maria look at her as if she were indeed mad, but their white opaque stillness filled a void inside her that had opened after Bryson's passing and allowed his death some meaning.

When she caught the golden eyes of Rafael Carmichael resting upon her face, she hoped the stones did not permit him to divine her thoughts.

The normal and ordinary seemed to have passed her by and this had been magnified again by her ordeal at the inn, but as she glanced around the room she saw there were things here in this house that were also unusual.

The backs of all the chairs were notched in patterns not unlike the rune stones and a book that sat open on the table held a raised print embossed into the paper.

On the mantel above the fireplace sat five small marble busts, each depicting emotion. Besides each sat a flower, the single blooms in tall glass vases and newly picked.

Arabella's language of flowers? She looked down at the buds in her grip.

There were no paintings at all on any of the walls.

'Did you enjoy the garden?' Winterton had asked her this. His expression held the hint of something she could not quite interpret.

'Very much indeed. If I closed my eyes I might have been anywhere.'

'Or nowhere,' Rafael Carmichael said as he stood, his hands against the chair. 'Smells are evocative, are they not? Winter has an aversion to peppermint and nothing will cure him of it no matter how hard Arabella has tried.'

Peppermint.

Every time she smelt it she thought of blood and breathlessness. Imagine what it must be like for him with years of long sickness to remember and the futility of his mistake.

'So we never plant it.' Arabella added this and the tone lightened. For a second though Flora had seen in the glance of James Waverley a truth that made her take in breath.

Shame. Guilt. All the things she had hoped for in her years of ruin, though now she did not wish to see them at all.

Perhaps the Carmichaels knew what had happened on the North Road? Perhaps he had told them? What must that be like to have good friends standing by you, through all your trials and difficulties, people you could be honest with and trust?

The *ton* with all its rules and propriety seemed shallow and foolish compared to these people. She'd never felt a part of society, but was always adrift and out of step. Here, with Lord Winterton and the Carmichaels, it was like having life breathed into deadness, an energy she had lost hold of returned in all its fervour.

Maria had moved on and she had been left behind, her sister's marriage taking away some of the closeness that they used to enjoy. Bryson had been her true confidant, but she had never wanted to speak of him with her family as his death had broken all of their hearts, the hole left by his passing unending and black.

But here amongst the flowers and laughter with Winterton and his friends she felt at home, comfortable, able to be herself.

Well not quite herself, she smiled, given the disguise

that she wore and the name that she sheltered behind. But no longer hiding her honest thoughts, no longer unable to speak in the way she wanted to, no longer ruled by expectations.

She had not thought it possible to live well outside of such strictures until today where the differences allowed one to flourish and thrive, like the blooms all around them and the flowers in her hands.

She liked it when Lord Winterton came to stand beside her, showing her a book.

'These are prints of some of the oldest known maps.' His finger traced the outline of the Americas. 'They thought you would sail off the edge of the world and into the land of monsters.'

Scaly green serpents hung at each edge of the paper, the ships depicted weathering storms tiny by comparison.

'When I sailed to America I remembered these illustrations as I stood and watched over the ocean.' He laughed and, with the sunlight blending the colours in his hair and glinting against the pale clear green of his eyes, Florentia knew she had never seen a man more vibrant. The thought struck her as a blow and she held her breath as she tried to look way.

But she could not.

This truly might be the last day that she ever saw him, the last time she heard his voice or knew his smile. She drank him in even as her throat thickened with sadness and it was Lord Winterton who looked away first, his glance flickering to Rafael Carmichael and his wife watching them from the other side of the room.

'Monsters of the deep hold a certain wordless eloquence, I always thought.' There was a quiet anger in his voice that was surprising. 'An adventure that I wanted.'

'And which he got, Mr Rutherford.' Arabella had joined them. 'Did you know you are in the company of a man who single-handedly saved a whole regiment of British Hussars from the clutches of the French and lived to tell the tale?'

'Barely.' This time there was no mistaking the fury.

'He was decorated for it, too, though I never saw you wear your medals, Winter. You should. If it were me I would wear them on my chest in pride and glory daily.'

'Old friends have the tiresome habit of telling one how to act and what to do, Mr Rutherford,' He gestured her to follow him through the wide doors. They came into another smaller garden filled with crocus and hellebores.

'You don't like to remember your past?' Florentia asked this even as she bent to smell one of the Lenten roses, needing to know something of him, something of who he had been. Something to hold on to after he was gone again.

'War is glorious only to those who have never lived through the middle of one.'

'But you survived?'

'But not well and the painting you made for me showed you knew that.'

Such a raw truth kept her silent. The things people did not say were as easily heard as those they did and she was good at listening to the spaces in between. It was where she had lived for years, after all, that awkward half-hidden part of life, an invisible quiet world of little consequence and no real substance.

The paintings had brought her back from the greyness and filled her world with colour again, repairing frayed edges with purpose and delight.

But here in front of her was a man who was also good at hearing the unspoken and who had ghosts of his own. Such a kinship made her falter and hesitate, a danger here that was almost touchable.

'The room inside and the gardens without are fashioned in a way to compensate sight?'

Clear green eyes blazed. 'Rafe's father died last year. He was blind. This was where he lived for his last months.'

'You were close to him, too?'

'I was. He was like a father to me.' He took in breath and carried on. 'Most people miss all the things you don't, Mr Rutherford. Did you know that?'

'Art is made in the carefulness of notice, my lord.'

'And in the regard of the concealed?'

She looked up at that, expecting accusation. Instead all she saw was a sorrow and when the Carmichaels came out to join them again Florentia was glad for it.

James felt the rope at his ankles and his wrists and the blood running cold down his back. It was into a pit of sorts that he had been thrown, the freeze of the dirt in the Cantabrian winter crusted with ice and snow and it was raining. He could feel the steady drip of it on his face when he looked up, trying to catch even a bit of the thin moonlight.

He'd been beaten every day since the French had taken him, with a beaded rope and with a musket. Something had been carved into his back in glass and that smarted more than all the other wounds that abounded across his body. His fingers ran across raised scoured skin, trying to read by touch.

Espion.

Spy. There was no clemency in such a word.

He would die here, unheralded and unknown. Just another soldier whose bones would grace the soil of Spain. And when the French Hussars came again he tipped his head and screamed into the night, his throat aching with the sound as he tried to stop all the pain that they inflicted...

He came awake suddenly into silence and to the softness of a mattress, the sweat dripping from him on to clean linen and the moon limning the world in silver.

He was in his bedchamber in St James's. Outside came the noises of a waking city. Only a dream. Again. He had had the same nightmare for years.

Pushing back the counterpane, he sat and held his head in his hands to steady the fury and the beat of blood. The Early Cheer Arabella had sent him home with were in a vase next to his bed. He clung to the smell of them like a man who was drowning, clung to their pureness and their beauty. The first flowers after the snow.

Florentia Hale-Burton was just like the blooms. Unexpected. Impossibly fragile. Today as they sat in the garden room at the Carmichaels' he had seen things that were particular only to her. The way she used her hands when she spoke, the dimples in her cheeks, the small freckles across her nose and the grace with which she moved.

He'd seen her take in the details, too, of the room, of Arabella and Rafael, of the flowers and the nicks in the wood on all of the railings.

An artist's eye, seeing the things that other people missed, understanding secrets and accepting them. When she had looked at the rune stones he had thought she might speak of her past then and there, the truth bursting out unbidden.

But she had not. She had simply held the flowers so tightly that the knuckles on each of her fingers were white with the pressure.

As they'd made to leave Arabella had pulled him to one side.

'Look after her, Winter. She is a treasure.'

'Her?' He was wary of Arabella's accuracy.

'When I was younger I, too, used disguises. Bring her back whenever you want and make certain that she is safe from what it is she is so very afraid of.'

Him. She was afraid of him.

He was glad Arabella had not asked Florentia's name or insisted on knowing her story and was relieved to finally depart before more of the truth surfaced. The girl who at the Carmichaels had chatted and laughed was on the ride home much more silent.

'I've hung your portrait in my library, Mr Rutherford. I like looking at it. Perhaps you might bring the Warrendens to see it. I know they enjoy your work and I would be pleased to show them.'

She nodded, but made no effort to pin him down to a time at all. Rather she looked away again and spoke on a different topic.

'The Carmichaels have the best of it, I think, living out of the centre of town. Kent is the same.'

'You will go back, then?'

'I will, my lord, for I have found out all that I needed to know here.'

'And the commissions?'

'I'll draw from what I have around me and be happy with it.' Her glance dropped away.

'I have noticed that your cough is much recovered, Mr Rutherford.'

'It is asthma, Lord Winterton, and it comes and goes.'

'A difficult affliction.'

'And one far less prevalent away from the pollution of town.'

'My cousin Tommy suffered from the same, but he lives in the Americas now with his wife, Acacia, and he says that the weather there suits him far better than it ever did in England.'

The slight start told him she had caught the reference. But she was almost as good at hiding things as he was. For a moment he wondered what would happen should he simply reach out and take her hand and confess everything before they reached the Warrenden town house, but this was neither the time nor the place.

He wanted to see Florentia Hale-Burton's eyes properly and the colour of her hair. He wanted to see the dimples, too, in her cheeks and run his finger across the freckles on the bridge of her nose.

'I doubt that I shall see you again, Lord Winterton.' The words came through his reveries. 'But I'd like to thank you for your generous payment for the portrait and also for taking me to see the Carmichaels today. They were lovely people.'

Lovely? Was that the sort of word a man would use? Flora wondered and looked out of the window.

'You will not return to London?' His query came quietly.

'It is a difficult place to fit in.'

'Yet all I've heard of you is salutary.'

She smiled at that and turned towards him. 'An insincere regard given that they barely know me.'

'My offer of you painting Atherton Abbey still stands.'

'I've taken enough of your money with the portrait, Lord Winterton. Any more would be a travesty.'

'It is not because of your agent's insistence in the accelerating value of an investment that I would like more of your work, but because of the truth I see within it.'

'Thank you.' Such a compliment was distracting because it was given so unexpectedly.

'I am heading west tomorrow to see to the last of the contracts on the Abbey and shall be away for a while.'

'Julia Heron said it was a beautiful house and expensive.'

'To me it will only be home,' he returned and she understood other things about Lord Winterton, things she had not considered at all before.

He had been without roots for years, but underneath the persona he presented to the world lay a vulnerability that was surprising. At least she had had Albany Manor and a family, her life closeted but safe. His had been transitory, hard and uncertain.

She wished she might have placed her fingers over the hand that rested on the seat beside her, the one with the scars across the knuckles, webbed in whiteness, but her sister's warning came to mind.

'He is a dangerous man, Florentia, and will be hard to dupe because he is like a flame and you are the

*moth. If you do not wish for discovery you would be
wise to never meet him again.'*

Maria had given her this advice as she had left this
morning on the trip to the scented gardens and she had
laughed off such concerns. But Winterton was harder
to read today, although far more open, and when he had
told her about his cousin Tommy she had felt a shock
that she knew he must have seen.

Was he playing a double game? Did he know who
she was? The horror of that thought made her sit forward, her heart beginning to thump and her mouth dry.

Another minute to Grosvenor Square and safety.
The anger in her warred with sorrow and that in turn
was followed by a pure and quiet grief. This was the
end of everything between them and all she wanted to
do was to go home.

Please God, do not let him smile or murmur words
that were conciliatory and impartial and final. She did
not wish to stay his friend. She did not want platitudes
or recriminations or even kindness.

These grey little feelings were nothing at all compared to the burning raw-red inferno that was consuming her now, her breath shaky and her throat tight
with tears. She wanted things he would never be able
to offer her and as she could not have those then she
wanted nothing at all.

Her father would simply expire should they come
face-to-face. He sometimes talked to her as he recalled
what had happened at the inn and his memory was surprisingly sharp and uncompromisingly bitter.

The number of people who'd seen the Viscount and
who would be able to identify him as the perpetrator
of a terrible crime was also worrying. Her maid Milly

was no longer in her employ, but Florentia had heard that she'd come to London to work in one of the houses here. The Urquharts, too, were a couple who might recognise him should they see them together and their tale would not be flattering. Her father's driver and the two footmen who had accompanied Papa north could also offer information should they be asked.

The truth was like a stone flung into a still pond, the ripples widening as time passed until no tranquillity was left. If Winterton was thrown into such a scandal, she did not know what might happen to him. Would the law be involved? Would he be thrown into jail and left to rot there or sent to the colonies as an indentured felon?

It was all dangerous suddenly, this secret between them, for she had no certainty that he would be safe.

When the carriage stopped she was pleased as his man opened the door to help her down. She did not tarry, but made her way inside with the utmost speed. Looking back, she was glad he had not followed and even more glad as the conveyance readied itself for departure and the horses stepped on.

It was over and finished. She would never need to see him again. Roy greeted her as he came from his library and looked down the corridor behind her.

'Is Winter here?'

'No. He had an appointment and needed to be gone. The painting is signed and paid for so there is no contract left that binds us.'

'I am glad to hear it for these matters are never without their messiness. Once I thought I knew Winter well, but now…' He shrugged. 'He is harder and more aloof.

There is something in his character that wasn't there when I knew him at school.'

She was about to answer when Maria walked in and asked them both to join her in the front parlour.

'The Duke of Northbury has sent an invitation asking for our company and that of Mr Frederick Rutherford to a ball he is having in a week. Inside there is a handwritten note to the effect that he would be most disappointed should we be unable to go. Your name is specifically mentioned, Flora. Well, Frederick's is, I mean.'

Roy looked horrified. 'The Duke was a particular friend of my father's. I can't see how we might decline this.'

Maria handed him the gilt-edged paper, the red-wax seal broken and beribboned in blue. 'I knew something bad would come of all this. I knew we should have left London sooner and now to be stuck with another charade. It is all just too, too much and you cannot possibly attend in those old clothes of Bryson's.'

'I think clothes are the least of our worries, Maria. The very least.'

Her brother-in-law's eyes ran across her face, the brown full of concern. 'What of you, Flora? Do you wish to do this or would you rather…'?

She did not let him finish. 'I have got this far, Roy, and no one could be more discerning than Lord Winterton.' Even as she said this, however, she felt vaguely sick. 'I am sure I can be convincing for one last outing if you feel it necessary to stay.'

'We will call my tailor in to measure you for a set of clothes befitting the occasion. We will also make it known that we will be leaving the day after the Northbury ball which will effectively stop any more invitations coming, no matter how important the sender.'

Maria tucked her hand through Florentia's arm. 'We will be there this time which will allow some sort of a barrier between you and the other guests and we won't need to tarry long. An appearance is all that is required. Still, it would be better if we tried not to engage others in conversation for there is only so much luck in the world after all.'

She stopped and the unspoken lay between them. *And ours could very easily be running out.*

Chapter Nine

It was a whirlwind week of fittings and bustling activity. The Warrenden tailor had come and measured her up for the clothes and, on a generous retainer from her brother-in-law's coffers, had been the very soul of discretion and confidence. If he guessed her figure was not one pertaining to a youth he made no mention of it whatsoever, fashioning the clothes around her form and fitting them with barely a word uttered.

Standing in front of the mirror an hour before they were all to leave, Flora looked at her reflection and was shocked.

This was what Bryson would have looked like had he lived. She could see the lines of him in her face and the blue of his eyes gazing back at her. The wig and the moustache blurred the resemblance a little, but at that second all she could feel was the unexpected closeness of her twin.

'I wish you were here,' she whispered. 'I wish you could help me.'

She smiled because all her antics and movements were completed with him in mind. The way he walked, and spoke and was. Without Bryson she knew she should never have chanced such a deception.

Her fingers went to a ring he'd worn that now sat on her hand. The gold was solid and real somehow, a circle that had not broken.

Would Viscount Winterton be there tonight? Would he come if he knew she was invited or was he still away seeing to the specifics of the property he was acquiring? She had not seen him since she had exited the carriage outside the Warrenden town house. But she had dreamed about him. She had dreamed they were before a beautiful country house in the sunlight and that he had pulled off her wig and kissed her, hard and true.

Ridiculous, she thought, and shook away the image. He was probably doing his very best to never see her again.

She had drawn him every single day, late at night when the others were asleep and when there was no chance of interruption. She had drawn him in colour as well as in all the shades of grey.

She hoped he would be there. She did. She wanted to meet him again and feel his eyes on her own. She wanted to ask of the portrait and of his new home.

My God, what was she thinking? James Waverley, Viscount Winterton, would hold no interest in who she was. Every woman in society was angling to catch his eye after all and with his investments in the lucrative timber trade he was exactly the sort of man the society mothers would want for their daughters.

The night suddenly seemed less of an adventure and much more of an ordeal to get through and when Maria came in with her new blue gown, her hair a cascade of ringlets, Florentia felt suddenly sick.

'I know that look, Flora, but you have to come. Roy would be devastated if you did not and we have already sent back our intention of attending.' She suddenly smiled. 'I never realised how much you looked like Bryson. It's nice, because I miss him.'

'Me, too.'

'If Father were here…'

'I doubt he will ever be well enough to return to society.'

'Maybe if your abductor had been proven dead he might have, but to never hear a word again and your reputation ruined as it was, I think he simply lost his will for life really. If Roy was to act like that I'd probably simply hit him over the head for I certainly wouldn't be pandering to his moods as Mama is want to suffer Papa's.'

The room was crowded when they arrived, the Duke of Northbury's town house one of the largest and grandest Florentia had ever seen. From one end of the first salon right along to the other there were lengths of blue shot silk hung with corded red tassels which in turn were threaded in jewels. In front of each hanging stood huge urns filled with flowers, the aged terracotta embellished with drawings of ancient Grecian gods. Arabella Carmichael would have enjoyed such bounty, Florentia thought, for many of the blooms were out of season and must have been brought in from warmer climes. She wondered about the cost of it all.

It was like a wonderful tapestry of colour and form and texture, a beautiful living painting that faded and reformed under the light of chandeliers and the shadows of quiet darker corners. With the music playing and the chatter constant Flora closed her eyes so that she could memorise it, for the grace and movement was a tableau she might never see again. But to paint it with strokes of energy and boldness…

'I thought you had returned to Kent, Mr Rutherford?'

Her eyes snapped open. Winterton stood before her, dressed this evening in black save for the snowy cravat at his neck, folded high across the scar.

She chastised herself for feeling so uncertain, her newly found bravery reduced by his presence. 'This is the last social occasion I have promised to attend, my lord, before I go home.'

'Then it is a fine choice. The Duke's soirées are always…interesting. The man has a genuine notion of the theatrical and a budget to indulge his very eclectic taste.'

As she glanced up at him she saw the bruise on his cheek had almost gone. The pale green of his eyes against his tan always surprised her.

'You are here with the Warrendens?'

'I am, my lord.'

A servant dressed in the exotic clothes of an Indian maharaja came and offered them wine, the golden tray he held inscribed in Egyptian hieroglyphics.

'One cannot be over-concerned about mixing up dynasties when the serving tools of the Raj are so very hard to come by.' Winterton stated this dryly when he saw her observation. His expression was distant, a man with a thousand masks and not one of them the truth.

The danger in him was shocking and for a second Flora forgot how to breathe, but stood there watching him, the thickness in her throat wrenching and unfathomable. When a striking and sensual woman stepped in from one side to take the Viscount by the arm she moved back.

'I have finally found you, Winter, and so many of my friends are asking for your company.'

There was a quick flare of anger in his eyes, but this disappeared as instantly as it had come. Tipping his head, he gave her his farewells and accompanied the newcomer away without any resistance whatsoever.

Maria joined her a moment later. 'The Heron girls have just asked me if my sister was still unsure about stepping into society. I told them she has no care for the deceptions prevalent here.'

'A brave rejoinder, perhaps, given our circumstances?'

Maria managed a smile. 'Winterton is always surrounded by females and looking at him I can understand why. He does seem to favour the Heron girls, but then they are awfully attractive.'

A bevy of the most beautiful women in society had indeed gathered about the Viscount and he by no means looked disconcerted. The hand of the woman who had spirited him away lay possessively upon his arm.

'James Waverley is soon to be thirty. Hopefully he will settle on someone to take as a bride if only to put all of these desperate females out of their misery.'

Florentia laughed, but she could hear the falseness in it as surely as her sister probably could. As she glanced across the room his eyes met her own and she stood transfixed at what she thought she could see. A fine regard and respect.

She took in a breath, the wig tight about her head and the stock at her throat constricting.

The other woman had turned to see what had caught Winterton's attention, anger crossing her brow, but, seeing only the thin form of Frederick Rutherford, merely smiled and turned away.

No competition there, Flora thought the gesture implied, the soft rounded womanhood relaxing into an amused benevolence.

When Roy came to claim Maria in a dance it allowed Florentia the chance to move into an alcove with long windows overlooking the garden.

She was glad for the moment of aloneness though she felt a presence behind her and knew that it was the Viscount. Without turning, she waited for him to come and stand beside her, the lights in the gardens reflected on both of their faces.

'Could I show you a painting, Mr Rutherford? I am sure you would find it of interest.'

'A painting?'

'It is in the Duke's library and he has allowed me the use of the room.'

'I am not sure...'

'It would just take a moment.'

She glanced around, trying to see her sister, but there were only strangers standing about them and, short of a rudeness, she could not dredge up any true excuse as to why she should refuse. He would expect her to be interested and so as he gestured to her to follow him she did so, down a short unlit corridor and into a chamber at the very end.

The painting stood on the far wall, the lights around it giving its darkness a particular space.

'It's a Van Dyke.'

She moved forward with amazement. 'I cannot believe that this portrait should be here, close enough for me to touch.'

'The Duke's great-grandfather gave a particular service to Charles the First, it seems, and the painting was his reward. It has been in his family's hands for years.'

Florentia moved closer to see the brush strokes and the small details of the work. 'The elegance and authority are traits in all of his works. He painted the King and his wife many times.'

'You are well informed, Mr Rutherford.'

Winter had moved up next to her now and close, the smell of sandalwood and freshly washed male easily discerned. The darkness around them and the silence was complete. Much further away she could hear the sound of music.

When he lifted his hand to run a finger across the line of her cheek she was shocked by such an intimacy.

'Your knowledge of the arts is beguiling.'

She swallowed, the horror of her situation unfolding. Was he attracted to her as a boy? Pray God, he would not take this further.

'You asked me once if I believed in Fate, Mr Rutherford. Perhaps this is ours.' His interest had fallen to her lips, a gentle tracing of the shape under the pad of his thumb.

She could not understand just what might happen next.

'Perhaps it is our fate to meet in the most unexpected of places and under the most dubious of circumstances.'

'Dubious?' Her voice was strained.

'Me and you…here. Like this. Alone. Do you not think it fortuitous?'

There was a new tone now in his words. One of humour if she might name it and careful question. A game of cat and mouse was the bread and butter, no doubt, of any spy, and he was rumoured to be a good one.

She could feel the breath of his words against her cheek as he spoke and his hand had fallen lower across her shoulder and down the line of her arm.

If he truly did not know her, then this game was dangerous, but if he did…?

'Do you ever play the rune stones, my lord?' She asked this because she knew the answer even before he shook his head.

'Then perhaps you should. For protection.'

'Against what?'

'Enemies come in all shapes and sizes and society holds a narrow view of what is right and what is wrong.'

He laughed at that and when he ceased he leaned across and whispered in her ear.

'Is this wrong? Are you my enemy, Lady Florentia Hale-Burton?'

Her world simply stopped, the whirl of colour turning grey and all balance lost under the pounding beat of her heart.

Dread rendered her speechless.

'If you expose me, Florentia, I will not deny the charges. Everything that has happened to you was my fault. I accept that.'

'Do you?'

'You tried to save me when we fell from the carriage even after all I had put you through. Why?' His words came soft and when she did not answer he carried on. 'I thought perhaps…' Again he stopped.

'You thought what?'

'That you might not have hated me as much as I believed. That there was a chance you could forgive me for what I had done to you and your family. What I am still doing to you, with your disguises and your secrecy.'

'Pity isn't a flattering word, Lord Winterton.'

'You think it such?'

'I have been an outcast for years. How could I think anything different?'

'Marry me, then. I can protect you from them all.'

She could not believe he could possibly have said this. 'Guilt is not a solid basis for a union, either. Even a ruined woman hopes for more than that.'

'Marry me and we will leave London and society. We will make a new life at Atherton Abbey.'

'And my family? You think Papa will give his blessing? You think he will not crow your name in distaste from every rooftop he could find when he sees your face? When he knows it was you who kidnapped me?'

'I think he will see sense and do what is the best for his daughter's reputation.'

'The best? The best.' She repeated those two words, sneering at him in a way that she knew was not attractive but she no longer cared. It was one thing to be married in love and quite another to be married in shame or duty. The best of a bad situation.

'No. I cannot marry you, my lord.' She could barely get the words out.

He wished he had said it differently. He wished he could take his words back and start again, this time not immured in guilt but in respect.

Florentia had removed her glasses and was wiping them against the silk in her waistcoat and for the first time he truly saw her eyes for more than a fleeting second.

He remembered them like a punch to the stomach. Their blue honesty. The grey at the edges. The flashing shards of anger mixed with sadness. He wanted to reach out then and take her hand to hold it warm against his own, two people beached up by history on to some sort of foreign shore that neither could fathom. Shipwrecked by uncertainty.

She was beautiful. He had always known that.

She had turned now and was out of the door before he could stop her, making her way into the busy melee of the main room. As he caught her up an old friend, Frank Reading, slapped him on the back.

'Been looking for you, Winter. I have some need for timber and I hear you are just the man to provide it.' His eyes went across to Florentia, who had replaced her spectacles and regained her composure.

'You're the artist, aren't you? I have been hoping to make your acquaintance for society is abuzz at your talent with a brush.'

'Mr Frederick Rutherford, this is Lord Frank Reading.'

'Pleased to make your acquaintance, sir.'

James heard the timbre of her voice lower and gain that certain cadence of masculinity. He had not realised how convincing she sounded as a boy until she had spoken to him in a different voice altogether.

'I don't suppose I could persuade you to make a painting for me, Mr Rutherford?'

'I am afraid not, my lord. I am leaving London for a

long while. Family commitments and the need for privacy,' she went on and left the words hanging.

'I hear you have done a portrait for Winter. I for one cannot wait to see it. From the whispered gossip it is magnificent.'

Florentia shrugged and James understood what her art truly cost her in just that small gesture. It was as if she did not wish to acknowledge or discuss the paintings she had left behind, a sort of bereft anger displayed on her countenance that was gone as soon as he recognised it.

Others had joined them, too, squeezing in around them, asking questions of him and of her, dissipating any closeness. He wished he might have simply lent forward and led her away, to take her into the garden in the moonlight and…kiss her.

That ludicrous thought made him swear beneath his breath in a single heartfelt curse. She had dismissed his marriage proposal summarily less than five minutes ago. She would hardly be interested in less.

The words had astonished him even as he had said them.

Marry me. He had never once in all his life uttered that to any woman before and there had been many vying for such an offer both in America and here. He could not believe how he had meant it either, how he had hoped that she might say yes.

Had Lady Florentia Hale-Burton upended his sense in some way as to render him into this man that he barely recognised? He had not seen her for almost six years, and still did not truly, for the disguise she wore was a good one.

Maria Warrenden had come out to claim her now

and they were walking back to the main ballroom, the light catching them both as it streamed through the large glass doors.

Florentia was so much thinner than her sister, more fragile, brittle almost. Was this his doing? He could see the platforms built into her shoes and he frowned at the shape of her legs through thin silk, glad that her jacket was of a long length and covered much of what he did not wish others to see.

He swore again. He had no right to such opinions, no mandate to even think such things. When he saw that Reading watched him thoughtfully he turned away and arranged his face into the more normal expression of indifference.

Nothing seemed quite right any more. It was as if his life had slipped a cog since meeting Florentia and he could not get it back on track. He wanted to follow her inside and talk to her again just to hear her voice and listen to her odd opinions.

God, she must be laughing at him now with his ill-considered marriage proposal and his patent desperation. Swallowing his brandy in three large gulps, he felt all the better for it.

Julia Heron was watching her intently from the small distance where she stood with a few of the other girls whom Florentia recognised from her first foray into society.

Just as she was about to walk away the Heron girl broke from the others and came directly up to her.

'You have the look of the Hale-Burton brother, Mr Rutherford. Bryson was his name. I thought to tell you before another does. I puzzled on the resemblance the other day when you came to our town house, but could not quite put my finger upon it. Tonight it is right here before me.'

Flora saw the frown deepen on Maria's brow. 'Ancestry often has that certain trick of stamping likenesses on those who come next, Miss Heron. My sister and I have often been mistaken for each other as well.'

'Your sister? I sometimes wonder how she is faring, Lady Warrenden?'

'She fares very well, thank you, although she is busy with her life at Albany.' Maria was quick in her reply.

'I had heard she was dabbling in painting?'

'She is indeed. Mr Rutherford here has been her tutor.' Her sister's answer held a note of panic that Florentia hoped Miss Heron did not detect and, setting her mouth in the grim line she had perfected over the weeks of playing the artist, she nodded.

'And how is it you are related to the Hale-Burtons, Mr Rutherford, to hold such a resemblance?'

'Loosely, Miss Heron. Our fathers were second cousins.'

'Just a trick of nature then?' Julia Heron opened her fan as she spoke and glanced out from behind it, a girl who knew her worth in the market place of the *ton*. 'Lord Winterton looks well tonight, does he not? I saw you speaking with him earlier and you both seemed most intense?'

'Art has its deep conversations and its age-old fascinations.' Flora tried to moderate her tone into one of indifference.

'Papa is still hopeful he may entice you into our home to draw us all.'

Maria interrupted. 'Mr Rutherford is returning to

the country the day after tomorrow. He will have no time at all to be able to consider taking on more work in London.'

The arrival of Roy allowed a natural end to the conversation and Julia Heron begged her leave and left them.

'I thought you might like a dance, Maria.' Roy looked to have had quite a bit to drink, his face flushed.

'If it stops you from taking another brandy for a few moments I think it is probably a good idea. But what of Flora?'

'Oh, I am sure I can lean against this wall without getting into any trouble.'

'Are you certain?' Her sister looked torn.

'Go and dance, Maria. I shall be more than fine.'

As they went she watched them, Roy's hand within his wife's, a sense of trust there and respect.

Marry me, then.

The three words reverberated through her body and she swallowed away the emptiness she had heard in them. How long had Winter known her secret? When had he guessed she was not as she seemed?

The Viscount was over on the other side of the room, talking with a group of men. She could see him easily for he stood a good few inches above everyone else. He did not look at all like a man who had just had a marriage proposal turned down as he threw back his head and laughed. Under the chandelier his hair appeared lighter and it contrasted markedly against the black in his clothes. Julia Heron was cosied up beside him and he appeared to be paying her a good deal of attention.

Another side of his character was present tonight. Here in the *ton* he looked at home and relaxed, a man who would welcome the discourse of others, a viscount whose lineage was easily discerned in every line of his body and in the indifference on his face. A man who was lauded and admired by others. A man far above her station in life in all the ways that counted.

She would have liked to have drawn him like this. Even as she stood there she could feel her fingers move across his form, picking out the strengths and that which made him unique. She would have fashioned him in charcoal, the thickness of it garnering attention, bold strokes of confidence and ease, the sombre clothes against his lighter hair, muscle pressing against superfine.

She wished she might have been standing there in a gown that was beautiful and feminine, her hair paler than his own and falling in long cascading curls. The cloth she had shoved into each cheek to try and change the lines of her jaw felt dry and foreign and she accepted a glass of wine from a passing waiter to try to alleviate that.

Marry me, then.

Had he even truly asked it? Without a scrap of knowledge as to who each other were and with a history between them that could only foretell disaster? What was he thinking? Why would he imagine it could be possible? Perhaps he felt sorry for her, their enforced proximity in St James's Square having the effect of allowing him a glimpse into her life since the incident at the inn? Guilt could be a factor. Or plain old pity. A man like him could not possibly have asked her in love.

She failed to see the drunk fellow weaving across the floor because he was behind her. She did not observe him clutch at the hangings of one curtain and drag it down so that it fell heavily in her direction, the banner from the pelmet above sheering away from splintered wood.

She did hear the screams, though, echoing through the room, and she did feel the moment something sliced through the fleshy part of her right calf.

A body landed on top of her before rolling away, the smell of alcohol strong, one burly arm rising to graze her cheek and leave it stinging. She felt the heavy tightness of the shock and the sharp agony of pain. A young woman to her left began to cry and the sound of the orchestra playing a waltz quietened with an awkward lilt until it had all but stopped, only the last strings of a wayward violin vibrating into the silence.

Her leg was bleeding all over the parquet floor of the Duke of Northbury's ballroom. Indifferently she wondered how much damage had actually been done to her and then all she felt was coldness.

Florentia Hale-Burton was on all fours trying to get up, her leg pushed beneath her in a strange fashion. He could tell she was hurt even before the curdling cries of those around her took away the sense of it. Through the gaps of all the colourful silk gowns between them James saw that the tie of the ugly black wig had come unfastened and the hair now fell in a macabre way down her face, the lifeless strands covering her like a shroud.

It was as though time simply stopped, the room full of horrified onlookers and the whispers growing even as he strode across to crouch beside the pale Lady Florentia Hale-Burton.

Her eyes met his own, the spectacles fallen and the

blueness in the light of chandeliers astonishing. Repositioning her hairpiece, he found her glasses and perched them once again across her nose, praying like hell that no one had noticed something was amiss.

'I am fine.' She did not cry or try to explain. No, instead she simply sat there, attempting to draw a steady breath, a slight still figure in the centre of chaos doing her best to be brave.

More and more people were coming to join the throng, their expressions shocked at the blood that was pooling beneath her on the floor.

'It is the artist, Mr Rutherford. My God, he has been injured and badly, too.'

Maria Warrenden pushed through the crowd, shouldering those who were close to let her through. Roy came behind, his face a mixture of worry and horror, but James had untied her neckcloth and was winding it about Florentia's knee just above the wound. When he knotted it tightly the bleeding on the fleshy part of her calf seemed to slow and he let out his breath. For this second she was safe, though he could feel the wolves gathering.

'Rutherford is very thin, is he not?'

'And remarkably young and girlish.'

'What is his story, exactly?'

Interest spread around them and as Roy's wife's gaze caught his own he simply bent down to lift Florentia into his arms, her lightness as surprising as the fact that she did not fight him but rather buried her face into his chest and stayed still. Winter hoped those in the room would see Florentia only as a young and sensitive youth who had been brought to tears by a shocking and unexpected accident. The blood helped her case, he supposed, though his anger mounted at the thought.

'Bring him through to our carriage, Winter. I have called for my driver to bring it to the front.' Roy Warrenden beckoned him and James was glad for the direction.

'Hold on,' he whispered to the shaking figure he held. 'It will only be another moment until we are out of here, I promise.'

But she did not answer as he walked along one side of the ballroom, people scattering before him, looks of horror and speculation on each face he passed.

Flora knew that Viscount Winterton did not wish for an explanation. Yet. He had looked at her in something akin to warning, the clear green eyes taking in everything.

She knew he was angry, but the mask that had dropped over his features allowed no certainty of anything else, no shared ground at all save for the recent congress of an artist and subject.

Later there would be questions, she knew that, but for now the shock of everything made her cold and shaky and she felt the first tears pooling behind her eyes.

Winter's clothing held the same smell as his jacket had all those years before. Citrus, amber and sandalwood, smoky-dark and rich. She watched him because she did not wish to shut her eyes, the stillness that was gathering in all the corners of her body frightening and complete.

When he laid her down on the seat of the conveyance she tried to scramble up into a sitting position, but he held her there, raising her injured leg and securing a blanket beneath it.

'I hurt my thigh once and this is what the army doctor did,' he gave as an explanation. 'You will, however, need to sit very still.'

Maria looked sick with worry and Flora was glad Roy was there to hold her sister's hand because at that moment she had no energy for anything or anybody else. Closing her eyes, she prayed she would not be ill all over the expensive clothes of James Waverley. Again.

Blood was still seeping through Florentia's trousers and her face was so pale Winter thought she might just faint dead away.

Maria Warrenden watched him, he could see the questions in her eyes and he hoped that her husband would have the driver ready to move off soon.

He had sent one of his men to summon a physician and take him to the Warrenden town house in Grosvenor Square. James prayed that the man might be quick in his task and that the injury sustained was not a substantial one.

She was cold, he could tell that, but short of pulling her into his own warmth all he could do was to allow her the heat of his jacket which he tucked around her. Her fingers curled across the edges of light wool and the shivering seemed to be tapering off a little.

With care he unstoppered his brandy flask. 'Take a good mouthful and you will notice a difference.'

But she simply looked away, ignoring the offer completely and rocking back and forth on the seat. He took a swig himself.

'Does the injury pain you?'

There was a quick nod.

'Then that is a good thing. Without that a wound is always thought to be far more serious. It was the same with me after I was injured out of Lugos.'

When he saw her tilt her head as though she was interested in his answer he carried on. Roy was still fussing around with instructions with the driver and Maria Warrenden was now standing beside the carriage with her husband.

'It was snowing and the pass was high. I thought when I did not feel the pain that I was simply freezing, but afterwards they said I was as close to death as they had ever seen anyone be before and survive it.'

Blue eyes came across his own, worry stamped within them. 'I am cold, too.'

'Don't worry. You always feel that after any accident.'

'I hit my head…and it's hard…to breathe.' Her teeth were chattering now and air that she took was compromised.

He remembered this from last time, the blueness around her lips and the way she spoke as if every word were difficult. Maria had climbed in now and was crying. Ignoring the noise, he simply placed his fingers against Florentia's throat and talked quietly.

'Breathe with me. Just quiet breaths. Don't try to take too much.' Her heart was racing so fast he could barely hear the silence between.

'Good. You are doing well.' He made his voice calm as she began to do as he asked.

Her fingers came up against his, searching for warmth, her slender artist's hands covered with a crust of blood from the accident. The whole side of one sleeve was drenched in red.

Florentia wished her sister might stop crying. She wished she were home in the grove of trees at Albany. She wished she might have curled up and slept in Viscount Winterton's arms and stayed there for ever.

So many differing wishes.

Bryson was in the mix, too, for this was how he had died, his leg bleeding out from the wound upon it after she had dared him to jump the fence. The tears she had held back so far spilled over. Winter wiped them away without saying anything.

And then there was a flurry of activity as Roy rejoined them, the horses called on and the carriage jolted into motion.

But the Viscount had disappeared. He was gone and Maria was there beside her, face crinkled with horror.

'I knew this was a foolish idea, Florentia. I knew that we should be caught finally and that more scandal could follow.'

Roy, sitting opposite, laid a hand upon her shoulder.

'Only an omnipotent deity could have had such a vision, my love, and if the upshot is that we all retire back to Kent, well, we were going anyway.'

'Everybody was looking at you strangely, Flora, and if they guess what we have been doing you will never be allowed to come back into society. You will always be an outcast and you will never sell another painting.'

'I don't think your bedside manner is h-helping me, Maria.' Her sister sat closer to her at that and took her hand in her grasp.

'There are things that are so very unfair in life and its time you had some luck.'

'Luck?' Flora winced as she moved her foot for her toes caught against leather and the shooting pains made her shake. Blood had begun to seep out again and was staining the seat. 'Where is the doctor? Will he come soon?'

'Winter has sent for a physician. He will be at the house when we arrive in a few moments' time, I am sure of it,' Roy said, his tone full of question.

'And the Viscount?'

Maria frowned. 'He left. Why do you ask about him?'

'He…helped me. Did you thank him?'

'I did. He seemed…more familiar than usual.'

Florentia lay back against the seat, the pain in her leg making her feel dizzy.

Chapter Ten

James called into the town house on Grosvenor Square the next morning because he had dreamed all night that Florentia Hale-Burton's health had worsened and he wanted to see for himself that it had not. The physician had assured him the lad was recovering, but he had seen the amount of blood she had lost and she was so very slight, after all.

Roy took him through to a bright room at the back of the house where Florentia was lying on a sofa, her leg raised on two pillows. Warrenden seemed tense and uncertain, giving James the impression that his presence here was as welcome as the plague.

Today Florentia's colour was better and he could see she had been reading. The lad's clothes she wore were less formal than those he had thus far seen her in and she wore no neckcloth or jacket. On his entry she scrambled up to a sitting position and the wince of pain across her brow at such a movement had him swearing.

'Winter has come to enquire about your health, Frederick.' The tone Roy used was strained, no doubt wary of further participation in such a charade. Still, James thought, he could use it to his advantage.

'I wonder if I might have a word with Mr Rutherford in private, Roy?'

Short of rudeness there was little the other could do but agree, for there was no reason whatsoever to refuse the request of a lord wanting a small and private chat with a younger man with whom he had done business. James was pleased Maria Warrenden was not about as he doubted she would have withdrawn without a fuss.

'I shall be in the room next door, Frederick, should you want me.'

Not far. Within earshot. A simple shout will have me back.

When the door shut behind him there was a deafening silence which Florentia sought to instantly fill.

'I am much recovered this morning, thank you, Lord Winterton.'

'James,' he drawled, trying to keep out the anger. 'I am certain we have long since passed the point of such formality, Florentia. Even Winter would do.' Unsure as to whether Warrenden was listening on the other side of the door, he kept his voice down and was glad when she nodded.

'I do not think your charade has been discovered. The gossip this morning is on the severity of the wound and of the amount of blood lost. I have heard no mention at all of more worrying things.'

'That was because you replaced my glasses and wig quickly and I thank you for that.'

He could see in her eyes as he looked away the shadow of his foolish proposal and he wished like hell that he had not made it.

'I must also thank you for sending your physician to attend to me. He was a c-competent d-doctor.'

Her niceties were disassembling under the burden of manners, the voice of the lad lost into a higher and sweeter inflection.

But he did not let this distract him as he came to the point. 'If the disguise you have donned as a boy is anything to do with my abduction of you all those years ago…?'

She stopped him. 'It is not.'

He frowned because her expression was showing the exact opposite. 'I do not believe you. I think you agreed to do my portrait because you wanted to understand exactly what sort of a man I was.'

She stayed silent.

'And when you found out that I was more than sorry for my part in your…numerous difficulties since and wanted to rectify them, you ran.'

'Rectify them?' Now she had found her voice.

'With marriage, and my offer still stands. It is the only honourable path that I can see to follow. A linkage of the Hale-Burton name to my own to ward off further controversy and awkwardness.'

'Controversy and awkwardness?' Her anger worried him as she scrambled up her face six inches from his own, blue eyes blazing. 'Your first marriage proposal was dreadful, Lord Winterton, but this one is even worse.'

'Is it?'

The control that he had held for ever suddenly snapped as he dragged her against him, his lips coming down across her own. He could not remember ever being so angry or so aroused, but as he slanted his mouth over hers he understood the danger that she presented.

He had kissed so many women, but this one was unlike any of them. It was like kissing quicksilver, one moment one thing and the next something entirely different. It was like meeting his destiny.

'Hell.' He broke away without explanation and moved back, breathing so heavily he could hardly find air. 'Hell,' he repeated again, the world turning on its axis.

'Fix up your moustache.' It was all he could think to say, the thin disguise unpeeling to one side of her mouth.

Florentia Hale-Burton made him into a man he no longer recognised, a dolt with the manners of an oaf. Beneath the door he saw the shadow of Roy Warrenden marching up and down.

'I realise that you can never forgive me for my appalling mistake all those years ago, so if it is money instead that you have a need of...'

'No.' She limped to the door and opened it, allowing him no recourse but to leave. Roy was outside, the look on his face dark.

'Thank you for coming to enquire about my health, Lord Winterton, but as you can see I am fine.'

For the first time ever Winter understood her prowess as an actor, no tremble in her words, no expression that would give away even a little of what had happened between them.

'Then I am glad for it, Mr Rutherford, and I promise that I shall not trouble you further.'

With a tip of his head he walked out of the house,

relieved to see his driver in place and the square empty of other traffic.

It was over. He had offered a fair and reasonable compensation to alleviate his own guilt, but she had not accepted it. Swallowing, he wiped the fabric of one sleeve across his mouth, trying to remove the sweetness of her lips from memory.

Florentia sat down heavily, her leg aching and heart thumping.

She hated him, hated Lord Winterton for his supercilious and patronising arrogance. To offer money and marriage in exactly the same breath and then to kiss her as if she actually meant something to him, his mouth hot against her own exploding into a feeling that was both dizzying and inexplicable.

She'd kissed him back, too, she knew she had. She'd given herself away before she had even had the chance to think. She could not even bear to imagine what might have happened had they truly been alone.

Swallowing, she looked up at Roy, her whole body shaking.

'I think you should not see Winter again, Florentia, and we will say nothing of this visit to Maria for it would only make her worry.'

'Thank you.'

'The Viscount is a man who always got his way. Even at school. The charm of the devil, we used to say, but there were darker parts in Winter, even then. He saw through your disguise?'

She nodded.

'At his house when you were drawing his portrait?'

'No, it was only afterwards.'

'Praise the Lord for that, at least. He's a womaniser. The very best that there is, by all accounts. His conquests are legendary.'

'Well, I am not one of them, Roy.'

'I am glad to hear it, Florentia. I do not think you could survive such an onslaught for his taste is eclectic and not at all salubrious. Maria was at pains to tell me that every unmarried woman in the *ton* is holding out for a chance to bear his name, like lambs to the slaughter.'

The irony of such an observation had her standing. 'Well, if you will excuse me I think I shall go and rest upstairs.'

'And tomorrow we will retire back to Kent?'

'Yes.'

She wished desperately and with all of her heart to be home.

James knew that the society wolves were circling and he needed to stop them. Already this evening at a soirée in Chelsea three days after the Northbury ball everybody he met had regaled him with the news of the artist's accident.

'Mr Frederick Rutherford is the talk of the town, Winter, and questions are beginning to be asked.'

Frank Reading was quick to tell him this as he came upon him in the card room about halfway through the night.

'Questions?' James tried to make his tone as nonchalant as he could.

'Questions such as how Rutherford is related to the Hale-Burtons given his likeness to the family. There is also another strain of mystery which expounds the theory that nobody in the *ton* seems to have met him before this.'

James understood well how gossip worked; the first stirrings, the quiet queries that then led to further unanswered puzzles and deeper mysteries. Part of him wanted to simply move away and leave Florentia Hale-Burton to cope on her own, but another and greater part found it hard to simply abandon her. Her problems had been caused by him, after all, and despite her personal anger at him he needed to make reparation.

'From what I have heard he is a second or third cousin to Albany's daughters and one who had only just moved up from the West Country.'

He sought to make the geography and the relationship as vague as he could manage it and was glad that the Honourable Phillip Wiggins had joined their group because the man was a notorious gossip.

James lent in to give his next words quietly. 'Rutherford has taken ship to the Americas, according to my sources, to try his chances in a new land. I think he felt after the incident in the Northbury ballroom he could no longer fit in here.'

'He did seem to take the injury rather to heart,' Wiggins said. 'Perhaps he was younger than we thought him to be, more emotional.'

'I am certain that could be true,' Winter returned, weighing the new theory with a heavy consideration, for anything to take the focus off Florentia Hale-Burton was to be encouraged.

Heron walked by and he felt the man watching him. For a moment it looked as though he might indeed stop and speak, but then he moved away. The anger in James twisted and it was all he could do to stop himself from confronting him directly.

'Warrenden is probably rueing the day the lad came into their life for all the problems he seems to have caused them. I know his agent is furious that he should have simply disappeared. Most inconsiderate of him, really. There was some talk about the younger sister, too, as I recall.' Wiggins offered this quietly as though he were trying to remember the particulars.

'The Albany girls have had their detractors for the scandal with the younger daughter was something that was never resolved.' Reading leaned in to add his piece. 'I myself always thought they seemed like nice and sensible girls. Very pretty, too.'

'Well, all that talk of scandal was a long time ago and it was a rather scrambled story.' Now James made his contribution.

'Scrambled?'

'There were no real witnesses to any of it from what I hear and Lady Florentia was back at her family home before nightfall.' James kept his tone light.

'Then why did she not return to society?'

'It's widely known that the Hale-Burton sisters never really fitted in here. My guess is the younger daughter did not wish to return and was glad for the conundrum. Kent was a sanctuary and she ran for its cover and protection.'

Wiggins nodded. 'Perhaps it could be true. Warrenden's wife is certainly direct to a fault, although he seems more than enamoured by her. Besides, Albany was always unusual and his wife was much the same. My own mother knew her at school and said she was strikingly unconventional.'

The conversation then moved on to other topics, but the first seeds were planted of a different theory and one which dismissed the sisters as uncommon rather than ruined.

It was all in the semantics, James thought, as he swallowed his brandy. A slight question, a skewered truth, the niggle of uncertainty and the hint of doubt.

Wiggins would talk as would Reading and those they talked to would talk as well. A widening pool of knowledge about Rutherford and the Hale-Burtons, about the artist's desperate flight to America and the sister's need for quiet down in Kent which, after all was said and done, was almost expected in a family as unusual as the Hale-Burtons.

This was how the world worked and how society made sense of itself. Years of intelligence in both Europe and America had at least taught him that.

He had heard that the Warrenden party had repaired to Albany the day after his ill-thought-out visit. He wished he might have heard how Florentia fared there, but with the history he had with her father he did not dare to enquire. Warrenden too, was another consideration. Roy had known something had been amiss the other morning though he was too polite to take it up further. But if his part in her abduction ever came to light…

The glow of the social occasion seemed dimmer without the clever and measured repartee of the youngest Hale-Burton. Every other woman here seemed dull, ordinary and witless. He wondered if he would ever see beauty again in the flirtatious shallowness of the *ton*, with its penchant to breed girls totally consumed with what they looked like and whom they would marry.

He wished he had met Florentia Hale-Burton properly in society six years ago, when all the world was before her and she could have chosen him on his merits.

He smiled at such fancy, for even an impoverished Earl's daughter might have had second thoughts about a man with no land or prospects and an army career that had left him in tatters.

And therein lay the crux of it all. He was richer now and the title was his, but his abduction had left her with a distaste for him and all that he had done.

Still, he could not allow his foolish mistake to erode his sense of justice. He would make sure that she was safe and back in the fold of the *ton* that was her heritage and then he would leave for Atherton Abbey to see out his days there and far away from the prattle of society.

A movement to one side of the room showed Benjamin Heron slipping out to the balcony. Perhaps tonight he could lay more ghosts to rest and, although a crowded ballroom was probably not the place to bring up his father's past, he none the less would use this opportunity to do so, feeling that there might never be another presented.

As he strode outside he saw the older man standing to one end of the small enclosure. In the lamplight Heron looked worn down, his face lined and frightened as he recognised who the newcomer was. That emotion made James wary for it was so unexpected.

'I wonder if I might have a word with you, Mr Heron?'

At that the man paled and sat on a small seat behind him, this reaction so out of character Winter wondered momentarily if he was ill.

'I knew you would come, Winterton. I knew that

one day this moment would arrive between us and I should be left asking myself why I had not been honest before it, why I had not been honourable. Alfred Perkins talked, didn't he? He told you about your father? He said I had something to do with his death?'

Lord, this conversation was going places James had no notion of, no true way of answering without blatant accusations. He decided to chance it. 'Did you?'

'William was my friend and had been for a very long time, but…' Perspiration beaded at his temples and on the top of his lip. 'But he betrayed me.'

'How?'

'He slept with my sister under the nose of her husband and got her with child.'

'When?'

'Twenty-two years ago. The boy gained his majority last year. I thought they should meet at least once and William should know the face of the son he had never wanted to acknowledge. A boy caught between dalliances…between a true identity. A young troubled man with needs of his own.'

This news was unexpected and life-altering. Winter had never had much in the way of family and here was a half-brother who was suddenly and shockingly presented.

'What was his name?'

'Trevellyen Hartington. He took my sister's husband's name though they were already distant when he was born in Wales.'

'And he did not return?'

'Not until early last year when he came to London. He wanted answers.'

'I should imagine he did.'

'He demanded to meet William and so I arranged it, but there was a quarrel and recriminations and unfortunately your father was deep into his cups. The meeting did not go well and to try not to attract the attention of others at the busy inn we walked down to the river bank for some privacy. When Trevellyen told your father he was off to the Americas William said he was glad to be rid of him and that he would never get a penny from his estate and there was a scuffle. They both fell into the river where the current was particularly strong and I did not see either of them again.'

The truth of what Heron was not saying began to sink in. 'You tried to cover up the evidence. You left my father's clothes in a pile by the water's edge and walked away.'

'His jacket, gloves and neckcloth. William had taken those off when he was shouting and I didn't want an investigation so I folded the clothes and left them there for others to find. In a neat pile because that way I thought there might not need to be an enquiry which could only hurt all those who were left behind.'

'So the constabulary would come to the conclusion of suicide?'

The older man nodded his head and there were tears in his eyes. 'I did it to protect my nephew Trevellyen and my sister and your father as well. I did that to protect everyone.'

God, thought James. There was a certain sense to what he was saying, even an honour if it could be called such. The man was outwardly sobbing now, the powerful and rich man reduced to a shadow. He prayed no one else would come through the unlocked door and see them here.

'Amelia, my sister, had two other sons and they have children as well. A lineage that would be tainted should all of this be known, a scandal to walk on down through the decades with them.'

'And what of my lineage?'

'Scandal is the Wintertons' life blood, do you not see? It is what makes your family stand out and be... different. But mine...? I have built the family finances on being...righteous, on toeing the line if you like, and I have three daughters who need husbands, one who is not even out of the schoolroom yet...'

The sniffing stopped and he looked up. 'I betrayed your father and my friend in his death and if it is my blood you demand, Lord Winterton, then I will agree to it. I will meet you at dawn in any location you desire.'

'You are talking of a duel?' James could barely believe the arc of this conversation.

'I would not draw my pistol against you.'

'You want me to kill you?'

'No. That is my burden alone.' Now he squared his shoulders and stood. 'I would use the loaded gun on myself.'

'God.' James went over to the balustrade edge, the greyness of the night creeping into his very bones.

'I decline such an offer, Heron. Your secret is safe with me and I do not demand your life for it.'

'Why?'

'William did not do the right thing for his son.' As James said this he heard the anger in each and every word. 'Or indeed for your sister. This way my father can repay at least some of his debt.'

Benjamin Heron had taken a handkerchief now from his pocket and was wiping his face briskly.

'Your father used to be like you before the drink ruined him and if there is ever anything that I can do for you in return for the keeping of this secret…'

Winter began to smile.

'Well, actually there is one thing that might balance the books, so to speak….'

He was glad to see Heron move forward and listen.

Chapter Eleven

Florentia could not believe the name on the card delivered into her hand by the butler at Albany Manor twelve days later.

'Mrs Heron, Miss Heron and Miss Caroline Heron have come down from London to call.'

Her sister clapped her hand across her mouth and whispered between her fingers, 'Why on earth would they travel all this way to see us unless…?'

The door opened, however, before Flora could reply, leaving them both to rise and meet the fashionably dressed new arrivals. Julia came across, offering her hand to both of them, a look of concern in her eyes.

'We heard the news about Mr Rutherford from Papa and came to see if we could be of any help. It is a sad fact of life when a man as sensitive and talented is harried out of society for an accident that was hardly his fault in the first place. If your own family suffers with the connection, well, that is even more unfair.'

'Indeed.' Maria seemed to have recovered her wits faster than Florentia had. 'What was it your papa had heard exactly, Miss Heron?'

'That Mr Rutherford has taken ship to the Americas in the hope of escaping the ugly gossip about his unfortunate wounds and that he did not intend to return. Ever.'

'Which is such a very long time.' Caroline Heron seemed determined to add her thoughts now. 'And it was hardly his fault, any of it.'

'Perhaps he imagined society might censure him for such sensitivity, but it is my opinion that an artist should be able to express himself in such a way and not be thought the less of for it.' Julia had taken over the conversation again, her clipped and rounded vowels horrified by such censure.

Flora, who had finally found her wits after the shock of entertaining the family in their parlour, wondered who might have spread such a rumour in the first place. 'Society can indeed be cruel...'

She left the thought hanging.

'Which is why we have come to see you.' For the first time Mrs Heron spoke. 'My husband is most insistent that our family be seen as the one to hold out an olive branch and ask if you all might like to come to a ball we are having in two weeks' time at our town house.'

'I am not sure, Mrs Heron.' Maria had the tone of worry and politeness exactly right. 'My sister has had her detractors in the past...'

Julia leapt in to clarify things. 'But we should be there to see an end to it, Lady Warrenden. You will all come as our guests of honour and no one would dare to question such an authority under our roof. Your relative, Mr Rutherford, has left England needlessly and unfairly, but as his cousin, Lady Florentia, the very least we can do is return you to the fold.'

Her eyes were worried and tear filled, leaving them in no doubt of her sincerity.

'It is of course such a shame that no one else now will see the talent of your cousin and be able to procure a portrait. But perhaps in time Mr Rutherford might return—?

Maria broke her off. 'No, Frederick is adamant he will never set foot on England's soil within his lifetime again and he is stubborn to a fault. I should never expect him back.'

'Those words were almost exactly Lord Winterton's, were they not, Caroline? He, too, was most certain Mr Rutherford would not be back. He saw the lad take sail apparently, in the dead of night on a rising tide. The Viscount said he barely took a thing with him, save his paints, of course, and one small leather case.'

Flora's heart had begun to beat quite violently at the name. Was it Winter himself who had started the gossip about Mr Frederick Rutherford? They had been hearing various versions of the same thing since they had returned to Kent and a further thread of their family's unusual outlook had been attached to that. Could Viscount Winterton possibly be trying to help them from afar?

Was this new development of invitations to the Heron ball his doing, too? Had he wangled the whole thing using his particular kind of cunning and deceit? She smiled, rather thinking he just might have.

When their visitors finally left two hours later Maria sat down next to Flora on the sofa and began to laugh.

'My goodness, Flora. Could it possibly be this easy to both be rid of Frederick Rutherford and reintroduce you to society?

'I don't know. Mrs Heron said that it was her husband who was most insistent on the help.'

'Can we trust them, do you think?'

'Do we have any choice?'

'Well, if we want this scandal associated with your name gone, I do not think so.'

Away from the prying eyes of others later that night Florentia allowed the tears fall.

Marry me, then.

Winterton's words came back, echoing as they had done in her mind every night since he had said them.

Yet he had not called in to see how it was she fared or even sent a note. Every time there was the sound of a carriage on the driveway she tensed up, but Winterton had stayed away, lost to her somehow, as if finally all the problems that seemed so attached to her name had scared him off and made him reconsider.

He knew that she had masqueraded as Frederick Rutherford, so the newest rumour of the artist relocating to the Americas was fortuitous and opportune, the protections winding around her in a way that was ingenious.

Spies operated in netherworlds and hidden places, shrewd resourcefulness a part of their code.

But if it was he who had circulated these new theories, then why had he been absent for nearly all of two weeks?

The answer came without doubt. He did not care and he would not come. Perhaps it was only guilt that led him along the path of atonement and reparation. A tit for tat, so to speak, and then his duty to her would be over. Having reintroduced her into society, he would leave her again in the same position as he had found her six years before, older perhaps and undoubtedly wiser, but still able to live a life and function.

'Every man is guilty of all the good he did not do.' The words of Voltaire echoed in her mind.

The kiss they had shared still sent a shiver down her spine every time she thought about it, thrills of want bursting unbidden. If he hadn't kissed her she might have been able to move on with more ease, to relegate what she hoped for into the impossible. But the desperate way in which they had come together suggested other things, headier yearnings and different anticipations.

Crossing to her wardrobe, Florentia hauled out the painting she had done of him all those years before and leaned it against a chair in the candlelight.

James Waverley watched her from within the canvas, his clear green eyes suggesting both pain and faith. His lips were full and sensual and the dimple in his chin was deep. She had fashioned his mouth in a way that she recognised.

Passion and lust had a certain ripeness that was unmistakable and distinct. When she ran her fingers across the thickness of paint it was almost as if she could feel the warm and living man beneath.

Winter. Even his name held a hint of mystery within.

'Come back,' she whispered to the likeness. 'Please come back and find me.'

The tears fell across her cheeks and she shook her head firmly. Life was not a fairy tale and she was not the sort of woman Lord Winterton would wear his heart on his sleeve for. Yet, she felt a bond with him that had nothing to do with guilt or shame. He had not betrayed her when he had discovered her charade. Indeed, if gossip was to be believed, all he had tried to do was help her become reinstated in the society she had been banished from.

Another chance. A further choice. Because of him.

Everything she wore was beautiful, so beautiful she felt like a stranger inside such finery as she stepped down from the conveyance and made her way into the Heron ball with her sister and Roy by her side.

The interior of the Heron town house was more opulent than she remembered, the world of the *ton* on show in a way it seldom was. English society tended to err away from showiness, but Benjamin Heron's wife was of German heritage and obviously held firm with the notion of excess and surfeit. The Heron sisters greeted them warmly as they made their way into the huge reception.

'You look lovely in that colour, Florentia. Yellow suits your hair.' Julia Heron took her hand and tucked it under her arm. 'Papa is most insistent that this should be a wonderful night for you and your family.'

'Thank you.' The turnaround of attitude in the Heron sisters was still as surprising as it was welcomed, but in a room like this Florentia knew she needed as many allies as she could muster.

Mr and Mrs Heron were equally as effusive as they bade her welcome.

'It is seldom we have the company of such lovely young women, Ana,' Heron remarked, his wife's smile showing an edge of strain as she looked at her own daughters.

Perhaps it actually could be this very easy? Perhaps with influential people like the Herons supporting her entry back into society anyone who dared to have it different would be silenced.

Roy and Maria made it a point to stand on each side of her as they walked into the main salon and as the seconds progressed into minutes and then to an hour Florentia allowed herself the luxury of relaxing. Maria must have been thinking along exactly the same lines as she leaned in to whisper her encouragement.

'Your dance card must be full by now?'

She nodded, for indeed it was. Every few moments since being here another one of Roy's acquaintances had stepped forward to inveigle a dance so when Timothy Calderwood came over she smiled at him.

'I could not believe you were here, Lady Florentia, and it is so very good to see you again.'

His voice was exactly as she had remembered it, a kind and friendly man whom she had immediately liked. Once.

'Is your wife here, too, my lord?'

A shadow fell over his eyes. 'My wife unfortunately caught a chill and passed away early last year. I am surprised you had not heard of it?'

Horror filled her. 'No, I am afraid I had not and—'

He stopped her. 'Celia was…fragile even before her sickness. She found life difficult, if you will, almost unbearable.'

Was he saying his wife had had problems? She was surprised when he reached for her hand and spoke with real feeling.

'I am sorry to have cried off all those years ago. I should never have been so cowardly, but I have paid the price for my intransigence.'

'You are forgiven, my lord.' She could think of no other words as she pulled her fingers away from his grasp and looked around. Maria was watching her.

'If you would honour me with a dance tonight, I would be very relieved.'

'Of course.' She wrote in his name beside a quadrille and was answered with a delighted smile.

'I see most of your card is filled and you are the talk of the *ton* this evening.'

'I hope not.'

He laughed and as she turned to look at him she caught sight of Lord Winterton across his shoulder observing her from further away in the room.

The Viscount was finally here? She had been looking for him ever since she arrived, but had seen no sign at all of him. Her heart fluttered and the blush that rose on her cheeks made Timothy Calderwood braver.

'I was hoping I might have the pleasure of a dance tonight for I had heard that you were coming.'

Winterton had turned now, making his way further down the room, another man beside him who was almost as tall as he was, and the disappointment that welled was painful.

'Perhaps we might even be able to resume our relationship where we left off?'

'Left off?' She could not quite get the gist of what Calderwood meant.

'I would be most grateful if you might let me call upon you at the Warrenden town house. Tomorrow, shall we say?'

Understanding dawned. 'Tomorrow would be fine.' She would instruct Roy to warn Calderwood off gently.

The first strains of a dance were beginning to be heard, an orchestra to one side of the floor tuning their instruments in readiness for the entertainment to follow, and as a young man stepped forward to claim the dance Florentia thanked him as he led her across the floor.

When Winter had first seen her a good half an hour ago he had been astonished all over again at how beautiful Florentia Hale-Burton truly was. But beyond that she looked happy, her golden hair knotted at her crown and falling in long ringlets down her back. He remembered the colour, all the wheat and gold and flaxen. He remembered her face, too, the dimples in both cheeks even when she frowned and the startling blue of her eyes. He kept his glance well away from her lips.

A myriad of young swains had stepped forward to petition her to place their names on her card and he thought that this was how she must have been once, lauded and fêted and admired, a golden girl of the *ton* before his ill-thought-out actions had ruined her reputation and any chance of a marriage. He was glad to see the Herons placing their weight into her re-introduction.

Smiling grimly, he caught her form as she was whisked past him in the company of Lord Alton Gower.

The man was a lecherous cad and Winter could not imagine what had made her agree to a dance with him in the first place. He was even more amazed that she was laughing at something he said, her dimples deep in the light of the chandeliers above. All about the dance floor other men watched her, a beauty without guile or pretence.

The pale peaked visage of Frederick Rutherford had been weary and cautious and in his persona she had seldom laughed or allowed her feelings to show.

What must it feel like to be suddenly free of all criticism, to be able to hold your head up in a society you had once belonged to and been a part of, before censure had torn you away from it?

The anger in him escalated until he wondered if it might be seen there on his face, in the burning fury and in the regret. The air he took felt restricted and when he realised his hands were tight fists at his side he made a concerted effort to relax them.

'You look…dangerous, Winter. Dangerous and beautiful.' The voice was Lady Elizabeth Hilliard, one of the most handsome women in the room. Years ago he had kept her company for quite a time until he realised that she wanted all of the things he could never give her. His love. His name and his loyalty.

'And if it is the Hale-Burton daughter you have your eye upon I might warn you that you have competition. Calderwood gives the impression of a decided interest given the loss of his wife and the history between them.'

'History?' he could not help but ask.

'They were all but betrothed once, it was rumoured. Lady Florentia's unfortunate incident put paid to that, of course. But now…she is risen from her shame and supported by some of the richest families in society. Who would dare mention her dark days in the face of such adulation? And true beauty has its own triumph after all, do you not think?'

Her laughter was harsh but not unkind and as her fingers threaded through his he allowed her to pull him towards the floor and into the first strains of a waltz.

'It is my favourite dance, Winter, and if I were to have the choice of any partner I am glad that it is you.'

'You were always a flirt, Elizabeth,' he answered.

'But I could never catch the only man who matched me,' she returned and pushed her body into his, the pure sensuality of the movement surprising him. 'We are each of us lost in some past tragedy, I think, something that stops us from living for this moment. You could have your pick of any woman here yet you do not stake a claim, and I suppose I am exactly the same.'

'Your philosophy is flawed. I have no interest in any of the ladies present and nor do they have any disposition towards me.'

'You see, Winter, that is what makes you so...appealing, this complete disregard for your allure and beauty. If you were a woman it might almost be seen as a practised vanity, but in a man...' Her laugh was merry and sweet even as the pressure of her fingers increased against his own. 'In a man such a lack of ego is overpoweringly sensual.'

Such nonsense annoyed him and he was glad when the music finished and he could lead her back to her friends. He moved away even as Elizabeth tried to detain him.

He was alone and he was drinking, a darkness in his eyes Florentia had seen before as they had travelled together. She wished he might ask her to dance or glance her way or nod his head in kinship and memory. Even friendship might do.

But he did not look towards her and as the night aged and each and every dance partner gave her the words that once she might have longed to hear, all she could feel was a growing disconnection.

She had kept one dance free just in case Winterton might cross the room and ask her, the empty space on her card taking on a greater importance than all of the others put together.

Yet still he did not come.

As she saw him move off in the direction of the balcony something in her suddenly set her own feet in motion. She intercepted him before he reached the double doors leading out into the night.

'My Lord Winterton.'

'Lady Florentia.' Careful, polite and distant. He looked as though he would have given anything at all to be able to avoid this meeting. He looked at her as though he had forgotten their kiss altogether.

'You are well?' Her words. She wanted to take them back as soon as she had uttered them.

'I am.' The silence between them howled with the awkward unsaid.

'And the portrait?'

'Is hung.'

'In the place above the mantel?'

He nodded and a muscle on one side of his jaw ground into movement.

'I am sorry.' She could not think how else to express all that had happened between them. Her hands bunched the golden silk of her skirt into tight fists. 'For this. For the lies.'

'You made a good-looking boy, but you are a beautiful woman. There is nothing at all to be sorry for.'

She had not expected such a compliment and felt a blush rise from her chest and travel in a bright heat across every part of her face.

The card was in her hand before she knew it and the pencil there poised above the one last space. 'Would you dance with me tonight?'

He looked down, his eyes dark and guarded.

'I saved it.' Another truth that she should never have confessed and just for a moment she imagined he might refuse. But he did not. A quick nod and then he was gone, back into the melee of the crowded room, away from her neediness and her desperation.

Had he agreed to the dance or not? Had he seen which number on the list it was she had kept for him and would he remember to come to claim her?

Maria was there then, her hand outstretched and a deep frown crossing her forehead.

'Winter is not a man to be played with, Flora. He is dangerous and hard.'

'You think that is what I am doing? Playing with him?'

'To ask a man like him for a dance is close to lunacy. Did you not see Lady Elizabeth Hilliard all but throwing herself at him not half an hour ago? He incites something in women here that is not…safe. Play with fire and you will be burned.'

Again.

The sound of her father's gun, the blood, the ache of flesh ripped open. The grasp of his fingers in her own. Holding on. Shaking. Every second falling into memory.

Sometimes she wondered why time had not softened

the horror of that moment, had not melded it into the history of the past where it could no longer hurt her.

'What is Lord Winterton to you, Flora? What makes you seek him out like you do?' Her sister's query was whispered and urgent.

'I painted his portrait. There is a connection.'

'Well, if you keep this interest up he most certainly will recognise you as the artist Frederick Rutherford, and if that happens no amount of cajoling on your behalf shall save your reputation.'

Flora felt the dance card in her hand, the edge of it cutting into flesh as she closed her fingers hard. He had promised her a waltz.

She swallowed and smiled, taking a glass of wine off the silver platter of a passing footman. If Lord Winterton came she would dance with him. If he took her hand she would follow.

Timothy Calderwood was there now, beside her.

'I think this is my promised dance, Lady Florentia.'

She did not even need to glance at her list to know that what he said was true.

'Calderwood looks like the cat who has the cream,' Frank Reading stated. 'But it is good to see the Albany girl so happy.'

Guilt wrapped around the heart of his anger as he made himself look away.

'Tonight every man in the room who is unattached or interested in changing their circumstances has made their feelings known. Lady Florentia has a full card and no shortage of compliments and it is a pleasing sight.'

Swearing softly under his breath, James finished his drink and laid the glass down on the polished surface of one of the tables marching down the length of the room; the delicate crystal meeting the hard marble with barely a sound.

He'd always lived with shadows. Seeing Florentia in the light of such adoration reinforced such a fact. He was damaged and scarred and the distance he held between himself and others had widened without his even knowing it. Arabella had warned him of such things and so had Rafe.

But tonight he was tired of fighting it, this inertia. Tonight as the music swelled about him and the golden dress of Florentia Hale-Burton caught in the light all he wanted to do was to be alone and outside away from the noise and the laughter.

He wondered if Reading had caught all he tried not to show as he turned away, the weary naked core of himself harder and harder to hide.

He was leaving, Florentia knew that he was and he had not come to claim his waltz for the first strains of the dance were being played. He had not even come to apologise for it either—a man who had asked her to marry him without any emotion at all and then failed to turn up for a single promised dance.

Timothy Calderwood on the other hand was hovering at her elbow and if she tarried he would see the gap. Claiming she needed a drink, she threaded her arm through her sister's and asked Maria if she would accompany her for a stroll about the room. Once away from Timothy Calderwood she unlaced her fingers and spoke quietly.

'Maria, you are the most wonderful sister in all of

the world but I am going to ask you now to do something for me that you may not quite agree with.'

'It is something to do with Lord Winterton, isn't it?' The retort was sharp.

'The Viscount has promised me this dance and I need you to walk with me over to him so that I can claim it, for I think he is leaving.'

'Roy said there is much unknown in Winter, Flora. He implied there are things that are hidden within him.'

'Please…' Flora swallowed as she asked this. 'Please will you help me?'

Maria looked stricken, her eyes wide and frightened. 'If he hurts you again…'

'Again?'

'Oh, Flora, I know you so much better than you think I do. All these meetings with Winterton. All your interest. The scar on his neck that he hides, the pull that he seems to hold over you and the drawing of the portrait…' She stopped. 'He was the lord who kidnapped you, wasn't he?'

'Yes.'

'Yet you still think this wise?'

They had reached the trajectory that brought him directly to them, another few seconds and he would be there.

'I do. There are many things you don't know about him, Maria, good things that I need you to trust me with. Please?'

'If this turns out badly…'

'It won't. But if I don't try, I will always regret it.'

Maria raised her hand and pasted a smile across her face, signalling her surprise at finding Winterton right there beside them.

'Lord Winterton, how very fortuitous for my sister was just saying that you had promised her this dance, and here you are. I shall leave you both to it and go and petition my own husband to join me on the floor.'

A warning placed around social niceties, but at least James Waverley could do nothing else but agree to accompany her into the waltz.

Florentia felt his arm beneath her elbow shepherding her through the throng of others, the warm sandalwood of his scent familiar and known.

'I realise you were just leaving, but I needed to speak with you. To explain.'

He had taken her into his arms now, the intimacy of the dance allowing them privacy, and she could not quite meet his gaze. All night she had stood up with a variety of lords and all night she had wished only for this one.

'I want to say that I absolve you from any wrongdoing, Lord Winterton. You owe me nothing more now. My own charade was ill advised and risky and I want to thank you for the story of a broken-hearted Frederick Rutherford scampering from London on a ship bound for the Americas. From all accounts the narrative seems to be your doing.'

'Says who?'

'Every one of the Heron women. Phillip Wiggins. My brother-in-law. The list goes on.'

He smiled at that, his teeth white against sun-burnished skin. 'I had forgotten and underestimated the temerity of the London *ton* in determining the source of any scandal. But be warned, Lady Florentia, a benevolent and sainted defender is far from who I am.'

Now there was no humour at all, the scars across

the knuckles of his hand across hers opaque beneath the lights. Her finger ran softly over one of the marks.

'Who hurt you here?'

He stiffened perceptibly and she turned her own thumb over when he failed to answer. 'This came from the inn when you fell to the ground beneath me. There was glass on the road and it cut deeply. Afterwards it was a memory. Often I would feel along the raised ridge of skin when I thought you were dead and pray for your soul. It helped, I think, to try and find forgiveness in something so very terrible.'

His green eyes met hers directly and they were full of pain.

He felt the shock of her words run through him like small daggers into the heart of his darkness. The scar. The one he had seen a score of times in the company of Frederick Rutherford took on an importance that was poignant.

But she did not truly know who he was.

He'd always been divided since he was little, one side of him turned to the light and the other to the shadows and fear.

His early family life was partly to blame, his own mother's indifference and bitterness part of the tableau, and his years of soldiering had deepened the dislocation.

Florentia had been damaged by him in a number of ways and yet she seemed to have survived in forgiveness, the elemental hell that he had thrown her into lessened by the mercy of a pardon.

God, he'd tried to understand people, but he had seldom managed the trick of it. Rafe and Arabella had been the closest friends he knew, but they were both as damaged as he was so perhaps they did not count.

Florentia on the other hand was blameless. An innocent thrust into notoriety by his poor actions and living out her years in the seclusion of the Kentish countryside, filling her mind with images of art in all its forms. He didn't deserve such goodness, that much was certain, and if he allowed her into his own particular ruin she could only be hurt further.

The most honourable path would be to beat a retreat and flee to leave her to the sort of life she had been born to, kind un-complex men and women who found joy in all the things he never had. Still he felt an ache surge in the very pit of his belly.

'I am leaving for Herefordshire in the morning and I am not sure when I shall be back.'

'I see.' Her words were small. He felt the breath of them against his cheek.

'London has palled in its delight for me and I yearn for more open spaces.'

She made no attempt at all in answering this.

'I have done everything I can to see that your reputation is recovered and tonight you are undoubtedly resurrected.'

'I am.' This was stated in a tone that held the promise of a fight. 'Like a phoenix.'

'A state of affairs that gives much delight to all of those around you.' Such a platitude made his mouth dry.

'I prefer you when you are at least honest, my lord. The patronising words of a man who knows he has slipped a noose whilst proclaiming its very beauty does not become you.'

'You will thank me for it one day, Florentia.'

'Will I, Lord Winterton?'

At that he stumbled, the misstep bringing her into him closer. He could feel the rise of her breasts.

Hell, would this dance never end? He could see others watching them and moved back again.

Roy and her sister were near now, a few feet away, Warrenden's wife's frown full upon her brow.

And then the music sidled into silence and the world crashed in on them again, pulling them apart, the uttered thanks, the quiet goodbyes. An inch, a foot, a yard away.

The smell of lavender followed him from the room and out into the night where he stood under the shadow of a tree and leaned against a wall.

'Please protect her. Please God let her be safe.'

It had been so long since he had prayed to any deity he could not remember the proper form of entreaty. But the wind heightened and the clouds scudded across the dull London sky and for just a moment he felt honourable.

Half an hour later the Warrenden carriage was heading back to Grosvenor Square.

Maria was unusually quiet and Flora knew there would be many difficult questions about the Viscount on arrival.

'Winter told me that he was off to the country on the morrow to visit the property he's just bought. Somewhere to the west, I believe.' Roy reached into his pocket for his flask. 'God, but I am so glad to be away from all that joviality. Calderwood looked enamoured by you, Florentia?'

'He used to be a long time ago before...' Maria stopped.

'Before my ruination.' Flora smiled gently. 'I think now he is only sad.'

'A frightened kitten, but at least a moral one.' Her sister's eyebrows raised as she looked straight at her.

They'd played this game years ago, divided people into various animal personas. And if Calderwood was now a moral cat, then Lord Winterton was a wolf. An alpha wolf, she amended, with his teeth fully bared.

She had seen the women there watching his every move, young women and old. He had that sort of aura that was undeniable and magnetic...

The leg that had been hurt at the Northbury ball was aching from standing for so very long and she wanted to be home in her room, alone to think.

Once they were back at Grosvenor Square, however, Maria came to her room and she looked anything but happy.

'You should have told me, Florentia, about Winterton. You should have said something.'

'So that you could warn me off him? So that I could not discover what sort of a man he was by myself?'

'And did you? Discover that?'

'He is remorseful for what he did. It was by mistake that he took me from Mount Street in the first place— he thought that I was his cousin's lover.'

'I don't think this is making me feel reassured, Flora.' Her sister looked shocked.

'He never hurt me, Maria. He protected me. He was kind and good and beautiful. When Papa shot him...' She stopped and lowered her voice. 'I have never ceased to hope that he would be alive and when I knew that he was… I felt whole again and so very relieved. He asked me to marry him in order that he might protect me.'

Maria sat, her pallor whitening. 'What answer did you give him?'

'He does not love me. He asked out of duty. What could I say?'

'My God, Flora. If Papa ever finds out that it was him…'

'He would probably die of shock. I have thought of that, too.'

'So where does that leave you?'

'I am not sure. Lonelier, I suppose. Less hopeful. He is leaving London and he wished me a happy life without him even as we danced.'

When Maria began to pace across the room Florentia felt a rising worry.

'When did he propose to you?'

'At the Northbury ball and also when he came to visit the Warrenden town house the day after I had been injured.'

'Twice? He has asked twice? You have never been able to see what is right in front of your nose, Flora, for you do not value yourself highly enough and it is time that you learnt to. There is something about Lord Winterton that is hardened and distant, but perhaps you are the only one in the world who might find his softness and retrieve your own happiness in the process.'

With that her sister kissed her on the cheek and retired, leaving Florentia to mull over and try to make sense of what exactly she had said.

Chapter Twelve

Winter rode across the lands of Atherton, the wind in his face and the promise of rain in the west across the Black Mountains.

For the first time in a long while he felt able to breathe, to take in the air that was somehow denied to him in London.

He skirted the rocky knife edge of the ridges, the narrow single track leading past peat bogs and cairns. Down in the valley he could see the Olchon River cutting into the land and further away the slopes of Hay Bluff rose above Hay-on-Wye, the barren summit clouded in mist.

He had bought Atherton Abbey because his maternal grandmother had lived her years out here at Craswell Village and this was where he had enjoyed some of the happiest moments of his childhood.

He understood this land like no other. He knew the birdcalls, the red kites, the kestrels and carrion crows and when he noticed the birds of prey riding the thermals on the edges of the hills he felt a familiar tug of memory and was comforted by such recollection.

He wished Florentia was here so that he might have shown her the majesty of the place.

Florentia. He could no longer make out what to do about her. Marry her or ignore her? She had refused his offers of marriage twice and yet he felt a pull between them that was undeniable.

He imagining how she would have drawn the outcrops and screes and the spring-line flushes. The birch and oak and alders stood in the valleys, the bushy slopes and the barren summits. Like a portrait. A portrait of an ancient knowingness, red-brown sandstone and solid bedrock.

Breathing out, he closed his eyes, taking in the particular smell of this corner of England. Here he felt whole again and healed.

Home.

An hour and a half later when he was back at Atherton Abbey he asked his man to begin hiring more of the local villagers in preparation for his move here permanently.

'And the furniture, my lord? What instructions do you have there?'

'Keep what is here and we will add to things as we see fit. The roof will need some work as will the salons in the west wing. Other than that a good clean and tidy should do it.'

They had reached the kitchens now and a small maid curtsied to them as they came into the room, a wriggling and rough sack in her hand.

'What do you have there, Mavis?' His factor's voice was stern.

'The last of the puppies, sir. No one wants the thing

as it is scrawny and sick and the old stable master told me to go and throw it into the lake.'

'Very well.' Kenning stepped back to let the girl pass, but James stood in her way.

'I will deal with the stray, Kenning. You may see to the other orders I have given you.'

It was so good to have the brushes back in her hand, Florentia thought, and to be in front of a canvas in a secluded section of Hyde Park. The Warrendens had re-established themselves again at Grosvenor Square a few days prior, Roy having urgent business to deal with in town.

She had taken up painting again, carefully and in isolated spots for she did not wish any notice from society.

Her maid sat on a wooden seat some twenty yards away. Her own seat was the grassy bank above a line of trees stretching into the distance.

Early morning in town had that certain light to it and she wanted to capture the nuances before the sun was higher and the day was dispersed. Hence she worked quickly, the pink blush on the horizon committed to paper and the deep green at her feet juxtaposed against it. Shadow and light. Cloud and grass. The hard edges of the trees seemed to float against an amorphous sky, like sentinels, and she was lost in the beauty.

'I did not expect to see you here, Lady Florentia?'

She turned to the voice and Winter was standing there, looking into the sun, a thin brown and white puppy on a leash at his side, its ears floppy and skin wrinkled. She could not help but smile as the dog pawed at her with one loose-skinned leg. The canine looked a lot less wary than the man.

'Her name is Faith. I acquired her unexpectedly.' It seemed as if he might turn away, his glance taking in the pathway behind, a man caught in a place he wished he was not.

'She is beautiful.' And she was, brown soulful eyes staring straight into her own.

'She has just eaten my best pair of boots for breakfast. If I had not brought her out to the park, I think my valet may well have murdered her.'

The humour was welcome and the clothes he wore countrified. She could imagine him on a horse with more dogs like this one running beside him and a magnificent estate in the background.

'Would your puppy sit still for a portrait, do you think? It will not take long.'

He motioned to the dog to lie down and she did.

'You have trained her to do this?'

'It's the first time she has obeyed any command since I got her a week ago. I doubt she would do so twice.'

Florentia used charcoal, the lines of a hunting dog appearing over the sweet-tempered calmness of the puppy.

'You work fast?'

'She is an easy subject.'

'Whereas I was not?'

'You have many layers, my lord, and each one is blurred by secrecy. Faith's face is open and simple.'

She did not look at him as she said this, the words coming easier with the charcoal in hand.

'I've been in Herefordshire at my new home.'

Her fingers stilled with the words and she looked straight at him then, the small scar above his eyebrow in this light much easier to see today and curling into his brow.

'The mark is from your books,' he clarified when he noticed such an observation, though when she frowned he carried on. 'The ones you hit me with on Mount Street. The ones that were in your bag.'

'I had just bought them at Lackington's. They were expensive books on art and difficult to find.'

'Perhaps I could replace them, then. If you gave me the titles, I could ask at the shop in Finsbury Square.'

Florentia swallowed and gathered her courage. 'I accept such an offer, but would you meet me there tomorrow at midday so I can show you exactly which titles are the ones I lost?'

The caution across his face was easily seen as she tore the picture of Faith from her sketching book. He reached out to take it.

'A peace offering, Lord Winterton. Between us.'

But when her fingers touched his she felt the sharp shock of that which was not so ordinary, a jolt of recognition that sizzled in every part of her body.

If he saw her reaction he swallowed any comment, his own face allowing no glimpse of emotion.

'I shall leave you to your drawing, Lady Florentia, but I will see you at Lackington's tomorrow, at twelve.'

When she nodded he left, the dog pulling at her leash as she gambolled across the long wet grass in front of him, its patterned coat darkening with the moisture.

Patricia, her lady's maid, had joined her now and looked at her with interest as she bent to collect her things. Packing her brushes into her leather bag, Florentia tried to act as natural as possible. But her heart raced and her breath became shallow and the knowledge that she would meet James Waverley tomorrow alone sung in her mind.

She dreamed that night of things she never had before. She was in his bed in an estate somewhere, a Gothic splendid house before a lake. The moonlight covered him as he came across her, his hair loose and his eyes pale, hands on places of her body that only she had touched.

'Love me, Florentia,' he had whispered, his voice broken with want.

'I do, Winter,' she had given back, and then there had been no space at all between them.

She came awake with a jolt in the pink room she always used at Grosvenor Square above the front entrance on the second floor.

She felt hot, disorientated and breathless, the time on the face of the clock on the mantel just past the hour of three.

Where was Winterton now? Did he prowl the nighttime reaches of town? Or was he with friends somewhere in a smoke-filled dim bar in a dangerous part near the river? Did he sleep alone? Did he ever think of her? Of their shared past?

Questions. So very many of them. Standing, she walked to the window to look over the square and the rooftops beyond. Her nightdress stuck to her heated skin and so she took it off, letting it drop to the floor around her ankles and enjoying the cool air that flowed across her nakedness.

She was glad the candles were out. Only the light of the moon came into her room, muted and silver, the paleness of her skin reflected in the mirror.

She was thin.

Was that a good thing or a bad one? Before the accident she had been fatter, more robust, but now no matter what she ate she remained the same weight. Thin.

She was also not a young girl any more, her twenty-three years soon to be twenty-four. Once she had imagined she would be a wife by this age and a mother. She had conjured up a house in the country with dogs and chickens and a garden of flowers that she would gather and bring inside in joyful colourful bunches.

And instead…

They had both been shattered by a mistake, their lives changed and turned on different courses, roads that they might not have taken otherwise. Him to the Americas. Her to painting.

Could they find their way back? To each other?

She smiled and saw the movement of it in the glass, blurred and indistinct.

'Please God, help me.'

To understand and to forgive.

Chapter Thirteen

He had barely slept on his first night back in London. The puppy had been fretful and afraid. He wondered for the twentieth time whether he should have brought the dog back with him as it was proving more than a handful. But when he had opened the sack and the small thin wet thing had fallen out of the folds of hessian he had had an instant recognition of himself as a child, confused, frightened and in desperate need of a proper guardianship. He'd taken the dog in his arms and placed it in his carriage on a blanket and it had sat deathly still beside him for all the hours of the journey back to London.

Once at St James's Square it had followed him up the stone steps, ungainly but with purpose, the small yelps of despair as he had deposited the dog on a rug by his bed only subsiding when he had dragged it up on to his counterpane. The shaking cold of fear pulled at other older memories and in the darkness he had allowed it under the sheets against his own body where it had settled in a long sigh until the early dawn.

When the bells of the small church a half a mile

away had rung the following morning he had been woken by the pensive dark eyes and the scratching tiny paws.

'Faith. I will call you that,' and he had laughed when the dog had tipped her head and listened as if the name meant something that she had not yet realised it did.

Permanence. For them both.

Now he was getting used to the small loyal presence and their bedtime routine. He enjoyed feeling the dog there beside him, warm and alive and responsive. Following him. Waiting for him. Constant and adoring.

The sketch from yesterday in the park was up on the wall beside the fireplace, two pins stuck into the top of the paper, Faith staring out from charcoal with all her rambunctious and impossible energy. The gift Florentia had of rendering the inside to be seen without was remarkable. She had done the same on his portrait, the one he kept in his library, the one he had shown to nobody save for Arabella and Rafe.

Such truth unsettled him, he supposed, and made him realise the extent he had withdrawn from the world.

Everything was turning upside down with an ever-increasing motion, like the points on a compass rose drawing him in. He wondered suddenly if he were like those cardinal directions and their ordinal intersects with their degrees of separation and interpretation of space. Scattered to the four winds but now drawing back, facing home and finding hope.

Was Florentia like some true north and he the filings lured in by a magnet no matter how hard he tried to escape her? For her own happiness, he said to himself, but he could barely believe it any longer.

He would meet her today at Lackington's and say what? I know I should stay well away from you, but I can't help myself? I can only hurt you again with all the things you do not know of me? The Spanish pit. His appalling childhood. His dislocation. The want to tell her all these things sat on his tongue like sharp points of the truth. Not once in years and years had he managed to sleep through a night.

'God,' he swore into the silence and Faith whimpered.

'Not you,' he said and held her as close and as tightly as he possibly could.

Standing in front of Lackington's waiting, all James could feel was dread. When the Warrenden carriage stopped before him he took in breath and watched as Florentia Hale-Burton alighted.

'I hope I am not late, my lord.'

'No. I am early.' He tried to alter his tone into one of light inconsequence, but failed.

'London and its demands makes things difficult,' she told him. 'The clothes. The hair. The shoes. The rules. There is hardly ever a stop to think about what one should do and what one should not. In the end it eats up all of your time and inclination.'

'What is it you would rather do?'

'Paint. Read. Think. Anything at all except look at myself again in a mirror.'

He laughed and was surprised by it, the sound so unfamiliar.

'Men do much better than women in the time-consuming business of appearance, Lord Winterton. For example, how long does it take you to get ready?'

'Today?' He thought about it for a few seconds and

then answered. 'A half an hour, perhaps. Less if I could have found one half of the pair of shoes Faith had run away with.'

She groaned. 'Make a guess as to the time of my *toilette*.'

He looked at the pink-sprigged day dress and the light green pelisse she wore above it. Her hair this afternoon was less fussy, the thick gold of it entwined in a smooth chignon beneath a small and jaunty hat.

'I do not dare. Too little and you will think I don't give you enough credit. Too much and you will imagine I perceive you as vain.'

'Of course, you are a diplomat with that particular knack of discretion.'

'No longer. I gave in my resignation last year before coming back to England.'

'Why?'

'Honesty has its degrees just as treachery does. Sometimes at the end I could not see much difference between them. *"I am myself indifferent honest."'*

'Hamlet?'

'Impressive.' His energy felt watered down and lost today, a weariness covering everything. 'The truth of espionage is that it makes you less trusting. After a while you only see the blackness in people and life becomes skewered.'

'So you are fighting your way back to the light?'

'Isn't that what you tried to show me in your painting?'

The blue eyes widened. 'Most people never understand such nuances.'

There was a certain sadness in him that was heavier this afternoon. He looked as if he had not slept well, dark bruising beneath his eyes.

'Have you ever drawn yourself, Florentia?' His query was surprising.

'Once. A long time ago.'

'I'd like to see it.'

Her arms around him, her nails digging runnels of blood into his skin. The flesh between them joined at the hip. She had drawn it a month after her accident when she believed him most likely dead. A violent depiction of a sexual encounter which even now made her blush.

'I doubt I will ever show you.'

'Do you always say exactly what you feel?'

'I used to once. Before…'

He took her gloved hand and held it, his fingers tight about her own and it was as if the world about disappeared into a swirl of greyness, the colour between them bold and true.

'Before I hurt you. Before I took you from one life and discharged you into another.'

'I was always out of step, Lord Winterton. You allow yourself too much blame for my fall from grace as it may have happened anyway.'

At that he let her go. 'People here admire you, Florentia, and they should. Because you are rare and honest and good.'

Surprise kept her silent, for the deep frown on his brow was at direct odds with the lovely compliment he had just given her.

Inside the bookshop was busier than she had known it and almost every patron looked their way. The Viscount did that to people, she thought, with his height and his bearing. He was a man who incited strong opinions, a man who would never be invisible or anonymous. Preferring such states herself, she hurried him through the lobby, pleased when they gained the stairs at the back of the room.

'The art history section is up here.' She tried to keep her voice neutral though every part of her was aware of the fact that once he followed her up they would probably be alone. Few others seemed to browse this section of the Temple and this was one of the reasons she'd always liked it so much.

'I've bought books here for years,' she began as they walked along the shelves towards a window at the other end of the aisle. 'They seem to have copies of things that one seldom finds anywhere else, you see, and so each time I visit London I invariably come to this place to browse. Mostly I buy, but sometimes I simply look. I can always find something that interests me even when I think I may not.'

'You talk more when you are nervous. Did you know that? You did it as Frederick Rutherford, too.'

'Oh.' The strangled sound escaped from her throat as she wrung her hands together.

'But you seldom speak about yourself. Almost everything I know of you comes from others.'

'I am not really that interesting,' she began, but he stopped her.

'Tell me about your childhood. What was it like?'

'The same as everyone's, I suppose, until my brother died in my arms.' She had not meant to say as much, but then she found she could not stop herself. 'For a long time I thought his death was my fault because I dared him to jump a fence, you see, on his horse. I made him do it even though he did not truly wish to.'

'Did he dare you to do things before his fall?'

'Often and often.'

'Then you both dared each other. It is the way of most siblings, I have heard, the way children grow and risk and learn. Surely you know that?'

And she did. Suddenly. It had been like a game to them. This fence. That gate. This ditch. That hedge. All of their lives they had egged the other on to new heights and further distances, to harder jumps and more difficult feats.

'Papa said I was the most undisciplined of his children. He said if it wasn't for me Bryson may still be alive.'

'Did you ever give consideration to the fact that had it have been your brother who lived your father might have said exactly the same to him?'

Truth. It came in shades from white to black and all the hues in between, like a spiderweb stretched across different facts and opinions and gathering them in. Piecing them together. Making sense of the little bits.

'If your brother was here now perhaps he'd be urging you to get on with living?'

We need to live a hundred per cent. Another catch phrase Bryson, Maria and she had often used. Perhaps her brother's death was not her fault. Perhaps Winter was right and her father was wrong. It could have been any of them who had come to grief at a high fence on a lonely road. She'd jumped that same hedge a few moments before and her horse's hooves had also clipped the tangled canes of wood. Relief filled her.

'Has anything so terrible ever happened to you that you have thought you might never recover from it, Lord Winterton?'

He nodded.

'Well, Bryson's death was like that for me. Before it I was someone else and after... I could not find my way back.'

'And now?'

'Now I can see a pathway.'

When she smiled at him joy lit up her eyes, a new warmth radiating in that dusty room ringed with books. Such joy held him spellbound, the lightness so foreign.

'As payment I will draw the house in the country you have bought for no fee whatsoever, my lord. Such a grand place would undoubtedly look well in a frame.'

'A discount that is generous.'

'A discount to thank you for always being kind to me.'

He could no longer simply ignore the harm he had done her. 'Especially after I did such a fine job of ruining you on the North Road?'

'Looking back, I think perhaps you did me a favour. If I had stayed in society I would probably be married to the Honourable Timothy Calderwood by now and wondering where my life had gone so badly wrong.'

'Words not entirely strong enough to compensate for my brutal kidnapping?'

She smiled. 'You tore my dress off and discarded it.'

'I did save you from the dogs.'

'After rendering me unconscious.'

He frowned. 'Yes, that was unconscionable and I even thought so at the time.'

'Why did you ask me to marry you?'

This question came right out of the blue and he decided to give her back the honesty she had given him, for he was tired of lies and pretence and caution.

'Because I wanted you, wanted you more than I have ever wanted anyone.'

Not quite the truth either, but he liked the way her eyes widened and the dimples on her cheeks were deep against the light. He did not say that she was his salvation, his last chance to find a link back to a world he had become disenchanted with. He did not tell her that every woman he looked at was only a pale reflection of everything she was. To him.

She hated the way he made her breathless and uncertain, lust burning across his face.

'My sister, Maria, says that you are like fire and that I shall be burned by you if I am not careful.'

'Careful?'

'Careful to remain distant, I expect she meant.'

'And is that what you would want?'

She did not look away at that, but stared straight into his perplexity. 'No, it is not. I am twenty-three years old, Lord Winterton, and what I want is for you to kiss me again.'

The run of confusion across his face almost made her turn, but she held to her course and did not flinch.

'I offered marriage and you refused twice? A kiss would have undoubtedly resulted from that.'

'It is not marriage I am angling for. It's the knowledge of the delight of passion that I require before I return once and for all to my life in the country. And in all the whispers that I have heard you are the master of such things.' She swallowed. 'I would, of course, require confidentiality, but then with the scandals that are known between us, I think…'

She did not finish.

'I'd be in no position to…gossip?'

'Exactly.'

That held him still. 'With no feelings at all involved?'

'Pardon?'

'A kiss might take you places you'd find addictive, Florentia. You might indeed want more. Much more.'

His fingers ran across her cheek as he said this, light and airy, barely touching. The timbre of his voice was deep, almost hypnotising, and a feeling began to build inside her that was astonishing.

His eyes were pale in the slanting light, the clear green in them turned velvet limed and fine. And then his lips came down in a hard need, his arms gathering her in, close and then closer.

She tasted exactly as she had before, of sweetness and of virtue, but it had been so long since he had felt those particular things he was careful.

They were in a public space and he understood the danger of being observed. Yet still his hand crept up into the gold of her hair and he tilted his head to come in more deeply.

There was a rush of connection, the red-hot wash of it pounding through his veins, making him reel slightly as he tasted further. His fingers cupped one breast rising ripe against the thin cover of silk and her neck arched in response. So very easy to simply take.

He pulled away. For his own safety. For a sanity that he could not understand, rationality and sense twisted into question over a complete void of control.

She was looking at him in the same way as he was probably looking at her, in shock and unrest, amazement in her blue eyes and her full lips swollen. His thumb wiped away a single tear that fell from her right eye down on to the alabaster smoothness of her cheek.

'Thank you.' Her words, whispered. 'I will always remember that.'

'God, Florentia, you slay me.'

Steadying her, he stepped well away, as far as he could move from her in the narrowness of the cubicle. He had never once in all of his years been concerned enough to put a woman's reputation above his own needs of the flesh. Women had thrown themselves at him, at this event and at that one. But they were always leavable, forgettable and interchangeable.

Until he had met Lady Florentia Hale-Burton with her cleverness and her honesty. He wanted to drag her beneath him and understand the lust he was consumed with, but he shook his head. Lust was the wrong word, but at that moment he did not wish to consider what might be the right one.

He could not do it wrong again. He could not hurt her or cause any hint of scandal. This time he must do what was exactly right for her because he had waited too long to rectify the harm he had once caused.

She felt him withdraw, saw the gleam in his eyes fade to some further-off place and the heartbeat at his throat settle.

Had the kiss been tepid to him, unenthusiastic, indifferent? After all of the women he was reputed to have been with, was her small offering laughable and pathetic?

She did not know the way of it. That was the trouble. She'd had no practice or tutorship in kissing.

The desperate need to be touched and taken consumed her, no consent in it save for a desire that made her feel beautiful beyond measure.

Her right breast still tingled with the feel of him, the out-of-bounds taboo so carefully disregarded. An ownership of the male domain. She could not imagine reaching out and touching him in the same way.

But, oh, how she wanted to.

And the most surprising thing of it all is she felt neither shame nor embarrassment in what he had discovered. She was tired of all the hiding and even here in a space so open she would have still allowed him exactly what he wanted to take.

But he had turned, his fingers trailing across the leather spines of a pile of old books on one of the tables, the edge of the scar on his neck so easily seen at the top of his neckcloth.

'Does your father come to London at all, Florentia?' His tone was measured.

'Hardly ever.'

'Your sister said he had been ill for a number of years. Was it since this?' One hand gestured to his wound, the pale green of his eyes bruised with anger.

'Yes.' She did not keep the truth from him or try to soften it. Her father had returned home from the inn and within a matter of days he had gone to bed. He'd barely left Kent since.

'And it was all a mistake. That was the hell of it. My cousin had bid me to bring his...lovebird up from London and I thought she was you.'

'You thought I looked like a woman of the night?'

The first glimmer of humour crossed his face. 'You were wearing a red dress and Tommy's lady was supposed to have been, too. I had not had much practice with identifying women like that, though of course on reflection you could not have possibly been one.'

'I am not sure whether I should be flattered or not by such a comparison.'

He smiled and began to speak again.

'When I finally woke up after the debacle at the inn the only reason I didn't up and die was because I wanted to say sorry to you. You had told me your name and who your father was.'

'Yet you did not come to Albany?'

'I was sick for a long time and largely penniless. I imagined the very sight of me again would send a young girl into hysterics and so I went to the Americas. When I returned I met your sister at a ball about a month after I got to London and then I received your agent's letter about the portrait. I knew there was some connection between Rutherford and the Hale-Burton household and I needed to find out what it was.'

'Why did you spread that rumour of Frederick Rutherford's leaving?'

'Because his disappearance made it safer for you.'

'Safer?'

'Acceptance in society is a nebulous thing. A word here and there in the right ear can do wonders and a quiet shift of understanding is often the result.'

'The right ear?'

'Mr Benjamin Heron was listening.'

'Which is why the family sponsored me at their ball. I always wondered how you might have accomplished that.'

'The Winterton family history is convoluted and dissolute. Sometimes such reckless disregard can be an advantage.'

'An answer that allows me no clue at all to your methods.'

'Heron did not kill my father. I think I told you once I thought he might have. My father did not commit suicide either.'

'An accident, then? A terrible accident with its own secrets attached?'

'You are too quick by half, Florentia. But then I always knew that.'

'Did you, my lord?'

'From the first time you came to my town house. I thought you unmatched.'

'A dangerous realisation given I was a boy.'

'I still think that.'

Such a confidence left a silence between them, stretching across surprise, and Florentia was about to talk again when she heard the sound of footsteps on the staircase. A moment later one of the men at the desk from downstairs came around the corner.

'We had hoped to still find you here, Lord Winterton. One of our best customers, Lady Ecclesfield, who heard you were here, was most insistent to have a short word. By all accounts she was a friend of your grandmother's.'

'Of course.' Winter's reply sounded forced and the frown across his forehead deepened as he saw the man waiting to accompany him down. Tipping his head in a gesture of polite social discourse, he spoke quietly.

'Thank you for your recommendations on the books

on art history, Lady Florentia. I shall be certain to keep such titles in mind.'

'My pleasure, Lord Winterton.'

When he took her hand he held it for a second longer than was appropriate. Florentia wished that he might never have let her go but a second later he was gone completely. Leaning back against a wall, she closed her eyes, taking in a good deep breath to steady herself. What had just happened? Had he felt what she had? Where did this leave them?

She did not dare go down just yet for she knew her cheeks would be flushed and her eyes glitter bright.

No man now would measure up again to this new knowledge of what was. All the suitors who had asked for dances in the past weeks faded into a grey oblivion against the crimson truth of James Waverley, Viscount Winterton. The hues around him were vibrant and rich, a violent boldness that left her gasping, the soft and sombre others cast into shadow by his light.

Closing the book before her, she repositioned her hat and tightened the loosened fastenings of her cloak. Once downstairs she looked around for Winterton, but there was no sign at all of him, the scene before her returned to a normal softness after the force and power of his parting.

Outside she smiled her thanks as a Warrenden servant helped her up into the waiting carriage and the horses moved on through the busy streets around Finsbury Square.

It was either over or just started, this game between her and Winter, and right now she had no idea at all which way the dice might fall.

* * *

Winter hailed a hackney cab and gave it his direction. He wanted to be away from Lackington's and away from Florentia because he honestly did not know what he would do next should he see her. Fall on to his knees and make a public spectacle of himself or simply take her in his arms and kiss her to find again the magic and the grace? He did not want to do either until he understood what the cost of any troth might finally be to her.

Albany was two hours south and he knew that if he made a start now he could be there before night-fall. His own conveyance would not take long to ready and he could find lodging tonight in some inn near the Manor. And yet other considerations kept rushing in.

The Earl of Albany had been largely housebound since his daughter had been kidnapped six years ago and from what James had found out he was a nervous man, inclined to odd turns of behaviour.

Roy Warrenden was often in White's in the early afternoon so Winter took the chance to find him, banging on the roof of his cab and changing the directions of his travel. He needed more information on the family and who better to give it than Maria's husband himself?

'I am very glad to see you here, Warrenden.' Winter slid into the empty seat beside him, removing the sheets of today's early edition of *The Times* as he did so.

'Are you indeed? I thought you might have come before this, Winter?'

'How so?'

'You are as astute as any man I have ever met in my life and I have been hearing the rounds of your well-placed gossip about the artist Frederick Rutherford. Florentia also confided in us that you now knew of her charade?'

Ignoring this, James formed his own query.

'How old was the brother? The one who died?'

Roy looked startled. 'I am surprised your numerous sources did not tell you Bryson was Florentia's twin. He died in her arms after mistiming a jump on his stallion. I think her heart was broken.'

'Hell.'

A twin.

There was in all his reading a special closeness between twins. How bereft Florentia must have felt at the loss of hers for every time she had spoken of her brother he had felt the sadness.

'Maria worries about her constantly, though I myself think she is far stronger than anyone imagines. To pull off the stunt of imitating Rutherford required nerves of steel and she did it well. Why are you now so intent upon protecting her?'

'I will leave it to her to tell you that. What I do want to find out is if you think the father is up to a personal visit?'

'From you?' Now Roy sat bolt upright and lowered his voice markedly. 'Lord, are you saying what I think you are...?'

When Winter did not answer he went on. 'Albany is self-centred and inclined to enjoy poor health. I think like all the other members of the family he does not enjoy society and an accident in the north allowed him the chance to opt out altogether. Which he has.'

'And the mother?'

'She is easier to understand, though she is also browbeaten by a husband who refuses to get truly well.

Maria and I do not see them often as a visit usually ends in my wife trying to cajole them back into the mainstream of life which, as you can gather, they do not take to kindly.'

'And how does Florentia fit into all this?'

'She supports them with the earnings she makes from her paintings, which will be sadly lessened now that Frederick Rutherford has disappeared to the Americas. I have tried to gift them money, but the Earl is too proud and too stubborn to accept it though Maria manages to get around some of that and slips help in now and again. Florentia has more recently had some offers of marriage presented which would alleviate all financial responsibility, but she has turned each and every one of them down.'

'Are there any more on the table that she might accept?'

'I don't know, Winter. Certainly I have young men of good heart and family calling on me daily. Whether she is interested is another matter entirely, for she is most reticent to talk of her personal affairs. Perhaps there is someone for whom she already holds a *tendre*? Should I take it from this conversation that you may be interested in throwing your own name into the ring?'

'Don't let her say yes to anyone until I have spoken with her. I need to go down to Albany tomorrow.'

'You could not speak with me now? I have taken over Albany's duty of vetting suitors, after all.'

'No. There is more to it than that.'

He could see the workings in Roy Warrenden's eyes and knew the minute his old friend had understood the truth.

'It was you? You were the one? The one who took Florentia? The bastard who changed all their lives?'

'Yes.'

'God.' He ran a hand through his hair and breathed out heavily. 'If I thought Florentia truly hated you for it, Winter, I'd want to run you through with the sharpest sword I own.'

'But you don't?'

'My wife told me the other day that her sister has not understood her destiny yet or the fact that you are going to be part of it and Maria is seldom wrong about anything. But what if Albany himself kills you? He'd hate you enough to do it, I think.'

'Then I'd be dead.'

Roy unexpectedly began to laugh. 'He's an academic, Winter. The heroics in the inn was his finest hour and I doubt such bravery will ever be repeated. Still, he keeps a loaded pistol in the drawer on the right side of his bed. If he reaches for it, I would duck.'

'Thank you.' Holding out his hand, he was glad when Roy took it.

Chapter Fourteen

Albany was a grand old manor perched on a hill and set back from the river which meandered before it, the banks resplendent with white arum lilies and tall blue flowers Winter did not know the name of. The family seat looked as if it were only just hanging on to the glorious earlier days by the fingernails, the cracks of time imprinted in the lines of the place. Like many of the old and titled names of the *ton* the Earl had obviously fallen upon hard times, and harder times still for his family, Winter imagined, with a lost entailment looming before them.

He'd stayed in the carriage until the village when he had asked for his horse to be brought around. With a light breeze and the promise of a warm day in the air he had enjoyed the exercise of riding. The worry of what this visit might bring also hung across him.

At the front door he was met by a slight older servant, his uniform too big for him. The fellow bowed as he took his hat and coat.

'May I tell the Earl who has come to call, sir?'

'I am Viscount Winterton.' Even with the threat of

what might happen Winter gave his true name. If the Earl chose to crucify him then that would be a punishment he would have to take, but he hoped he might talk the fellow into an acceptance of all that had happened.

'Very well, my lord, but the Earl is upstairs in his chamber and so it might take a little while to rouse him. If you would like to go into the library, perhaps, there is wine there and I will have the cook bring you some sustenance after your journey.'

'Thank you.'

He proceeded to follow the man a little way down the corridor. Standing in the middle of the empty room as the servant hurried off once again, Winter saw many of the things that Florentia had never told him. Her father kept a library that would have been the envy of every thinking man in Europe and the paintings on the wall were like no others he had ever seen.

He corrected himself. The portrait hanging now above his desk in St James's Square held the same freedom of lines and boldness of colour. Florentia's work. He walked over to the nearest canvas that presumably depicted her parents. They were both slight and lost looking. The wife had her hands firmly fixed in the husband's and on her breast was embroidered a picture of a boy.

Bryson? There was a startling likeness in his features to that of Frederick Rutherford. No wonder she played the part so well, he thought to himself. She was emulating a dear and lost twin. The poignancy of that thought made him swallow.

'The Earl will see you now, my lord, in his suite of rooms. I shall take you up.'

The runners were threadbare and there were several

spindles missing from the grand staircase, but a frieze had been carefully painted all the way up on the hand-rail, one of flowers and plants and entwined leaves, the same arum lilies and blue blooms in the design that he had seen by the river.

The curtains were drawn as he stepped within the bedchamber, so for just a moment he did not see the man sitting in a leather chair by a fire that was blazing even in the considerable warmth of the morning.

'Lord Winterton?' The voice was steady and pleasant. 'Thank you, Murphy. I will see to our visitor now.'

Winter waited until the butler had left before moving in further. The room had a smell of mustiness and sickness, a carbolic astringent scent laid on top as if even with all the cleaning in the world the underlying malady could not be erased.

'I do not have many visitors these days and was wondering…'

The words faded off as the man got a good look at him.

'You? Is it you? My God, I have seen your face for all of the days since we met, every night in the darkness, every moment as I eat.' He had stood up now, though his right hand was still anchored to the solidness of the chair, as if on letting go he might fall unstopped to the floor. Sweat poured down the old Earl's forehead and beaded on his top lip. 'You are not dead and buried all these years, but alive?'

Winter could not quite decipher his tone. Albany sounded shocked and shaky, his hands trembling. He had expected fury and he was being met with stupor and distress instead.

'I have come to apologise for taking your daughter,

my lord. It was a mistake which I have regretted immensely ever since.'

'A mistake?' Now the older man sat on the bed again, quite abruptly. His mouth worked up and down without sound as he swallowed.

'My cousin had asked me to bring his…paramour up from London. She was to be dressed in red and standing on the corner of Mount Street at the hour of five o'clock. She was blonde and I was warned would be feisty, but it was for her own good that he wanted her out of London so my orders were to insist until she came.'

'My God.' Anger seemed more apparent now and Winter's eyes flicked to the cabinet there with its two small drawers.

'I did not know about the scandal that ensued. I have been away in the Americas for years and came back to England only a few months ago. If I had known…' He stopped. What would he have done? Confronted the Earl so soon after he had almost been killed by him? Returned from the Americas? He was glad he had not had to make that choice.

'Have you seen my daughter? Have you seen Flora?'

'Yes.'

'And she knew you?'

'She did, Lord Albany. Though I had trouble knowing her. She was dressed as a lad. An artist, Frederick Rutherford.'

He nodded. 'Maria has told me of it.'

'I want to make things right with your family. I have come down to see if I might have your blessing in asking your daughter for her hand in marriage.'

'My blessing?'

'I want to protect Florentia. I want to make sure that she is always safe. I am wealthy now and have a large property in Herefordshire as well as extensive land in the Americas. I will see she never goes without and is always happy. I would swear it to you on my life, my lord.'

There was silence and then Winter noticed the tears that were falling down the older man's cheeks. Breathing in deeply, he tried to take charge of the situation.

'I am sorry for all the harm I have caused you and your family, Lord Albany. It was unprincipled and unacceptable and if you feel my presence here is too much for you to bear then of course I will leave.'

But Albany shook his head. 'I am not crying with sadness, Winterton. These are tears of happiness. Instead of the horror of killing someone in my mind every and each minute, now I can be free.'

'Free?'

'To live again. To feel again. Repentance has given way to absolution and sorrow to joy. I am unfettered from the guilt of taking a young life for here you are standing before me.'

Of all the things Winter had imagined of this meeting this was not one of them. 'And your daughter?'

'It is up to Florentia to decide if she wants you. She has been lonely for so many years, but she has also found a great gift in her painting.'

'Of course.'

'May I ask you something before you leave? Something personal?' He waited for a nod. 'Your throat was ripped to threads and there was so much blood at the inn. How did you survive?'

'With luck and determination. Your daughter tried

to help me as I fell and I wanted to give her my apology in person.'

'And have you?'

'Yes.'

'Then you have my blessing to try and see your way to right such a travesty, Lord Winterton.'

Florentia was sitting in the garden at the Warrenden town house watching the sparrows playing in the blossoms of an apple tree. She had been out here for a good while now, trying to decide in the quiet of nature just exactly what she should do about Winter.

She had thought to send a letter, but had decided not to. What could she say after all? *You kissed me and I was wondering if you might do so again? Please.*

She smiled, but a welling unhappiness stuck in her throat, making her feel sad and furious at exactly the same time.

Winterton had left London according to Roy. Did that mean he had left for good or would he be back? Timothy Calderwood had offered her marriage as had a dozen other men of the *ton*. They had trooped in to see Roy at every hour of the day and she had ceased to even answer her brother-in-law when he had called her to his study after each departure and asked her if she had any interest in pursuing the latest request.

She had not been able to paint or sleep or eat wondering what might happen to her now that Winter was gone. He had ruined her reputation last time, but this time it was even worse. This time it was her heart that lay in tatters at his feet.

The sound of voices inside the house took her attention. It would be Maria probably returned from her afternoon tea or Roy from his men's club where he went most afternoons to read the paper and meet friends. The normal everyday noises of a marriage and a house that reflected the happiness of Lord and Lady Warrenden. Her sister was more content than she had ever seen her and her own uncertainty was magnified because of it.

The door opened to the garden and the butler came forward with a card.

'Viscount Winterton has called upon you, Lady Florentia. Shall I ask him to come into the garden?'

Shock ran through her, but she waited perfectly still as his footsteps came closer. She did not wish to look up and find something in his face that would shatter her. She did not wish to see a return to tepid friendship or the more sombre shades of some awful truth she could not cope with.

'Thank you for seeing me. I know that you are here alone and I hope it is a good time to speak freely.' His voice was deep and husky; the voice her father had left him with.

At that she did look up and saw his eyes were full of trepidation. That alone frightened her more than anything else could have for he had always been so sure every time she had met him. She decided to get in first.

'If you are here to apologise for the kiss we shared, Lord Winterton, I do not want to hear it.'

'Pardon?' Now he looked perplexed.

'At Lackington's.'

'Why should I apologise?'

'You shouldn't and I am most certainly not sorry for it.'

'You aren't?'

'I liked it a lot.'

When he laughed she thought she might begin to cry, but he stepped forward and took her hands, drawing her up before him and then falling on to one knee.

What on earth was he doing? Could he possibly be…?

'Will you marry me, Florentia? I know I have been instrumental in many of your family's problems, but I swear to make it up to you, all of it, for every day of my life.'

'Why would you want to?' This time she heard other things beneath his words. Desperation. Anguish. Worry.

'I have always been alone, but lately I have become lonely because of you. Talking with you, dancing with you, seeing you smile, watching you paint. I can't imagine my life any more without you in it.'

She could not believe his words. Was she simply imagining this happening out of hope? 'You are asking me to be your wife, but this time because of love?' She whispered it. To say it out loud might take the truth away.

'I am if you will have me.'

'Yes.' The word came unbidden in a cry of sheer joy, disbelief making her shake. She could hear her heartbeat in her ears and feel the shallow quickness of breath. Then his mouth covered hers and she understood magic as he showed her without words his troth was indeed honest, the same swell of desire beaching across her.

'I love you, Winter. More than life itself.' She said this as he finished the kiss, his hands cradling her face.

'I don't want to wait, Florentia. I can't. We can be wed quickly by special licence if you would wish it.'

'I would.'

'I don't deserve you, God knows that, but I will never give you up. Not for anyone or anything. Yes is for ever by me, Florentia. Know that.'

'My father…?'

'I went there to Albany to ask him for his blessing. I needed this to have everything right because the last times…' He didn't finish.

'It was all so very wrong.'

She could feel the smile on his lips as she pressed against him.

'I have dreamed of this moment every night since I first saw you.'

'Good, for so have I.'

When he kissed her again it was different. This time as the warmth of his breath touched her skin she looked at him and saw things there that were now unhidden. The heat in him shocked her.

'I want you.' Her words came slowly and with feeling. She felt dampness on her skin and the running whorls of want inside like living things, dancing to a tune she had not heard before.

Everything was brought into focus. The clear green of his eyes. The streaks in his hair pale from sunshine. The stubble on his chin that showed her he had not shaved since early dawn. He smelt of the outside, of exercise and horses, of leather, sweat and hard riding.

His hands were not those of an idle lord either, the palm toughened in a way that spoke of work and toil and labour. Such a hard and lean masculinity made her smile. When his thumb ran over the fullness of her lips she marvelled at the way she responded to him.

'I never forgot you for all of those years.' His words, broken with hope. 'I remembered you every single day.'

Tears came, brimming in her eyes. 'What a waste,' she answered, but he shook his head.

'Not that, Florentia. For me it was an apprenticeship in love.' He held her hair and tipped her chin up, his tongue touching where his thumb had just been. 'I did not know what it was like to lose your heart to someone until I saw you again. Even as the lad Rutherford, I loved you.'

The intensity of his eyes drew her in, the sheer longing and veracity.

'Because without each other it was so hard to exist?' She thought of her empty days and nights, of the long and lonely years and of the painting in the back of her wardrobe that crouched in truth. Her fingers came up and touched a living breathing cheek in the same way she had caressed her canvas. He leaned into her.

'I have missed you.' Her words, fractured with conviction.

Closeness. Certainty. Desire and faith. They melded into an emotion that made her shake until his mouth came down and he allowed her to know just what she meant to him, nothing at all held back.

She answered his desperation with her own, opening wider and threading her fingers through the length of his hair.

Here she was. Her. Florentia Hale-Burton. It was staggering and astounding. The colour of scarlet and blood and fire. The hue of daring and determination and power and courage. Her. Risen in flames from the ashes. Regenerated and reborn. No longer hiding and afraid and ruined.

And then she could no longer think at all.

She was all ripeness and softness and woman, her curves sweet and full, the plump flesh of her breasts, the long line of her throat, the creamy smooth of her skin. Breaking off the kiss before it went so far he would not be able to stop going further, he brought her into his arms and kept her there.

Florentia stripped him to the bone, his naked longing exposed and vulnerable. She was so very beautiful with her innocence and her honesty, all the shades of gold across his hand in her hair and her eyes reflections of a summer sky.

An eddy of wind blew around them, lifting the fabric of her skirt and further afield he could hear the sound of horses and voices as the everyday reality of London broke again into their paradise.

With remorse he let go of her and stepped back, back to where he could only watch her, the dappled sun on her hair, the joy on her face.

'I cannot wait long, Florentia. For you.'

Then her sister was there, stopping as she saw him, her face expressing worry as well as anger.

'I hope everything is well with you, Flora?' The query hung in the air. 'I did not know visitors were expected.'

'I have come to ask your sister if she would do me the honour of becoming my wife, Lady Warrenden.'

'Your wife. Your wife?' Now there was only amazement in her visage. 'Oh, my goodness.'

Florentia took up the conversation. 'I have said yes,

Maria. We are to be wed as soon as we can. By a special licence.'

Maria Warrenden's hands were stretched across her mouth, the same dimples her sister sported deep on each cheek. 'Does Roy know?'

Florentia shook her head. 'You are the first to hear our news although Winter has asked Father and he gave us his blessing.'

Now she simply shrieked as she rushed forward, enclosing her younger sister in her grasp, the blue in Maria's gown complementing the yellow in Florentia's.

Her parents came to London the following day for a stay in the Warrenden town house and for the first time in years her father looked happy. When he asked her to the library later in the evening she knew what it was he would want to speak to her about.

'Lord Winterton came to see me, Flora. He is a good man. A moral man. He apologised sincerely for his mistake and tried to explain to me what had happened. When he asked for your hand in marriage I gave him my blessing.'

'He told me, Papa.'

'And the blinkers of my stupidity and shame through all those years simply fell away. I had not killed a man, which was a relief that was indescribable, and he had given me a second chance to get better and live again. Do you love him?'

'I do, Papa.'

'Roy said you have had many requests for your hand, but have barely glanced at any of your swains until Winterton. He implied James Waverley has been...fairly dissolute, I think is how he phrased it, but that he had turned over a new leaf and has eyes now only for you.'

'He is a friend of Roy's. From school.'

'Yes, he told me that, too. There is one worry that niggles at my mind, however. In London all those years ago there were witnesses. If any should come forward and name him…'

'I am not letting my one hope of happiness go on a chance, Papa. If that happens we will deal with it.'

'Your mother said I was to fall on my knees and thank the Lord above that you are happy, my dear, so perhaps that is what I will do. The years of our hardship are over and even with Albany entailed it shall no longer be of any significance.'

'Perhaps Bryson has been looking over us, Papa.' This time when she mentioned her brother her father smiled.

'Like our guardian angel. I like that thought.'

When he came forward to envelop her in his arms Florentia did not pull away.

The wedding had been small and quick.

It was a quiet ceremony at a chapel close to the Warrenden town house, a bunch of white roses in an opaque green vase at the altar.

Fine spring weather had swept in from the south, the sun shining through a stained-glass window.

Flora wore a gown that she and her sister had found in a shop in town, and one that with only a slight alteration had fitted her perfectly.

It was of light blue silk and matched the colour of her eyes, the bodice trimmed in cream lace and ribbon. The skirt cascaded wide from the waistline and sleeves of organza were ruched at the shoulders and fell almost transparent to her wrists. In her hair she had flowers, the ivy pulled through her curls where they were caught in a cream band of more silk. Bryson's ring hung about her neck in an ornate clasp of rose gold.

'Do I look…enough?' She turned to ask this of her sister as they stood in the small vestibule.

'You look beautiful, Flora. But more than that you look happy.'

'I love him, Maria.'

'And he loves you back. Every time he looks at you I can see it.'

'How was I so lucky?' She barely liked to ask this.

'You deserve it. You complete each other. Two halves who have been alone for a long time. Now come, I can hear the music and it is time.'

The wedding party was a very tiny one. Maria and Roy would be there, of course, and her parents and Roy's elderly mother.

Winter had only invited Rafe and Arabella. Seven people.

'So you have everything, Florentia. Something borrowed in the family garter. The old is taken care of in Bryson's ring and something new and blue in the dress. Talismans have their detractors, but for the grand occasions I have always believed in them to protect one against the Evil Eye.'

Her mother had stated this before they had left for the chapel. 'We do not want you rendered barren, my dear, so be sure to be mindful of the old rhyme.'

Barren. Flora blushed because tonight she would no longer be an innocent. Tonight she would go with Winter to his town house and she would know all the intimate delights that she had never had the measure of.

'Love lights the marriage bed, a glorious pyre.'

She saw Lord Winterton as soon as she walked through the doors. He was dressed today in a navy blue jacket and beige trousers, the white tie at his neck arranged more formally than she had ever seen him wear one. When he turned to look at her the beauty of him took her breath away and her father at her side stopped to observe her.

'Are you sure, Florentia? This is what you want?'

'It is, Papa, with all my heart.'

She would never forget the moment her father gave her over to Winter. James Waverley's fingers were warm and strong and they clasped hers in a way that let her know that they were in this together, that whatever happened in all the years to come they would both face it. With the height of his neckcloth she could see no glimpse at all of the scar. She wondered if that was deliberate.

The candles smelt of rose oil and the play of leaves from the tree near a window sent shadow against the opposite wall.

A setting that showed layers of beauty and of truth. Like her paintings. Deceptively simple. Unthinkingly complex. The colours of polished wood, the gowns and the bower of blooms a vibrant mix of shades that melded to create a perfect backdrop.

Us. We. Together.

When Winter squeezed her hand she turned to smile at him and knew the sort of happiness that was as complete as she could ever imagine.

* * *

He took her home as the day dimmed into dusk and Florentia felt an excitement that made her tingle.

She smiled as they passed the chair opposite the grandfather clock in the lobby. She had known very little of the Viscount personally when she had first come here to make his portrait and the rumours of his past had been rife. His parents were notoriously difficult, she knew that from the endless gossip of them, people who had never settled in love or in life. His own shifting lifestyle had probably come about as the result of such flagrant disconnection.

'Would you like to see how I hung your painting?' he asked, taking her from those thoughts as they veered off down the hall to the right.

The portrait had been framed in a way that showed it off to its very best advantage, the gilded and elaborate plaster moulding bringing out the tones within and giving relief to the subject and its colours.

'Is the frame French?' she asked as she walked closer.

He nodded. 'I found it at Christie's.'

'A perfect match.'

'Like us?' His eyes were darker tonight, clouded by high emotion as he reached out for her hand, lips warm on the back of her fingers. Stamping an ownership. Demanding much more than simple talk.

'I would never hurt you, Florentia.'

'I know.'

'But I want the sort of marriage my parents did not have. A true one and real. Nothing held back. A love match.'

'I want it, too.'

At that he nodded and drew the first pin from her hair. She stood there and let him make a careful deconstruction, the ivy loosening as more pins followed the first.

Her hair unravelled to her waist. She saw the colour and length of it in the shadow of his eyes even before one hand came up and knotted the fall hard in his grasp. Pinned into his want, she tipped her head back and met his gaze squarely, her mouth falling open and her lips dry.

'Let me love you, Florentia.'

'Yes.' Her breath shallowed behind the word, consent a yielded surrender.

His fingers on her cheek were soft, feeling the contours, understanding flesh. When they wandered to her ears, she smiled. Today she had on her grandmother's pearl earrings, the gold filigree in them intricate and beautiful.

'These suit you, my love, and I shall buy you whatever else you would like in the way of jewellery.'

Her skin rose at his touch and as his eyes locked into her own he took her into his arms, tight and true.

'I love you,' he whispered. 'I love you so much that it hurts.' Her breath quickened as his fingers slid against the thinness of silk, finding the bud of her nipple with his thumb and moving across it. She arched into the caress, the body's own music true and deep.

He did not halt as she came into her release, but felt the rumbling echoes of flesh when she cried out loud, the low and guttural sounds rising from the depths of a feeling that brought sweat to her brow.

And then she was limp, her head resting on his chest.

'Not here.' It occurred to him that his mastery as a lover was being tested even as he said it, lost in a feeling that was unfamiliar.

He was desperate, more desperate than he had ever been in all of his life to please her, the silk and shadows of his past melded into this one unprecedented moment when he felt the control he was famous for slipping. Slipping so far away that he carried her up the stairs and into his bedchamber like a green lad, fingers fumbling at her fastenings, a row of pearl buttons and stays and ribbons and hooks. He ripped the last layer of flimsy lawn and then his hands were on her breasts, ripe and firm and his.

Even language was deserting him. A blue garter was around her right thigh, trimmed in cream ribbon. She was the most beautiful woman he had ever seen in his entire life. Perfect. Unflawed. Glowing in the candlelight, burnished in wheat and ivory and gold.

Dipping his head, he tasted her, one pale pink nipple coming full into his mouth. Sweet and salty. Then he felt her hands thread into his own hair and bring him in closer.

'Sweetheart, I can barely think with the wanting.'

'Then don't,' she said and reached for his own nipple, flicking it as quickly.

A measured equal taking. That thought made him hard for the years of his own whispered prowess had left him always as the instigator, the leader. Here she was, an innocent finding in the tiny nuances her own sensuality and giving it back to him without any shyness whatsoever. When she leaned over and bit him as he had done her he simply lifted her up in his arms and took her to bed.

Always he was careful and thorough and clinical. Always he followed a pattern, a routine, a method. Habitual, customary and ordered.

Today passion simply ruled him, pronounced and random, the haphazard and arbitrary desperation taking his breath into large unruly gulps and his erection as hard as stone.

When she suddenly looked up and smiled, he had the impression that she knew his thoughts almost as if he had spoken them out loud.

He was beautiful. As beautiful as any man she could have drawn, with the long lines of his body and the dimple in his chin. Bur there was something else there that held her, too. A vulnerability and a tenderness, addressed only to her and translated into flesh.

He had not removed his clothes though she was naked. But he was frenzied and when his hands pushed down his trousers she understood that he would be fully garbed when he took her. He met her eyes then, his manhood poised at the edge of movement.

'I…don't want…to hurt…you…'

And he pushed in, the length and breadth of him. When she cried out he held very still, engorged now inside, the thick ache of him unfamiliar. Exposed.

Above her the ceiling was moulded plaster and the chandelier sported candles in cut crystal. She strove for the details, for the tiny things she could see that might take her mind from the pain, for the colour of the beadings, for the top of the velvet curtains around the four-poster bed, ruched into dark gold and burgundy.

And then he moved again, slower this time, a gentle rolling rhythm interspersed with quicker pushes and a feeling grew that she could not stop, like a wave gathering force, building, peaking and breaking upon some far-off shore, taking her with it, the fire and the ice, the beauty and the grace. Just her breath now and his in the room, all else forgotten as she closed her eyes and only felt. Him. His force and his power. Taking her in the way lovers had for all of time immemorial, sacrificed upon an altar of delight she had no name for.

Endlessly primal and beautiful and astounding.

She felt as if the beating heart of her lust was there in the room as a physical form, scarlet gold, orange and black. White was present, too, the colour of safety and innocence.

She had always seen life in terms of colour.

And finally the quiet crept back in, breaths shallowing, hearts calming, the movement of his fingers across her gentle and comforting. Close and content, the outside sounds of the night, the last bird calls, the roll of a carriage wending its way past, a servant moving through the corridor, the last sparks of flame in the grate.

Anchoring them to this life, returning them from the other.

'Thank you, Florentia, for your gift of innocence.' His breath warmed her shoulder. 'I think I should have been gentler.'

She answered him with a simple shake of the head. 'You were perfect.'

She felt the movement of a smile against her hair.

'I lost control. It is something that has never happened before. Usually…' He stopped and so did the movement of his fingers across her naked back. 'I have not been without women in my life, but the rumours that multiply my conquests many times over are false. I want you to know that. There's never before been anyone special. Until now, here with you.'

Raising herself up on one elbow, she looked at him, the neckcloth in disarray and the scar beneath easily seen. 'I drew you after the inn in oil on canvas in the dark and sombre colours of grief. For years the study has been hidden away, but every now and then, and more often of late, I have taken it from its hiding place and felt the lines of you.' Her first finger hovered over his jaw and his cheek before rising to his nose. 'It's as if I knew you through my drawing, like a ghost or a spirit, always there. A protection against life and the living of it. A guardian.'

'And do I measure up? Now?' The fullness of his lips were emphasised by candlelight as he asked his question.

'When Bryson died I thought in my heart that my world would be frozen and dead for ever. I thought that the beauty in life had gone with him and that there was nothing left to live for.' She saw him watching her, a small frown between his eyes.

She had to tell him, had to make him understand. 'Now I think life has grabbed me and made the blood run again and even that makes me feel guilty because in the minutes you hold me close and safe I forget Bryson. Completely. Forget all that he was and will never be again. I allow him to die.'

'It's what you paint, isn't it? His death. Again and again. I saw your work on the walls of your father's library.'

'He was my twin. Without him I was only half until you came and made me whole again. And it is a dangerous place to be in, this hope, because were you to leave as well...' She didn't finish because she couldn't.

He felt his heart lunge and shatter. Into pieces. A thousand hearts all beating just for her.

'It's for ever, Florentia. This. Us. As long as we both shall live and beyond that if I am able. There will never be another for me, I promise you that.'

'Thank God you didn't die when Papa shot you.' Her hand reached out to trace the scar and he stiffened. No one had ever touched his neck before and he had never come to any woman's bed without his shirt on. 'Can I see it? Can you undress to show me?'

Winter did not hear any pity in her voice and if he had he would have refused. All he heard was interest in the outcome of a piece of time in history that had changed them both. Besides, she'd just told him of some of her secrets and fears and he felt that there should be an equal sharing in return.

Sitting up beside her, he made his decision, but it was with trepidation that he untied his neckcloth and undid the buttons of his shirt. An armour that had been in place for so very long was difficult to remove and he knew the marks beneath the cloth on his skin to be shocking.

Please God, let her not be repulsed, he found himself beseeching to a deity he had barely prayed to for years.

'It's not a pretty sight...' He told himself to stop and be silent. No manner of words would lessen the shock of it and apologies and confessions would only make things worse.

So when he turned so that she could see the full

wreckage of his back and shoulders and neck he felt the shivers of shame turn with him.

'Esp…ion…?' He heard her pronounce the word and felt her finger trace the letters in flesh.

'Spy,' he returned, hating the hope in his voice. 'Under Moore in the First Peninsular Campaign. I was caught, you see, and held…' His voice broke as the memories he tried never to recall weighed down upon him.

'And these?'

Now he felt her gaze and touch on the long horizontal scars that covered his upper back.

'From being whipped. Like a dog,' he continued and made himself go on. The honour had left him a long time ago and the three days in the pit of hell had made him a different man altogether.

Detached. Indifferent. Callous. Cold.

'What of here?'

The softness of her fingers was now on the bands of white scars around the top of his arms.

'Ropes. They bound me and when I fought the ties tightened and stripped off the skin.'

He turned then and stopped her hands from finding more, simply by holding them together on her lap.

'I am damaged and ruined, Florentia. Much more so than you should ever think and if such wreckage is something you feel you could not stomach to look at, then…'

Her lips closed over his mouth, her small tongue finding in his silence what he had found in her. She did not hold back or half-heartedly try to reassure him that things were all right, that he was not too much damaged, that the scars were small or the shame was nothing.

Instead she simply gave him back his life in the one way she had just re-found hers.

I was only half until you came and made me whole again.

She had told him of it before, but now she was showing him, her lips on the mark at his neck careful and gentle and kind before moving on to those on his back. Not as if she might simply erase them with her attention, but as if to her they were only just a part of him, a part of them, a part of the life he had led.

'Let our past lie in the same bed, Winter, where we can allow it some honour before we forget it.'

The tears fell down his face before he could stop them, he a man who had never cried, not once in all the years of his hardships. Not when he was young and unloved and lost. Not in the pit with the French soldiers who liked nothing more than to hurt him. Not even in Tom's house after the debacle at the inn. His eyes welled with relief and release and gratefulness that he should have met a woman who could finally understand him.

Florentia with her wisdom and her difference, with her honesty, intelligence and enlightenment. How, after twenty-nine years of being alone, had he finally found a woman who was his?

Such a question staunched the sadness and brought a half-smile. He had found her by ruin and deceit, by accident and charade, by luck and by design. She had sought him out to understand just who he was and he had agreed on the portrait to get closer to the truth of who he had been. Two ends to the same question. Pole opposites whom Lady Luck had finally favoured because they belonged together.

Standing, he shrugged off the rest of his clothes and then lay down beside her. Her hair fell like a curtain of spun gold on the sheets and the long line of one leg came across him. Her eyes were the colour of skies in summer and seas on a quiet and favoured wind. They were the blue of cornflowers and sapphires and tourmalines.

'When I look into your eyes, Florentia, I can see right through you.'

'Into my heart?'

He laughed.

'And beyond.'

'Show me what you can see, Winter.'

His hand fell across her stomach and downwards and then he drew her a picture of all of the feelings in the world.

And that night he slept in her arms from midnight until dawn, all of the broken nights' sleep he had known for years lost in a calming slumber and warmth.

When the bells of London rang and there was birdsong he could not believe that it was six o'clock on the old timepiece on top of the mantel.

'Florentia?' he whispered her name.

'Yes?'

'Love me?'

'I do.'

Chapter Fifteen

It was the very last ball of the Season and as Florentia and Winter had virtually stayed away from any formal social occasion since being married they decided that they would attend the Bell-Harris soirée before leaving town to live permanently at Atherton Abbey.

Winter had bought her a gown for the evening's entertainment from a dressmaker who was newly set up in London and the current favourite of this Season. It was a deep navy interfaced with cream and gold, the sort of dress that took two maids and a great amount of time to get her into. Florentia felt like a princess.

Maria and Roy had been down in Kent in Albany for the past ten days and her parents had returned to London with them and were to come to the ball. The first time her father had been out in proper company for six years. She was pleased he had made such an effort to be in their lives again and her mother was bathing in all the marital bliss of her two daughters.

Faith had taken to her father like a duck to water and had gone down to Albany with them. She would be back this evening, too. Winter and Flora had missed their energetic and excitable puppy and were looking forward to seeing her.

Flora's life had fallen headlong into a wonderful place. Winter was everything she could have ever dreamed of in a husband and a visit to Atherton had revealed a home of beauty and substance. The Carmichaels were to visit them in Herefordshire the following week and Arabella had promised that she would show Flora how to begin her own garden.

She played with Bryson's ring that she still wore around her neck on the long golden chain.

Pride goeth before the fall.

The quote came from nowhere, but it unsettled her and made her worry. Was it even possible to stay as happy as she now was for ever? Or was there some celestial truth that balanced out luck and ill fortune so that one did not have too much and another too little?

She breathed out and looked at herself in the mirror. Money did have a particular way of softening all the edges and presenting one in a light that was…peculiar. That was the only word she could think of. She could not imagine walking anywhere in a dress such as this or indeed even relaxing in it.

One night, she whispered to herself. This night. And then we will be gone.

As soon as she arrived she felt an undercurrent that she did not recognise. Winter by her side felt it, too, for his hand tightened across hers and he stiffened.

'Your parents and your sister are not here yet. Were they expected to be late?'

'I did not think so.' Her own glance took in the many corners of the room trying to find them. 'Perhaps the journey took longer than they imagined. There has been a lot of rain lately.'

He nodded and led her over to the side of the main room to stand near a pillar that had been decorated in gold ribbon and the leaves of some plant she did not recognise.

Julia Heron came over to her side immediately.

'Papa said to tell you that he would like a word, Lord Winterton, if I was to see you before he did. He is over by the dining table in that far corner. I could wait here with your wife if you wish me to?'

Green eyes skated over her own and she saw in their depths a worry. 'I'll be gone only a moment, Flora. If you stay here?'

'Of course. I shall talk with Julia for we have much to catch up on.' She tried to keep her tone as light as possible, but a dread had wrapped itself around her heart and would not let her go. She squeezed her hands so tightly together that the crescents of her nails began to sting as they dug into the back of her fingers.

'What is it your father wishes to say to my husband, Julia?'

'I think it is a warning. There has been some gossip…' She stopped and smiled tightly. 'But I am sure it is all a misunderstanding and will be resolved forthwith.'

'A misunderstanding?'

'There has been talk that the Viscount may not have a reputation quite as spotless as others believe it to be. Nonsense, of course, and as it only requires a firm denial there will no doubt be a swift ending to any rumour.'

The kidnapping. Florentia knew without a doubt

that this was what Julia spoke of. Had the Urquharts talked? Had their marriage finally been the catalyst that allowed the couple to put together memory and come out with accusation? She looked around to see if she could see Winter and was glad to find his tall form threading its way back through the crowd and towards her.

His face was a mask of indifference and she knew instinctively that he was furious. Still, as he reached her he kissed her hand, all attention and easy smiles.

Deception and deliverance was all in the charade, he had told her once, and he was a man who understood the shifting sands of complicity.

'I hope everything is all right?' Flora tried to match her tone to his. 'For the orchestra should be striking up a waltz soon and I would love to dance.'

He looked at her at that and she knew he understood in her airy conversation that she perceived the truth of what was happening here.

Julia looked relieved. 'The Urquharts are such prattle mongers and such a far-fetched accusation could not possibly be true.'

'Gossip holds a life of its own, Miss Heron.'

'Which is exactly what I said to Percy Urquhart when I saw him the other day. Why on earth would Florentia marry a man who had ruined her? What possible motive would she have for doing that? He did insist that the scar you carry on your neck, Lord Winterton, substantiated the stories he had heard. Some fracas in an inn by all accounts. Papa assured him it was all made-up shilly-shally and that you were at that time busy with army matters.'

Flora felt her husband's hand tighten about her fingers. Together they might weather this if the Urquharts did not make a scene and accuse them directly.

A moment later she knew the futility of such a hope.

'You have a fine sense of the absurd, Winterton, by creeping into the *ton* with your newly earned money after causing such an outcry all those years ago. To kidnap a young lady and throw her into your carriage as you did was reprehensible and lawless. You deserve to be hanged for it. No offence, Lady Florentia, but if he is coercing you in any way now would be the time to admit it.'

His voice boomed out. Not a quiet assassination of character but a very public one. Flora held on to Winter's hand as if it were a lifeline in a rough and dangerous sea.

'I think you are mistaken, Urquhart. Or drunk.' Now Winter's talons were out as well, though his voice was much more quiet than that of Percy Urquhart.

'I can prove it. We were walking with Dan Collins that day and he is here standing beside me. He says it was you, too, and would sign any legal form to swear so.'

Around them other voices were adding to the allegations, a wealthy and respected family of the *ton* like the Urquharts against the dissolute and far more scandalous Wintertons. The taint of new money was undoubtedly in the equation, too, and the *ton* had cut their teeth on the dreadful antics of James Waverley's father.

He was like a wolf surrounded by a pack of yapping hounds, all out to draw blood and make menace. But if she noticed the darkening of his pale green eyes she doubted anyone else would.

Fight or flight. That realisation made her sick for she knew Winter would attack until he could do no more. For her honour. For their family. It was not his name that would keep him fighting, but hers. If he lost this battle she would lose her own protections and she knew he would never allow that.

Another voice suddenly rose across the others and when she turned she saw her father and mother with Maria and Roy pushing through the crowds.

'You are an idiot, Urquhart, and you always were.' Her father's tones were clear. Her family had come to stand beside them now, forming a ring around Winter. 'If there is anyone in all of this world who would know the whelp who tried to kidnap my daughter it would be me. I shot the man in the shoulder. I saw him die right there in front of me, his blood running across the cobblestones in a river and I have been brought to bed with regret ever since. For the taking of a life. A young life, for the man could not have been more than twenty. So do not talk to me of such foolishness, for in the death of Florentia's abductor lay a sorrow for my family that is still new and green. I remember his face as if he were here standing next to me, the dark brown eyes, the light hair, that longish face. The screams of anguish as I dispatched him to hell. No insincere and foolish assertions shall ever take that from me.'

'Perhaps I remember wrongly, Lord Albany.' Collins spoke. 'I, too, think his hair was lighter and his eyes darker. In fact, I am sure of it now.'

The crowd wavered and withdrew, the chatter building of Albany's loss, a high penance for a concerned father. The ground swell of opinion changed and altered. It was suddenly not Winterton and Albany who were at fault here, but the mean-minded and imprudent Urquharts.

Winter felt the change and knew the support of a family who had much reason to hate him. He was overwhelmed by such assistance because it had been seldom in his life that he had ever felt such succour from anyone. Save Florentia.

His wife shimmered beside him in her navy gown, her hair against the darkness of fabric like silk and honey. He had felt her fear and her terror, yet not in one tiny movement had she shown it to anyone. No, she had stood beside him and held his hand as she smiled, unmovable and solid.

With a family like this around him he could do anything.

Roy slapped him across the back as the others chatted. 'You owe the old Earl a drink,' he said quietly.

'I do.'

'Maria told me that I was to bring a knife tonight and if it came to a fight I was to use it on whoever threatened you.'

'You knew of the Urquhart allegations?'

'They have been swirling for a week or more now around the salons of London town according to Frank Reading. I found that out when we arrived yesterday afternoon from Kent.'

'God.'

'It's over. Albany saw to that quite nicely, I think.'

The Earl had come across to him now. 'That is the last of it, Winter. We will never mention any of this again.'

'Thank you.' The shake in his voice was clear, but Florentia's father ignored it as he stopped a footman with a tray of newly poured wine and asked for it to be shared around.

'Let us drink to the future,' he said as they all took a glass. 'To the years ahead. May they be full of laughter, wisdom and wine.'

Winter tipped his head and drank deeply and when he looked over Florentia was doing exactly the same.

'It's finished. The past cannot touch us again.'

'Not after your father's performance. One of the finest actors I have ever seen in a theatre or out of one.'

She laughed. 'He was often in plays before he met Mama. I think it was she who put a stop to it.'

'He was magnificent. Perhaps your own talent as a thespian comes directly from him?'

She felt his feet pull away from underneath Faith's stomach. The puppy had crawled on to the bed the moment they had arrived home and they had no heart to remove her.

'A family is a wondrous thing,' he said softly after another moment, 'for it comes in all forms. A wife who is as beautiful as she is clever. A dog who does not know the meaning of obedience. A father-in-law who looks like an owl and has become an eagle. Maria with her worry. Roy with his knife. Your mother. They were all there today for me, by me, supporting me despite the truth being exactly as they knew it wasn't. Without them…'

'That will never happen. The thing about a family is that for good or for bad you have them for ever.'

'I love you, Florentia. I love you more than life itself.'

She felt him turn and his arms came around her to pull her close. Bodies had eloquence, too, she decided as his strength closed in and she knew without words exactly what it was that he promised.

* * * * *

THE DISSOLUTE
DUKE

I would like to dedicate this book to my sister-in-law, Susie.

Thanks for being a fan.

Chapter One

〜◦⦿◦〜

England—1831

Her brothers would kill her for this.

Lady Lucinda Wellingham knew that they would.
Of all the hare-brained schemes that she had ever
been involved with, this was the most foolish of the
lot. She would be ruined and it would be entirely
her fault.

'Just a kiss,' the man whispered, pressing her
against a wall in the corridor, the smell of strong liquor on his breath. His hands wandered across the
line of her breasts, and in the ridiculously flimsy
dress that she had allowed Posy Tompkins to talk
her into wearing, Lucinda could feel where his next
thoughts lay.

Richard Allenby, third Earl of Halsey, had been
attractive at London society balls, but here at a country party in Bedfordshire he was intolerably cloying.

Pushing him away, she stood up straight, pleased that her height allowed her a good few inches above his own.

'I think, sir, that you have somehow got the wrong idea about my wish to…'

The words were cut off as his lips covered hers, a wet, limp kiss that made her turn her head away quickly before wiping her mouth. Goodness, the man was almost panting and it did not suit him at all.

'You are here at the most infamous party of the Season and my room isn't far.' His fingers closed across her forearm as he hailed two others who looked to have had as much to drink as he had. Both leered at her in the very same way that Halsey was. A mistake. She should have fled moments ago when the chance had been hers and the bedrooms had not been so perilously close. In this den of iniquity it seemed anything went, the morals of the man whose house it was fallen beyond all redemption.

A spike of fear brought her elbow against the wall, loosening Halsey's fingers and allowing a hard-won freedom which she took the chance on and ran.

Twisted and narrow corridors lay before her. There were close to twenty bedchambers on this floor alone and, moving quickly, Lucinda discovered double doors at the very end. With the corners she had taken she was certain those following would not see which door she had chanced upon and without a backward glance she turned an ornate ivory handle and slipped into the room.

It was dark inside save for a candle burning next to the bed, where a man sat reading, thick-rimmed glasses balanced on the end of his nose.

When he looked up she placed one finger to her lips, asking for his silence before turning back to the door. Outside she could hear the noise of those who followed her, the uncertainty of where she was adding to their urgency. Surely they would not dare to try their luck with any number of closed doors? A good few minutes passed, the whispers becoming less audible, and then they were gone, retracing their steps in the quest for the escaped quarry and ruing the loss of a night's entertainment. Relief filled her.

'Can I speak now?' The voice was laconic and deep, an inflection of something on the edge that Lucinda could not understand.

'If you are very quiet, I think it might be safe.' She looked around uncertainly.

A ripe swear word was her only answer and as the sheets were pushed back Lucinda saw the naked form of a man unfold from within them and her mouth gaped open. Not just any man either, but the scandalous host of this weekend's licentiousness: Taylen Ellesmere, the Sixth Duke of Alderworth. The Dissolute Duke, they called him, a rakehell who obeyed no laws of morality with his wanton disregard of any manners and his degenerate ways.

He was wearing absolutely nothing as he ambled across to the door behind her and locked it.

The sound seared into Lucinda's brain, but she found she could not even move a muscle.

He was beautiful. At least he was that, his dark hair falling to his shoulders and eyes the colour of wet leaves after a forest storm at Falder. She did not glance below the line of his neck, though every fibre of her being seemed to want her to. His smile said that he knew her thought, the creases around his eyes falling into humour.

'Lady Lucinda Wellingham?'

He knew her name. She nodded, trying to find her voice. What might happen next? She felt like a chicken in a fox's lair.

'Do your three brothers know that you are here?'

Her shake of the head was tempered by a lack of breath that indicated panic and she could barely take in air. Every single thing had gone wrong since dawn, so when her hands tried to open the stays of her bodice a little she was glad when they gave, allowing breath to come more easily. The deep false cleavage so desired by society women disappeared as the fasteners loosened, her breasts spilling back into their natural and fairly meagre form. The lurid red dress she wore fell away from the rise of her bosom in a particularly suggestive manner and she knew he observed it.

'Choosing my room to hide in might not have been the wisest of options.' He glanced tellingly towards the large bed.

Lucinda ignored the remark altogether. 'Richard

Allenby, the Earl of Halsey, and his friends gave me little other choice, your Grace. I had the need of a safe place.'

At that he laughed, the sound of mirth echoing about the chamber.

'Drink loosens the choking ties of societal pressure. Good manners and foppish decency is something most men cannot tolerate for more than a few weeks upon end and this place allows them to blow off steam, if you will.'

'At the expense of women who are saying no?'

'Most ladies here encourage such behaviour and dress accordingly.'

His eyes ran across the low-cut *décolletage* of her attire before returning to her face.

'This is not London, my lady, and nor does it pretend to be. If Halsey has indeed insulted you, he would have done so because he thought you were... available. Free will is a concept I set great store by here at Alderworth.'

The challenge in his eyes was unrepentant. Indeed, were she to describe his features she would say a measured indolence sat across them, like a lizard playing with a fly whose wings had already been disposed of. Her fingers went back to the door handle, but, looking for the key, she saw it had been removed. A quick sleight of hand. She had not seen him do it.

'As free will is so important to you, I would now

like to exercise my own and ask you to open the door.'

He simply leaned over to a pile of clothes roughly deposited on a chair and hauled out a fob watch.

'Unfortunately it is that strange time of the evening: too early for guests to be properly drunk and therefore harmless and too late to expect the conduct of gentlemen to be above reproach. Any movement through the house at this point is more dangerous than remaining here with me.'

'Remaining in here?' Could he possibly mean what she thought he did?

His eyes lightened. 'I have room.'

'You have known me for two minutes and half of those have been conducted in silence.' She tried to insert as much authority as she could into her announcement.

'All the better to observe your…many charms.' His green eyes were hooded with a sensual and languorous invitation.

'You sound like the wolf from the Grimm brothers' fairy tales, your Grace, though I doubt any character from a nursery rhyme exhibits the flair for nudity that you seem to display.'

Moving back from him, she was pleased when he pulled on a long white shirt, the sleeves billowing into wide folds from the shoulder. A garment a pirate might have worn or a highwayman. It suited him entirely.

'Is that better, my lady?'

When she nodded he smiled and lifted two glasses from a cabinet behind him. 'Perhaps good wine might loosen your inhibitions.'

'It certainly will not.' Her voice sounded strict even to her own ears and her eyes went to the book deposited on the counterpane. 'Machiavelli's *Il Principe* is a surprising choice for a man who seems to have no care for the name of the generations of Ellesmeres who have come before him.'

'You think all miscreants should be illiterate?'

Amazingly she began to laugh, so ridiculous was this conversation. 'Well, they are not usually tucked up in bed at ten o'clock wearing nothing but a pair of strong spectacles and reading a book of political philosophy in Italian, your Grace.'

'Believe me, degeneracy has a certain exhausting quality to it. The expectations for even greater acts of debauchery can be rather wearisome when age creeps up on one.'

'How old are you?'

'Twenty-five. But I have been at it for a while.'

He was only a year older than she was and her few public scrapes had always been torturous. Still he was a man, she reasoned, though the double standards of behaviour excusing his sex did not even come close to exonerating his numerous and shocking depravities.

'Did your mother not teach you the basics of human kindness to others, your Grace?'

'Oh, indeed she did. One husband and six lovers

later I understood it exactly. I was her only child, you see, and a very fast learner.'

She had heard the sordid story of the Ellesmere family many times, but not from the angle of a disenchanted son. Patricia Ellesmere had died far from her kin. There were those who said a broken heart had caused her death, but six lovers sounded particularly messy.

'What happened to your father?' She knew she should not have asked, but interest overcame any sense of reticence.

'He did what any self-respecting Duke might have done on discovering that his wife had cuckolded him six times over.'

'He killed himself?'

He laughed. 'No. He gambled away his fortune and then lost his woes in strong brandy. My parents died within a day of the other, at different ends of the country, and in the company of their newest lovers. Liver failure and a self-inflicted shot through the head. At least it made the funeral sum less expensive. Two for the price of one cuts the costs considerably.' His lips curled around the words and his green eyes were sharp. 'I was eleven at the time.'

Such candour was astonishing. No one had ever spoken to her like this before, a lack of apology in every new and dreadful thing he uttered.

Her own problems paled into insignificance at the magnitude of his and she could only be thankful for her close and supportive family ties.

'You had other relatives…to help you?'

'Mary Shields, my grandmother, took me in.'

'Lady Shields?' My God, who in society did not know of her proclivity for gossip and meanness? She had been dead for three years now, but Lucinda still remembered her beady black eyes and her vitriolic proclamations. And this was the woman whom an orphan child had been dispatched to?

'I see by your expression that you knew her?' He upended his tumbler and poured himself another. A generous another.

He wore rings on every finger on his left hand, she noticed, garish rings save for the band on his middle finger which was embellished with an engraving. She could not quite make out the letters.

A woman, no doubt. He was rumoured to have had many a lover, old and young, large and thin, married and unmarried. *He does not make distinction when appetite pounces.* She remembered hearing a rumour saying exactly that as it swirled around in society—a diverting scandal with the main player showing no sense of remorse.

The Duke of Alderworth. She knew that most of the ladies in society watched him, many a beating heart hoping that she might be the one to change him, but with his having reached twenty-five Lucinda doubted he would reform for anyone.

Foolish fancies were the prerogative of inexperienced girls. As the youngest sister of three rambunctious and larger-than-life brothers she found herself

immune to the wiles of the opposite sex and seldom
entertained any romantic notions about them.

Surprisingly, the lengthening silence between
them was not awkward. That astonishing fact was
made even more so by the thought that had he pushed
himself upon her like Richard Allenby, the Earl of
Halsey, she might have been quite pleased to see the
result. But he did not advance on her in any way.
Outside the screams of delight permeated this end
of the corridor again, women's laughing shouts min-
gled with the deeper tone of their drunken pursuers.
A hunting horn also blasted close, the loudness of it
making her jump.

'A successful night, by the sounds. The hunters
and the hunted in the pursuit of ecstasy. Soon enough
there will be the silence of the damned.' He watched
her carefully.

'I think you are baiting me, your Grace. I do not
think you can be half as bad as they say you are.'

His expression changed completely.

'In that you would be very wrong, Lady Lucinda,
for I am all that they say of me and more.' A new
danger cloaked him, a hard implacability in his eyes
that made him look older. 'The fact is that I could
have you in my bed in a trice and you would be
begging me not to stop doing any of the tantalising
things to your body that I might want to.'

The pure punch of his words had her heart pounding fast, because in such a boast lay a good measure
of truth. She was more aware of him as a man than

she had ever been of any other. Horrified, Lucinda turned to the window and made much of looking out into the gardens, lit tonight by a number of burning torches positioned along various pathways. Two lovers lay entwined amidst the bushes, bare skin pale in the light. Around them other couples lingered, their intentions visible even from this distance. The intemperance of it all shocked her to the core.

'If you touch me, my brothers would kill you, most probably.' She attempted to keep fear from the threat and failed.

He laughed. 'They could try, I suppose, but…' The rest was left unsaid, but the menace in him was magnified. The indolence that she imagined before was now honed into cold hard steel, a man who existed in the underbelly of London's society even though he was high born. The contradictions in him confused her, the quicksilver change unnerving.

'I came to the party with Lady Posy Tompkins and she assured me that it was a respectable affair. Obviously she and I share a completely different idea of the word "respectable" and I suppose I should have made more of asking exactly where we were going before I said yes, but she was most insistent about the fun we might have and the fact that her godmother was coming made it sound more than respectable…'

He stopped her by laying his finger across the movement of her mouth. 'Do you always talk so much, Lady Lucinda?'

Her whole body jerked in response to the touch. 'I

do, your Grace, because when I am nervous I seem to be unable to stop although I don't quite remember another occasion when I have been as nervous as I am right at this moment, so if you were to let me walk from this room this instant I should go gladly and find—'

His mouth came to the place where his finger had lingered, and Lucinda's world dissolved into hot colourful fragments of itself, tipping any sense of reality on its head and replacing ordinariness with a dangerous molten pleasure.

Chapter Two

Tay just wanted her to stop talking, the edge of panic in her voice bringing forth a guilt that he hadn't felt for years. The slight curve of her breasts fitted into his chest and he liked the softness. Usually he had to bend down to women, but this one stood only a few inches below him, her thinness accentuating her willowy figure in an almost boyish way.

Her nails were short and the calluses between her second and third fingers told him she was left handed and that she participated in some sort of sport. Archery, perhaps. The thought of her standing, aiming at a target and her blonde hair lifting in the breeze was strangely arousing. He should, of course, escort her from Alderworth post-haste and make certain that she was delivered home safely into the bosom of her family.

But he knew that he would not, and when he took her mouth against his, another feeling surfaced which he refused to dwell on altogether.

He did not imagine she had been kissed much before because her full lips were held in a tight line and, as he opened her mouth with his tongue, her eyes widened.

Eyes of pale blue etched with a darker shade— eyes a man could lose himself in completely and never recover from.

Softening his assault, he threaded his hands through her hair, tilting her face. This time he did not hurry or demand more as the heat of a slow burn built. God, she smelt so good, like the flowers in an early springtime, fresh and clean. He had become so used to the heady over-ripe perfumes of his many experienced *amours* that he had forgotten the difference.

Innocence. It smelt strangely like hope.

Sealing his mouth across hers, he brought his fingers behind her nape. Closer. Warmer.

The power of connection winded him, the first tentative exploration of her tongue poignant in a way that made him melancholy. It had been a long time since he had kissed a woman who watched him as if he might unlock the secrets of the universe.

Lust ignited, an incendiary living torch of need burning bright, like the wick of gunpowder snaking down through his being. Unstoppable.

'Are you a virgin?'

He knew she was by the way she was breathing, barely enough air to fill her up, lost in the moment and her lips parted. 'Yes.'

'Why the hell did you come to this party, then?'
The layer of civilisation that he had tried to keep in
place was gone with the feel of her, but there was
no withdrawal as he asked the question. Rather she
pressed in closer and shut her eyes, as though trying
in the darkness to find an answer. He felt the feath-
ery waft of her breath in the sensitive folds of his
neck and wondered if she was quite as innocent as
he presumed. If this was a game she played, then it
was one that he had long been practised in and she
would need to be careful. His hands went around her
back of their own accord, like a pathway memorised.

Salvation.

The word came unbidden and blossomed into
something that he could not deny and his pulse began
to quicken. It had been years since he had felt like
this with any woman and surprise spurred him onwards.

He twisted her and his mouth fell lower, laving
at the skin at her neck, his attention bringing whorls
of redness to the pale. Her breath matched his own
now, neither quiet nor measured, for the power of
the body had taken over and his thumb caressed the
budding hardness of one nipple through crimson silk.

She arched back, thighs locked tight, her breasts
twin beacons of temptation.

He wanted her as he had never wanted another
in all his life, the feel of her, the softness, her hair
light-spun gold against his dark. With a small motion he had her bodice loosened and his palm around

the bounty of one breast, cupping flesh, stroking the firmness. He needed her devoid of clothing, wanting pure knowledge without a covering. If she had not been the lady he knew she was, he would have simply ripped the garment off from neckline to hemline, and transported her naked to his bed to take his fill. His mouth ached for the intimacy of her curves.

'The taste of a lover is part of the attraction,' he stated simply as he raised his head, watching as understanding dawned. Uncertainty chased on the heels of wariness, but still she did not pull away as he thought she might. Only a slight frown marred her brow, measuring intent without any fear whatsoever. A guileless allowance.

Such an emotion was something he had rarely experienced. His reputation had protected him, he supposed, and kept others at a distance. But Lucinda Wellingham was different and more dangerous than all of the sirens who had stalked him across so many years. The connection between them was unexpected and startling as it drew him in, his body tightening in the echo of an old knowledge. His head dipped and he brought one soft peak into his mouth, the force of the action ripping stretched red silk and the seam shirring into uncountable and damaged threads. He liked the way she arched into him, her fingers combing through his hair, nails hard-edged with want, taking his offering and giving him back her own.

His hands now moved from the rise of her bottom around the front to feel for the hidden folds of womanhood, the silk only a thin barrier to taking. He pressed in to find her centre.

'No.' A single word, moaned more than stated, but enough.

'No?' He had to make certain that that was what she had meant, his breath coming thick with need. She shook her head this time, sky-blue eyes devoid of everything, a frown on her forehead and her chest rising and falling.

No, because she could not envisage what a yes might mean? No, because he was a man with enough of a reputation to destroy her?

Breaking away he moved back, the anger in him mounting with a pounding awareness of guilt. The road to ruin was a short one and he knew a lady of her ilk would have no possible defence against his persuasions. Suddenly his own chosen life path seemed seedy and vulgar.

'I will take you home.'

She did not repair the damage to her dress as she watched him so that one breast stood out naked from the loosened fabric, a pink-rosebud nipple beckoning against scarlet silk. With her glassy eyes and stillness she was like a sensual and pliant Madonna fallen from heaven to land at the feet of the devil. Indecision welled, but he had no shield against such goodness, no way to safeguard his yearning against her righteousness.

Stepping forwards, he readjusted her gown, retying the laces on the flimsy bodice so that some measure of decency was reinstated. He could do nothing to repair the ruined seam and his eyes were drawn to the show of flesh that curved outwards beneath it, calling for his attentions. Swearing, he took a blanket from his bed and laid it around her, the wool almost the same shade as her hair. Then he collected his clothes, pulling on his breeches and placing a jacket over the shirt. He did not stop for a cravat. His boots were shoved on stockingless feet at the door as he retrieved the key and unlocked it.

'Come, sweetheart,' he murmured and found her hand, liking the way her slender fingers curled around his own.

Trust.

Another barrier breached. He yearned for others.

Outside it was quiet and, as the stables materialised before them, a lad came to his side.

'Ye'd be wanting the carriage at this time of the night, your Grace?' Disbelief was evident in the query. Normally conveyances were not sent for until well into the noon hours of the next day. Or the one after that.

'Indeed. Find Stephens and have it readied. I need to go to London.'

When the boy left them Lucinda Wellingham began to speak, her voice low and uncertain. 'My cloak is still in the house and my hat and reticule. Should I not get them?'

'No.' Tay wanted only to be gone. He had no idea

who would talk about her appearance at one of the most infamous and least salubrious parties of the Season, but if he had her home at the Wellingham town house before the morning surely her brothers would be able to fashion a story which would dispel all rumour.

'My friend Posy Tompkins might wonder what has happened to me. I hope that she is safe.' She did not meet his eyes at all, a contrite Venus who had tripped into the underworld unbidden and now only wanted to be released from it.

'Safe?' He could not help laughing, though the sound was anything but humorous. 'No one at my parties is safe. It is generally their singular intention not to be.'

'Enjoying herself, then?' she countered without missing a beat, the damn dimples in her cheeks another timely reminder of her innate goodness.

'Oh, I can almost swear that she will be that. The thrall of a good orgasm is highly conducive to contentment.'

Silence reigned, but he had to let her know. Who he was. What he was. Her muteness heartened him.

'I am not safe, Lady Lucinda, and neither am I repentant. When you came to Alderworth dressed in the sort of gown that raises dark fantasies in the minds of any red-blooded man, surely you understood at least that?'

Tears glittered and Tay swore, causing more again to pool beneath the light of the lamp.

'Lord knows, you are far too sweet for a sinner like me and tomorrow you will realise exactly just how close to ruin you were and be thankful that I took you home, no matter the loss of a few possessions.'

Asher, Taris and Cristo would not have called her sweet. Not in a million years. She was a failure and a liability to the Wellingham name and she always had been. That was the trouble. She was 'intrinsically flawed'. The gypsy who had read her palm in a stall outside the Leadenhall Market had looked directly into her eyes and told her so.

Intrinsically flawed.

And she was. Tonight was living proof of the ridiculous things she did, without thought for responsibility or consequence. With a little less luck she could have been in the Duke of Alderworth's bed right now, knees up around his bare and muscled thighs and knowing what a great many of the less principled women of English society already did. It was only his good sense that had stopped her, for she had been far beyond putting a halt to anything. With just a little persuasion she would have followed him to his bed in the candlelight. Shame coated her, the thick ignominy making her feel ill. Such a narrow escape.

An older man came towards them, carrying a light, and behind him again a whole plethora of busy servants. Lucinda did not meet their eyes as they observed her, plastering a look on her face that might pass for indifference. Goodness, how she hoped that there was none amongst these servants of Alderworth who might have a channel of communication into the empire of the Wellinghams.

At her side Alderworth made her feel both excited and nervous, his heat calling her to him in a way that scorched sense. When his arm came against her own she did not pull away, the feel of him exciting and forbidden before he moved back. She took in one deep breath and then let it out slowly, trying to find logic and reason and failing.

His gaze swept across her with all the intensity of a ranging and predatory tiger.

Within moments the conveyance was ready to leave, the lamps lit and the driver in place. Without touching her Taylen Ellesmere indicated that she climb up and when she sat on a plush leather seat, he chose the opposite side to rest on, his green eyes brittle.

'It will take us four hours to reach Mayfair. If you are still cold...?'

'No, I am fine.' She pulled the blanket further about her, liking the shelter.

'Good.' Short and harsh.

Glancing out of the window, she saw in the faded reflection her stricken and uncertain face.

What did the Duke of Alderworth make of her? Was he as irritated by her uncertainty as he was with her intemperance? She could sense he wanted her gone just as soon as he could get her there, a woman who had strayed unbidden into a place she had no reason to be in; a woman who did not play the games that he was so infamous for.

Why he should hoist himself into the carriage in the first place was a mystery. He looked like a man who would wish to be anywhere but opposite her in a small moving space.

It was the kiss, probably, and the fact that she did not know quite how to kiss a man back. Her denial of anything more between them would have also rankled, an innocent who had played with fire and had burnt them both because of it. Granted, two or three forward beaux had planted their lips on her mouth across the years, but the offerings had always been chaste and tepid and nothing like…

No, she would not think about that. Taylen Ellesmere was a fast-living and dissolute rake who would be far from attracted to the daughter of one of London's most respectable families. He had all the women he wanted, after all, loose women, beautiful women, and she had heard it said time after time that he did not wish to be shackled by the permanency of marriage.

She shook her head hard and listened to what he was saying now.

'I shall deny that you were at Alderworth tonight should I be questioned about it. Instruct your brothers to do the same.'

'They might not need to know anything if I am lucky...'

'It is my experience that scandal does not exist in the same breath as luck, Lucinda.'

A strange warmth infused her as he said her name. She had never really liked 'Lucinda' much, but when he pronounced it he made it sound...sensual. The timbre of some other promise lay on the edge of his words.

'Believe me, with good management any damage can be minimised.'

Damage. Reality flared. She was only a situation to be managed. The night crawled in about them, small shafts of moonlight illuminating the interior of the coach. Outside the rain had begun to fall heavily, a sudden shower in a windless night.

Taylen Ellesmere was exactly like her brothers, a man who liked control and power over everything about him. No surprises or unwanted quandaries. The thought made her frown.

'I do not envisage problems,' he said. 'If you play your part well, there should not be—'

A shout split the air, and then the carriage simply rolled to one side further and further, the wild scrunch of metal upon wood and a jerking lurch.

Leaping over beside her, the Duke braced her in his arms, protecting her from the splintering glass as it shattered inwards, a cushion against the rocking chaos and the rush of cold air. He held her so tightly she felt the punching hardness of metal on his body, drawing blood and making him grimace.

Then there was only darkness.

Lucinda was in her own room at Falder House in Mayfair, the curtains billowing in a quiet afternoon breeze, the sounds of the wind in the trees and further off in the park the voices of children calling.

Everything exactly normal save for her three sisters-in-law dressed in sombre shades and sitting in a row of chairs watching her.

'You are awake?'

Beatrice-Maude came forwards and lifted Lucinda's head carefully before offering a sip of cold lemonade that sat in a glass on the bedside table. 'The doctor said he thought you would return to us today and he was right.' She smiled as she carefully blotted any trace of moisture from Lucinda's lips. 'How do you feel?'

'How should I feel?'

Something was not right. Some quiet and creeping thing was being hidden from her, crouched in the shadows of truth.

'Why am I here? What happened?'

'You don't remember?' Emerald now joined Beatrice-Maude and her face was solemn. 'You don't remember an accident, Lucy?'

'Where?' Panic had begun to consume her and she tried to sit up, but nothing seemed to work, her arms, her legs, her back. All numb and useless. The feel of her heart pumping in her chest was the only thing that still functioned and she felt light headed at the fear of paralysis.

'I cannot move.'

'Doctor Cameron said that was a normal thing. He said many people regain the use of their bodies after the swelling has subsided.'

'Swelling?'

'You suffered a blow to the neck and a nasty bang on the head. It was lucky that the coach to Leicester was passing by the other way, because otherwise...'

'You could have been there all night and Doctor Cameron said you may not have lived.' Eleanor, her youngest brother's wife, had joined in now, but unlike the others her voice shook and her face was blotchy. She had been crying. A lot.

This realisation frightened Lucinda more than anything else had.

'How did it happen?'

'Your carriage overturned. There was a corner, it seems, and the vehicle was moving too fast. It plummeted down a hill a good many yards and came to rest at the bottom of the incline.'

Agitation made her shake as more and more words tumbled into the chasm of blankness her brain had become.

Beatrice took over, holding her hand tightly, and managing a forced smile. 'It is over now, sweetheart. You are home and you are safe and that is all that is important.'

'How did I get here?'

'Asher brought you back three days ago.'

Lucinda swallowed. Three days. Her mind tried its hardest to find any recollection of the passage of time and failed.

And now she was cast upon this bed as a figure of stone, her head and heart the only parts of her body that she could still feel. A tear leaked its way from her left eye and fell warm down her cheek into the line of her hair. Swallowing, her throat thick and raw, she had the taste of blood on her tongue.

Screaming. A flash of sound came back through the ether. *Screaming and screaming. Her voice and another calming her. Quiet and sad, warm hands holding her neck so that she did not move, the night air cold and wet and the rain joining blood.*

'Doctor Cameron said it was a miracle you did not move another inch as you would have been dead. He says it was fortunate that when they found you, your head had been stabilised between two heavy planks of wood to restrain any motion.'

'Lucky,' she countered, the sentiment falling into question.

They were not telling her the whole of it. She could see it in the shared looks and feel it in the hushed unspoken reticence. She wondered why her brothers were not here in the room and knew the answer to the question as soon as she thought it.

They would not be able to hide things from her as

easily as her sisters-in-law, although Cristo was still most efficient at keeping his own council.

'Was anyone else hurt?'

The hesitation told her there had been.

'There was a man in the carriage with you, Lucy.' Emerald now took her other hand, rubbing at it in a way that was supposed to be comforting, she supposed, though it felt vaguely annoying because her skin was so numb.

'I was alone with him?' Nothing made sense. What could she have been doing on the open road at night and in the company of a stranger? It was all too odd. 'Who was he?'

'The sixth Duke of Alderworth.' Beatrice took up the story now.

'Alderworth?' Lucinda knew the name despite not remembering anything at all about the accident.

My God. The Dissolute Duke was infamous across London and it seemed he kept to the company of whores and harpies almost exclusively. Why would she have been there alone with him and so far from home?

'Does Asher know he was there?' She looked up at Emerald.

'Unfortunately he does.'

'Do other people also know?'

'Unfortunately they do.'

'How many know?'

'All of London would not be putting too fine a point on it, I think.'

'I see. It is a scandal then and I am ruined?'

'No.' Beatrice-Maude's voice was strong. 'Your brothers would never allow that to happen and neither will we.'

Lucinda swallowed, the whole conundrum more than she could deal with. Eleanor and Emerald watched her with a certain worry in their eyes and even Beatrice, who was seldom flustered, seemed out of sorts.

Intrinsically flawed. The words came from nowhere as she closed her eyes and slept.

Chapter Three

Tay Ellesmere sat in the library of the Carisbrook family town house in Mayfair and looked at the three Wellingham brothers opposite him.

His head ached, his right leg was swollen above the knee and the top of his left arm was encased in a heavy white bandage, as were his ribs, strapped tightly so that breathing was not quite so agonising. Besides this he had myriad other cuts and grazes from the glass and wood splintering as the carriage had overturned.

But these injuries were the very least of his worries. A far more pressing matter lingered in the air between him and his hosts.

'You were dressed most inappropriately and Lucinda was barely dressed at all, for God's sake. The scandal is the talk of the town and has been for the past week.'

Asher Wellingham, Duke of Carisbrook, seldom minced words and Tay did not dissemble, either.

'Our lack of clothing was the result of being thrown over and over down a hill in a somersaulting carriage. One does not generally emerge from such a mishap faultlessly attired,' he drawled the reply, knowing that it would annoy them, but short of verifying their sister's presence at his party he could do little else but blame the accident.

'We thought Lucinda had gone with Lady Posy Tompkins to her aunt's country home for the weekend. I cannot for the life of me imagine how instead she ended up alone in the middle of the night with the most dissolute Duke in all of London town and dressed as a harpy.'

'Did you ask her?'

'She can remember nothing.' Taris Wellingham broke in now, his stillness as menacing as his older brother's fury.

'Nothing?'

'Nothing before the accident, nothing during the accident and nothing just after the accident.'

Hope flared. Perhaps it might give him an escape after all. If the lady was not baying for his blood, then her brothers might also give up the chase should he play his cards well.

'Your sister informed me that she was trying to reach the Wellingham town house after being separated somehow from her friend. She merely asked me to give her a lift home and I immediately assented.'

'Her reticule, hat and cloak were returned to us from your country seat. A coincidence, would you not say, to be left at the very place you swear she was not.'

Cristo Wellingham's voice sounded as flat as his brothers'.

'Richard Allenby, the Earl of Halsey, has also told half of London that she was a guest at your weekend soirée. Others verify his story.'

'He lies. I was the host and your sister was not there.'

'The problem is, Duke, Lucinda is facing certain ruin and you do not seem to be taking your part in her downfall seriously.'

Taylen had had enough.

'Ruin is a strong word, Lord Taris.'

'As strong as retribution.'

Asher Wellingham's hand hit the table and Tay stood. Even with his arm in a bandage he could give the three of them a good run for their money. The art of gentlemanly fighting had been a lesson missing from his life, the tough school of displacement and abuse honing the rudiments of the craft instead. Hell, he had been beaten enough himself to understand exactly the best places to hit back.

'We will kill you for this, Alderworth, I swear that we will.' Cristo spoke now, the sound of each word carefully enunciated.

'And in doing so you may well crucify your sister. Better to let the matter rest, laugh it off and kick any suggestions of misbehaviour back in the face of those who swear them true.'

'As you are apt to do?'

'English society still holds to ridiculously strict rules of conduct, though free speech is finding its way into the minds of men who would do better to believe in it.'

'Men like you?' Taris stood. His reported lack of sight was not apparent as he stepped towards the window, though Tay saw the oldest brother watch him carefully.

Care.

The word reverberated inside him. This was what this was all about, after all: care of each other, care of a family name, care in protecting their only sister's reputation from the ignominy of being linked with his.

Protection was something he himself had never had. Not from his parents. Not from his grandmother. And particularly not from his uncle. It had always been him against a world that hadn't taken the time to make sure that a small child was cherished. The man he had become was the result of such negligence, though here in the salon of a family that watched each other's backs the thought was disheartening.

He made his way around a generous sofa. 'I have an errand to attend to, gentlemen, and I find I have the need of some fresh air. If you will excuse me.'

* * *

'What do you make of him?'

Asher asked the question a few moments later as Cristo crossed to the cabinet to pull out a bottle of fine French brandy.

'He's hiding something.' Taris accepted a drink from his brother. 'For some reason he is trying to make us believe there was only necessity in our sister's foolish midnight tryst in the carriage with him and that she was never at Alderworth.'

Cristo swore. 'But why would he do that?'

'Even a reprobate must have his limits of depravity, I suppose. Lucinda's innocence may well be his.' Taris drank deeply of the brandy before continuing. 'He studies the philosophy of the new consciousness, which is interesting, the tenets of free speech being mooted in the Americas. Unusual reading for a man who purports to be interested in nothing more than sexual mayhem and societal anarchy.'

'I don't trust him.' Asher upended his glass.

'Well, we can't hit a man wrapped in bandages.' Cristo smiled.

'Then we wait until they are removed.' There was no humour at all in the voice of Asher Wellingham, Duke of Carisbrook.

Lucinda wheeled herself to the breakfast table, her muscles straining against the task and her heart pounding with the effort. It had been almost two weeks since the accident and the feeling that the doctor had sworn she would recover was finally coming back, though she had been left with a weakness that felt exhausting and a strange and haunting melancholy. Now she could walk for short distances without falling over, the shaking she had been plagued by diminishing as she grew steadily in strength. The wheelchair was, however, still her main mode of getting about.

Posy had spent much of the past week at the town house, her horror at all that had happened to Lucy threading every sentence.

'I should never have taken you to Alderworth, Luce. It is all my fault this happened to you and now…now I don't know how to make it better.' Large tears had fallen down her cheeks before tracing wet runnels on the pink silk of her bodice.

'You did not force me to go, Posy. I remember that much.'

'But while I was safely locked away in our bedroom, you were…'

'Let's not allocate any more blame. What is done is done and at least I am regaining movement and energy.'

It had taken Lucinda a good few days to convince her friend that she held no malice or blame, Posy's numerous tears a wearying and frustrating constant.

Asher was sitting in the dining room, reading *The Times* just as he usually did each morning, and he folded the paper in half and looked closer as something caught his interest.

'It says here that the Earl of Halsey has suffered a broken nose, a black eye and twenty stitches in his cheek. The assault happened in broad daylight four days ago in an altercation outside the livery stables in Davies Mews right here in Mayfair. There were no witnesses.'

His glance strayed to Lucinda's to see how she might react. The whole family had tiptoed around her since the *unfortunate happening* as though she might break into pieces at any unwanted reminder of scandal and she was tired of it. Consequently she did nothing more than smile back at her oldest brother and shrug her shoulders.

'Footpads are becoming increasingly confident, then.' Emerald took up the conversation as she buttered her bread. 'Though perhaps they do us a favour, for isn't he the man who has constantly insisted Lucinda was underdressed at the Alderworth fiasco? Without his voice, all of this could have been so much easier to deal with.'

Lucinda knew Richard Allenby, of course. He had always been well mannered and rather sweet, truth be told, so she had no idea why he should be maligning her now and in such a fashion. Yet a shadow lingered there in the very back of her mind, some nebulous and half-formed thing trying to escape from the darkness. Wiping her mouth with the napkin, she sat back, the food suddenly dry in her mouth and difficult to swallow.

'You look like you have seen a ghost, Lucy.'

'What exactly was it that the Earl of Halsey said of me?'

'He has been spreading the rumour that you may have been intimate with Alderworth at his home. He says he saw you in the corridors on the first floor of the place, searching for the host's bedchamber.'

Her brother's tone had that streak of exasperation she so often heard when speaking of her escapades, though in this case Lucinda could well understand it.

'Intimate?' The shock of such a blatant falsehood was horrifying. 'Why would he tell such a lie? Surely people could not believe him?' Wriggling her foot against the metal bar of the wheelchair, she checked for any further movement. Over the past few days the tingling had gone from her knees to her feet as the numbness receded.

'Unfortunately they are beginning to.' Asher's voice no longer held any measure of care.

'What does Alderworth say?'

'Nothing and that is the great problem. If he denied everything categorically and strode into society the same way he strode into Wellingham House, people might cease to believe Richard Allenby. But instead the man has disappeared to the country, leaving chaos behind him.'

'Alderworth came here? To the town house?' Lucinda frowned. There was something about him that was familiar, some part of him that she remembered from...before. 'What did he want?'

'Put bluntly, he wanted to be rid of any blame

as far as your reputation was concerned. He made that point very plain.' Asher put his paper down and watched her closely. 'The man is a charlatan, but he is also clever. The slight whiff of an alliance with us might be profitable to him.'

'Alliance?' Lucinda's mouth felt suddenly dry.

'A ruined reputation requires measures that may be stringent and far from temporary.'

'You mean a betrothal?' Horror had Lucinda's words whispered. Low. She had heard all the stories of the wicked Duke. Everybody had. He was a man who lived by his own rules and threw the caution most others followed to the wind.

As her heartbeat quickened, memory fought against haze and won. Dropping the teacup she was holding, she stood, liquid spilling across the pristine whiteness of an antique damask tablecloth, the brown stain widening through the embossed stitching even as she watched.

The naked form of Taylen Ellesmere came through the fog, unfolding from a rumpled bed, each long and graceful line etched in candlelight, the red wine in a decanter beside him almost gone. She knew the feel of his skin, undeniably, for they had been joined together pressed in lust, his velvet-green eyes close as he had leaned down and kissed her. No simple chaste kiss, either, but one with a smouldering and virtue-taking force.

Shock kept her still, as she looked directly at her oldest brother.

'What is wrong? You look…ill.' Real concern crossed his face.

'I am remembering things and I th-th-think everything Richard Halsey is saying of m-me might indeed be tr-true.'

Her weakened legs folded beneath her just as Asher caught her, the hard arm of the chair slamming into her side.

'You are saying you lay with Alderworth. Unmarried.'

'He was naked in his bedchamber. He touched me everywhere. The door was locked and I could not leave. I tried to, but I could not. He took the key. He was not safe.' A torrent of small truths, each one worse than the last.

'My God.' She had never heard the note in her brother's voice that she did now, not once in all her many escapades and follies. His fractured tone brought tears to her eyes as she felt Emerald's hand slip into her own and squeeze.

'You will marry my sister as soon as I can procure a special licence and then you will disappear from England altogether, you swine.'

Asher Wellingham had already laid a good few punches across Tay's face and Cristo Wellingham was still holding him down. Not the refined manners he had imagined them to have, after all, each blow given with a deliberate and clinical precision. His nose streamed with blood and he could barely see out of his left eye. The two front teeth at the bottom of his mouth were loosened.

'If you kill me…a betrothal might be…difficult.'

Another blow caught him in the kidneys and, despite meaning not to, he winced.

'You will tell Lucinda that it was completely your fault she was at Alderworth in the first place and that your heinous, iniquitous and pernicious sense of social virtue was lost years before you met her. In effect, you will say that she never had the chance of escaping such corruption.'

'C-comprehensive.'

'Very. But as long as you understand us we will allow you to at least take breath into another day whilst we try to mitigate all the wrong you have heaped upon our sister. She is distraught, as you can well imagine, and names you as the most loathsome of all men. A reprobate who took advantage of her when she was drunk.'

'She told you that?'

'And worse. But although she might hate you, she also knows that you are the only man who can restore her shattered name in society when you marry her. In that she is most adamant.'

'A sterling quality in a bride.' Even to his own ears his voice lacked the sting of irony he usually made an art form of.

'Well, you can laugh, Alderworth, but if you believe we will let you anywhere near Lucinda after the ceremony is performed then you have another think coming. You have already done your damage. Now you will pay for it.'

Tay coughed once and then again, his breath difficult to catch. When the younger brother allowed him to drop heavily to the floor he felt the arm that had been hurt in the carriage accident crack against hard parquet, pain radiating up into the shoulder socket.

Ignominiously he began to shake and he swore. It had been a long time since he remembered doing that, his uncle's face screwed up above him in the wrath of some perceived and tiny insult, the summer winds of Alderworth hot against the wounds that lashed his back. Bleeding, everywhere. No mercy in the beating.

Standing uncertainly and holding on to the edge of a chair, he raised himself before them. 'Your sister's memory is faulty. I did not touch her.'

'She says exactly the opposite, and anybody who knows Lucinda knows, too, that straightforward honesty is one of her greatest strengths.' The embossed ducal ring on Carisbrook's finger caught the light as he moved forwards. 'Frankly, given the number of your dubious guests who have not ceased gossiping since the accident about what went on at Alderworth, I find your whining and feeble excuses insulting. A man worth his salt would simply own up to his mistakes and take the punishment he deserves.'

From experience Tay knew when to stop baiting a man who would hit him until life was leached from truth. He nodded an end to the dispute and saw the answering relief on Asher Wellingham's face.

'We will pay you to leave a week after the wedding. A considerable sum that should see you well on your way to your next destination. After that, you will never again set foot anywhere near London or our family.'

'Alderworth is almost bankrupt. Your father's debts were numerous and you will not have enough equity to continue the repayments after the year's end.' Taris had taken up the reins now, from a sofa near the fireplace, his voice steady and quiet. 'You have been trying to trade your way out of the conundrum, but your bills are becoming onerous and a lifestyle of indolence is hardly a profitable one. Accept our offer and you might keep your family inheritance for a few years yet. Decline and you will be in the debtors' prison by Christmas.'

'Will your sister know?'

'Indeed. Lucinda wants it.' Cristo stepped forwards, disdain in his eyes. 'She wants you out of her life for ever.'

Marriage as a bribe to keep the Alderworth estate. Tay thought of its roofline under the Bedfordshire sky, the golden stone against the sun and hundreds of acres of fertile and green land at its feet. His father had forsaken the place, but he could not. Not even if the alternative meant selling his soul.

'Very well.' His voice was hoarse and he felt his honour breaking, but he swiped the feeling away as a quill was inked and a parchment made ready. He was the only Alderworth who could save four hundred years of history and Lucinda Wellingham hated his very guts.

Chapter Four

Lord Taylen Ellesmere, the sixth Duke of Alderworth, had the appearance of a man who had been in a particularly rough boxing match when Lucinda saw him for the first time at the top of the aisle in the small chapel in London's Mayfair.

He did not turn to look at her, his profile granite-hard, his left wrist encased in a bandage and a large cut running along the whole side of his jaw. The muscles beneath the wound rippled with anger, a barely held wrath that was seen in the straightness of his posture and in the rigidity of his being. His hair was shorter, shaved almost to the skull, a single white, opaque scar snaking from the edge of his right ear to his crown. One eye was blackened.

Even Asher looked slightly taken aback by his appearance, but at this stage of the proceedings there was little anyone could do.

The die was cast after all. She would marry the

Duke of Alderworth to redeem her place in society
and he would marry her because her brothers had
made him do so. She had sinned and this was the
result. Love existed nowhere in the equation and the
empty pews in the chapel reflected the fact. Her siblings and their wives sat on her side of the church,
as well as some close friends, but on his side…there
was nobody.

Lucinda speculated as to who might stand up as
his witness, the question answered a moment later
when Cristo moved across to him. Her youngest
brother looked about as unhappy with the whole
thing as Asher was, a duty performed out of necessity rather than respect.

Every other Wellingham wedding had been a joyous affair, celebrated with laughter and noise and
elation. This one was sombre, quiet and dismal. She
wondered how long the Duke of Alderworth would
stay in London after the ceremony and just what
words she might use to explain away his absence.
Asher had said that he would remain in the capital for
a week or more, so that appearances could be upheld.
After that they would be glad to see the back of him.

Her brother had breathed this through a clenched
jaw as if even a day in the company of her soon-to-
be husband would be one too many.

Lucinda swallowed away dry fear. This was the
worst mistake she had ever made, but the consequences of her own stupidity had brought her to such
a pass, her whole family entwined in the deceit. She

wanted to throw down the bouquet of white roses interlaced with fragrant gardenias and peel off the ivory gown that had been quickly fashioned by one of London's up-and-coming modistes. The veil helped, however, a layer of lace between her and the world, sheltering confusion. A week ago she would not have been able to walk or to stand for such long periods, but today the utter alarm of everything allowed her to keep any pain at bay.

Posy Tompkins stood to one side of her, her face drawn. Her friend had been nothing short of horrified about the consequences of their ill-thought-out visit to Alderworth and had been attentive and apologetic ever since. She claimed she had managed to avoid the worst of the excesses by locking herself in her room.

'Are you sure you want to go through with this, Luce?' she whispered. 'We could disappear to Europe together otherwise. I have more than enough money for us both. We could go to Rome or Paris to my relatives.'

'And be for ever outcast?'

'It might be better than…' She stopped, but Lucinda knew exactly what she was about to say.

It might be better than being married to a man who looked for all the world as if he was going to his own funeral. With an effort she lifted her chin. It was not as if she was happy about anything, either, although some quiet part of her buried deep held its breath as green eyes raked across her own, the red streak in one of them bright with fury.

'This is 1831, Luce, not the Middle Ages. If you truly do not wish to do this, you only have to say. No one can drag a reluctant bride to the altar even if the alternative is enormous scandal.'

'I do not think your words are helping, Posy.'

'Then let me call it off. I can say that it was completely my fault I took you to Alderworth in the first place and procured the dress and…'

But the minister had begun to speak in his low, calm voice and Lucinda knew that to simply walk out on her last chance of salvation would be to cut herself off from a family that meant the world to her.

She had brought this upon herself, after all, and she just could not think of another more viable solution. A marriage ceremony. A week of pretence. And then freedom. Lord, she would follow the straight and narrow from now on and, if God in all his wisdom allowed her the strength to get through these next hours, she would promise in return an eternal devotion to His Good Works.

When Tay took a quick look at his bride-to-be he saw that under her veil her hair was plaited in a crown encircled by pale rosebuds. Today she seemed smaller, slighter, less certain. The lies she had spun about them, he supposed, come home to roost in front of the altar, no true basis for any such betrothal. He was glad of the lace that covered her head because he did not wish to see her deceitful eyes until he had to. The gown surprised him, though. He had thought she might balk at making any effort whatsoever, but the dress fitted her perfectly, spilling in a froth of whiteness about her feet. A dainty silver bracelet adorned her left wrist, four small gold stars hanging from it.

A continual whispered dialogue with the bridesmaid began to get on his nerves and he was glad when the minister, dressed in flowing dark clothes, called the place to order.

Everybody looked tense. The bride. The brothers. Even the minister as he held his hand up to the organist and called for quiet.

'Marriage is a state that is not to be entered into lightly, or with false promise. Are you happy to continue, Lady Lucinda?'

Tay bit down on chagrin. Of course she would be. His title was one factor and her ruin was another. He wished the man might skip through to the final troths and then all of this would be over.

But he did not. Rather he waited until the bride before him nodded her head without any enthusiasm whatsoever. 'Then we are here today to join this man and this woman in the state of Holy Matrimony…'

For ever and for ever. It was all Tay could think as he gave his replies, though his parents had never let such pledges inhibit them in their quest for the hedonistic. For the first time in his life he partly understood them and some of his disillusionment lifted.

But it was too late for such understanding now,

with his years seemingly destined to run along the same chaotic and uncontrolled pathway as those that he had sworn he would never follow. He was his father's son, after all, and this was a universally ordained celestial punishment for what he had become. The thought calmed him; fate moving in ways which allowed no redemption and if it had not been this particular sticky end that he had met, then undoubtedly it would have been another.

'Will you, Taylen Andrew Templeton Ellesmere, take Lucinda Alice Wellingham as your lawfully wedded wife…?'

The words shook him from his reverie. Her middle name was Alice and it suited her. Soft. Pale. Otherworldly.

'I will.'

Resignation tempered his pledge.

When Lucinda Wellingham gave the troth her tone was shaken, a thin voice in a house of God that held no message of joy within it.

And finally it was over.

Because it was expected he turned to face her and lifted the veil slowly. The church had been a place of refuge for him as a child and he still believed in the sanctity of religion despite everything he had become. The woman who stood there, however, was different from the laughing brave one in his bedchamber in Alderworth. This girl had dark rings beneath her lashes and eczema on her cheeks. Her eyes were flat blue orbs with no sparkle at all and the bump on her head from the accident was still visible. Exhaustion wove paleness into her skin.

As hurt as he was. A shared damage.

He felt his hand move to touch the wound and stopped himself. Theirs was a marriage in name only and the Wellinghams had been insistent that he understood this was for public consumption. A week or two at the most and then they wanted him gone. Her brothers had said that was her wish, too, his bride who, after uttering only lies, would not carry out even the pretence of a union once her ruin was minimised.

A travesty. A perversion. A shameful parody of something that should have been finer. Lord, the notion that survival justified the use of immoral means to achieve the required end was rubbing off on him in a melancholic and peculiar discontent. *'He who neglects what is done for what ought to be done effects his ruin...'* Machiavelli. The memory took him back to the night she had burst uninvited into his room, her colour high and the red dress low across her breasts.

Tay wished Lucinda Wellingham would take his hand again and hold it as she had at Alderworth, her fingers entwined into the worth of him as if she knew things that nobody else had ever discovered. He shook his head hard at such nonsense and she chose that moment to look at him directly, pale blue searingly condemnatory, the lies between them settling into an uncrossable distance.

'It cannot be easy to be the bride of ruin.' His words made her flinch, but he did not take them back. He wished that amongst those gathered there had been one person who might have welcomed his company. But there wasn't. All the wives of the Wellinghams had drawn Lucinda into their bosom, their eyes slicing across his like sharp knives—a rancorous truce, the white flag of surrender raised across his spilled blood and bruising. If he had by chance dropped dead due to some unforeseen and dreadful ailment he thought a party might have ensued, this veil of pretence transformed into a celebration of death.

He had never felt so unwelcome anywhere.

The shake of Taylen Ellesmere's head made Lucinda turn away, the tears she felt smarting at the back of her burning eyes threatening to fall. He did not look contrite or penitent or even slightly apologetic. He looked implacable and indifferent, this man who had disgraced her through fine red wine and a callous disregard for innocence, and was now making no effort whatsoever to assuage such poor behaviour.

The Bride of Ruin, indeed. Her husband now. Judas. Shylock. Marcus Brutus.

Lucinda could not even bear the thought that he might reach out and touch her.

She had been destroyed and she could remember none of it. She had been deflowered by a master with only the slightest jolt of memory remaining. Her brothers stood around her, a wall of masculine prickliness, sheltering her from the canker this betrothal had spawned, her sisters-in-law stalwart in the next ring of protection.

Alderworth had not apologised to them. Rather he had laughed in the face of their accusations and sworn free will was a liberty that all were entitled to.

Free will to take an innocent beneath him and to ravish her under the influence of strong wine; free will to take her to his bed and to say nothing to obliterate the raging gossip that swirled around the circles of society.

Lucinda Wellingham, the harlot. Lucinda Wellingham, intrinsically flawed.

Like the spoilt centre of a fruit, she thought, and was glad Posy Tompkins had also pushed in beside her because at least her friend's perception of the nuptials was laced with some sense of excitement.

'You will be free now, Luce. A married woman has so many more liberties.'

'I doubt another invitation will ever land upon my mantel, Posy.'

'Then we shall hold our own soirées, brilliant cultured gatherings that shall be the talk of the town.'

'Like courtesans?' Lucinda could not take the sting of it from her words for, all of a sudden, the whole world seemed meaningless and hollow. Posy had no notion of the signed agreements designating the boundaries of this marriage. She had not told her.

'Taylen Ellesmere is titled and handsome. There will be many a woman who might envy you such a husband. Believe me, be thankful he was not old and grey with no teeth and bad breath.'

Despite everything Lucinda smiled. Trust Posy to see the bright side of it all. Taking her friend's hand, she held her fingers in a tight grip and turned away from the worry of her family. The promises had been given and the deed was done. The only way on from here was upwards and Lucinda swore that when she was finally free of all this she would never allow her life to be mired again in such a shambolic wreck of betrayal.

'The wedding breakfast has been set up, Lucy. Asher asked if you would come now so that we can get this…finished with.' Beatrice spoke softly so that no one would overhear. The Wellinghams could manipulate to avoid disaster, but they wanted no others to understand that they did so. The twenty or so outside guests who had strong ties with the family beamed at her from one corner of the room of Falder House.

They had been invited to make this farce seem… legitimate. With the knowledge of what might happen next her brothers had at least given her back her shattered name. But after this she would only garner pity; the bride who was left summarily by a husband who had never loved her.

Threading through the room, Beatrice, Taris and

Asher led the assembly along to the blue salon. If she had wondered before at the control her brothers liked to wield, she understood now the very essence of it. The tables were dressed lavishly, the settings of the finest bone china and sterling silver. French wine had been brought up from the cellar. No shortcuts to encourage gossip. No small errors that might make the invited guests wonder. Nay, beneath the polite banter another reality lingered, stronger and unmistakable, but only if your name was Wellingham.

Taylen Ellesmere was sat next to her, his nearness making her shake, though when his leaf-green eyes brushed her own she felt…dizzy and disorientated.

Some worry leaked through her anger, a quiet emotion in a room full of tension. Bruising lay beneath his one blackened eye and there was a cut upon his bottom lip that she had not noticed before. Despite it all his beauty shone through, no slight comeliness, either, but a full-on barrage of masculine grace.

Unnerved, she shifted the lengthy veil which had pulled in beneath her, the lace of the Carisbrook's heirloom fragile in the play of sunshine from the window. She felt as though the breath had been knocked out of her lungs by one hefty punch of misgiving, but another truth also lingered.

Her husband was not all evil. There was a goodness in him that no one had discovered as yet.

She knew this as certainly as night followed the day, even though on his left hand beside his marriage band other rings glinted in the light—perhaps reminders of love from other women he had once admired before he had been made to marry her by her brothers? His name was always linked to paramours, after all. Was there one who he might have wished was standing here now in her stead?

Her cheeks itched with the eczema she always got when misgiving consumed her and the idea that her good name might be salvaged by such a course of action suddenly seemed foolish and ill advised. She wished she did not feel so shamefully heated by his presence at her side, the indifference she sought so far away from this undeniable awareness of him.

'The carriage accident hurt us both? I have been told how very lucky I was in not being killed by it, for with only a small movement things could have been so very much worse and I may never have walked again or even spoken and according to Doctor Cameron there might have—'

He stopped her by raising one hand. 'Are you nervous?'

For the first time she could ever remember in her whole entire life, Lucinda blushed. She felt the slow crawl of blood fusing her cheeks and held her hand up to the heat.

'Why would you say that?'

'Because you confided in me once that you talk too much when you worry.'

Her mouth dropped open.

Such a private honesty and one that she had never let another soul be privy to. She seldom shared her secrets, keeping them close to her heart instead, safe from derision or discussion. When and why had she told him such a thing? Perhaps the wine had made her speak? The exasperating fact of her lack of memory was both tiring and worrying.

'Surely you remember. It was just before I kissed you.'

Should she tell him that only a minuscule recollection remained from the time that they had shared in his chamber? *His nakedness. The wine. His mouth upon her breast. Her nipples hardening.*

Now that was new. Sitting up, she tried to remember some more, but couldn't. A new resolution firmed. He had taken her maidenhood without her consent and now would pay for it.

The laws of the land were there to protect the innocent and every Lord in his position had been brought up to acknowledge such a code. Ethics safeguarded chaos. When such tenets were broken, this was the result: a hasty marriage between strangers, flung together by the flimsy strands of expedience.

'I was foolish to come to your house in the first place, your Grace, and more foolish to stay. This is my penance.' She kept her tone distant, formal, just a polite conversation. When she leaned forwards she caught sight of herself in the wide shiny silver of an unused platter. Her cheeks were worse, even in the few short hours since leaving her chamber. She doubted she had ever looked quite so awful and her groom's handsome visage just made everything a hundred times more humiliating. Shallow, she knew, but in all her girlhood fantasies she had not imagined herself appearing so very bedraggled at her own wedding feast.

Lord Fergusson came up behind them, placing one hand on each of their shoulders. 'If you can have a marriage like I had for forty-three years, then you will be well blessed.' His old eyes brimmed with kindness.

Tay Ellesmere simply looked across at her. Answer this as you will, he seemed to be saying, shards of irritation noticeable.

'Indeed, Lord Fergusson,' she replied, remembering Mary-Rose, his beautiful wife, who had passed away suddenly the previous summer.

'But may I offer you a few words of advice? What you put into a marriage is what you get out from it and agreement is the oil that smoothes the way.'

'Then with all the agreements between us, ours shall run most smoothly,' Alderworth observed.

He had changed the meaning of the word 'agreement', but Lord Fergusson did not understand his reference. Her new husband's hands were in his lap. Fisted. Not quite as indifferent as he made out to be. Another thought struck her. Every knuckle had been grazed as though he had only recently been in a fight. Was that why his eye was black and his jaw cut? Please, God, let it not have been her brothers who had hurt him.

'I knew your uncle, Duke.' This was said tentatively. 'The Earl of Sutton.'

'Unfortunate for you.' Her groom's tone was plain ice and Lord Fergusson left as quickly as he had come, a frown on his face as he scrambled away.

'He is an old man who would do you no harm, your Grace, and he has only just lost his wife. Besides, this is a wedding and people expect—'

He broke in before she had finished. 'What do they expect, Lucinda? All that is between us here is dishonesty and farce. The charade of a marriage and the farce of a happy ever after. And now you want me to lie about an uncle who was not fit to be around children, let alone one who—' He stopped suddenly, his green eyes as dark as she had ever seen them, fathomless pools of torture. The real Taylen Ellesmere who lived beneath all he showed to the world was evident, the pain within him harrowing.

'You speak about yourself as a child? This uncle, the Earl of Sutton, he was your guardian?'

Only horror showed now, though the shutters reflecting emotion closed even as she watched and the implacable ruthless Duke was back.

'Enjoy your day, my dearest wife, because there are not many left to us.'

With that he stood and walked out of the room.

Chapter Five

God, she knew. Lucinda Alice Ellesmere was
guessing his secrets as easily as if he had written
them down for her, one after the other of sordid truth.

He should have remained silent, but the old man
and his useless dreams had rattled him, made him
remember his own hopes as his mother and father
had spat and hissed each and every word to the other,
unmindful of a small child who heard the endless
malice and rancour. He had promised himself he
would never marry and yet here he was, chained to
a family who would like nothing better than to see
him dead and buried.

'If you slope off now you won't get a penny, Alderworth.' Cristo Wellingham came to his side, the
room they were in empty. Unexpectedly Lucinda's
youngest brother produced a cheroot. 'You have the
look of a man who might need one,' he said, offering
a light and waiting as Tay took the first few puffs.

Smoke curled towards the ceiling, a screen of white and then gone. Tay wished he could have disappeared as easily as it did and, closing his eyes for a second, he leaned back against the wall, enjoying the first rush of its effects.

'I look forward to the day when the guilt of your sister's lies finally brings her to her senses.' The exhaustion in his voice was disconcerting, but the day had taken its toll and he was tired of the pretence.

'When you will likely be squandering what is left of your blood money in some poverty-stricken dive, remembering the ill that you did to a blameless innocent and wondering how you came to such a pass.'

He laughed at that. 'You did not enjoy a few of your wife's charms before marrying her?' A shadow rewarded the query and so he continued. 'I kissed your sister and brought her home. That was all. If she insists otherwise, then I say she lies.'

'With a reputation as disreputable as your own, a lack of belief in anything you say cannot be surprising.'

'Then allow me one boon, Lord Cristo. Allow me the small privilege of some knowledge of how your sister fares once I have gone.'

'Why would you want that? You have made it plain enough that a substantial payment constitutes the sum total of your care.' He stepped back. 'There won't be more from where that came from, no matter what you might say.'

'You will always hold her safe, then?' Tay had

not meant to ask the question, but it slipped from him like a living thing, important and urgent, the last promise he might extract before he was gone.

'Safer than you damn well did,' came the reply, but in Cristo Wellingham's dark eyes puzzlement flickered. Using it to his advantage, Taylen pressed on.

'If I wrote, would you give her my letters?'

'Yes.' Ground out, but honest. When Lucinda's brother turned and left he was glad he had been given even that slight hope of contact.

Lucinda felt exhausted by all the smiles and good wishes given with such genuine congeniality that the scandal disappeared into a God-ordained union that restored the balance of chaos in a highly regulated world. A violation covered up. A wrong righted. A happy ending to a less-than-salubrious beginning.

She had been surprised at the way the Duke of Alderworth had stood next to her for the past twenty minutes, his manner with the guests at odds with his self-proclaimed lack of interest in polite society. Perhaps he, too, had finally seen that in a good show of pretence there lay freedom. When his arm touched hers the full length of warmth seared in, the shock of contact electric, her breath held still by an awareness that she had felt with no other before him.

If only she might remember what a night in his bed felt like. The very idea made her frown, because in it she sensed she was missing something important.

'You look concerned.' Alderworth used a gap in the line of well-wishers to address her directly.

'It seems for all your reputation, people here are inclined to give you a second chance. I was wondering why.'

'Perhaps it's because you stand up as my bride, a Wellingham daughter who might deign to lend her name to my sullied one.'

'No. It is more than that. They accord you a certain begrudging respect, which is interesting.'

'Vigilance might be a more apt word!' Unexpectedly he smiled at her, the green in his eyes relaxing into gold, and with the colour of his skin burnished into bronze by the outdoors and his dark hair so shortened, he looked...unmatched. Her brothers were handsome, but the Duke had some spark of incomparable beauty that set him apart from everyone else Lucinda had ever seen.

The vapidity of her thoughts held her mute.

'Frowning does not suit you as much as laughter does,' he remarked.

'Of late there has not been too much to be delighted by.'

'I am sorry for that.'

'Are you?' Even amidst a crowd of family friends she could not leave the question unvoiced.

She saw him glance around to check the nearness of those in his vicinity before he gave a reply.

'I lived with lies all of my childhood, Duchess, and do not wish to encourage them. If you insist on such deception then that is your prerogative, but I will never understand it.'

Both her new title and his unwarranted anger made Lucinda step back, the same scene she had remembered at the breakfast table a week ago replaying over and over in her head.

His nakedness, the red wine, the feel of his warm skin against her own. The door locked and the key hidden. No opportunity to simply leave.

'London is a haven for gossip, Duke, and because of your actions my name has been slandered from one edge of it to the other.'

'A reputation lost for nothing, then.'

Lucinda paled. Did he speak of her virginity in such scathing terms? She was glad her brothers were nowhere nearby to hear such an accusation.

'For nothing?' She could barely voice the question. 'You are a reprobate, your Grace, of the highest order and the fate that flung us together at Alderworth will be regretted by me for the rest of my life. Bitterly.' There was no longer any conciliation in her tone.

He had the temerity to smile. 'Then it is a shame you did not make full use of our evening together and understand the true benefits that uninhibited sensuality can bring. Better to have enjoyed a night in my bed learning all you needed to know about the art of love and regretted it, than repenting the "nothing" you have been crucified for.'

Shocked, she turned on her heels and left him, not caring who saw her flee. He would castigate her for her poor performance in bed when she could recall none of it. Her blood rose to boiling and she hated her pronounced limp.

'Are you feeling well, Lucinda?' Emerald waylaid her before she had reached the door.

'Very.' Even to a beloved sister-in-law she couldn't betray him entirely, a trait she did not understand at all.

'Alderworth will be gone before the end of this week and you will never need to see him again.'

The absurdity of such a statement suddenly hit her, the first glimpse of her life after today. Was she destined then to always be alone, marriage-less and childless? Would she now linger in the corner of society with those hapless spinsters who spoke of unrequited love or of no love at all? Not ruined, but blighted by her lack of adherence to the normal conventions and suffering because of it.

The headache she had been cursed with all day bloomed with a fierce pain, blurring her vision. A migraine. She had had them badly ever since the accident.

Understanding her malady, Emerald took her hand and led her from the room, the familiar flight of stairs to her childhood bedroom welcomed. A refuge. A place to hide.

With care Emerald helped her undress and pulled down her hair till it fell about her waist, the heaviness of it causing her temples to throb harder.

'Marriage has made everything worse, Emmie.' The ring Alderworth had brought with him glinted on her finger and she looked down at it. A single ruby in white gold. Surprisingly tasteful. 'Before it was only my reputation immured in the sludge, now it is my whole life as well.'

'When your head does not ache as much and you realise you can once again participate in all the things you love doing, the world will look rosier.'

'As a widow? As a wife? As a spinster for ever doomed to sit in the corner, waiting for a husband who is gone?'

'You are saying that you wish he would not disappear?' Her sister-in-law's voice was sharp.

'No.' Shaking her head violently, she remembered Taylen Ellesmere's caustic disparagement of that which had been between them. She also remembered the way it had felt when their arms had touched and he had not pulled away.

She shook away the thought with a hard anger. Her husband saw her as a woman to be pitied, a poor excuse of a girl with her puritanical take on life and her inability to embrace his darkness.

They would ruin each other. It was as simple as that. All she wanted was to be between cool and crisp linen sheets, the world dissolved into dreams and ease and far from the reality of being bride to a groom who had not said even one kind word to her across the whole awful charade of their wedding day.

The Bride of Ruin. Indeed, she was exactly that.

'Lucinda is in bed with a headache and won't be joining the family again this evening. To say that she is disappointed in you would be putting it mildly.'

Asher Wellingham stood before Tay, a glass of brandy in a sizeable goblet in his hand. He did not offer the chance of the same to him. Taris Wellingham leant against a window in the far end of the library. As reinforcement, Taylen supposed, the quiet stillness of the middle brother as alarming as it always was.

'You will be allotted a chamber here, Alderworth, to allay any rumour or gossip. Then you will accompany Lucinda to the Parkinsons' ball tomorrow evening. The Duchess and I will attend as well, to make certain that you play the part of a doting and besmitten groom.'

'Another staged affair, then, though I cannot quite understand what you plan to do about the legal fact of our union in the future. Marriage is usually for ever.'

'Death negates a marriage.' The words were said without any emotion whatsoever as amber eyes met his own.

'You are threatening me?'

'I am the head of a family who is trying to make sense of a senseless act of treachery.'

'Treachery? I kissed your sister once and then

bundled her into the carriage to bring her home. An accident prevented us from reaching this town house. Where is the treachery in that?'

'I am more inclined to believe my sister's version of the story above your own.'

'The ravished, ruined version?' Tay could not help his sarcasm and the Duke of Carisbrook's brow furrowed.

'If I hear even the slightest hint of rumours that you say differently, I will make it known you demanded money from us for the sole purpose of your own benefit. Blackmail, if you will, with no thought for your innocent bride.'

'A fabrication that will have me drummed out of London whilst you condemn Lucinda to the life of a nun?'

'Better a nun than the harlot you have already made her.'

'Better than a misguided girl who invents tales to trap me?' Tay had had enough of carefully tip-toeing around the issue and the gloves were off.

Intent darkened his adversary's eyes. 'You came into our lives by an accident, Alderworth, and you can depart on one just as easily.'

'More threats?'

Turning away from Asher Wellingham, Taylen took in a breath. Let him strike like a coward and see what happened next. He had had it with headaches and warnings just as he had had it with utter lies. This was his wedding night and the only one he might damn well ever get, given these ridiculous edicts, yet here he was trading insults with his...new brother-in-law. Such a thought made him maudlin.

He could not win any concessions here tonight when tension, mistrust and fury coated every word between them. Better to wait until the morrow and have a conversation with his new bride that was long overdue.

'I am returning to my own town house and, short of rendering me unconscious and tying me up to a bed here, you can do nothing to stop me going. I will be back tomorrow after midday in the hope that your sister will be well enough to sit down and talk sense. Make sure that she is here, Carisbrook.'

As the door closed and Alderworth's footsteps receded into the distance, Taris rose. 'There is a note in his voice that concerns me, Ashe.'

'How so?'

'He seems to genuinely believe he is the innocent party.'

'The guilt of the damned is never simple. His is just more complicated than most.'

Taris drained his glass. 'Emerald said that Lucy never wants to see him again.'

'A difficult emotion, given that a marriage ceremony has just been performed and he was promised a week.'

'We might be rid of him if we were to leave London at first light and make for somewhere he could not find us. I think both parties need some time to take stock of what has happened and see a way through this. I doubt he would make a fuss with the threat of the removal of the promised remuneration hanging over his head.'

Possibilities roared between them as the fire carved shadows across the ceiling. A clean break would make certain that Lucinda was safe and it would also calm the troubled waters until they might make something else of the conundrum. The fine strong brandy in each of their glasses after such a harrowing day made their best intentions seem more…persuasive, less high-handed.

Always they had cared for their little sister, rescuing her from this scrape and then that one, smoothing down conjecture and controlling any whispered gossip. Always, until now.

'Have we made a mistake, do you think, insisting on this damn marriage?' Asher's voice was grave, copious liquor and contrasting emotions clouding certainty.

'Too late for second thoughts.' Taris swore even as he said it, a ripe curse that reverberated around the library. 'We did what we could. It is far past time for Lucy to understand the repercussions of her mistakes.'

'Loneliness might be one of them.'

'Aye, it might. But better than being tied to a man she loathes, I'd be thinking, and if we play it right he will be gone and she can get on with a new sort of life. These awkward alliances happen all the time, but with good management they can be manipulated to appear to be nothing like they actually are.'

'Successful?' Sarcasm dripped from the word.

'I was thinking more along the lines of moderately satisfactory to both parties concerned. Lucinda gets her freedom and Alderworth his money. At least it is a way past ruin.'

Chapter Six

⸺⧾⸗⸗⧼⸺

Hands kept shaking her awake, insistent and un-relenting.

'Come, Lucy, we need to be up and about, for Asher wants us out of London by daybreak.'

'Why?'

Taking a quick look at the clock on her bedside table, Lucinda determined it to be very early in the morning. The birds had not even called yet and Emerald looked in a hurry.

'Alderworth is rescinding his promise to leave. He seems to think you will be accompanying him north to his estate.'

Sitting up, Lucinda pushed the covers back, the bruises on her legs dark against the whiteness of the sheets.

'He wants that of me?'

Her sister-in-law shrugged her shoulders. 'Given his character he probably wishes to haul you off to Alderworth and keep you there.'

'Like a prisoner?' Tremors of fear made her feel ill.

'Of course not. But it might behove us to make certain that he understands exactly what you do want.'

'Nothing. I wish for nothing between us.'

The wedding dress stared at her from its hanger across the wardrobe door, the white, pristine silk more than she could bear. Getting up, she threw the thing into the cupboard, the veil of gauzy lace joining it.

One day when she was ninety and her brother's children's children asked her about her life, she might tell them that the worst moment of all was the one where she had caught sight of herself in the mirror in her bedroom the morning after her nuptials. And when they asked her why, she would say because that was the moment she realised there would never be another chance of happiness for her.

'I will have the housekeeper dispose of the gown, Lucinda, so that you do not need to see the garment again.' Emerald's eyes were a stormy turquoise, but tenderness lay in the hand that came to fall over hers. 'We shall get through this together as a family, for your brothers have ways to right all the wrongs.'

'Divorce is not an easy passage…'

'Annulment, then? That could be an option.'

'I rather think that might have come too late, considering my returning memories and society's talk. I should never have married him at all.'

'Then we just need some time to think about it,

some quiet time away from the pressures of London. A solution is always available to any problem and this one will be no different.'

'What if Alderworth comes to find me at Falder and demands my return?'

The silence told her that there was some other thing afoot.

'We are not going to Falder?'

'No. We are making for Beaconsfield and then to a house on the south coast. You can live there with a stipend if you cannot stay close to town.'

'Away from the Duke of Alderworth?'

'He is a dangerous adversary, Lucy. Until we can formulate a plan to keep you safe, it is better to keep you apart. I think such a man would insist on his marital rights.'

The blood simply drained from her face as she contemplated that truth. Would the Dissolute Duke want to take her to his bed? Again? Her imagination ran wild. If she was already pregnant from her ignominious ruin, how would this change things? The very thought of it had her reaching for her thick night-wrap.

'I do not want to see him, Emmie. Asher is right. I wish for some distance between us so that I can indeed think.'

Tay sat in his study with the curtains open and a quarter-moon outside in the heavens struggling to find clear sky through banks of high-billowed cloud.

She had left. Lucinda Wellingham had gone with her family from London, running in the early dawn to a place that was not Falder. He had found out this little information from a stable hand he waylaid on the way home from their town house, though the boy had no inkling of their true destination.

His bride had, however, left a note, the words written in his memory like some morbid poem of rebuttal.

I hope that you will allow me a few weeks to recover from the accident and to consider my options.

Please do not come after me. I will not receive you.

If you need to contact me, Cristo will forward any communication and I will answer as I see fit.

The missive was signed formally. *Lady Lucinda Wellingham.* She had not even used his name.

Lifting a glass of brandy to his lips, he upended it, the quiet tonight a pressing and heavy one. The purse of the Wellinghams sat on the desk in front of him, a considerable sum representing a new life, somewhere far from England, perhaps? The Americas beckoned and so did the East Indies. Here he was struggling to keep ahead of the many and mounting debts his father had left him, every pound he made subtracted twice over by the ones he owed. Another few years at this rate and it would all be gone. Alderworth, the extensive land and buildings around it and the London town house, disappeared into the gloom of history.

A new life summoned—a refurbishment of the soul and one with a beguiling promise. The choice was simple. Stay here and fight the power of the Wellinghams for a wife who did not want him, or leave on a new tide and chance his hand at something different. He had never travelled away from the shores of England before, the duties of being the caretaker of Alderworth taking all his attention. If he left half of the Wellingham money here in an account to be drip-fed into the estate just to keep it afloat, perhaps he could build other possibilities?

Flat blue eyes came to mind, the anger in them directed only at him. Lucinda wanted neither his name nor his title and, as tiredness settled, it took too much will to quarrel.

His parents had frittered away their lives together in acrimonious exchanges and he did not wish to do the same. No, far better to welcome change and simply vanish.

His eyes strayed to the band on the third finger of his left hand. To have and to hold from this day forth, his wife had promised as she had placed it there...

Dragging the gold across his knuckles, he threw it into a drawer in the desk. A relationship that had begun in untruth and blossomed under duress was now ended in deceit. He would journey to a far-off corner of the world which laid no claim to the stifling conventions of a society immured in manners.

And then he would be free.

The journey south was hurried and long and as the carriage swayed against a wind from the sea, Lucinda thought that her life from now on might be exactly like this flight into obscurity.

She could not go back and she could not go forwards, the worry of seeing Taylen Ellesmere again precluding any early return to London. Emerald and Asher both looked as tired as she did, the last weeks resting on their faces, worn down by worry. At least the beginning of her menses had come that morning and there was some relief to know she would not be bound to Alderworth by a child. But even that relief was tempered by sadness as she faced the possibility that she might never ever be a mother.

'The air here is so much better than in London, Ashe.' Emerald's observation was falsely cheerful, just words to fill in the heavy silence.

Lucinda nodded and tried to smile, though she doubted that her brother would be fooled by such a forced joviality. With a cursory glance at the sky, Asher brought the subject back to the problem they were all thinking about.

'In a month you can come back to Falder, Lucinda. I will employ guards to make certain Alderworth comes nowhere near you and at least it will be a more familiar setting. I doubt, however, that London will be a destination available to you for a good long while yet. Society has a great need to feed off scandal and this one…' He left the sentence unfinished.

She nodded to please him, but the ache in her breast threatened to explode into an anger she did not recognise. She wished with all her heart that she had not been persuaded to go to a house of such ill repute in the first place, for all that had followed was the result of one injudicious decision.

'Visiting Alderworth was more than foolish,' she muttered and Asher looked up, the pity in his eyes almost her undoing.

'I have left word to have Alderworth followed so any movements that alarm us will be monitored. Let us hope he has the sense to retire to that estate of his and never again leave it.'

'You think he will stay in England?' As Emerald asked the question something passed between Asher and her—a warning, were Lucinda to name it. A quiet notice of caution with an undercurrent of intent.

Goodness, had her brothers shanghaied her husband already and thrown him on to a ship sailing far from Britain before disgorging him on to some unknown foreign shore? Her mind ran all the possible injuries that Taylen Ellesmere might sustain.

'If you have hurt him…' she began and stopped, dread making her question what it was she was going to say. Ellesmere should mean nothing to her. She should be glad that he would disappear for ever, yet concern lingered.

'He is at liberty to go where he wants. There was no duress in it.'

'You paid him?' Suddenly she understood. 'You bribed him to leave?'

When he nodded, she looked away. Ruined and humiliated. She vowed that there would never be another time when she allowed a man to hurt her.

Tay watched the coast of England receding into only mist. The sea birds called around him as the canvas of the sails caught the wind, turning the ship east, and an excitement he had not felt before quickened his breath and made him lift his face to the heavens.

Free.

For the first time in his life the debt of Alderworth did not weigh him down with its constant demands and a new horizon beckoned.

A place to make a different mark, a land where no one knew him. The mantle of the past slipped away into the gathering breeze and his fingers curled around the guard rail, holding on to the rusted steel as though his very life depended on it.

'You look as though you could do with a drink.' A tall red-haired man stood next to him, the collar of his coat raised against the weather. 'Where are you headed?'

'Anywhere a fortune is to be made,' Tay answered, a plan formulating as he spoke. He needed money to come back. He needed good hard cash to retrieve his life and make it work in the way he wanted it to. His glance took in the bare third finger on his left hand as the stranger spoke again.

'I am bound for North Georgia. They say that the gold there is easy to retrieve and the veins are rich. Two years I have given myself to find it and my wife, Elizabeth, is already counting down the days.'

'You have experience of mining, then?' A small worm of an idea began to creep up into possibility.

The other nodded. 'With farming as it is I have needed to supplement my income from the family estate by other means. I could do with a partner if you are interested. A flat fee for the tools we will need and that will be it, save for lots of hard work and a good dollop of persistence. A sense of humour might help, too.'

The screech of a gull above had them looking up, the big bird wheeling out of the sky towards them, its wings outstretched as it landed on a point at the top of the ship. Hitching a ride or having a rest?

Choices.

They came from the most unexpected places and from the most unexpected people. Putting out his hand, he felt the firm grasp of the other.

'Tay Ellesmere.' No title. Nothing to tie him to the England he was leaving. A different man with another life.

'Lance Montcrieff. From Ridings Hall in Devon.'

Lucinda walked along the cliffs of Foulness Point and watched the ocean waves break across the beaches below, never-ending tides, washing the land clean of all that it had left there the day before. A constantly refreshed canvas, the flotsam of life taken away to another headland in a different place, redefined and transformed.

As she was not. Two years of isolated country living had left her struggling with her identity, Falder and its environs beautiful, but never changing. Her physical strength had returned finally, though her memory had never followed. Oh, granted, she still had headaches sometimes and when she was tired her vision became a little blurred, but the bone-wearying fatigue had dissipated and in its place a haunting curiosity had risen.

She wondered where in the world the Duke of Alderworth might now be. Cristo had given her a letter a good year ago and she had opened it with shaking fingers.

His description of a town in the North Georgia mountains in the Americas had been interesting, but had left her hollow. He had written nothing of his feelings or of his intentions or of any new relationships he might have formed. A half-page long, and wholly factual, the message could have been written for anyone.

He had signed it Tay Ellesmere. No title. Just the diminutive of Taylen. *Tay.* She had run the word a thousand times off her tongue ever since reading it and hated herself for doing so.

She wanted him back. She did, out here in the

wind and with the sound of the ocean all around her. She wanted to feel his skin against her own in that particular way he had of heightening her senses and making her feel alive.

Dead. She had been dead since he had left, on an early morning ship out of St Katherine's Dock, Asher had said. Sailing for the Americas and a new life without any of the burdensome encumbrances that he had been tied to in England and so unwillingly.

Paid to take ship from London and never return? She had heard that, too, when she had listened in to a conversation between Taris and Asher. All she had picked up in their tones was relief that Alderworth was gone and so she had tried to forget him, banishing all thoughts of a husband from her mind.

And failing.

She hated this limbo she was in, caught between marriage and widowhood, and never a chance of moving on. Sometimes she hated Taylen Ellesmere so much that her skin shook with the loathing.

A voice calling took her thoughts away and she saw Lord Edmund Coleridge, a friend of Cristo's, walking towards her.

'Cris told me that you would be here,' he said as he came close. 'He also said that I was to ask you for a dance tonight at Graveson.'

'Florencia's party?' The house had been awash with busy hands since it had been decided to throw a birthday party for Cristo and Eleanor's oldest daughter.

'Seven is an important number. She has asked her father if she might invite Bram Crowley to help her celebrate.'

'Young love.' Lucinda smiled and shook her head. Brampton's father owned the property bordering Cristo and Asher's holdings and, although the family were not titled, they were by all accounts very rich. Florencia had liked him from the very first moment she had arrived with her mother, and the boy had done much to bring a frightened and retiring child out of her shell.

'I hope you might save a waltz for me, Lady Lucinda.' Edmund took her hand, surprising her. 'I would dearly like to get to know you better.'

'I am married, my lord,' she returned quickly. 'There can be no gain in aiming your sights at me.'

His laughter floated on the wind around them, a happy, free sound that made her relax.

'Your brother told me that you were forthright and now I believe him. I will swap you one waltz for the chance to tool my greys around the Falder course on the morrow.'

'A difficult thing to refuse. Did Cris also tell you of my passion for horses?'

'He did indeed. He said I was to expound on my expertise in archery as well.' His eyes lost their humour as he continued. 'It is just a dance I beseech, Lady Lucinda, and the chance of friendship.'

For the first time in a long while Lucinda allowed a man to hold her fingers for more than a second without pulling away. There was none of the magic there that she had felt with Alderworth, but it was not unpleasant, either. With blond hair blowing in the wind and his dark eyes soulful, Edmund Coleridge had his own sort of appeal. Lord knew she had heard he was popular with all the young ladies of society and she could see how that could be so.

But he did not smell of wood-smoke and lemon and his eyes were not the colour of the wet forests at Falder. Nor were they underlaid with a thrilling lust that made her whole body sing.

Lucinda wore a new gown that evening, a red silk that was edged in gold. Such a combination might have been showy, but the dressmaker had played up the under-lights in the silk and matched them exactly with the trim.

'You look beautiful tonight, Lucy.' Emerald was the first to see her as she came downstairs, and indeed as she caught a reflection in the large mirror at Graveson she did look…different.

Sorrow had stalked her for so long since the fiasco in London that Lucinda had almost got used to its sombre presence. Tonight, however, her spirit was lifted. Perhaps it was because of something as uncomplicated as the beautiful gown or the fact that Eleanor's maid had fashioned her hair in a new style. Or perhaps it was just the fact of a family celebration and the excitement of Florencia, Cristo and Eleanor.

Edmund Coleridge was the next one to compliment her and he did so with a raft of words.

'I could compare your hair to moonbeams or sunlight or to the sparkling fall of water over rocks, my lady.'

Despite the flowery rhetoric, Lucinda laughed. 'Please do not, my lord.'

She liked the warmth of his hand and the smooth feel of his skin. His hair tonight was Macassared and it suited him; made him look more dangerous. She shook away the thought. Safety was what she was after. The consequences of following reckless paths had ruined everything, after all, and she had promised herself to walk a discreet and scatheless way in future.

'Your niece has been asking after you. I think she wants to give you something.'

As if on cue Florencia appeared before them, a beautiful gardenia in hand. 'Everyone has to wear one tonight, Aunty Lucy, because they are my very favourite flower.'

Lucinda noticed the bottom of the stalk had been wrapped in brown paper, a pin secured in the folds.

'Is this your handiwork, my love?' she asked as she took the bloom and smelt it.

'Mine and Mama's.' Her dark eyes crossed to Edmund. 'But you are wearing yours upside down.' A wide smile lit up her face as Coleridge knelt and fashioned his flower exactly as she wanted it.

'Is this better?'

'Much. Now I just have to find Uncle Taris. I think he is hiding from me because he thinks flowers are for girls.'

With a whirl she was gone, with her little basket of gifts and a jaunty lilt to her step. Lucinda remembered back to when she had first met Cristo's daughter. The change in her demeanour was heartening and it seemed Coleridge was thinking exactly the same thing.

'Cris is lucky with his family and is happier than I have ever seen him.' The flower had wet the fabric of his coat where water seeped through the paper, but he only wiped it away.

Edmund Coleridge was a kind man, a good man with high principles and moral worthiness. She caught Eleanor watching them with a smile on her face and thought briefly how easy it might have been had she chosen a man like this one. Her family liked him, society lauded his goodness and he observed her as though he was inclined to know her better.

When a waiter passed with a tray of drinks in tall and fluted glasses she picked one up and drank it quickly before returning for a second.

'My brother knows his wine. French, I should imagine, and very smooth.'

The first flutter of warmth stirred in her stomach, the drink relaxing a tension that was ever-present in her life. More usually she stayed away from anything that might not allow her control, after her last débâcle, but tonight she felt able to risk it.

She nodded as Edmund Coleridge took her hand and asked her to dance. A waltz, she realised, as he led her to the floor, the slow languid three-beat music swirling across her senses.

He was thinner than his clothes suggested, but as her fingers came across the superfine of his jacket a sense of masculine strength made her breath come faster. It had been so long since she had touched a man like this.

Taylen.

Swallowing, she made herself stop. Alderworth was not here and would never be so. He had gladly gone to the Americas, paid handsomely by her brothers to abandon any husbandly duty. The ache in her chest made her breathe faster.

'We can sit this out if you would wish to?'

Concerned dark eyes washed across her own.

'No. I would like to dance.'

The music of the orchestra was beautiful and the smell of the gardenia wafted up from her gown. She had to learn to live again, to laugh and to dance and to touch a man without pulling back. The wine was beginning to weave its magic and at the side of the room she could see Asher and Emerald watching her without worry marking their eyes.

Two years of dislocation. The silk of her chemise felt cool against her skin and Edmund Coleridge's fingers curled with an increasing pressure around her own.

Claimed. Quietly. She did not look up at his face.

Too soon. Too quick. She wished the fingers that held her own were covered in golden rings, an old scar visible just beneath the crisp white cuff of shirt.

Taylen.

Sometimes she could smell him, at night when everything was still and when she reached into the deepest place of memory. Lemon, woodsmoke and desire. She bit at her bottom lip and sent the thought scattering, leaf-green laughing eyes and short dark hair dissolving into nothingness.

'Will you come back to London soon?'

Another voice. Higher.

Edmund.

'I am not entirely certain. My brothers think that I should, but...'

'Come with me, then. Let me take you to the Simpson Ball.'

Now his interest was stated and affirmed, the *perhaps* that Lucinda had been enjoying transformed into certainty. The game of courtship had begun, all chase and hunt, and her heart sank.

'I am a married woman, my lord.'

'A married woman without a husband.' The dimples in his cheek made him look younger than he was, an amiable and gracious man who had taken the time and effort to try to humour a woman of little joy. Cristo's friend, and a man that her other brothers approved of, all the parts of him adding up to a decent and honest whole.

She allowed him the small favour of bringing her

closer into the dance so that now his breath touched her face.

'I should like to see you laugh, Lucinda.' When his thighs pushed against her own, the pulse in his throat quickened. Coleridge was so much easier to read than Alderworth had ever been, his secrets hidden in an ever-present hardened core of distrust.

Breaking off the dance when the music finished, Edmund led her into the conservatory at the head of the room. Stars twinkled through the glass overhead and myriad leafy plants stood around them in the half-light.

She knew he would kiss her even before he leaned down, she could see it in his eyes and on his face, that desire that marks even the most timid of men. She did not push him away, either, but waited, as his lips touched her own, seeking what it was all lovers sought, the magic and the fantasy.

A light pressure and then a deeper one, his tongue in her mouth, finding and hoping. She felt his need and tried not to stiffen, understanding his prowess, but having no desire for a mutual understanding. Just flesh against flesh, the scrape of his teeth upon her lip, his wetness and the warmth. Ten seconds she counted and then twenty until he broke away, a flush in his cheeks and a hoarseness of breath.

Sadness swamped her as he brought her in against him. Nothing. An empty nothingness. Wiping away the taste of him when he was not looking, the weft of cotton felt hard against her mouth.

'Thank you.' His words. Honourable and kind.

Even as she tried to smile an aching loss formed, the mirthless harbinger of all that she had wasted. Alderworth had ruined her in more ways than he knew. Edmund Coleridge was exactly the sort of beau she should wish to attract and yet…

'Perhaps we should go inside. It is chilly out here.' The shaking she had suddenly been consumed by was timely.

'Of course, my dear. A dress of silk is no match even for a summer evening. I should have realised.'

Manners and courtesy. The smile on her face made the muscles in her cheek ache as she accompanied him into supper.

'Edmund seems more than taken with you, Lucy.' Cristo approached her as she returned from having a word with Beatrice. 'He is a good man who has long wished to know you better.'

'Well, I am sure he is besieged by all the lovely young women in society. His manners are faultless and he is such congenial and unaffected company.'

Cristo frowned. 'Such vacuous praise is usually an ominous sign…' His dark eyes watched her, the gold in them easily seen in the light from the chandeliers above.

Lucinda rapped him with her fan. 'I am not in the market for a…dalliance.'

He laughed at that, tipping his head up with mirth, the sound booming around them.

'I hope not. It was something more permanent Edmund was angling for, I would imagine.'

Taking one of her hands, he chanced offering advice. 'If you do not choose to move on with your life soon, Lucy, the opportunities may not keep coming.'

'You speak of suitors as if I were a widow, Cris.' Anger tinged her words and she was surprised as he shepherded her from the salon and down the corridor to his library. Once there he poured himself a generous brandy, restoppering the decanter when she turned down the chance of the same.

'Another letter has come.'

The words shocked her. She felt the blood drain from her cheeks and her heartbeat race.

'From Alderworth? When?'

'Last week. The mark on it is from Georgia.'

'Yet you did not think to give it to me sooner?'

'I knew Edmund would come tonight and he had asked me for the chance to court you. I had hoped…'

'Hoped for what? Hoped that the law might have dissolved all that was between me and Alderworth? Hoped that I might finally find a man that you all approved of? Hoped that the scandal of my disgrace may have been watered down by the pure goodness of your friend? That sort of hope?' Her voice had risen as she shook away his excuse. 'Where is it?'

Digging into a drawer at the back of his desk, Cristo laid an envelope down on the table. The writing was large and bold and not that of her husband, for the hand was completely different from the one correspondence she had received. Her excitement faded.

Lady Lucinda Ellesmere.

Graveson.

Essex.

Lucinda held her fingers laced together so they would not snatch at the paper. Was Taylen dead? Was this a missive to tell her of an accident or an illness or of the wearying of soul and a final resting place?

Had he married again, had children to a new lover, found gold, lost a hand, suffered a horrible and gruelling death in the throes of dysentery or smallpox or the influenza?

Finally she moved forwards and picked it up. 'Have you told Ashe of this?'

He shook his head.

'Then please do not.'

'You need to be careful, Lucy. Alderworth is a reprobate and a liar. He uses women for his own means and does not look back over his shoulder at whom he has hurt. Coleridge, on the other hand, is trustworthy.'

The sound of the orchestra winding up an air and the deep voice of Asher took them from the moment.

'The speeches.' Lucinda was glad for the interruption.

'We need to return to the ballroom.'

Folding the note, she stuffed it into a small compartment on one side of her reticule. Cristo made no comment as he gestured her to go before him and doused the lamp on his desk.

As soon as she was able to escape the party without raising any eyebrows Lucinda did so, climbing the steps to the room she had been allotted at Graveson with a mixture of hope and trepidation.

She could feel the presence of the envelope in her bag almost as a physical thing, prickling inwards.

Gaining her bedroom, she asked her maid to unhook the buttons at the back of her gown and, feigning tiredness, dismissed her. Locking the door behind the departing woman, Lucinda sighed with relief as she leaned back against heavy oak, free at last to see just what the letter from Georgia contained.

With agitation she slit open the top of the paper, carefully and precisely so as to do no damage to anything within.

A newspaper clipping confronted her, the folds of print displayed in such a way as to show a headline.

'Ellesmere strikes gold in fine style'.

The hazy distorted ink spoke of Tay Ellesmere celebrating with a great number of women in some sleazy saloon, the text citing details of a raucous party lasting well into the early hours of the morning, the guests invited unsuitable and rowdy.

As infamous as his soirées at Alderworth? Unchanged. Unabashed. She was in England pining for something that he had not spared a thought for, while

he partied with women who were probably inclined
to give away any and every favour he would want.

Swallowing, Lucinda let herself slide down the
door frame where she sat pooled in red silk, her first
finger tracing the exploits of a husband who on each
turn of events seemed destined to disappoint her.

Another smaller piece of paper suddenly caught
her eye and she lifted it up.

Lucinda
I presume that this is your runaway husband.
Perhaps, given the goodly amount of his newly
found claim, you should be seeking him out
again.
I have sent this letter to Graveson in the
hope that your brother might pass it on as I
have no notion of your new address.
Yours
Anthony Browne

Screwing up the paper, Lucinda crossed the room
to the fire, hurling the letter into the flames. The
paper caught at one edge and blackened, embers
glowing red before turning to a dull and dusty ash.

Anthony Browne, the brother of a school friend.
She had always detested him.

Her glance returned to the newspaper cutting.
If she had any sense she would consign this to the
fire, too. But she didn't. She hated the tears that

fell down her cheeks and the gulps of grief that she tried to quieten.

He would never stop hurting her, Taylen Ellesmere with his wild and ill-considered chaos. Another episode in a far-off land, his name slandered and his intentions dubious.

This was the man she had married, unstable, volatile and lawless.

Wiping the moisture away as a tear slid unbidden down the newsprint, she cradled the missive in her palm before bringing it to her heart.

'Where are you?' she whispered into the night.

Chapter Seven

London—1834

The gold coins were heavy in Tay's hand as he hoisted them up on to the desk. They clinked against the dark mahogany, solid and weighty, the letters of the Federal Mint at Atlanta imbued in red ink on the fabric of the bag.

'Here's the return of your bribe, Carisbrook, with more than interest in full. Now I want my wife back.'

Asher Wellingham stood as the words echoed around his library. 'You accepted our sum to disappear for ever.'

'Your expectation, Carisbrook, not mine. My Duchess and I shall leave for my country estate first thing in the morning and you can do nothing to stop us.'

'Over my dead body, you bastard.' Without warning the Duke was at Tay's throat before he had time to react, the chair beside the desk overturned and the strength of his fingers cutting off breath.

But Taylen was a good ten years younger than Lucinda's oldest brother and had more in muscle. His time in Georgia had also given him plenty of battle practice. With a quick twist he rolled away, fists up and waiting as the other angled in.

'I don't want to hurt you, Carisbrook. All I want is what is mine.'

'My sister isn't yours.'

'In God's eyes and anyone else that counts, Lucinda is my wife.' He had not meant to get into an argument, but the history between them was murky and here, in this same room he had been pummelled over once before, he found it difficult to temper back wrath.

'We should have killed you when we had the chance.'

Tay laughed and then moved quickly as a punch almost connected. He couldn't afford for his dinner dress to be bloodied as his next pressing destination was a ball. Waiting for his chance, he moved in, fingers reaching for the arteries of his adversary's throat.

It was over in two minutes, the point of pressure allowing an easy end. The fights in Dahlonega in Lumpkin County had been rough and a lucrative stake in gold at Ward's Creek in the North Georgia mountains always had to be defended. He almost felt sorry for the Duke of Carisbrook laid out on the floor but, when he checked, his breathing was deep and regular and tomorrow he'd barely feel any effects. Save embarrassment, probably, but he'd given Tay a good measure of the same treatment almost three years ago so Tay could not be remorseful.

Straightening his jacket, he caught sight of the clock at the end of the room. Ten-thirty. His wife was spending the evening at the Croxleys' ball in Culross Street and it wasn't far. He smiled. Almost too easy.

Letting himself out of the library, he closed the door behind him. Then he took his hat and cloak from the waiting servant and thanked him with a coin before walking into the night.

He was back.

She knew he was from the frantic whispers swirling around the ballroom, his name on the edge of every one of them.

'The Duke of Alderworth is here, returned from the Americas and twenty times richer than his father ever was.'

Lucinda felt all the eyes upon her as she stood near a pillar in the Croxleys' ballroom, Posy Tompkins to one side gripping her hand. Three years of dreading this very moment and it had finally arrived. The breath congealed in her throat and her heart beat so fast she was certain she would keel over.

No. She would not faint or fall or run. None of this was her fault, after all, and she would not allow Taylen Ellesmere to make her feel that it was.

'He is coming this way, Luce.' Posy barely managed to get the words out. 'And he is looking straight at us.'

'Then we shall give him exactly what he does not expect,' she replied, plastering a practised smile upon her face. Almost simple to do, she thought in surprise, the warmth of greeting a foil to the inquisitive faces turned her way.

'Your Grace.' Lucinda tried to make her tone convivial, a meeting of acquaintances, a trifling and inconsequential thing—a figure from the past to whom she had given no consideration since last seeing him.

'Duchess.' His voice had deepened in the years between their forced marriage and this unexpected return. 'I did not think to find you here in town.'

He was still beautiful. His hair was much longer than when she had seen him last and it made him look even more menacing.

Intimidating.

It was the only word she could come up with to describe him as he stood before her, dressed in black from head to foot, save for the white cravat at his neck fastened loosely in the style of a man without much care for fashion.

'Do you still enjoy the art of untruthfulness?'

The effrontery of such a question almost undid her and she answered with one of her own. 'Do you still enjoy despoiling innocents on a whim and all in the name of free will?'

A fiery glint in his eyes was seen fleetingly in a face hewn from cold stone.

Urbane and distant. Anger made her fists ball at her side, though she unclenched her fingers as soon as she realised what she was doing. She was pleased Posy had had the sense to retreat so that their conversation remained private.

'I had heard that you were back in England, your Grace.'

'Your brothers gave you the news, no doubt,' he returned, taking her hand in his own and pulling her towards the dance floor. 'But come, let's confuse the wagging tongues and stand up together. It will give us some space to talk.'

Short of creating a scene, Lucinda allowed herself to be led into a waltz, his arm encircling her back and drawing her towards him.

'The gossips have placed you on the Eastern seaboard coast of the Americas for many years, your Grace, taking part in all the temptations the cities there have to offer, no doubt.'

He laughed, a deep rumble of amusement; a man embedded in scandal and savouring it. Her ire rose unbidden. She had seen the evidence of his immorality, after all, in the headlined cutting Anthony Browne had sent her.

'Your brother Asher said much the same to me when I saw him this evening.'

'You have been to the Wellingham town house already? Why?'

'Paying my dues,' he replied obliquely, 'and stating my intentions.' He stopped for a moment as though gathering the gist of what he might next tell her. 'Not every one of them, though. I saved the best proposal of all for your ears only.'

A streak of cold dread snaked downwards. 'You want a divorce, no doubt?'

At that he laughed, the sound engulfing her.

'Not a divorce, my lady wife, but an heir, and as you are the only woman who can legitimately give me one the duty is all yours.'

She almost tripped at his words and he held her closer, waiting until balance was regained. Their eyes locked together, no humour at all in the green depths of Taylen Ellesmere, the sixth Duke of Alderworth.

He was deadly serious.

Shock gave her the courage of reply. 'Then you have a problem indeed, your Grace, because I am the last woman in the world who would ever willingly grace your bed again. Surely you understand why.' Disappointment and anger vibrated in her retort as strains of Strauss soared around them, the chandeliers throwing a soft pallor across colourful dresses resplendent in the room. The privilege of the *ton* so easily on show.

Scandal had its own face, too!

It came in the way his fingers held her to the dance even as she tried to pull away, and in the quiet caress of his skin over hers.

Memory shattered sense and the salon dimmed

into nothingness; the feel of his hands upon her nakedness, the smell of brandy and deceit and a wedding quick and harrowing in that small chapel.

Even the minister had not met her eye as he said
the words, 'To have and to hold from this day forward...'

Taylen Ellesmere had stayed less than a few hours.

Her husband. A different and harder man from
the one who had left her and now back for a legitimate heir. She wanted to slap him across his cheek
in the middle of the ballroom and he knew it. It took
all of her will not to.

'If there wasn't a male left in Christendom save
for you, I still would not—'

He broke over her anger.

'I will gift you the sole use of the Alderworth
London town house on the birth of our first son and
pay you a stipend that will keep you independently
wealthy in fine style.'

Blackmail and bribery now. She shook her head
against such a promise, but did not speak.

'One heir and then the freedom to do whatever
you want for the rest of your life. A safe haven. The
power of independence and autonomy. One heir
whom you shall have the right as a mother to raise
until he is ten. Eton should see to the rest.'

'And if the child is a girl?'

'Then I will dissolve all contracts and allow you
what I offer regardless. I would not tie you to such

a bargain for ever should you in good faith produce only a female Ellesmere.'

She frowned, barely believing the words she was hearing. 'There are other women here who would jump at your offer, your Grace, if you obtained a divorce and remarried.'

'I know.'

'Then why?'

'Salvation.' He gave no other explanation as he smiled at her, the deep dimple in his right cheek caught in the light. So very beautiful.

Lucinda felt the muscles inside her clench.

Freedom for the use of her body? He had had his fill once and she was no longer young. The very memory of it all took her breath away.

'I will not rape you if that is what you are thinking.'

'A mutual consent may never happen, your Grace.' She put as much disdain into the words as she could manage.

'I stake all my gold on the fact that it will.' His voice was overlaid with a certainty that was worrying.

Could she do it? Play the whore to a husband she could not trust and sell her body for a freedom she had never had? The girl she had been almost three years ago now would never have considered such a monstrous proposition, but the woman she had become did.

'I want it in writing. I want a hundred pounds for

every time I lie with you and a hundred more for every month it takes to become pregnant. No one must know of this bargain of ours, however, and in public you will only sing my praises. Do you understand? I shall not be the subject of any scorn whatsoever, for if my brothers ever found out exactly what you have proposed…' She could not continue.

'They would offer more threats.' He said this not as a question but as a truth. 'However, I would like to add one more condition of my own. For the conception of an heir I would require the whole night in my bed, at a time of your choosing. No rushed affair. I wish to lie in the moonlight and know your body as well as you know it yourself. Hedonistic and unhurried.'

She turned her face away so that he would not see what she imagined might be there—horror vying with avidity. The muscles deep inside throbbed in a promise that was like the echo of memory. She would not show him the hurt or the anger or the plain recognition of the choking shame she had lived with since he had gone.

She would tell him none of it until she could take the papers for the town house and fashion a separate existence.

Salvation, he had said. Perhaps it would be hers as well, this unexpected departure from being beholden to her brothers' generosity and benevolence. The gossip that had never died down as she thought it would, but had followed her with every step that she took.

The forgotten wife. The abandoned bride. The willful Wellingham sister whose reckless antics had finally caught up with her.

'My carriage will collect you the day after tomorrow from Wellingham House and bring you up to my seat. It would be an early departure so you would need to make sure that you are ready when it arrives.'

She shook her head, sense returning in the indifferent way he gave her instruction, like a Lord might order his valet to set out his clothes. 'My brothers will stop me.'

'Then it is up to you to persuade them otherwise. But know that we are married in the face of God for ever. I have given you my terms of agreement and I would never consent to a divorce.'

When the music stopped he escorted her back to her place near the pillar and into the company of Posy.

'I shall expect you to be ready by nine o'clock on Thursday with any luggage you require. I will join you later on the Northern Road.'

Without further word, he left.

He had done it. He had struck the bargain that he needed with less difficulty than he might have imagined. The line of the Ellesmeres of Alderworth would be saved.

Tay breathed in hard even as he walked through the crowd, wondering why it was he felt so damned uncertain. His wife still wore the ring he had given her, he noticed. The rest of her fingers were bare. The scar on the back of her hand was faded now, but under the light from the chandeliers he had still been able to see it. The carriage accident had left marks inside and out. Shaking his head, he cursed.

She was a hundred times more beautiful than she had once been. He remembered her eyes to be darker, but they were the blue of the early spring-time sky, bright with promise. Her curves had matured as well, and her skin was still silky smooth and pale. He brought the edges of his jacket further around his body, angry at the reaction she so carelessly extorted from him.

Looking back from the doorway, he tried to find her in the crowd and there she was, taller than most of the other women present and graceful. Her bones were small, the thinness in her arms giving the impression of a dancer. The dark-blue gown she wore with a froth of lace at the neckline emphasised the colour in her eyes.

'Hell.' He swore and as if on cue Jonathon Wigmore, the Earl of St Ives, joined him.

'Is it the swarm of admirers around your wife you do not like, Alderworth? You might need to get used to that, for since her return to London last year every man with any sense has courted her. Lord Edmund Coleridge, of all the swains, has been the most constant fixture. She allows him more of her time than any other. We all thought you were gone, you see.'

'So you were amongst her ranks of admirers, too?'

'Indeed I was, though with little success, I might add. Her brothers are ruthless in the protection of their sister.'

For the first time since arriving back in England Tay smiled and meant it. He had something to thank Asher, Taris and Cristo Wellingham for, after all.

'There was always something damn fine about Lucinda Wellingham. I could never understand why you left when you did.'

'I was twenty-five and foolish.'

'And now?'

'Now I am older and wiser.'

The first notes of the next dance made it hard to hear and Tay watched as his wife was handed into a quadrille by Coleridge, the look on his face suggesting that he was escorting a rare and valued treasure. He looked away as her hand rested upon his shoulder and she allowed him a closeness that was improper.

Deceit came in a beautiful package with every appearance of veracity. He recalled his entrapment by the Wellinghams with an anger that was as raw as it had been all those years before.

Turning, he left the house and hailed a hansom carriage for he had not bothered with his own. Habit, he supposed, and the habitual saving of pennies even though he could now afford any number of carriages that he wished. Sitting back on the seat, he closed his eyes, the quiet noise of the hooves of the horses echoing in the street.

His wife was beautiful. But it was something else

that he saw in her pale-blue eyes. Sorrow lingered there now, the sort of sorrow that had been the hallmark of his childhood: fear overlaid with caution. It did not suit her, this new wariness, this vigilant and all-encompassing apprehension.

Breathing out hard, he cursed the Wellingham brothers their heavy-handedness, but at least, according to Jonathon Wigmore, they had kept Lucinda safe. Tay knew if he was to have any chance of successfully taking his wife to his own estate he would need to get one of them, even begrudgingly, upon his side.

Taris was the one he would target. The middle brother would not grab him in a headlock and try to pummel the daylights out of him with his failing sight and he was tired of defending himself physically every time he came into their company.

A group of women standing on a street corner beckoned to him through the window, the sort of women who had been two a penny in the gold-mining towns of Georgia. Good women some of them, with hard-luck stories almost the same as his own. There was not much to separate success from ill fortune and he had never been a man to judge another's way of dealing with the varied hands that life dealt.

He had always felt alone. Right from the first moment of perceiving that his parents saw him as a nuisance rather than a blessing and had sent him off to anyone who would have him, little care taken in making certain of the reliability and soundness of their protection. He would never bring his own children up the way his parents had him. He would love them and cherish and honour them.

He laughed to himself, although there was no humour in the sound. The heirs he hoped for were poised precariously between his wife's hatred and her brothers' aversion.

He suddenly and sincerely wished that everything could just have been easy.

Lucinda had seen Taylen Ellesmere walk for the door in the company of Jonathon Wigmore some five minutes ago.

All she wished to do was to leave, to run from the farce and close the door against gossip. But to do so would be adding to it and so she stayed, her conversation amenable and her smile bright. Only Posy watched her with any idea of the truth and she made a point not to look in the direction of her best friend at all.

Tonight she was the woman she had fostered so diligently to appear to be since she had arrived here a year before. Poised. Mannered. In such armour she was left alone, the figure of pity waiting plaintively for a husband who she thought would never return diminished into the new persona.

And now he had returned, taller and more imposing, striding into her life as if he had not left it and demanding the production of an heir. As she bit down on her disbelief, the reality of all she had agreed to seemed far more terrible without him here in front of her, yet in the recesses of places she had long since neglected a sense of excitement moved.

She would lie with him for all the long hours of the night. Had he not said so himself? A half-formed smile lifted her lips, and when Edmund Coleridge came to claim a dance she curtsied prettily and allowed him her hand.

Later as Lucinda lay in bed she replayed the conversation she had had with Taylen Ellesmere over and over in her mind.

He had promised her the freedom of deciding the time that they would lie together and he had also promised that she would enjoy it.

Such arrogance was something she would normally find most unappealing, but with Taylen Ellesmere there was a certain truth that saved him from sounding smug. Besides, when he had danced with her at the Croxleys' ball the touch of his skin against her own had made her feel…excited. Excited for the first time in years, the vibrating possibility of it all leaving her breathless.

He did not wish for a quick tumble, either, but had stipulated the promise of a whole night. It was not some momentary and sordid tryst that he was proposing, but the vow of a lengthy coupling that was…unimaginable. She was beyond the first flush of youth and had never known the things that he spoke of. A sad statement of fact, but true. Pushing back the sheets, she took off her nightgown and wandered across to the mirror on the far wall of her room.

She was not a siren with her small breasts and thinness, but everything looked to be in place, did it not? Turning to one side, she tried to make her stomach extend outwards by arching her back so that an impression of fullness was gained. What would it feel like to hold a child inside her? His child? One hand fell to the curve and she smiled and straightened, her hair falling away from her body in a long and pale curtain. Taylen was probably used to experienced, curvaceous women, women who knew what to do to make a man feel…more than she could. How would she compare to them? The smile on her face was lost.

A knock on the door had her scrambling for her nightdress and dressing gown.

Emerald walked in as she called out for her to enter and her sister-in-law did not look pleased. The conversation they had had when she had come home, she supposed, and the discussion about her intentions of joining Taylen Ellesmere.

'You do not need to leave with him, Lucy. I would bet my life on the fact that Alderworth is bluffing and if you call it he will be forced to back down completely.

'Ellesmere is not a man you can play with, Lucinda. He reminds me of the sailors on the *Mariposa*: harsh, raw men with blood on their hands and childhoods that have crushed any kindness from them. He is worse than your brothers.'

'He is not a pirate, Emerald. He is a Duke.'

'The difference only of a title. If he wants something, he will get it. I hope that thing is not you, for if he hurts one hair on your body I will—'

Lucinda interrupted her. 'I am married, Emerald, and I want to know what that feels like. I want a child and I want a home that is mine.'

'This one is yours.'

'No. It is Asher's, a ducal residence that is passed down across the generations to the next inheritor of the title. I do not wish to still be here when I am thirty and that is not far away.'

Unexpectedly Emerald began to laugh. 'Asher is hardly sleeping for the worry of what will happen and here you are actually wanting what it is he thinks you do not. Do you love Alderworth?'

'I barely know him.'

'But you are happy to take the chance of doing so?'

'Yes.'

Silence reverberated around the chamber for one long moment and then two. 'I wish to give you something.' Emerald reached into the bodice of her nightdress and slipped a necklace from around her throat. 'I have no more use for this, Lucy, but I swear that it is a formidable talisman.' She placed the green jade carving in Lucinda's outstretched hand. 'For happiness,' she explained. 'An old woman in Jamaica gifted it to me and I rarely take it off. But I want you to have it now because in wearing it I will feel that you are safe.'

Lucinda's fingers closed around the treasure still warm from Emerald's skin. 'A well-paid-for heir' did not quite seem in the spirit of the happiness the jade was imbued with, but she said nothing.

'And one more thing, Lucy. Men are simple, remember that, and you will know exactly what to do to please them.'

In the light of the candles with her hair down and her turquoise eyes bright with promise, Emerald had the look of an enchantress from one of the story books of Lucinda's childhood.

'Simple?'

'Happy with small pleasures. Sex. Food. And love if it is honest.'

Which mine is not. She almost said it, but didn't, choosing instead to slip the necklace over her head and position it above the warmth of her heart.

Taylen met Taris Wellingham at the pub of the Three Jolly Butchers in Warwick Lane and was glad when Lucinda's brother dismissed his servant to another, distant table on his arrival. He had sent the note to Taris after breakfast, hardly daring that he might heed it.

'Thank you for coming. I know it is short notice.'

Wellingham laughed. 'The idea of meeting you in a crowded pub allayed my concerns that the engagement would become physical, Alderworth. Words, however, can have the same effect of wrapping their meaning around your throat and squeezing.'

'Free speech in the broadest sense of the term?' Tay could not help but feel a certain respect for the man's intellect as he replied.

'Exactly. What is it you need?'

'I have asked your sister to come with me to Alderworth Manor tomorrow, and she has agreed.'

'You have asked her already?'

'Last night at the Croxleys' ball. She has agreed.'

'Then there must have been a strong reward to entice her to such a promise. She is not apt to sing your praises about anything.'

Disconcerting opaque eyes watched him with all the focus of one who could see to the heart of the matter clearly.

'Lucinda hates you. How plain do you need to hear it in order to go away, Alderworth, or are you one of those obtuse men who fancy they see hope where there is none and would batter their heads against a brick wall for the rest of their days rather than facing a truth they do not wish to hear?'

'Going away is no longer an option for me.' Tay kept his voice low. 'Lucinda is my wife according to the letter of the law and under the authority of the Church, and I would never agree to a divorce. Besides, I have enough money to care for her now and the desire to do so.'

'Desire?' Unexpectedly Wellingham leant forwards and one hand shot out to entrap his in a grasp that was unyielding. A surprising accuracy, too, given his lack of sight. 'Desire to bed our sister again and then leave her? Desire to beget an heir upon her and then be on your way into the shady corners of the world when nothing turns out quite as easy as you expected it to? That kind of desire?'

Had his wife already spoken to her brothers about their bargain? Surely not. His hand ached with the force of strong fingers wrapped into flesh, but he did not pull away. Let the bastard see how little anyone could ever hurt him again. Aye, Taris Wellingham could break every damn bone in his hand and he would allow himself no reaction.

And then Lucinda's brother let go, simply sitting back against the fine leather chair and lifting his glass to drink as if nothing had happened.

'My *desire* to protect your sister is none of your business, Lord Wellingham.' Taylen did not make any effort to accord the words politeness, scrawling them instead with the seedy innuendo her brother had read into their meaning.

The show of force from the older man was a smokescreen. He could do nothing legally to stop them leaving and he knew it. Threading his hands in his lap to prevent himself from retaliation, Tay waited. This meeting was not going anything like he had hoped that it would.

'With a name slathered and immured in depravity, it might be hard to protect anyone or anything, Alderworth. Your history of wildness and debauchery does not make for good reading and a hundred men and women of the *ton* would swear you are the Devil incarnate. No.' He shook his head. 'If we are looking into the etymology of words, I doubt *protection* in your book has the same meaning as it does in mine.'

The stubborn anger in Lucinda's brother's voice was more than evident—a man who was at the end of his tether and showing it. Taking in a breath, Tay took a different tack. 'Does Carisbrook know you have met me here this morning?'

'He does. His instructions were to stick a knife through the place where your heart should be.'

'Explicit.'

'Very.'

Tay detected the beginnings of a smile. 'Then perhaps we could forge a bargain that might suit us all.'

'Indeed?' The tone was not encouraging, but he needed to get at least one of the Wellinghams on his side and he had long admired Taris.

'I propose that my wife continues to reside in your family's town house for the next few weeks on the condition that I can escort her to various public functions of her choosing. That will allow you to see that I am not as black as you might paint me and give her time to see that I am not the bastard she thinks I am.'

'Asher has control of Lucinda's assets and all of her money.'

'Good.'

'And you will get none of it.'

His words were bland, no true reflection at all of the topic under discussion.

'All I want is a chance.'

'I can promise nothing without talking to my sister. I will, however, be advising her to run as fast and far away from you as she can and to refuse to partake in further dialogue or to accept other correspondence. If it is simply a case of enough money to be rid of you, then we have the means…'

'It isn't.'

'I thought not.'

He raised one arm and his man came immediately to his side. 'If Lucinda feels she would be interested in finding out more about the sort of man she has married, then I will not stop her and neither will my brothers. But it will be her decision, Alderworth, not yours.'

When Tay nodded and held out his hand, Taris Wellingham failed to respond. Laying his fingers upon the pristine white cloth covering the table, he stood as the other did and watched him leave, a tall dark-haired man who made his way with his servant beside him across the salon of a busy public bar, his lack of sight completely hidden to all those observing him.

Chapter Eight

'You do not have to go to this ball with Alderworth, Lucy. We can fight any allegation he might make through the courts and completely ruin his name.'

Taris took her hand and tears pooled behind Lucinda's eyes at both the familiarity and the safety.

'The Church recognises the sanctity of holy marriage and Taylen Ellesmere made it clear that he would never agree to a divorce.'

'Then let us talk to him again…'

'No.' She was most adamant about that. There was nothing more to be said. The Duke of Alderworth had offered her a proposition and freedom looked admirable after years of being shackled to a missing husband. All her friends, save Posy, were married and bearing children whilst she had wilted, growing old upon a shelf of her own making, withering into someone she had never thought to become.

She could bear it no longer, this middle land of no

choice at all, and, standing here in her best dress of light-blue shot silk, she knew that she wanted more.

'I need the chance to understand the only husband I am ever likely to have.'

She did not tell Taris that she had never been the slightest bit attracted to any other suitor in all her years of being out in society or that there was something about Taylen Ellesmere that made her heart run faster. She did not say that his green eyes had a promise in them she had found shocking because of her own capacity for response or that when he had spoken of the things he might like to do with her body at the Croxleys' ball she had finally felt…aroused.

Beatrice, from her place on the other side of the room, joined in the conversation.

'You are sure that this is what you wish, Lucinda? Alderworth seems both dangerous and alarming, a man who might be hard to tame.'

'He is my legal husband, Bea.'

'Your husband of only a few hours.' Her sister-in-law's voice was tight, though beneath it lurked a tone that was surprising. If Lucinda could have named it, she might have chanced humour.

Taris interceded. 'If there is ever any danger and you feel…'

'I am going to a ball a half a mile from home, Taris, with hundreds of people I know all around me. How could that possibly be dangerous?'

'Alderworth will not come here to get you?'

She shook her head. 'He said he would wait for

me at the Chesterfields' in Audley Street because he does not wish for another contretemps. Every time one of you meet him someone has been hurt so I can well understand his point.'

'Then I will ask you to give him this.' He pulled a letter from his pocket sealed in an envelope. Looking over at Beatrice, Lucinda knew the pair must have fashioned the missive last night when she had returned with the news of her imminent departure, a plan that had been changed that very morning to include at least two weeks in London.

'What is in it?'

'A warning. If Alderworth does anything to hurt you, anything at all, Asher, Cris and I will hunt him down to the very edges of the earth.' He swiped one hand through his hair, pushing back the darkness and looking as angry as she had ever seen him.

Goodness, if her brothers had any inkling of the agreement she had consented to regarding the conception of an heir, she doubted that they would have sent only a note.

The Chesterfield town house was one of the prettiest in Mayfair and one of the grandest, too, the sweeping drive of white pebbles leading to an imposing portico. Two men in livery stood at attention at each side of the wide flight of steps, Taylen Ellesmere between them, the darkness of his attire in complete contrast to the bright scarlet jackets they sported. He came forwards as he saw her and opened the door of her carriage, gesturing the Chesterfield servants away and shepherding her down a side path lit with lanterns, where they were hidden by trees.

Tonight he was dressed in charcoal, his long-tailed coat and breeches of the best-quality superfine. His cravat was loosely tied, no artifice in it, the snowy white of the fabric showing up the darkness of his skin and hair. A tall man and graceful with it. Where he touched her arm she felt the heat of contact. The ring she had given him all those years ago lay on his wedding finger and the small spark of recognition made her feel warmer. She was sure he had not been wearing it yesterday.

'I did not think you would come.' Lucinda could smell strong drink on his breath as he turned and stopped.

'I have a message for you.' In his company tonight she felt…uncertain and she hated the fact that she did. But in a crowded ballroom she knew she could simply slip away if she needed to. The thought calmed her as he turned the envelope over and looked closely at the writing. Breaking the seal, he opened the letter, reading it quickly before handing it back to her. 'This concerns you.'

Alderworth. One wrong move with our sister and you will pay for it.

The message was unsigned, but the parchment had the Wellingham insignia emblazoned at the top, an eagle argent on sable.

'You are fortunate in your protection.' His voice was an echo of some lost thing, surprising her.

'My brothers have been the most wonderful support in the world but…I am tired of being for ever thankful.'

Sacrilege to even utter such a sentiment, but she did, the words running into the silence between them like sharp daggers. Taking a breath, she looked around her at the other carriages coming up the drive. She was glad for the privacy the trees here afforded them.

'And the proposition I gave you yesterday?'

'You said you would not rush me, your Grace.' This time she looked directly at him, catching his eyes with her own in challenge.

'So formal?'

'We are strangers, you and I, who have been tied by the binding agreement of a marriage that is to neither of our liking. I barely know anything of you.'

'Which might be a good thing,' he returned, his words overlaid with just a tinge of regret. It was enough for Lucinda to press her conditions further.

'I couldn't tolerate the sort of parties you have made famous. An endless list of drunken guests parading through the places I reside within would be abhorrent to me and until…'

She could not finish because he leant forwards to take her hand, stroking the palm with his thumb so that small *frissons* of desire ran in ever-increasing strength up her arm.

'Until you are ripe with child?'

The shocking reality of the words made her pull back. That she could even have thought to control a man like Taylen Ellesmere, whose very world was so far from her own, was naïve.

'You may well laugh at our situation, your Grace, but I know that you accepted a large sum of money from my brother to disappear for ever. It is hard to trust a groom who only thinks to profit substantially from his bride.'

He looked away, a muscle in the side of his neck rippling with the tension only the guilty could feel. Asher had told her last night of the enormity of the sum Tay Ellesmere had taken and for a moment she had thought to rescind every agreement between them completely. But she had not. *Why* was a notion she found difficult to fathom, the thought of being tied to a man who had gained much fiscally from her misery more than demeaning. Lucinda waited for him to explain, to find some honour in his actions and clarify his reasons, but he stayed silent.

She felt the breaking of hope almost as a pain.

He was greedy and he was reckless. He was also dangerous, distant and intimidating. But there lay beneath the image he showed to the world other shadows, too, quieter and more beguiling. Tragedy was one such veil. She had seen it once when he had spoken of his uncle.

Secrets and silence stretched between them, the

sound of the world around distant, though her heart-beat drummed at a frantic rhythm in her ears.

He could not bring himself to say he had paid her brother back each and every single penny twofold, penance for the only time in his life where his integrity had been held to ransom. Not now. That would come later, far away from accusation and dishonour and the reality of an enticement he had succumbed to in desperation.

Breathing out hard, he tried to take a stock of things. His estranged wife looked a little like his mother used to, beautiful and prickly and angling for a fight, wanting high emotion to wreck what little peace he had left.

God. Patricia Ellesmere had used every single second of her life to make it harder for those near her and as her son it had often been him. Tay did not want acrimony and argument. He did not want greed and wrongdoing to punctuate everything that he was now, leaching out contentment and serenity.

Had he made a huge mistake by coming back after all, searching for an elusive something he could not quite forget? Almost three years of separation had hardened Lucinda. He could see it in her eyes. She was a different woman now, less innocent, more worldly.

'If it is of any use, I would apologise for the way I left. Excuses can only go a certain way in the alleviation of great pain so I won't bore you with them.'

'I have not heard even one explanation as yet, your Grace.' Her blue eyes were reflected in the silk of her dress, almost a match in colour.

'The dukedom was bankrupt.'

Surprise crept across her face. 'Surely my brother did not promise to rescue the Alderworth estate in its entirety?'

'No. He gave me the chance to do that myself. I hit a rich seam of gold in a river at the foot of the North Georgia mountains and had the luck to sell my claim for a tidy sum. After that I invested in the only services on a gold field that truly raise capital, the transportation facilities. The fortunes in mining are random, you see, but the large profits in the adjoining industries are not.'

'So you have arrived home rich?'

'I have.'

'And because of it you feel the need of an heir.'

He nodded.

'An unbroken line?'

'Precisely.'

'The saying that one person's luck is another's misfortune comes to mind.' Her mouth was a single tight line of fury.

She spoke as the forgotten wife who was suddenly recalled for duty a thousand days after he had left her. Such a thought was sobering, the contract for an heir stretching between them.

'If there is someone else who has gained your affections whilst I have been away, then I would—'

She did not let him finish. 'There isn't.'

Tay could not even begin to understand the relief he felt at her answer.

'After…us…I was largely left alone by others. Ruin has its own particular brand of isolation that is not easy to shake off. Besides, your reputation for debauchery and sexual experience meant all were wary.'

'When did you return to London?'

'Last year. My brothers insisted on it and their influence paved my way. It was all going well until…'

'I came back.'

She nodded and looked aside.

'Why, then, did you agree to come with me?'

He thought for a moment that she might not answer, as her eyes flinted in anger, but then she did, her voice shaking. 'Because anything is better than the stigma of abandonment.'

'I should not have let your brothers threaten me. I should have stayed and taken you to my home.'

'And forfeited your gold?' Her tone was neither soft nor conciliatory. It was hard and biting. 'No, your Grace, your promised largesse will go a long way in allowing me the freedom of a future I want.'

Tay shifted his stance and looked at her closely. She made him feel like the low-life he had not been, her lies cornering him into defending himself before her brothers, the licentious duke who had ruined a favoured sister.

Only he hadn't.

He had bundled up a woman who, with little persuasion, would have been easy to bed, but instead he had ordered a carriage and driven her home.

He had been paying for it ever since, by God, because the Wellinghams bore a grudge with great persistence, even one based on deceit.

He had sent his own correspondence, too, of course, a few careful letters explaining his daily routines and the harsh beauty of the countryside around Dahlonega. His wife had never written back. Not once. Tay wondered if Cristo Wellingham had stayed true to his promise and delivered the notes.

He could ask her, he supposed, pull the truth out of lies, but he had no more stomach for it and an idea hatched in the lonely fields of American dreams made little sense here.

The brothers' latest missive sizzled in his hand full of threat, the careful illusions of their wedding day dissolved here into only disappointment.

For them both.

'When we go to Alderworth Manor you will be given your own suite of rooms. I shall not presume on you for anything save for the fulfilment of our bargain.'

He turned away as she nodded and felt his body respond in anticipation of all that was implied.

I shall not presume on you for anything save for the fulfillment of our bargain.

A duty that had turned into obligation, the giving of her body for a sum of money and the promise of future freedom. A chore and a task that sounded onerous tonight. Lucinda couldn't decide just where she had lost all sense of herself: at Alderworth Manor three years ago or here, hurtling towards her marital requirements, only a womb for rent.

She could find no common ground with a husband who was a stranger, forged in hatred and anger by a family that gave no credence to close bonds or honest discourse.

'If I come, I would need at least a few weeks to settle in.' She blurted the words out, each one running on top of the other in a stream of quickness. 'I could not just be…'

She found it hard to finish.

'Pounced upon?'

Humour laced the query and she was glad for it, but still she pressed on.

'I would also require some sort of kindness, your Grace.'

This time he did laugh. 'How many men have you slept with, Lady Lucinda?' He did not use her married name and she did not answer. The corded arteries in his throat were raised in the dim light.

'I realise, of course, that you are used to faster women, women who would think nothing of sharing around their charms and making certain every man got their portion, but I am not of that ilk, your Grace, and if you think that I might change…'

'I do not wish for that at all.'

'Oh.' All of the wind went from her sails and she stood there, exposed and waiting. 'I need at least a few weeks,' she repeated, the quiver in her demand easily heard. Should she have bargained for more time? A month. A year?

'Very well.' His voice was hoarse, a promise co-erced only under duress. When he turned and offered her his arm, she could do nothing other than take it as he walked her back to the portico. Joining other couples who made their way up the wide stair-case, the light from the lamps showed up his face as a handsome and distant mask.

Lucinda had not understood just exactly what it meant to be at the side of a man who was the most vilified and envied Duke in all of London. When their names were called as they stood waiting to go in, she heard the distinct murmur of surprise and a momentary lull in conversation of the three hundred or so guests present.

'The Duke and Duchess of Alderworth.'

'Notoriety has its own set of drawbacks and this is one of them.' His voice was soft and steady, not a care in the world showing as he smiled at those who might crucify him. 'Let us just hope that your unblemished pedigree shelters you from some of it.'

'With an attitude like that it is a wonder you still receive invitations to anything at all, your Grace,' she replied.

'No one wants to be the first to leave the lofty

ducal title off their guest list and especially now they know all the coffers are full.'

'How full?'

The tone in his voice changed somewhat as he replied. 'Full enough to call in the chits of men with fewer morals than I have.' As she pulled back he made an effort to lighten such darkness. 'Full enough so that you could order as many gowns as you desire and I would barely notice, Duchess.'

'Tempting.'

His hand closed tighter in a movement that claimed her as his wife and Lucinda was pleased not one of her brothers was present as they walked down into the crowd. Edmund Coleridge was at the front of the group and smiled at her fondly, but she did not encourage him to come forwards because a small part of her worried that Alderworth would slice any tenderness to pieces should he know of it.

The Beauchamps, Lord Daniel and his French wife Lady Camille, were the first to receive them.

'I had heard you were back, Tay. How long are you here for?'

His brown eyes were kind and Camille Beauchamp seemed just as welcoming. Perhaps this evening would not be as difficult as Lucinda had thought it, her husband's reputation melding with her own to produce some sort of a halfway point of acceptability.

'Only a few weeks.'

'Then you might come to see us before then.' Camille joined the conversation for the first time, her lilting French accent beautiful. 'My husband made a point of telling me that you speak French well, your Grace. I should enjoy a conversation in my native language.'

More couples drifted over towards them, amongst the group an old school friend of Lucinda's. Annabelle Browne was as effusive as ever.

'Why, I just absolutely cannot imagine what it must have been like for your husband to have spent three years in the Americas, Lucy. My brother, Anthony, was in Washington for only a small amount of time and he was most forthcoming about the primitive state of the place.'

'I suspect that Alderworth managed,' she returned.

'The gold fields were dens of iniquity, I am told. It was a shame you could not have been there with him, to guide him through the pitfalls.'

'Oh, I am certain my husband was able to navigate them by himself, Annabelle.' The cutting she had received from Annabelle's brother came to mind and in an effort to change the topic she looked around at the others present. But Annabelle Browne was as persistent as she was dull-witted.

'Tony says the Duke was lucky in his windfall and that he left Georgia under a cloud.'

'A cloud of what?'

'Suspicion. His partner in the mining venture, Montcrieff, was killed and there was some discussion as to who would have benefitted most from such a tragedy. It seems Alderworth did.' She smiled sweetly, setting Lucinda's teeth on an edge.

'I am certain had there been anything untoward, the constabulary would have moved in.'

'But they did, you see, that is my very point. Tony said that your Duke was supposed to come before the courts in Atlanta, but—'

She stopped, aware of Alderworth's glance upon her.

'I was freed, Miss Browne, as an innocent man. The law has its uses after all, even though most of the time it is an ass.' His smile was languid, the creases in his cheeks deep against his tan and in a room full of men who had spent the good part of the day getting ready for this evening's entertainment he looked untamed—a ranging wolf amongst dainty chickens. The vibrant green of his eyes added to his menace.

Annabelle turned red and for a moment Lucinda viewed the world as Taylen might have, the innuendo and aspersion on his character a constant presence. She made herself smile as she faced her husband.

'It is most trying when people insist on passing on false rumours, do you not think, Duke?'

'Indeed,' he returned, and they both watched as the woman gave her goodbyes and dragged the man she was with away.

'I do not need you to defend me,' he said as Annabelle Browne moved out of hearing and the anger in his voice was sharp.

'Do you not, your Grace? I should have thought the very opposite.' She stood her ground as he loomed above her.

'Doubts begin to creep in if one crows one's innocence too loudly, I find.' He was back to his most infuriating best.

'It is more than doubts that hold those in this room enthralled in the saga of the Alderworth family. Were I to name it I might chance…fear.'

A small flicker of doubt came into his face. 'Do you fear me then, too?'

'No.' Surprisingly she did not. The answer tripped from her tongue in truth as their glances met and held, a living flame of heat that curled around sense and wisdom. She should fear him because every single thing she heard about him compromised all she had known before and just as they were finding a footing together some other new and terrible story pushed all accord aside leaving only this…attraction.

It would never be enough, she knew, tragedy and disaster trumping proper judgement and good sense. But she could not help it.

Intrinsically flawed.

And she was.

Lucinda was looking at him as though he might stab the next person who came to talk to them. The aspersions just aired, he supposed, as the face of Lance Montcrieff rose up in memory, an accident with their rudimentary stamp mill in Ward's Creek slicing through his thigh just below the groin.

It had taken less than ten minutes for him to bleed out, despite Tay's efforts to staunch the flow, and Tay had held his hand through every long and harrowing one of them, willing his friend to live even as breath dulled and stopped. Gold took no account of the integrity of its victims, for if it had it would have been him lying there with cold blue on his lips and death in his skin, thousands of miles from home.

Another loss. Another brush with the law. Another woman without a husband, another child fatherless.

Swallowing, he pulled himself back into the ballroom on Audley Street with its chandeliers and wide curtained alcoves, marbled pillars and liveried servants.

A gentle England that had not been his for a long, long time. He had forgotten its beauty and peace, he thought, as his wife swayed unconsciously to the beat of music, deliberately not looking his way.

'Would you dance with me again?'

He expected her to refuse, but she did not. Instead he found her fingers within his outstretched hand and then they were on the floor amongst the other couples, the music of a waltz beginning.

He had always liked the way she fitted into him, her head just under the curve of his chin, liked how she allowed him to lead her, an easy flowing dancer with a light and clever step.

He did not usually dance at these social occasions, but spent the hours in the card rooms drinking away the night.

'How did the man in America die? The one Annabelle spoke of, I mean?' Her query was soft and he could think of no other of his acquaintance who might have asked this question so directly of him.

'His name was Lance. Lance Montcrieff. We set up a stamp mill outside Dahlonega to crush the ore from the tunnels and release the gold. When the sapling holding the structure broke and it all came down on him, he never stood a chance. We were ten hours from the nearest township, you understand, and a lot of that was over rough terrain.'

'Why did they blame you?'

'Gold has the propensity to make fools of every man and a rich claim incites questions. I was the one who would profit most from his death, after all, and there was no one else about to vouch that my story was true.'

Her breath hitched against the skin at his throat. Another truth she did not want probably. Another way she would be disappointed in him.

'Trouble never seems very far away from your door, your Grace. Do you ever wonder why?'

Shaking his head, he was amazed when she let him pull her closer, their bodies now touching almost like lovers. The firm daintiness of her breasts rubbed against his chest and he pushed his groin against her own in a quiet statement of intent.

Slender fingers tightened on his hands. Their bodies talked now in the smallest of caresses, almost accidental, never hurried—a slight pressure here, a small stroke there, too new for words, too fragile for any true acknowledgement. Taylen had never been in a room before and felt so removed from everybody in it. Save her. Save his wife with her straightforward questions and her unexpected allegiance.

'What is Edmund Coleridge to you?'

'A friend who has helped me to laugh again.'

'That is all. Just the laughter?' He did not care for the hesitation in her words or the sudden stiffness in her body.

'Why all these questions, your Grace?' She smiled as she asked, a smile that made her look so beautiful, with her deep-set dimples and pale spun-gold hair, that he had to glance away.

'My father may have had no problem with being cuckolded, Duchess, but I most certainly do.' He did not like the unease he could so plainly hear in his words.

'Three years of absence makes your insistence on celibacy rather hard to take, your Grace. Perhaps I should inform you that a woman, contrary to belief, has as many needs as a man.'

'Needs I wish to fill, sweetheart, and tonight if you would let me.'

He felt shock run down through all the parts of her body in a hot and hard wash, and was glad for it. If he had been anywhere else save in a crowded ballroom, he could have used such a reaction to persuade her to take a chance on him. Such an easy seduction. He had done it so many times before, after all, and not one woman had ever held complaint.

Yet as he gritted his teeth those faceless paramours dissolved into the ether just as they had done for a while now, lost to him and formless, lovers with the word skewered into only faithless lust. The broken promises of his childhood bound into the present.

When the music stopped they came apart and he was glad for the distance as he went to find a drink.

Lucinda felt giddy. A ridiculous word, she knew, but it explained her lack of certainty entirely. Taylen Ellesmere threw her into a place that was without compass, directionless and wanton.

Wanton? Another word she smiled at. Tonight her vocabulary regarding misdirected emotions was growing and she did not wish for it to stop. Already she looked for him across the room, tall and dark amongst a sea of others.

She was like a moth to his light, fluttering unheeded, waiting to be burnt. Her brothers had warned her, her sisters-in-law had told her stories about him and none of the tales had been kind. Yet still some invisible bond drew her to him, the wedding ring circling her finger a part of it, but nowhere near the total. Her nails dug into the soft flesh of her palms as she pondered her intentions.

What did she want of him? She could not even begin to name it.

Posy Tompkins came to her side and took her hand. Lucinda liked the warm familiarity of the action.

'You look beautiful tonight, Luce, and I think that fact has something to do with the return of your mysterious husband. Edmund has already been whining to me about your lack of attention.'

'You never liked him, Posy. I am not certain why.'

'He is a boy compared to the Duke of Alderworth, a boy who in the end would disappoint you.'

'And you think that the Duke would not?'

'I think he has been misjudged by society. I think he is strong like your brothers and honourable in his way. I think, if you gave him a chance, he might surprise you.'

'You were always the romantic, Posy.'

'To find the happiness you haven't had ever since your wedding, Luce, you might need to allow Alderworth some ground for compromise, for a bending is better than a breaking. If it were me, I would grab him with both hands and never let him go.'

'Fine words from a woman who has sworn off relationships for ever.'

Posy's more normal optimism was sliced by a sadness Lucinda had sometimes seen in her friend before. 'He reminds me of a man I knew a long time ago, in Italy.'

Their conversation was interrupted by the arrival

of the Elliott twins, their voices louder than they needed to be.

'Lucinda, it is so wonderful that your husband is finally back. You must be thrilled that he has returned after all this time?'

Elizabeth Elliott was as effusive as her sister, Louise. 'Everybody is talking about him, of course, and it seems he has arrived back in England a lot richer than when he left it. Perhaps you might both come to our ball on Saturday night—for Edmund Coleridge had already said that he will be there.'

The questionable undercurrents of the *ton* at play, Lucinda thought, and was glad when Posy took charge.

'I had heard a rumour that you are to be married, Lady Elizabeth. Is it true?'

A scream of delight and then much was made of a ring on the third finger of her left hand. Lucinda scanned the room for any sign of her husband and was disappointed when she could not see him at all. Had he simply left or was he in the card room, drinking himself into oblivion and losing a fortune? The excitement she had felt before was suddenly changed into cold hard worry and she did not like the feeling at all.

Ten minutes later she made her way to a large terrace overlooking the garden and was about to walk out on to the edge of it when a scuffle and shouting at the far end caught her attention. Richard Allenby, the Earl of Halsey, was pummelling someone on the ground, a number of others around the prone body adding their particular attentions. Turning away in order to find somebody to help, she saw the profile of the person they were hurting suddenly in the light.

'Taylen.' Shouting, she moved forwards, catching the group unawares, each one of them looking towards her with a varying degree of disbelief on their faces. Then she was amongst them, sheltering her husband with her body and daring them to go through her person to get to him.

Blood was on his nose and his chin, a long cut across the back of his head and a metal bar lying down beside him. He looked groggy and dazed, his collar crooked and his jacket torn.

'You have no business here.' Allenby's voice. She turned to face him with pure wrath.

'No business, Lord Halsey?' Her hand came out to push him back. 'Will you hit me next, then? Do you creep up on defenceless women as well as men?' She stooped as she spoke; her fingers found the bar and she raised it above her head. 'If anyone comes closer, I will use it on them and I will scream the place down as I do it, you understand. And then when people come running I will tell them exactly what I saw; a bunch of cowardly thugs beating up a badly injured, half-conscious man in their midst and enjoying it.'

Silence reigned except for the breath of her husband, taken noisily through blood and mucus, then they were gone, all of them, the door to the ballroom shutting, leaving them alone.

She leant down to him, his blood staining her blue silk as she tried to mop up his face with her hem. Her hands shook with the shock of it all and she made an effort to still them.

She knew the moment he came back into full consciousness because he stiffened and tried to stand, coming up to his haunches in a way that suggested great pain and swaying with the movement.

'The bastards hit me from behind.' His fingers worked around into his hair, finding a gash as he looked at the bar. 'They used that, I suppose. Halsey always was a coward.'

Lucinda thought that his pupils looked larger than they should be, green shrunk into darkness. He blinked a lot, too, as though his vision was impaired and he was trying to find the way to correct it.

'There are stairs at the other end of the terrace. If we went through the garden, we could get to the road to find your carriage.'

'You would come with me?'

'Of course I would. You need help.'

'If people see us, they will talk.'

When she laughed it felt free and real and good, a surprising discovery with the trauma of all that was happening around her. 'They talk now, your Grace, and there is too much blood to go back into the ballroom. If they see you like this, everything will be worse.'

Nodding, he came up into a standing position, though his hands used the balustrade to steady himself, to find his balance. 'I have ruined your gown.' His top lip was thickening even as he spoke.

'A small consideration given all of the others.'

The music had begun again, calling those present to the dancing, and Lucinda was pleased for it. With so much happening inside it would be far less likely for a guest to take the air on the terrace. Placing her arm across his, she led him down the steps, the small pathways amongst the plants lined with white chip stone which made it easy to traverse in the moonlight. Before a moment or so had passed they were out at the gate and Lucinda hailed the Alderworth conveyance, which languished further down the road, the driver throwing a cheroot to the ground and stomping it underfoot before climbing up into the driving box.

Another moment and they were inside with the door closed behind them and, for the first time since finding her husband at the feet of his assailants, Lucinda took in an easy breath. They would not be discovered like this, battered and bloodied after such a scandalous attack. They were safe.

Reaching into her reticule, she found a handkerchief. 'Here, let me help you.'

His hand came out as he shook away the offer, anger evident in his refusal.

'Why would Halsey waylay you in the way he did?'

Taylen Ellesmere raised his head slightly and had the temerity to smile.

'Because, once upon a time, I did just the same to him.'

Chapter Nine

'You crept up on him like a coward and knocked him out?'

He shook his head and then clutched at the side of it.

'With a whole group of others to help you do your dirty work?'

'Of course not.'

'You used an iron bar on his scalp and hit him with it from behind, allowing him no chance to defend himself, and when he was down you kicked at his face?'

He seemed to suddenly lose patience with her questions, leaning forwards to take her hand into his.

'Thank you, Lucinda.'

'You are welcome, Taylen.'

His blood had made his palm sticky and he was careful to wipe her fingers with the tail of his shirt when he let go. Such a simple action and so much imbued within it. She looked away so that he would not see the emotion on her face. Outside the London streets were as busy as usual, nothing changed. Inside her world had shifted, though, the touch of his fingers against her own different now, more familiar. His smell. His warmth. The breadth of his thighs as they pressed against the velour on the seat.

'My parents always believed in the concept of treating everyone as an enemy. Tonight I forgot.' The words were said concisely, as if he would place a point on each one of them.

'Advice like that makes me wonder whether such people have the right to offspring. Surely no child deserves to be brought up under such a cruel misconception.'

The sound of his laughter filled the small space, allowing accord to push through shock and anger. 'Are you usually so forthright, Duchess?'

'Indeed I am, Duke. My family would tell you that it is one of my greatest faults.'

His head shook as the Wellingham town house came into view, the action shadowed on the wall of the carriage behind him by the light from the portico. His hair had worked free from its leather strap and lay around his shoulders, darker than the darkness.

'But I would not. Free speech has always been a particular preference of mine. I think it a residue of being raised by parents who never said what they actually thought.'

'Because they were trying to protect you?'

He laughed again and was about to say something more when a movement on the stairs before them caught his attention. 'It seems we have a welcoming party.'

Lucinda's heart sank. With the blood from his nose still smeared across his face, a rapidly darkening eye and a thickened lip, Taylen Ellesmere looked exactly like the reprobate her brothers had good reason to think that he was.

'I won't come in. I doubt my body could take another beating.' The dispassionate and cynical Duke was back, no warmth in his eyes at all as the footman opened the door and the light spilled upon them.

'A further rowdy night of fighting, Alderworth?' Asher's question was layered with disgust.

'Someone has to subdue the scum of London. It may as well be me.'

'No, it isn't as you think it—' Lucinda began as she stepped down from the coach, but her husband cut her off.

'I will see you tomorrow, Duchess. Thank you for the most interesting of evenings.'

A rap with his cane on the roof had the horses moving, the perfectly matched pair of greys gathering speed as they disappeared down the road.

'His blood has ruined your gown.' Asher ground the words out as they walked back inside.

'Halsey did it. Halsey and a group of his cowardly friends. They caught him alone on the terrace at the ball in a planned attack. He had no chance against them.'

A look crossed her brother's face, dark and unexplainable, and a terrible idea suddenly occurred to Lucinda.

'You did not pay anyone to do that to him, did you, Ashe?'

'Halsey is a weak-willed and arrogant sycophant. If I wanted the job done, I would do it properly myself.'

'Well, don't.' She stood to her tallest height in her stained and crumpled gown, the shock of the evening on her face and an anger boiling beneath everything that was dubious. 'Hurt Alderworth, I mean. I am tired of being the forgotten wife and I want at least the chance to…' She stopped, not quite able to voice what it was she did want.

'The chance to what?' His dark eyes were filled with an urgent question.

'To…know something of the man I have married.'

With that she swept past, making for the staircase and the privacy of her room.

Tay held a hand close against his chest. He was sure a few of his ribs were broken and knew they would hurt like the devil in the morning. Breathing shallowly, he leaned forwards, finding in the movement a slight relief. The wedding ring he had retrieved that morning from the bottom drawer of his library desk felt solid on his finger.

Lucinda had seen him helpless at the feet of a pack of cowards who had crept up on him as he was lighting a cheroot, the evening with his wife making him less vigilant than he normally was. Usually the *ton* avoided any contretemps or whiff of scandal, but Lucinda had come forwards with her integrity and her honour, admonishing grown men with words that he could not have bettered.

Like a fierce and urgent angel. Lord, he was the sinner married to a saint and with his past it would be her paying for such loyalty again and again and again. The shock in her eyes, her trembling fingers, her ruined gown and disappointment scrawled in deep lines across her brow. He had seen her stiffen when her oldest brother had come out to meet them. Another mortification. He smiled at the word and then regretted it as the skin on his top lip stung.

Without Lucinda here everything hurt, badly, a cold emptiness closing in about him. He would not meet her tomorrow or the day after that, for he needed time to nurse his wounds and to try to find some idea as to where to go to next.

He could not keep putting his wife into danger or see her compromised by his own lack of regard for the law and there were more of the ilk of Halsey out there than he would have liked to admit.

Remembering Lucinda's words in the carriage as she had tried to explain to him why he was nothing like Richard Allenby, he smiled. No one had ever been on his side before, not like that and in the

face of such damning evidence. The feeling was…
warming.

Shaking his head hard, he told himself to put such
nonsense aside. Twenty-eight years had taught him
a few home truths and one of them was to depend
upon nobody.

Treat everyone as an enemy.

His mother and father's son after all, the words
scrawled into his flesh like a tattoo. Ineradicable
and permanent.

Lucinda did not see Taylen Ellesmere the next
day or the day after. No note of explanation came.

Her brothers had ceased to talk of Alderworth
whatsoever, hoping perhaps that by ignoring him
he might go away, but she haunted the wide front-
window bays like a wraith, glancing out each time
a noise caught her attention or the sound of hooves
echoed on the street, her breath catching with every
newcomer turning into the square, eyes picking out
their livery with interest. He might be laying low, but
the bargain for an heir that they had struck between
them still simmered underneath everything, calling
through the silence.

'You seem jumpy.' Eleanor sat on the small sofa
in the blue room working on a tapestry.

Smiling half-heartedly, Lucinda picked up her
own needlework, but the stitches blurred before her,
the counting of each one difficult today.

'I did not sleep well last night or the one before

that.' Goodness, that was an understatement. She had lain awake almost till the dawn, worrying.

'I could make you one of my tonics if you like. It is bound to help you relax.'

As Lucinda shook her head to decline the offer, the needle pierced her finger, drawing blood, yet instead of wiping it away she watched as the red of the wound spread into white cotton. Other blood came to mind. The injuries Taylen Ellesmere had sustained were substantial and damaging and she wondered how he fared now. Who would tend to him and make certain he was not becoming worse? His breathing had been laboured, after all, and she was sure his nose had been broken.

Standing again, she walked to the window, unconcerned as to what Eleanor might make of her distractedness. Outside drizzle coated the world in grey, a few leaves falling on the gardens with their ragged yellow edges brittle. Like her. She felt the tension in all of the corners of her body, scraping away contentment, panic close to the skin. Tears pooled at the back of her eyes. One step forwards and then two steps back. She was tired of the uncertainty and the confusion.

'Is the contretemps at the Chesterfield ball worrying you?' Eleanor came to stand beside Lucinda, the palm of her hand making contact.

A nod brought the hand fully around Lucinda's shoulders.

'Cristo thinks Alderworth may have been the one

to deal with Halsey three years ago, which would explain the attack upon him in Mayfair after the carriage accident. He said that he may have misjudged him.'

'Alderworth would not thank him for the compliment were he to hear of it, Eleanor.'

'Because he is prickly and distant and completely unmindful of a reputation that is hardly salutary? Or because he likes to hide behind an image that is not entirely the truth?' The tone in her words was a worried one. 'His grandmother used to hit him, you know. Hard. She thought such training would make a man of her grandchild because her own daughter had become such a biting disappointment with her many lovers and her drinking.'

Bile rose in Lucinda's throat as she turned to her sister-in-law. 'Who told you that?'

'Rosemary Jones, my maid's older sister. She works at Falder now, but as a young girl she was employed by Lady Shields at her home in Essex.'

'Many children are punished, Eleanor.'

'Not in the way he was. According to Rosemary, he spent months away from the family in a hospital in Rouen after one particular incident. Then his uncle took him away.'

'An uncle? Which uncle?'

'Hugo Shields, Lord Sutton, I think was the name mentioned. His mother's brother. Rosemary did not see any of the family again because she was asked to leave. The old lady had some inkling of her disapproval, I suppose, and did not wish to be reminded of an unsavoury period in her life.'

Goodness. The whole horror of everything began to mount inside Lucinda. Between a heavy-handed grandmother and a brutal uncle, the small Taylen Ellesmere never had a chance, just as he did not now with the building censure of a society that barely knew him.

'I think I will take the carriage out, Eleanor. I need to see my milliner about a hat.'

'I will tell your brothers that you have a few errands to do, Lucy. I know there are a pile of library books well overdue from Hookham's Lending Library if you would not mind dropping them off for me.'

'Certainly.' She smiled as Eleanor did. Both knew that the Ellesmere town house was only a few hundred yards from the mentioned establishment, a distance easy to walk.

The door of Alderworth House opened almost instantly after her maid rang the bell, a tall man ushering them into a room which was light and airy, the windows looking out on to a garden filled with greenery. A mismatched set of a sofa and two chairs were arranged before the fireplace and there were faded areas on the walls where pictures had been removed and never replaced. Lucinda wondered why the Duke had not had the place refurbished after his windfall in the Americas.

'I'll tell his Grace you are here, your Grace.' Elles-mere's butler's face flushed at the recognition of her name and he seemed to hesitate for a moment as if he could not quite decide what to do. 'It might take a few moments,' he managed finally. 'A maid will bring tea and cakes into you while you wait.'

'Thank you.'

Claire, her maid, stood by the door, her face a careful blank canvas. She was probably balancing the luxury of the Carisbrook houses against the fru-gality here, a topic that would be faithfully reported back to the downstairs staff at the Wellingham town house to mull over and discuss. Lucinda wished she might have asked her to wait with the carriage, but to do so would have invited questions.

She heard a cat howling outside somewhere close. Further afield the faint trip-trop of a carriage wending its way was audible above the ticking of an ancient ornate clock in the corner, its glass face shattered on one side and the time running a good half an hour slow.

The piece had already boomed out twice before the door opened again and Tay Ellesmere stood there, formally dressed and his gait stiff. His hair was wet, giving the impression he had just bathed, and it was pulled back into a tight tail falling to his shoulders. One eye was ringed in black whilst the white of the other had changed into a violent red, deeper marks of the same colour snaking into his hair at the tem-ple. He smelled of soap and of lemon, a combination that was appealing, but all she could think of were Rosemary the scullery-maid's words: a small battered child lost behind hard green eyes.

'I am sorry. I did not realise we had arranged a meeting.'

'We had not, your Grace. It is just the last time I saw you it looked as though your injuries were worse than you let on and I thought to check to see if you were…well?'

'I am. Entirely.' The puffy edge of his right eye had made it close at one end. Lucinda wondered if it blurred his vision because he squinted as he watched her, the tick in his swollen eyelid clearly visible.

'I see.'

She wished with all her heart that they might have a moment in private. He seemed to understand her reticence as his glance took in the servants. 'Bingham, would you take the Duchess's maid to the kitchen and find her something to drink.'

'Very well, your Grace.' It took only a moment for the room to be cleared and the door to be shut behind them.

'A walk in the park would be out of the question, I suppose?' She kept her tone light as she broke the awkward silence.

'Unless you want me to scare small children.' His smile went nowhere near his eyes. 'Why are you here?' Tiredness draped the query.

'I have waited for you for the past two days and

when you did not come I wondered if you had the medical help that you needed…'

'I do.'

He did not even look at her now.

'What was the reason for your attack on Halsey all those years ago?'

That brought his attention back. 'Allenby broke one of the most important rules of my house.'

'Which was?'

'What goes on at Alderworth stays there.'

Disappointment welled. So it wasn't solely because he had been trying to protect her, after all.

'It seems to me enforcing such a rule would require much effort?' The sharpness in her voice was not becoming, but she could no longer hide it. 'Why seek more battles when you had enough of your own to fight?'

'Usually I am more handy with my fists than you saw me to be at the Chesterfields', and making certain scandal does not follow each of my guests home has not been unduly onerous before.'

Today Taylen Ellesmere was exactly the Duke his title proclaimed him to be, the solemn answers at odds with his damaged face and eyes. He stood strangely, too, straight-backed and erect, the pose making her wonder what other injuries he had sustained under the ministration of Halsey and his cronies.

'But scandal follows you regardless, your Grace. Your own reputation has been the talk of the town for years.'

He moved towards her and reached out his hand, one finger tracing its way down her cheek.

'Every opinion should be allowed to be given freely, I believe, but it is wise to remember that what is said is not always the truth.'

The warmth and the strength of him flooded into her being, a touchstone in the scattered uncertainty of her life, drawing her home.

Hold me closer, she longed to say, as if their history together melded only into the bright promise of this moment, but his hand fell back instead.

'If you don't wish to be in my company for a while, I would quite understand. I cannot promise that there will not be another contretemps, you see, and if you were to be hurt because of it...'

He stopped.

'I am no weak-willed girl, your Grace. Were I to be pitted against your own skills with a bow and arrow I may well win the competition.' She held her palms face up. 'I have the calluses to prove it.'

For the first time that day true humour crept into his face. 'My Diana.' The words were whispered and then regretted. She could see the wariness in his eyes.

'Do you have any other family at all, your Grace?'

His brow creased at the subject change.

'Why do you ask?'

'You seem so alone sometimes. I only wondered if there were others you might rely on.'

He shook his head and crossed to pour himself a

drink, lifting a brandy decanter to offer her one as well. Declining, she waited until he began to speak.

'I have an aunt, but I lost any contact with her years ago.'

'A fading line, then?'

His smile was wicked. 'Which brings us back to our agreement.'

The heir. With a thick cloak on, servants just outside the door and her maid presumably returning at any moment Lucinda also smiled. 'A broken nose and cracked ribs have probably put paid to any designs you might have on me at the moment.'

His laughter filled the room, deep and resonant. 'Injuries such as these have not stopped me before.'

'I read of you once. A story in a newspaper when you had first struck gold.'

'Where did you get it from?'

'An old school friend's brother sent it to me. The author of the piece made certain that the readers understood that the women you were partying with were…" She could not quite find the word.

'Fallen?' He provided it for her. 'The difference between the *ton* and those who ply their bodies for money on the street corners of hopelessness is smaller than you might imagine. Believe me, I know it to be true.'

Was he speaking of his childhood? she wondered and braved a question. 'How did your uncle hurt you?'

'Badly.'

A truth, without an embroidered qualifying word attached? Lucinda could barely believe his honesty.

'He should have been shot.'

'He was.'

'Oh.'

The words were on her tongue to ask by whom, but the gleam in his green eyes stopped the question. She wanted amiability and agreement to be between them, even if only for this meeting.

'Would you ride with me tomorrow, your Grace? In the park. I usually go early before the crowds arrive.'

'Yes.'

She could hear the voices of her maid and one of the Ellesmere servants in the hallway coming closer. 'Shall we say nine o'clock?'

He reached over and rang the bell, the same man she had seen before hurrying back in. Claire also rejoined them, standing behind the sofa, a heavy frown upon her brow.

'Thank you for taking the time to see that I was regaining in strength, Duchess, and please do give my regards to your family.'

'I will, your Grace.'

So formal. So many undertones. She hoped with all her heart that her maid would say nothing of the visit to Asher's valet before she had had the chance to tell her brother.

'I went to see Taylen Ellesmere today,' Lucinda announced at dinner just as the main course was being served. On the journey home she had decided that honesty would be the best ploy with her family and bringing things out into the open was far better than having them simmer and boil over in the shadows.

'How is his face?' Emerald asked, her smile belying any more sinister purpose.

'I do not know if his nose is broken, though the boots of Halsey's minions did a good job of trying to do so. Both his eyes are blackened and there is a sizeable cut to the back of his head. Perhaps other injuries linger beneath his clothes. He certainly moved as if they did.'

'Trouble follows him like a stray dog after the meat man.' Her brother's voice was wary.

'I remember a time when it seemed to follow me with as much tenacity.' Emerald looked directly at Asher and the spark that ignited between them had Lucinda glancing away. Passion in a marriage bed was something she had never experienced, the burn of it rolling across ordinariness and lifting everything up. Every one of her siblings had that sort of feeling with their partner and she was suddenly tired of her own lack of hope for the same.

'I have asked the Duke to accompany me on my morning ride in the park tomorrow.'

'And he has agreed?' There was no warmth in her brother's query whatsoever. 'You may regret allowing a man who seems to find a fight at every oppor-

tunity, unprovoked or not, back into your life, Lucy.'
Fury raised the tone of his voice.

'He is my legal husband.'

'A matter that was supposed to be resolved three
years ago by a large sum of money. We hoped never
to see him again and we would not have, save for a
lucky strike in a Godforsaken goldfield miles from
England which allowed him to crawl back.'

Lucinda stood, breath coming almost as fast as
her heart was beating. 'Perhaps that is divine inter-
vention, then. Gold for gold and the recommencing
of an ordained union promised before a minister of
the Church. Surely when you hatched this plan of
matrimony a small part of you thought that it might
just…stick?'

Asher stood now, too, and Lucinda was glad that
the table lay between them, a solid wide slab of oak
that divided the room down its length.

'God damn it, you are my sister and I was only
trying to protect you.' For the first time in memory
her oldest brother sounded…defeated, the strain of
the last week showing on his face in deep lines of
regret.

'And you do that well, but I do not wish to live
with you for ever. I need to find my own life, too.'

'I will gift you Amberley Manor in Kent, then.
That estate is more than ample for your needs. You
can stay there with a stipend if you cannot stay here.'

'But I will still be beholden to your generosity,
don't you see, and with no recourse to marriage again

it will always be that way. For ever. Until I am old and childless and alone.'

'So you would agree instead to give the benefit of doubt to a Duke who displays neither morality nor virtue? A man you hate?'

'Eleanor seems to think he is more virtuous than any of us might realise, Asher.' Emerald came around the table to stand by Lucinda, her turquoise eyes deep pools of worry. 'She says that the servants at his London town house have a great deal of regard for him.'

'You imagine that is enough?'

'Cristo said Alderworth dealt with Halsey when he was spreading rumours of Lucinda's...dalliance. He seems to believe Halsey waylaid him to pay him back. If that is the case, we ought to be thanking him, not maligning him.' She stopped for a moment before carrying on. 'It is also rumoured that Alderworth still supports the wife and children of his mining partner, killed in an accident in America. Only an honourable person would do that.'

Unexpectedly her brother began to laugh. 'Lord, Emmie, if we want to find out about anyone it would be wise to ask you first.'

'All I am saying is that he may be a good man whom you have not given a chance to.'

'A good man who locked my sister in a room against her will and hád her way with her. That sort of a good man?'

'Well, if Lucy finds that she cannot bear him, then

she can take you up on your offer of Amberley. It is not medieval England after all. Alderworth cannot keep her anywhere against her will.'

The thought that he might do just that showed on Asher's face as a dark uncertainty, but the heart of his argument had been taken to pieces and Lucinda knew that Asher would allow her the freedom she asked for. However, when she exchanged a smile of gratitude with her sister-in-law, she saw in the turquoise eyes a quick burst of puzzlement and pity before she turned for the door.

Chapter Ten

As Lucinda brushed away a curl that had escaped her bonnet in the wind, a movement to one side of the park caught her eye.

Taylen Ellesmere watched her from a distance and she waited as he threaded his way towards her on a large dark stallion.

'You ride well,' he said as he reached her. Today his bruising looked less and he moved with more ease, though his right eye was still brutally red.

'You have been watching me?'

'I had heard you had a good seat.' His left hand shifted on the reins and the rings on his fingers caught in the sun, underlining the differences between them. Such adornment seemed an over-embellishment and foreign, though she was pleased to see that the ring she had given him as a wedding vow still lay amongst the others. He hailed from a world that was so far removed from her own that Lucinda wondered if she might ever truly know him.

When he saw where she looked he stilled, the vigilance that seldom left his eyes easily seen.

'I ride here most days when I am in town, your Grace. It is a freeing thing.'

'I have also heard it said that you tool a barouche like a champion.'

She laughed. 'Taris taught me.'

'You are fortunate, then, in the care your family gives you.'

She wished her brothers had heard the compliment he gave them, for perhaps then they might not have been quite so averse to any communication. The breeze caught at a line of oaks to one side of the path, sending a scattering of green leaves into the air.

'I think the early morning shows Hyde Park at its best,' she chanced when he did not deign to speak.

'Indeed. My grandfather loved it here, too. It was the closest he ever got to a peaceful and solitary life given my grandmother's disposition, for he spent all of his hours wandering the parks and gardens when he was in town.'

'He sounds kind.'

'He was.'

'How old were you when he died?'

'Six and a half.' So precisely known, Lucinda thought.

'I met Lady Shields a few times. She seemed difficult.'

'And now she lies beside my grandfather in consecrated ground for all of eternity.'

'Matrimony being the most onerous of bonds to break away from?' The sting in her voice did not become her, but his last words made her wonder if that was what he might think of their union, too.

He was quiet for a moment. 'There are things about marriage that one could find…addictive.'

She thought he meant sex and stiffened, but when he kept on talking she knew that that was not what he was alluding to at all.

'A person to watch your back and be on your side no matter what happens is one of them. I do not think I thanked you enough for doing just that the other night at the Chesterfields' Ball. No one ever has before.'

Again she saw behind the mask, a quick glimpse of a man she could love. A lot.

'I was glad to help.' So precise and stilted. She wished he would dismount and reach out to thank her with his body, but he did not, his attention caught by others riding behind them.

Shifting in his seat, his horse shied to one side and he gentled him. A few other souls had now ventured out on the same pathways, tipping their hats as they passed and looking back with more than interest on their faces. Tay knew the gossip mills had been grinding ever since his return to England and that the betting in the clubs were riding fifty to one

he would have his estranged wife beneath him before the week's end.

He might have enjoyed the irony of it all, but such
a gamble cut too close to the quick and fifty to one
still seemed like damn long odds. He hoped that the
Wellingham brothers had no knowledge of the punt-
ers' flutterings.

The stakes were rising and he could not get Lucinda to himself until at least after the promised two
weeks.

Breathing deeply, he bid his horse on and was glad
when his wife followed his lead, the path wider now
and more conducive to a canter. There was nothing
like a ride to free a soul of tension and the heavy
muscles beneath him were soothing and easeful.

Lucinda rode like the youngest sister of three
brothers who had all left the mark of their tutorship upon her, fluid and daring, and he allowed her
by him so that he might watch. She did not flaunt
her gift, but every movement and command had the
sort of controlled gentleness that even great horse-
men struggled to achieve as she galloped in front of
him. Her laughter rang in the air as she pulled in her
mount, waiting as he drew up beside her.

'I don't know of another female who can ride with
the expertise of a jockey.'

'You disapprove?'

'Far from it, my lady wife. I hail it. At Alderworth
you will find fine tracks to ride along, though the
stables have been largely depleted.'

'But you will replace them with new stock?'

He shook his head. 'To get the production from the land up and running again is my first priority.'

'You do not sound as dissolute as they say, then.'

'It is my experience that no one is ever as good or as bad as society might paint them.'

A slight flush crawled into her cheeks. 'Expectations are certainly bonds that tie you down. The Wellingham name held me captive for years in that I could never truly be myself.'

'And now?'

'When everybody disapproves so firmly of my actions, it gives a freedom to do just as I want.'

There it was again, that sadness. The accident, a hasty marriage and his three years away had all had their part in drawing a melancholy hue over her pale-blue eyes. Ever since they had met they had hurt each other, Tay thought, his demands for an heir adding to the burden. He was suddenly tired of it.

'Lucinda. Luce.' A sound from a distance had them both turning. A young woman hailed them from her mare, her groom left far behind.

'My friend, Posy Tompkins. You will remember her from the wedding.'

'She was the one who brought you to Alderworth in the first place?'

When she nodded Tay thought he had a lot to thank Miss Tompkins for. He watched as she came closer.

* * *

Lucinda wished that they had ridden further into the greenery where they might have been more alone to talk. Already she could see the intrigue on her friend's face.

'I have been following you,' Posy said as she joined them, 'and I still think you should not take such risks on a horse, Lucy. How many times have your brothers admonished you not to gallop so fast?'

'Oh, I lost count months ago.'

'The doctor told you another bump on the head could be dangerous…'

'He did?' Taylen Ellesmere sounded nothing like he had a few moments prior. Nay, now he sounded exactly the same as Cristo, Asher and Taris.

Posy nodded. 'He said that she was to lead a careful and circumspect life and that he had seen many a patient becoming gravely ill if they did not heed his advice.'

The green in her husband's eyes displayed no humour now whatsoever.

'Something about blood vessels bursting, I think he said. The walls of the brain are thinner where they have been damaged. Because of that it is easier for them to erupt again.' Listing the medical information using her fingers, she bent down each one after every fact stated.

Posy did not look at her, but at Alderworth, an expression that Lucinda recognised on her face. The same look she had seen in their earlier days when together they would stage outlandish tragedies for the family to watch, the curtains in the downstairs salon of Falder fashioned into a theatre. She was baiting Alderworth for some reason and Lucinda could do nothing at all to stop it.

'Posy is exaggerating and I hardly think that will happen, your Grace—' she began, but Taylen interrupted her.

'Are you a physician now, too?' The tone in his voice was furious.

'No.'

'Then you should heed a warning from a man who is obviously qualified to give it.'

'And never race along the gullies and cliffs at Falder? Never clear another fence in my life?'

'If that is what it takes to be safe from any danger, then yes.'

Posy's laughter brought an end to the bickering. 'Asher has used the same arguments as you do so many times, your Grace, but to no avail.' Posy raised her eyebrows as Lucinda frowned at her and smiled congenially at Alderworth.

Amazing, Lucinda thought. Posy had never approved of any of her suitors. Not one. It was the creases in Taylen Ellesmere's cheeks, she supposed, and the way the light played upon his eyes—a man who was no one's lackey. The only white he wore was in his cravat and it showed up the tan of his skin. She could suddenly imagine him far from London in the back country wilds of Georgia, traipsing across swollen rivers and steep craggy mountains. Any information she had ever read on goldfields described them as hard and dangerous places, spawning hard and dangerous men.

'My brothers have this idea that I need to be looked after all the time. I find it easier to simply get on with my life in the way that I wish to and allow them to do the same.'

'In other words, you do not tell them of the danger you are placing yourself in.'

'Exactly, and I would appreciate your discretion in the matter, too, your Grace.'

'Then I hope you will at least have the sense to walk your horse home.' He tipped his hat. 'Miss Tompkins, it was my pleasure.'

Then he was gone, cutting across the park on a path Lucinda seldom used, body rising and falling with each movement of his horse in an effortless display of skill.

'Alderworth rides well, Luce.'

Anger seeped into her reply. 'Why would that be important to me, Posy? If it was left to everyone else, I should be in my drawing room at home, pursuing the gentle arts of needlework or playing music.'

Or lying in bed on my back, trying to produce an Ellesmere heir.

She bit down on chagrin.

'What the hell are you doing here, Alderworth?'

'White's is my club too, Wellingham, and I want a chat with you.'

Cristo Wellingham did not assent, but neither did he get up and leave. Rather he sat with his drink in hand and waited until Tay had taken the chair opposite.

'Your sister is recklessly galloping in Hyde Park when, according to a Miss Posy Tompkins, her doctor has expressly discouraged such behaviour.'

The other took a large swallow of his brandy before putting it down. 'And now you want to stop her?'

'I do.'

'Well, good luck with that. Asher's response was to take her horses away for a month, but she only hired other more dangerous ones. Taris endeavoured to send a man with her every time she used the stables, but she gave him the slip more times than not. I took her to Graveson where she rode along the beaches until she got bored with them. A number of approaches, you see, and none of them worked well or for long because she is as stubborn as a mule and twice as difficult.'

'A true Wellingham, then?'

Cristo tipped back his head and laughed. 'If you were not such a bastard, Alderworth, I might even like you. What is in it for you, anyway, this sudden and touching concern for my sister?'

'I do not wish to be a widower.'

Again Cristo laughed. 'You have not as yet been a husband and, if my family has its way, you never will be.'

Ignoring the criticism, Tay went straight to the heart of the matter. 'What else interests her?'

Cristo leant forwards, a frown on his face. 'She enjoys archery. No danger and a quiet walk to the target. She is also inclined to drawing. But be warned that if you play false with her emotions this time, Alderworth, there won't be any second chances.'

'Word has it that you got one with your wife.'

'Word has it you were in gaol in the Americas for taking the life of another.'

'Gold makes bad men greedy and rumour is always overstated.'

'As greedy as you were when you hived off with the Wellingham booty after despoiling our sister?' The quiet of Cristo Wellingham's words belied the fury inside each one.

'You know as well as I that I have paid every pound of it back and Lucinda was an innocent when I left her, no matter what she remembers.'

'Edmund Coleridge may have changed that, of course.'

Tay's fist came down on the table. 'If I hear even the slightest of whispers from him saying anything of the sort, then he will be a dead man.'

'I will tell him when I see him next. He is a personal friend of mine.'

'You do just that.'

Swallowing the last of his brandy, Taylen stood, the peers of the realm of England watching him over their tipples. The Alderworth ducal title sat squarely on him, but he had never felt that he belonged here, the stuffy manners and pretensions of these men so far from his own road in life.

He wanted to get back to Alderworth and he wanted to take his wife with him. The face of Edmund Coleridge rose into his consciousness and he stalked from the room.

Coleridge was kissing Lucinda's hand when Tay met her next at an afternoon soirée at the house of Daniel and Camille Beauchamp.

His wife had not frequented the pathways of Hyde Park that morning to take her exercise. He had been waiting, after all, but as the minutes had turned to hours he knew she would not come.

He was therefore both relieved to find her here and furious to see who she was with, for the man was virtually making love to her with his lips and she was allowing it. Her compliancy had him grating his teeth together. Hard.

'Duchess.'

She frowned and he was pleased to see worry in her eyes. 'Duke.'

Coleridge made no attempt at all to distance himself from her side and Taylen looked at him pointedly as his wife began to speak.

'Cristo said you might want to talk to me.' The statement left Tay speechless. 'He said you had a proposition you would like me to know. Something about spending my days in the parlour with my embroidery or being coddled in the garden painting flowers?'

'Your youngest brother has a sense of humour.'

'You went to see him after our meeting in the park? You went to tell him about my galloping when I so expressly asked you not to?'

Coleridge was taking in every word between them with interest and Tay had had enough. 'Would you excuse us?' Without waiting for a reply he shepherded his wife to an end of the room sheltered from the notice of others by a narrow alcove.

'I did not expect you to be so…underhanded,' Lucinda said as they stopped, her eyes shimmering with anger. Taylen changed tack altogether.

'I told your brother I did not fancy living alone for the rest of my life if anything were to happen to you. Did he tell you that as well?'

She shook her head.

'Edmund Coleridge wants you in his bed.'

'A fact that makes him little different from you then, your Grace.'

He ignored her criticism completely. 'Yet knowing that, you still allow him to court you openly?'

'He is a friend. I allow him friendship.'

'Your brother thinks he would like to be very much more.'

'It sounds like you had a long discussion about me. Pity I was not there to set wrongs to right, but then my siblings have always been more than quick to make judgements about the suitability of my various beaux.'

'Various?'

'Indeed. You didn't expect me to be pining for the company of a husband who did not think to remember that he had a wife for three long years until the necessity for a legitimate heir brought him back?'

The four small stars on her bracelet sparked gold as her hands underlined her words.

'The newspaper cutting you spoke of, the one in the paper from Georgia. It was not as it was reported. Since marrying you I have always respected my vows and I have not…cheated.' He finished each word with a sharp honesty. The muscles in his jaw rippled with the effort.

Damn, Taylen thought, what the hell had made him confess that to his estranged wife here in a crowded room in the middle of a public soirée?

He was known for his waywardness and his belief in free speech and action, flamboyant and untempered by the conventions attached to society life. He had lived his whole life in the pursuit of the hedonistic and the liberal, escaping the dreadfulness of his childhood with fine wine and finer women.

Until he had married!

Then something had happened that he could not explain. His libido, long since more than active, had simply dried up and he found it difficult to touch a woman without thinking of his parents' licentiousness. Six lovers had trooped through his younger life on his mother's side and many, many more than that on his father's. And they had left their mark.

He remembered the chaos as if it were yesterday and had vowed every moment of his early years never to repeat it if and when he finally married.

His hands tightened at his sides, fisting into hardness. It was why he had returned to England, after all, to understand just exactly what it was that simmered between him and this woman he had been forced into a union with.

Lucinda, the only wife he was ever likely to have and to hold. If it had not all been so deadly serious he would have laughed at his conundrum. A sinner caught by a saint and made impotent to boot by the memory of his parents' unfaithfulness.

Nothing made sense any more and had not done so for a long time. He wanted his certainty back and his conviction and one small part of him understood that only with Lucinda at his side might he be able to regain it.

It was the reason he had pressed her so hard with his need for an heir—a way to bring her to him on his own terms. A way to bed her.

Lucinda could not believe what she had just heard. The Dissolute Duke of Alderworth was telling her he had been faithful to her memory? All those years. All those temptations. Three thousand miles from home and a stranger in a land that was as harsh as it was different and yet he had never cheated? A Duke who was known for his dalliances and excesses? She was astonished.

'Why are you telling me this?'

'Because I want to know that any child we do have is actually mine.'

The anger in his voice contradicted everything he was confessing. One moment she understood him and the next…

'I was brought up with a father who never believed that I was his, you see, and treated me accordingly. Seeing what such distrust does to a man, I should not like to repeat it.' No softness lay in his brittle green eyes, the bruising around them adding to his menace. 'It is not necessary that you like me when you provide me with an heir, Duchess, but I do need to be certain that you have not allowed another the same delights.'

My goodness, she could barely breathe with her anger and confusion, the joy of the disclosure eradicated completely by a reading of her character that was hardly salubrious.

He imagined *her* wanton? The pulse in her throat was beating like a drum as she stood speechless. At that moment she hated him with a passion and she could not keep the emotion from showing on her face.

'I shall be leaving London for Alderworth on the morrow. I will send the carriage back for you when I have word that you wish to join me.'

He was disappearing again, the tenuous truce that

she had felt between them across the last week dissolving. Even in the face of her fury she could not just watch him go.

'What time will you leave?' Her voice sounded broken and hoarse.

'In the morning. There is no point in staying here longer.'

'Then I will come, too.'

For the first time a spark of life entered his eyes. 'Very well. My carriage will be at the Wellingham town house at ten o'clock. Be ready.'

He did not speak again before he turned and walked away, Edmund Coleridge joining her the moment he was gone.

'You look pale. If Ellesmere has threatened you—?'

'No.' She did not let him finish. As a friend of Cristo's she realised he might know more of the relationship she had with Alderworth than others did. 'I think I am just tired.'

Taking a breath, she tried to regain her lost composure, all the while her eyes scouting to check if Taylen Ellesmere was still anywhere in the vicinity.

'I am retiring to Bath next week with my family, Lucy. If you should wish to join us, you would be more than welcome. My mother would enjoy having you to stay, I am sure.'

Edmund's eyes were warm with promise, but Lucinda knew she could no longer lead him on with hopes that would never come to pass.

'I am sorry. I shall be rejoining my husband at Alderworth tomorrow. It has just been decided.'

'I see.' He stepped back. 'Does Cristo know what you intend?'

'Not yet, but he will.'

'He won't be pleased.'

Ignoring his condemnation, she carried on. 'I wish you well in your Bath sojourn. I imagine it is lovely there at this time of the year.'

Platitudes, she knew, but her husband's unexpected confession had taken her from one place to another.

Taylen Ellesmere had never cheated on her, but had held their marriage vows safe and close. She felt the smile blossom on her face as she gave Coleridge her goodbyes and went to find Camille Beauchamp to thank her for the soirée.

Chapter Eleven

'I would feel far happier about all of this if you would take a few of the Wellingham servants with you.'

Lucinda shook her head at Taris's words. She did not want those in the employ of her brothers to see the truth of the relationship she had with Taylen Ellesmere, for undoubtedly such a detail would leak back to Falder. She was pleased when the conversation was interrupted.

'The Alderworth conveyance is here, my lord.'

'Very well. See that Lady Lucinda's luggage is stowed on board.'

Taris turned to her as the butler left. 'Asher and Emerald have decided not to see you off and Eleanor and Cristo were called back to Graveson yesterday afternoon. Perhaps it is best that it is just us.'

When her middle brother stood she went into his embrace, his arms warm around her, the solid strength and honesty of him so very familiar. Part of her wanted to hold on and stay here, under the shelter of home and family, but another part needed something different and that was the voice she was heeding.

Disengaging her arms, she moved away, trying to keep her emotions in check.

'I shall send word as soon as I am there to let you know that I am safe.'

'It is not the journey worrying me, Lucy, but the man who you will live with at destination's end.'

The amber in his eyes was clouded and she could see worry there. It broke her heart to sense her brother's concern. Just another betrayal she had heaped upon the family. Beatrice, however, was smiling.

'Go with hope, Lucinda, and find the way of your life.' She pressed a small package into her hand. 'I have wrapped up a book for you I have recently enjoyed.'

And then Lucinda was outside, the façade of the town house behind her in the wind. Looking up at the third-floor window, she fancied she saw Asher, but the shadow was gone before she had time to be certain.

One step, two steps and then three, her feet like leaden weights dragging towards the carriage. Taylen Ellesmere sat inside and gave Taris a cursory greeting which was given back with an equal lack of warmth. When the door was closed between them, her brother's open palm splayed out upon the window.

I love you. She mouthed the words, but knew that he would not see them. Biting down on the soft flesh inside her bottom lip, she sat back as the horses gathered their rhythm.

'I am not taking you away for ever, Lucinda. You may return any time you wish to visit your family. The carriage shall be at your disposal whenever you have need of it.'

She nodded because she did not trust herself to speak and he swore beneath his breath.

'My own family was not close so it is something of a novelty to see such affection in others,' he offered finally as she kept her silence. 'In fact, I would say loathing was the nearest term to describe any family dynamics that I recall.'

'That must have been difficult for you.'

'Well, it was always easier when distance parted us.' He smiled through the gloom of the day, a laconic devil-may-take-it smile that negated all that she had ever heard of his upbringing. 'I would be farmed out to others, with no thought given to my schooling. My life truly began when I eventually got to Eton.'

A new and interesting turn. 'How old were you?'

'Twelve. My parents had died the year before, but I was an independent child for my age so their deaths barely affected me.'

'Callous.'

'I prefer to call it practical.'

A dead end of insults slung across lies.

'One of the maids at Falder used to work for your grandmother at about the same time you did not return from France.'

He stiffened and Lucinda felt a creeping coldness. A muscle along the bottom of his jaw ground out movement when she chanced a peek at him.

'Rosemary Jones made some mention of your uncle.'

This time he sat forwards, his hands together so that his fingers were entwined in the position Lucinda remembered placing her own in one of the favoured games of childhood.

Here is the church and here is the steeple…

Ditties that he would not have played as he was fighting for his life in a hospital bed in Rouen.

'She said that you were often hurt.' This was blurted out before she lost her courage altogether.

'All children need to stand corrected in the name of good behaviour.'

His eyes flinted, the anger in them causing her to simply fold. She could have said more, could have told him everything that the maid had confided, but it was too soon and the facts were too raw.

'Of course they do, your Grace.' She sounded like a thousand other wives in London who only wanted a life that was peaceful and easy, the truth tearing what contentment was left into pieces.

Outside the road ran along fields of green and the sky was blue, a cold blue, the colour belying the temperature. It was chilly inside the carriage, too, and she was pleased for the woollen blanket that was over her lap.

She wondered where the accident in the carriage had occurred when they had come this way all those years ago. She had been told the name of the place, of course, but with no little memory left of the time, she could be certain of nothing. Still she felt a familiarity, a knowledge of having passed this way before and she was glad that the journey would be only a few hours in length.

Taylen Ellesmere had ceased to make any effort at conversation at all, his glance drawn by the views outside, his face a blank mask of indifference. If he remembered the accident, he did not show it.

Over the past week she thought she might have been getting closer to him, but this morning they sat opposite each other like strangers hurtling towards a new life together and one it seemed that neither of them wanted. When her fingers closed around the jade talisman of happiness that Emerald had bequeathed her, she frowned.

She wished she might ask him to explain more of his surprising confession from yesterday and that this time instead of anger there could be dialogue. But his expression stopped her from such an action and so she turned to look out at the countryside.

Alderworth was a substantial mansion built of stone and wood, the wings around a large central edifice a matching image of each other. The parkland it sat in was extensive, rows of old trees stretching as far as the eye could see. A lake of some proportion lay at the bottom of a rise, the old stone walls radiating out from the driveway alluding to another, more ancient dwelling.

Lucinda had come last time under the cover of darkness. She knew because Posy had filled in many of the details of the visit that she had forgotten. She hoped that the servants would not remember her and that enough time had passed for the incident to be consigned to history and to never be recalled.

'When my parents were alive they used to line the servants up around the front driveway every time a guest came to stay in a sort of skewed sense of importance. I have never been so formal.'

'It looks…' She could not quite voice what she meant to say.

'Less than well cared for?' His eyes took in the lines of the house. 'Much of the money at the moment is going into increasing the production of the agricultural yields.'

'Cristo has been doing the same at Graveson.'

'Then perhaps we have more in common than I thought.'

'So there are no more parties here?'

He turned towards her and Lucinda felt breathless. 'The shallow follies of youth have much to be accountable for. I spend money on far more important things now.'

Like the production of an heir?

She almost said it. Almost blurted it out, so that it was there in the open instead of seething underneath each and every word, a contract penned in pragmatism and shame. Instead she smiled, in a tight and vapid way, the movement taking the humour from his eyes.

'You will have your own set of rooms and a maid to see to your needs. The house has suffered across the years from inattention but I am aiming to see it restored.'

'You love Alderworth, then?'

'History is to be valued,' he answered in a measured way. 'If too much of it is left to waste, there will be no lessons to be learnt by those who come after us.'

The topic of the heir again, winding into conversation and strangling any hope of accord. Best to remember that she was not here as the cherished new wife of a Duke who would love her, but as the sole hope of ensuring that a questionable family name might march into yet another decade of unbroken lineage.

When the carriage stopped and Lucinda was helped out by a servant who welcomed her, she was achingly aware that Taylen Ellesmere neither took her arm nor gave her the courtesy of any introduction as they walked inside.

Not quite the wife he wanted, but at least the country air made her feel stronger and more in control.

Everything here was in need of attention: the flaky stone, the gardens, the few servants in their old and faded uniforms. Ellesmere had not lied when he had proclaimed the finances of Alderworth had suffered.

But beneath the lack of care, peeling paint and rotten woodwork was a beauty that lay in the very bones of the place, the house's roofline raised to the sky in a proud exclamation of old wealth.

The quality of the timber was undeniable, the ornate cornices alluding to a time where such frippery was the vogue. She vaguely remembered parts of it from the last time she had been here and did her best to recollect more, but to no avail. Darkly fashioned paintings of ancestors stared down from the walls in every room, sombre harsh people whose eyes seemed to follow this new generation with a disapproval that was tangible.

Two large portraits of his parents had pride of place above the fire surround in the main salon and Lucinda saw the small holes a dart might fashion in both of them before she had looked away, not wishing to pry further. A green *chaise-longue* with carved mahogany feet took up the space in a bay window, the sun lightening the fabric in all the places that it had touched, leaving the seams dark.

Taylen Ellesmere had disappeared almost immediately, leaving her in the hands of a middle-aged housekeeper, Mrs Berwick, who had hurried her up to the first floor and finally to her bedchamber, a room nearly at the very end of a long corridor. She had pointed out a pile of bath cloths and two decanters with brandy and whisky, equally filled on a table by the bedside.

An evening tipple? The single glass provided looked spotlessly clean.

'There is a light meal set out for your lunch in the small dining room, your Grace, and dinner will be served at six. When you require a maid to help you dress you only have to ring the bell and she will come.'

The bed was tiny, a child's cot that gladdened her heart, for there was no possible way her large husband could share it with her.

After the accompanying luggage was lifted into place she thanked the two men with a smile. Around the edge of the room stood many tallboys and wardrobes, the array of old furniture giving the impression that many of the unwanted accoutrements of the Ellesmere lineage had been dumped here, a last resting place before being disposed of or burnt.

When the woman didn't leave, Lucinda knew there was something important that she wished to impart to her. 'The master has brought new life to Alderworth, your Grace. The house may not be as magnificent as it once was, but the farm cottages have been refurbished and the people here appreciate his endeavours. He is a good man despite all that might be said of him in London.'

The woman hurried out after she had delivered her words, a swish of skirt and then gone.

A good master who was appreciated here? Lucinda turned the words on her tongue, liking the endorsement.

Nerves had taken away hunger, so she walked to the window to gaze down upon the gardens, the formal lines of hedges lost in the march of time. No one had tended to anything, it seemed, the wild and rambling roses climbing in a tangled heap of runners with the occasional misshaped flower blooming amidst green. The hand of good fortune had disappeared a long time ago from the estate of Alderworth, leaving disorder in its place. Her mind dwelled on the fact that her husband was a Duke who would make sure others were well housed before he turned his attention to his own living quarters and she smiled.

A movement caught her eye in the very far corner of her view. Ellesmere was hurrying towards the stable courtyard a little way off, his demeanour brisk. He had dispensed with his jacket and his hat and the white linen of his shirt stretched across the muscles of his back, his dark hair trailing across it. Another came out to meet him, a small round man waving his arms madly as if in some important explanation. The Duke in contrast stood perfectly still, a quiet centre in the midst of all that moved about him.

Taylen Ellesmere did that often, she thought, as though testing the air, like a deer might in the high hills of some undisturbed place just to make certain of safety.

Then a horse came forth, a stallion of a height Lucinda had not seen before, the lines of Arabia in its form. She saw her husband run his hands across its flanks, quiet and gentle, before he mounted, easily managing the skittish response of the animal. The Duke of Alderworth looked as though he had been born there, the flow of man and beast joined in a languid and perfect balance as he turned towards the hills beyond the gardens and disappeared.

Then there was nothing, only trees and leaves and the scudding clouds across the afternoon sky wending towards a dark forest in the distance.

She wished she could open the doors that led out on to a balcony to see if she might catch more of a glimpse of them, but they were nailed shut—another oddity in a house full of neglect. Lifting her hand, she wrote her initials on the inside of the window. With a flourish she surrounded her name with the shape of a heart and then rubbed the whole thing out, her fingers made dirty by the dust on the glass.

Falder, her family home, had the lines of love running through it, generations of Wellinghams enjoying the promise. Each day a legion of staff cleaned it from top to toe until it was polished and gleaming, the small decay of everyday living repaired before any damage had the chance to spread further.

The sun broke out quite suddenly, enhancing the green in the fields behind. Here in the rolling hills of

Bedfordshire and far from the expectations of London there was a certain peace and freedom she had not felt in years. It lay, she supposed, in the march of time drawn across a fading splendour. Once Alderworth would have boasted grandeur and sumptuousness, but there was a mellow truth about its present-day meagreness that was beguiling.

Finding her satchel, she drew forth her drawing equipment and laid a parchment on the desk, liking the feel of charcoal, the dusty ease of a long-time friend calming in the face of the unknown. She drew, from memory, the house and its lines and Taylen Ellesmere on the horse, his hair against the wind, his forehead strong.

She stopped after sketching his eyes and rested because the quickness in them was disconcerting, knowing, a question framed in them that held all her own fears naked in the afternoon light. She wanted to rub them out, wanted to scrawl across such eyes with a hard strong stroke, but she couldn't. Couldn't countenance destruction of such raw and angry beauty. His lips followed, full and generous, lips that had offered her the promise of liberty for the price of a child. Yet he had qualified such an unexpected option with salvation and loyalty and she believed he had meant it.

Placing one finger across the drawing, she felt an easing of spirit, a lessening of tightness. A slight question of flesh? Revealing. Unforeseen.

'Taylen.' She whispered the name into the quiet

and even as she watched his lips seemed to turn. Upwards. The black of charcoal moving in a way it never had before. Living. Breathing. Laughing. She did not dare to impart more form to his figure as she buried the sheet of paper in her sketchbook.

A flash of some hidden thing ripped through Lucinda, beating at truth. The headaches she had had after the accident had largely gone, yet here they threatened to return in the same intensity as they had whilst convalescing.

A room came through the fog, a room at the end of a long corridor and a man sitting in bed and reading.

Spectacles. She had the vague idea it was Alderworth. She squinted her eyes to try to remember the title of the book in his hands because she thought it was important in some way. But no more memory surfaced.

Rising, she picked up her cloth bag from the place she had left it in one corner and extracted the wrapped present that Beatrice had bequeathed her in the moments before her departure from London. A novel confronted her as she ripped off the bright blue paper and a note was threaded with ribbon around the cover.

Lucy,
The dependence of women on marriage to secure social standing and economic security can be underpinned with something far more wonderful. I have a suspicion that you will find

what I allude to with Taylen Ellesmere. Anne
Elliot certainly did in this story.
All my love,
Bea

Jane Austen's *Persuasion*. She had not read this
book and was glad for the chance to do so here,
though Beatrice's note seemed more than odd. She
knew her brothers hated her husband with a passion and had thought her sister-in-law might have
felt the same.

Something wonderful? Such hollow hope was
layered with a reality far from any such truth, the
unfamiliar environment here increasing her homesickness.

When tears welled up behind her eyes she did not
try to stop them as they ran down her cheeks and on
to the small book across her lap, blurring the inked
note in Beatrice's handwriting.

Taylen waded naked into the lake behind the
house and waited as the icy water numbed his feet
and his legs, the shadow of Valkyrie reflected in the
silver before him, low in the water. He had named
this dash of raised-up land as a boy and had used
the island as a fortress many times, a stronghold
against a coercive uncle and a place to assuage the
remnants of betrayal.

'Betrayal.' He whispered the word to himself and
watched how the warm air fogged. He had never

had a chance against his mother's brother with his corrupt tastes and easy smile. The fact that he was a child whose parents saw responsibility only as a nuisance and had gladly given up any claim on a son who was alternatively badly behaved or withdrawn aided such tendencies.

Innocence was such an easily taken commodity and Taylen knew that his had gone a long time ago.

Like the small hut he had built on the rise, left to the birds and the ghosts and the wind. Only echoes in the inlets and silence in the few remaining trees, the black outline of wood sharp against the dusk where it had fallen at an angle against the sky. No longer a shelter.

Picking up a handful of sand, he let it filter through his fingers—Alderworth soil, the mark of a thousand years of ancestry imprinted in the earth. His land now, to have and to hold as certainly as a wife brought from London under the dubious flag of obligation.

He shook his head hard, the strands of wetness falling into his line of vision before he wiped them away. The air here strengthened him and gave him resolve. Lucinda would be sitting in the room beside his and wondering what exactly might happen next. He hated the fact that she would be frightened, but there was no other way of resolving this impasse, and he knew without a single doubt that had he left her in London her brothers would have made certain any access was limited.

Lord, but was it any better here? The whole place teetered under a strange spell of melancholy, the staff left reduced to a bare handful of overworked servants.

He had left it too long to return, he supposed, but the memories here had always repelled him, the child without rights struggling inside the man he had become, dissolute and uncaring. Swallowing, he fisted his hands hard against his thighs and lifted his face to the rain that had begun to fall in a mist.

Back. Again. This time with a spouse who distrusted him and the threat of retribution from the Wellinghams should he ever hurt her.

A flash of lightning above the hills to the east reflected in the lake. A sign, perhaps. A portent of battle.

That evening Lucinda came down the wide staircase with a feeling of disbelief, her heart tight and her stomach filled with butterflies. The dress she wore was her newest, light-yellow silk shot through with gold, the *décolletage* on the prim side of fashionable heightened by a line of frothy Brussels lace, her arms covered by a shawl against the cold. Her hair was pinned to her head in a tall and elegant chignon, with a few curls left to frame her face, that had taken a maid a good hour to complete. On her feet were slippers of fine calf leather, the lacings drawn in tight.

The Alderworth servant accompanying her

stepped back as they came into the front salon. In the ensuing silence a bead of sweat traced its way between her breasts to fall across the skin above her ribs.

Taylen Ellesmere was already there, dressed entirely in black, the collar at his neck open. A gentleman at home and at leisure or a man expecting a woman to entertain him?

'Duchess.' His teeth were white and even and perfect.

Part of her wanted to run, wanted to lift the embroidered fall of silk and make for the safety of her room, negating any contract between them.

I do not think he would stop me if I went! The thought came from nowhere but it was there in his eyes, soft velvet with a sort of pity.

She did not wish for that. Raising her chin, she walked through the opened door and tried not to flinch as it shut behind her.

His eyes took in her gown and her hair, his expression tightening. 'I have something to show you,' he said as the silence lengthened. 'It is this way.'

He did not take her hand or shepherd her forwards. He did not touch her at all, but walked in front through the long corridors of the place to a room filled with books. Two glasses sat on a desk with a bottle of white wine chilled in a bucket of ice.

Intentions, she supposed, a heady amount of alcohol to loosen the restraints of almost thirty-six months of distance.

'Please, take a seat.'

She chose a chair with enough room for one person. Unexpectedly, though, he pulled a stool over to where she was and sat in front of her. A shaft of light bathed him, turning his hair to shining raven black. Like the cut sides of coal. He was the most handsome man she had ever met. She could not dispute that fact.

'I was not intimate with you three years ago no matter what you might say, Lucinda. I put you in the carriage before anything could happen between us and tried to take you home. If it had not been for the accident, I would probably have succeeded.'

Lucinda felt her insides curl. Taylen Ellesmere had always used words well to suit his intentions.

'You were in bed. I remember you...touching me?'

'You ran into my room to escape from the Earl of Halsey. I kissed you once. That was all.'

'No.' She shook her head. 'You lie.' Her eyes flicked to the line of her breast though she could not bring herself to voice all that she remembered.

His fingers at her nipples, the feel of him hard against her skin in places no one had ever touched before. The full naked size of him as he stood before her. Shocking. Thrilling. Forbidden.

Reaching over to the wine, he poured her a glass, fine crystal, and the stem vibrated under the pressure of her fingers as she took it. As easy to break as her innocence had been?

'Perhaps a drink might refresh your tangled memory,' he toasted, shattering the bubble of *détente* completely. A sharp bud of shock took her breath as hard eyes gleamed, the warmth of his glance searing through silk.

Her face was pale, the smile she had forced upon it tightly stretched.

A small droplet of wine lay on her top lip. Once he might have leant over and licked it away, but he had never been a man to take a woman against her will and the wariness on Lucinda's face was easy to read. Drawing back, he opened the folder on the table beside him. There was a file fat with the transfer-of-ownership documents tucked inside the front cover. He pushed the papers across to her.

'I have signed the town house over to you already. The terms allow you sole use of the place until you die. Then it shall revert to our heir…or heirs if sins of the flesh are as enjoyable as I think you will find them to be.'

Worry brought lines to her forehead and the tip-tilt of her nose against the light made him look away. He remembered running his finger down the gentle slope and on to the plump rose of her lips. Once she had watched him as if he were the only man in existence. Once she had taken his breath away with a single stolen kiss. Now suspicion and wariness were the only expressions that he could read and the disappointment was disquieting.

'I have a pouch, too. A hundred pounds for the first time you lie with me and a hundred more for every time after that.' The heavy thud of the leather purse sounded on the file, like the promise of Antonio's flesh from the pen of Shakespeare. A pound for a pound. Payment for an heir.

Her teeth worried her bottom lip and shadowed eyes perused the bounty, but she did not reach out, leaving the largesse exactly where it was. Then she lifted her glass and had a generous gulp of wine before chancing a second and a third. Tay wanted to warn her of the strength of the draught, but in the circumstances he refrained. A relaxed Lucinda would be so much easier to handle than an angry one.

'So you are saying that when I become pregnant the bargain will be fulfilled?'

The catch in her voice nearly broke his will and for a moment he thought to nullify everything and walk away. 'A doctor will need to verify your condition, of course.'

'Like a brood mare,' she returned. Against the candlelight her pale hair shone and her eyes were back to flinty, fighting blue. During all his travels amongst the most beautiful women in the world he had never seen another like her.

He did not want her subdued. He wanted her like this. In bed she would be magnificent.

The thought had the flesh in his trousers swelling and he cursed, feeling like a boy again with no control over any of it. If he had any sense at all he would reach out now and strip her naked, demanding the rights all husbands received at the marriage altar and be done with any bargains. It was a God-given privilege, after all, and he had paid for her in blood and in gold.

He knew she saw the thought, too, for her hands tightened.

'I would never hurt you.' It was suddenly important that at least she knew that.

'Then let me go.'

'I can't.' Two words that stripped the life out of everything and his heart beat faster than ever it had during the bleak and lonely watches in the Americas when death could be forthcoming in one moment of inattention and often was. With care he reached out to gather a long curl of pale flaxen, turning it in his palm as the light caught wheat and gold and silver. 'I can only hope for release from the demons that have hounded us for three long years. Will you be brave enough to trust me?'

'Do I have any other alternative?'

He shook his head and the pulse at her throat slowed marginally—small signs of surrender.

To take the charade further he allowed her glance to escape from his own, falling out of contact. Eyes can take much from the soul, he thought, as she jammed her hands into the yellow silk of her skirt. He hoped dinner would be served soon. Eating would ease the tension that words were failing to do. How often had he plied an adversary with food and wine before picking the flesh of secrets clean away from the bone?

The thought that he did not wish to hurt Lucinda in any way at all left him struck dumb with shock.

Her innocence again and her goodness. He had had this same trouble in his bedchamber three years ago with the heady sighs of sexual release reverberating all around them—wholesomeness like some sharp-edged sword smiting evil with a conscience he had never felt so keenly before.

She was very warm. A fire burnt low in the grate, sending out a glow of red, and she was too hot even in her light clothing. She loosened her shawl. The scent of herbs wafted in the air around her. Lavender. She would never again smell the bloom without thinking of this moment, the documents and money spilled across the table before her, sordid rewards of lust.

'Marriage has left us both in a difficult position,' he continued, 'a no-man's land, if you like, precluding any other relationships we might wish to pursue. But if we use the situation wisely, we may at least enjoy it.'

The shock of his words made her draw in her breath. She was twenty-seven years old and, apart from one night three years ago, her sexuality had lain dormant and curdled.

Until now! Until a husband straight out of the

pages of some improper and implausible fairy tale had walked back into her life and demanded this.

The Duke of Alderworth was not soft or quiet or gentle. He was hard and strong and distant, his eyes devouring her and the lavender blurring her senses. When she shook her head he laughed and broke away.

'May the Lord above help us then if you think we might spin this out for all of a week, Duchess.'

Such brutal masculine honesty reminded Lucinda of her brothers and a further ache of homesickness claimed her. 'The trouble is that I do not know you at all, your Grace.' She had agreed to come to this place, agreed to the things he had said. She could not pull back now. But she did need time to adjust.

'I thought you had made it plain to everybody that you did. Intimately. Your three brothers at least will swear to it.'

'Much of what happened before the accident is lost to me,' she continued as if he had not spoken, 'though I know in my heart that you enjoyed far more than the mere kiss you acknowledge.'

He stood very still, watching her. 'More?'

'You wore no clothes.'

'I had retired for the night and you surprised me. There is no crime in that.'

'There were red marks upon my breasts.'

Laughter reverberated around the room, his face made years younger by mirth. She had not seen him like this before, humour sparkling and a dimple in one cheek.

'Fine breasts they were, too.'

Now he *was* lying, for she knew she had none of the form of those women of society whose charms were followed by the eyes of men.

'You think it cannot be so?' He walked across to her and traced his fingers down the line of her bodice, his touch running softly over the skin above the lace.

'You are a beautiful woman, Lucinda, and the pleasures of the flesh have their own reward.' The sensuality in his tone was beguiling and his touch made her draw in her breath. But she was neither gullible nor stupid.

'Lust is a base and shallow emotion, your Grace. It could never be enough to sustain a marriage.'

'You would want more?' He said this in such a way that Lucinda knew the thought of love had not occurred to him at all. Probably he found the softer emotions laughable—sensations that were as foreign to his world as easy and gratuitous sex would be to hers. The gap between them was a widening abyss.

'Hell and damnation,' he said, pushing back the hair on his forehead. Another opaque scar lay under the hairline and the anger on his face was unhidden.

Love.

She was speaking of that. He knew that she was and cold dread seeped through him.

Love only hurt. Enjoyment was better, of the mind or of the body it mattered not which. Enjoyment allowed the ease of parting when it was time to say goodbye and move on to the next place or person. Enjoyment was not the trap that love was.

Lord, he was paying his wife enough for such enjoyment and he was even biding his time to enable her to get used to the idea. He did not know of one single person who sustained their marriage in the way that Lucinda seemed to think was normal, the congeniality of two souls for ever linked.

This was the stuff of fairy tales and operas and the books that flooded out of the Minerva Press. He had read one once, just out of interest, and laughed at such an implausible nonsense.

His uncle had whispered the word in his ear, too, as he had hurt him. 'This is because I love you, Taylen. Only that.' The last time Tay had kicked the bastard hard in the balls as he had lunged for him and run to the door. The key hadn't turned, though, stuck in the lock as his fingers fumbled to release it and Hugo had caught him easily, holding his shaking body close and telling him he loved him over and over.

That was love. That was his memory of love, bound by blood and hurt to all the adults in his life, until one day they had simply washed their hands of him and sent him off to boarding school.

His deliverance. The few canings there were nothing compared to his regular and systematic abuse at

Alderworth, and in the summers when all the other boys save him returned home the masters had allowed him the free run of the place. To read. To walk. To fish.

Lucinda was watching him closely and it was disconcerting with his past rushing in between them.

'Our bargain consists of a hundred pounds each time you lie with me, the end coming when you conceive an heir.'

He knew such words would cut the talk of love to ribbons, but the sweat had begun creeping up his body. He needed to get away before she understood more about him than he wanted anyone to know and there was no kind way to say it.

He gathered the heavy leather pouch and the papers he had meant to have her sign. 'I find I am not hungry, Duchess. My servants will see to your evening meal.' With that he left her.

Chapter Twelve

A sound woke her, a groan muffled by something, but close. Lucinda sat up in bed and listened, the moon coming in through a gap in the curtains. It was night-time and late. She had spent a short time in the dining room and then retired upstairs as soon as she was able. She had seen no further sign at all of the Duke of Alderworth.

Another cry had her up on her feet and she walked to the door, placing her ear against the wood and listening. No footsteps hurried along the passageway, no hint of someone else hearing and helping. An owl called from the trees that marched in a line up a hill near the mansion, plaintive and lonely. Otherwise there was only silence.

Her feet were becoming cold on the parquet floor and she was about to get back into bed when a further sound came. This time she recognised the voice. Her hands opened the door and she was through it in a second, slipping through the unlocked door of the adjoining chamber. For a second dizziness made her clutch at the oak, this room familiar somehow and dangerous.

A candle burnt on a low bedside table and her husband was caught in a tangle of sheets, his hard body brown against the white, not asleep and not awake, but somewhere in a halfway place that was haunting.

'Wake up.' She shook him, the opened shirt he had on drenched in sweat, but his hand pushed her away. Not gently, either, but Lucinda had been raised in a house full of brothers and she pushed back.

'Wake up.' Louder now and more insistent. The bottle in front of him was drained and the smell of strong drink lingered around the room.

On the floor lay a book in Italian, the corners on one page turned down. A pile of other tomes in English, Italian and French sat in a nearby pile: Voltaire, Rousseau, Dante, Thomas Aquinas, Adam Smith and Machiavelli's *Il Principe*. Another flash of him reading this same book came to mind, the room draped in shadow save for a single candle. Before. She strained to recall other things, but could not.

'Taylen. Taylen. Wake up.' He came to in an instant, one moment boneless and the next ramrod stiff, the distant and vigilant Duke back in place.

The redness in his eyes was marked, the green of his iris darker against the colour. 'I shouted out?'

'Loudly. No one else came.'

Looking away, he reached for a fob watch positioned near the candle and checked the time. When his shirt dropped down a little as he stretched, Lucinda gasped. A whole row of scars slashed into the smoothness across the top of his back and she could barely believe the damage.

However, if he saw her looking he gave no sign of it, shrugging his shirt on further, fingers on the collar pinching both points of it inwards. His hands shook so much Lucinda thought that he would not be able to hold it closed.

All his rings had been stripped off, save their wedding ring and she wondered what that might mean. Sweat glistened on his face and his hair was plastered to his forehead, a worrying unsteadiness visible as he pushed himself up.

'Are you drunk?'

He laughed at that and shook his head. 'If only it was that simple…'

'Nightmares, then? When I was a child I had—' He stopped her with an impatient flick of his hand.

'I will ask Mrs Berwick to place you in another room in the morning. That way you will not be disturbed again.'

'This happens every night?'

'No.' He was so quick in his answer that Lucinda knew he lied.

'Exercise helped me. My mother insisted I rode each day for hours and after that I slept so much better at night.'

She could tell he was listening and so she carried on. 'I was a wilful child, you see, and always in trouble. My mother thought it would have been best had I been a boy, but I wasn't.'

A slight upturn of his lips had her carrying on.

'My brothers would be assigned each in turn to watch over me. Ashe and Taris were far older than I was and they took the duty seriously. Cristo was more my age and seemed to get in worse scrapes than even I was capable of. Alice was not a woman to be too bothered with children, you see. Her garden was her great love.'

'And your father? Where was he when all of this was going on?'

'Overseeing the running of the estate. Ensuring the lineage of the Wellinghams remained financially viable. He died of a heart condition when I was young. I would probably have been a disappointment to him had he lived.'

'Were I a father I would hold no impossible expectations of my children.'

A father! There it was again, that same old hint of why they were both here. She could see he also was reminded of the fact because his eyes turned smoky and he pushed himself up out of the bed.

He had fallen asleep in his clothes and his boots, the rumpled linen of his shirt sticking to his skin where the sweat had gathered. The nightmares had carved deep lines of desolation across his face. Almost as deep as those on his back. Could they be the

marks of a careful and judicious beating adminis-
tered to a child with as much hatred as was possible?

She held her breath with the enormity of it all,
watching as he poured himself a generous glass of a
drink that did not look alcoholic and finished the lot.
Her nightgown felt insubstantial and she wished she
had stopped to put on the matching negligee. Outside
the moon was low and the night was dark, a mounting wind throwing the branch of a tree against the
glass in his window.

'Tomorrow I shall take you riding…sedately.' For
a moment she could not quite understand what it was
he spoke of. Then she did.

'My mother will be smiling down from Heaven.'

'Or warning you away from me as all your brothers have done and hoping like hell that you heed her.'

'You keep on telling me that you are not safe.'

Walking to the window, he pulled back the curtain of heavy burgundy velvet.

'Come and look, Lucy.' It was the first time he had
called her the name that her family did and she went
across to him. He did not touch her, but positioned
himself behind, his breath warm against her neck.

'As far as the eye can see it is Ellesmere land.
From the hills against the sky here to the place where
the moon shines on the lake there and behind the
house a thousand acres yet again rising through the
valleys. This is the safety that my father squandered
and my mother cared not a jot for. This was the
reason I took the money from your brother to dis-

appear after our wedding. It was never meant as a slight to you.'

'A precious bequest?'

She felt him nod.

'If it were Falder I would have done exactly the same.'

'Thank you.' His hand came down upon her shoulder, the pressure gentle at first and then building as it slid across silk and shadow to rest on the sensitive skin at her neck. She wanted to lean in and keep him there, all the pent-up loneliness bursting forth into a simple need.

He was dangerous and difficult and menacing. He was also the only lawfully wedded husband she was ever likely to have. When he turned her slowly, the greenness in his eyes was darkened by half-light and gentle honesty, a man woken up by his past and trying to come to terms with his present.

His confession of faithfulness in the Beauchamps' salon made her braver and she brought her arms up around him. She could feel the welts of the old scars, the cotton in his shirt hiding nothing. Drawing one finger along the length of a twisted ridge, she suddenly had an image of the past. She had wanted him then as she did now.

'I remember pieces. I remember this.'

His only answer was his mouth upon hers and then she forgot everything as his tongue slanted inwards. Pure masculinity found her essence through touch and taste and she knew in the first second

of his onslaught exactly what it was all those society women who watched him through their hooded
glances had known.

He was both tempered steel and quicksilver, the
opposites melding wonderment and delight and he
wanted from her what men like him had wanted from
a woman through the centuries since the very beginning of time. The quiet kiss she had thought to offer
was overtaken by a storm of sensation.

There was no sense in it left, no moderation, no
limit on the depth of her feeling, no careful pru-
dence. All there was were heartbeats and warmth.
Unable to understand what was happening, she simply closed her eyes and let him take, the magic finally in her grasp.

Her bosom heaved as he moved closer, drawing
his thumb along the edge of her throat and across the
bones of her chest. When he sucked at his forefinger
and ran it fast over one nipple, she arched back, her
nightgown leaving nothing hidden, and the languid
glassy abandonment of passion showed in her eyes
before she closed them. His woman. Paid for and
bought. Legally bound until the very end of time.
No confines on anything. He could use her exactly
as he willed.

He wanted to rip away the rest of her clothes and
have her there now upon the floor, emptying himself
into her time and time again until there was nothing left of three years of desperation and urgency.

The more worrying thought that a woman like this could in some way inveigle herself into a corner of his heart confused him. He felt as if he could tell her things he never wanted another to know and break covenants that he had always kept.

Carefully he pushed her back, his thumb running across the soft line of one cheek and then the swelling of her lip. Bewilderment lay in her eyes, demanding explanation, but the nightmares always left him exhausted—too exhausted to deal with the complex labyrinth that was a relationship.

'Why is it like this between us?' Her question, dredged from the depths of need.

'I do not know, sweetheart, but now is not the hour to find out. It is time you were back in your bed.'

She looked away, pulling the silk of her gown back into place at her neck, a prim and proper covering of what had been there only a moment before. Her hair had escaped the loose plait she had worn when she had entered the room and fell in waves across her shoulders, the paleness caught between candle and moonlight and the length emphasising her slim height as it fell to the curve of her waist.

His fingers tightened against his thighs and he wished she would leave, shutting the door behind temptation because if she stayed much longer he did not trust himself enough not to reach out and remove any choice.

'Goodnight.' Her voice was strained and low and a few seconds later she was gone.

* * *

Lucinda sat on her bed, trying to catch her breath, her heart pounding in her chest.

She wanted him. She did. She wanted him to show her what it was that had boiled between them when he had kissed her. Her fingers traced down the line of her bodice, cupping one breast through the layers of fabric, feeling the same things that he had. The thought had her standing because she had never been a woman who was overtly sensual, the men in London society leaving her with no true desire other than a residual and slight interest in what happened between the sexes. Nothing more.

Until now.

Different. Alive. Aching everywhere. For him. The skin around her nipples tightened as she imagined his mouth upon them, the place between her legs throbbing in anticipation. The jade Emerald had bequeathed her lay between her breasts. For happiness, her sister-in-law had promised. She wondered what this emotion she felt now was. Certainly there was an excitement that was foreign and wonderful.

Could one be married in lust and not in love?

Would that be enough?

Or might the agreements between them eventually ignite the sort of marriage her brothers had, the forever-and-ever sort that lasted through thick and thin?

Her husband did not seem to think so and yet he had kissed her in a way that made no sense of the distance he offered. His heart had raced as fast as hers, she had felt it where their skin had touched, the heat in his eyes belying the aloofness he brokered.

When he had stood behind her at the window, offering an explanation why he took money from her brother, she could almost imagine him standing there as a loving husband who cared for her feelings and who wanted her to understand that it was not insult but truth he sought.

She wiped away the tears in her eyes with the back of her hand, a quick angry movement because such a maudlin wallowing was useless.

She had been lonely for years, lost in her own company amidst a family who all had partners. The shared glances, the careful smiles, the way a hand was given in complicit understanding. These were the things she had never discovered, never desired until now.

The moonlight drew mottled, patterned trails across her skin, paleness overlaid by shadow. The artist in her enjoyed the line and the beauty of the design, but the woman only saw the desolation of solitude.

How would she be able to go through with this bargain of conceiving an heir if every part of her wanted so much more than he would give?

Chapter Thirteen

Lucinda spent the morning on her own. There had been no sign of her husband at all, no movements from his room. She knew this because she had been listening most carefully, getting up to place her head against the door at any sign of noise.

Mrs Berwick bustled in just before twelve.

'The master was asking after you, your Grace.'

'The Duke is up already?'

'Indeed. Riding across the top valley would be my guess, on that black horse of his that goes like the wind.'

Lucinda crossed to the wardrobe to find her bonnet and coat. Within a moment she was on the front portico, Mrs Berwick pointing out the formal gardens and the small pathway to the Ellesmere stables.

Finally she was alone, the wind on her face and the sun appearing from time to time between ominous banks of high, dark cloud.

A dog joined her on her walk a little way into the tumbled-down garden, his coat mangy and his head hanging. She could not even make a guess as to its pedigree, for the animal had the head of a Labrador, the body of a much thinner hound and the hairiest and longest of legs. Usually she was frightened of dogs, as she had been bitten badly once at Falder and had not been much in their company since, but this animal with its trusting brown eyes, its odd shape and a tail that curled twice before tucking under its back legs was so comical it was comforting. All day she had been alone, so when the animal's wet muzzle came into the curl of her fingers she laughed.

'Who are you?' Her voice brought it to a stop.

'His name is Dog.' Taylen Ellesmere was suddenly behind her, his riding clothes splattered with mud and no sign on his face at all to indicate he had any memory of last night. Perhaps he had felt nothing. Perhaps for him the kiss had been like one of the many others he had bequeathed to countless beautiful women across his lifetime.

'Is he yours?' Lucinda hoped that the rush of heat on her cheeks did not show.

'My carriage almost ran him over on the London riverfront and so I had him brought up here.'

'When?'

'The first day I arrived back in England, a month and a half ago now. It seemed a sign,' he added, an unexpected lopsided smile having a strange effect on the area around her heart.

'A sign of what?'

'A sign indicating that I was meant to stay. An anchor, if you like.'

'Mrs Berwick told me you had concentrated your efforts on bringing the farm cottages up to a habitable standard.'

'The estate needs work, though there are some who do not like what I am trying to accomplish.'

'Change always polarises people. Asher says that often.'

He smiled, and nodded. 'In a year I could have Alderworth profitable again…' He stopped, a sense of wariness in the words. 'But you probably have no interest in such things?'

His query trembled into the space between them.

'On the contrary. If this is to be my home, I could help you.'

'Our home.'

And just like that she was back again into breathlessness, enchantment shimmering in the air between them.

'Do you have your riding clothes?'

'Of course.'

'Then come with me and I will show you Alderworth from the hills.'

'Now?'

Nodding, he called the dog back to his side, its mangy spine rising into his hand where he patted it.

'Give me ten minutes,' she answered before breaking into a brisk walk.

* * *

Taylen stood and watched her leave, desire seeping into a cold dread.

Hugo Shields seemed to reach out from the grave and deny him any thoughts of hope, years after he had died with a bullet through his heart. His uncle had gone into his afterlife muttering the threats he'd made such an art form of whilst living, insults softening into pleas and then whimpers as the life blood had run from him. Tay had allowed him no forgiveness, simply watching with distaste and relief as he took his last and final breath. The Italian nobleman, who had shot Hugo as a card cheat, had taken ship back to the Continent that very night and a youthful Taylen had never spoken of the incident to anyone.

Secrets and lies. It was who he was, what he had become, and no amount of longing could change it. It was why the nightmares never left him, but spun into the release of sleep like a spider gathering corpses. He could not hide the darkness inside him from Lucinda and if he tried to…

He shook his head. He would have to be honest, for he owed her at least that.

The dog's whining made him tense.

With her riding habit in place Lucinda rejoined Taylen at the front of the stables.

The large black horse she had seen at a distance from the window of her room was twice as impressive close up. She stayed a good ten feet away from him as she looked over the lines of his body.

'He is beautiful. What do you call him?'

'Hades. My father brought his grandsire out from France after winning a lucrative hand of faro.'

Taylen Ellesmere never seemed cowed by scandal; rather he threw any caution in the face of the wind and challenged comment. Attack was better than any defence. He used the maxim like an expert.

'Your family is unusual.'

'There isn't much of it left.'

'The very opposite of mine, then. Sometimes I used to think there were too many Wellinghams, but now…'

She trailed off, but he finished the sentence for her. 'Now when you see the alternative it makes you realise how lucky you are?'

'I think that is true. They are not so bad, you know, my brothers. It is only that they are trying to protect me.'

'From further ruin?' He smiled unexpectedly, the green in his eyes paler today than she had ever seen it. The Dissolute Duke who watched over his estate out of a duty he could have refused, but didn't.

Sometimes her husband was so very like her brothers. Confusion made her ramble.

'It is good to be away from town and Alderworth is a beautiful place despite the disrepair or perhaps because of it, I think, although I can imagine my mother's displeasure at the state of your garden.'

'I would be more than happy if you wish to oversee any repair, Lucinda.'

She laughed. 'Gardening being such a quiet and docile hobby…'

'At least it might stop you from galloping *ventre à terre*.'

She knew he would kiss her before he leaned over. She could see it in the way his face softened, humour changing to some other thing less discernible. As the wind lifted her riding skirt and blew the falling leaves into eddies around their feet, she simply closed her eyes and felt his warmth against hers and his solidness, his fingers on the skin of her arm, stroking down to catch her to him, no questions left. Just them with a beautiful horse standing behind, the yellow sandstone of the stables pitted with age and the peace of the early afternoon settling in.

This kiss was different from the one they had shared the night before. This kiss came with all the knowledge of what they both wanted—nay, what they needed from each other.

They came together with a hard edge of disbelief, thrown into a storm of movement, his hand around the back of her head, his body pressed against her own. This time she did not limit what she gave in return, her teeth biting down and tasting the power of abandon. She was not careful or circumspect or quiet. She was all woman released from the fetters of years of manners and demeanour that denoted a

Wellingham daughter, the expectations of society a distant and unpleasant memory.

She could no longer care. Her fingers wound through his hair as his tongue came inside her mouth, rough and urgent, no quiet asking in it as he held his hands on each side of her face.

This was what she wanted, the taking and taking, moulded into desire, the loss of self in a thrall that held no end. A moment or an hour? It was his choice. She would have lain down upon the grass beneath the roses if he had asked her, opening to him, accepting the roaring release of a womanhood for ever tied to agreements and conditions and plain cold reason. Respecting the fact that he was a man caught in the complexities of family and trying to make the best of it, she could deny him nothing.

Nothing. Her mouth widened as he came within, tilting her, his breath hoarse and raw, his thumb on the nape of her neck as she arched back and simply enjoyed.

He could not remember ever revelling in the company of another as much as he did his wife. He had never had a confidante before, a person who might guard his back against the world despite everything that was said of him. The wonder of it was humbling.

Lucinda kissed like the most skilled of all courtesans, allowing him things most ladies didn't, gentle softness dispensed with under a building and aching need. When her teeth came down on his lip he smiled, the pain of it inciting urgency as he took her breath into his own, swallowing her air and exchanging it for his. He bound her mouth in a tight seal of authority, pressing down so that she had to trust him. She did not fight, though her eyes flew open, watching, glazed into submission, waiting while he fed her breath.

He had never felt such a compelling insistence for any woman, not in all the years of his life enjoying the fruits of a reputation he had earned at the hands of parents who taught him not to care for anything or anyone. So very easy to take and to leave.

But with Lucinda there was a betrothal that was impossible to break before man and before God, the edicts written in the law of the land and handed down through many centuries of union.

Unions that produced the next generations, heirs who could hold the great estates in the palms of their hands and care for their longevity as no outsider would ever be able to.

His heirs. Their heirs. The children of Alderworth who would follow in his footsteps. An agreement bound by time and gold.

Breaking away from her, he ran his hands through his hair and swore. This was not how it was supposed to be, this desperate need to be inside her, a sense of for ever in his thoughts that was as scary as it was impossible.

No one had ever stayed at his side through thick and thin, through richer and poorer, through the vagaries of trouble and the inadequacy of laws. No one at all, save Lance Montcrieff, who had died trying to show him such friendship was possible even as the last piece of life had bled from him, warm on the dusty turnings of earth and in a land that was far from home.

His breath felt shaky and he turned from his wife's sky-blue gaze, not wanting her to see things he had shown to no one before. Give a little of yourself and be punished for it. Trust another and that emotion would be thrown back as corruption and abuse. Or loss.

After his grandmother's betrayal he had allowed his uncle to see his vulnerability when he had come to collect him from the hospital in Rouen. Then another sort of deception had begun, one worse than his grandmother's heavy hand, one wrapped in soft bare flesh and whispered words. It was then he had understood that love equalled pain and shame. When he had finally rid himself of his uncle's depravities he had found a different enjoyment of the flesh. One that required neither trust nor honesty. One that allowed him the freedom to move on from a woman before there was ever the chance of more than a way to pass the hours of his life, superficial, numerous and unimportant.

'I know there is a lot I need to learn about the art of kissing…?'

He stiffened as he faced her, hating the worry so evident in her voice.

'But I no longer wish to wait to make an heir. I want to know where a kiss like that one might lead to next, Taylen. I am twenty-seven years old and I do not wish for another single day to pass before I know.'

Raw and honest with her chest heaving, Lucinda reminded him of everything that was good in the world.

'Now?' He did not recognise his own voice.

She nodded, a small hint of nerves, but still she stood before him, unflinching.

Tay could not believe she might mean it and yet in the aftermath of their kiss his body had hardened and risen. He took the chance of waiting no longer by simply holding out his hand.

Her fingers laced about his own, intertwined.

'Come, then.'

Calling to his man to unsaddle Hades, he strode back through the gardens along the white shell paths, ten steps and then twenty, always assuming that she would pull away. She did not.

He walked through the main salon at the bottom of the house, the servants watching them, a strange juxtaposition of the normal and the absurd.

A bargain.

A payment.

An heir.

He had never felt as he did at that moment, leading his wife towards his bedchamber and knowing what would happen once they got there.

Mrs Berwick asked him a question and he answered, the warmth of Lucinda's fingers burning need into his soul. He saw his wife's eyes were lowered lest the truth of what lay inside was seen. Speaking in words that were empty, his mind replayed other words, stronger words, words that would change both of their lives for ever. He felt as if they were tied by a quivering single thread, its quicksilver need running through all the parts of him. Forcing him on.

Up the stairs they climbed, Lucinda's breath strained. Not from exertion, but from anticipation. He almost smiled then, although humour was far from what he felt.

Then through the door they went, the heavy oak of it shutting behind them and the locks turning. The noise elicited a small involuntary flinch from Lucinda, but she did not speak. Pocketing the key, he moved away, dropping the contact, needing the space. For the first time in a life filled with indulgence and dissoluteness he did not know where to begin.

His wife did it for him, undoing her jacket buttons one by one, her small hands mesmerising. The shirt beneath was of the finest linen, inset with lace, her flesh peeking through where the pattern of the stitches changed. He stepped forwards.

'Let me?'

She nodded, stood still as he drew her hair into his hands and released the mass of gold and wheat from restraint, running his fingers through the curls so that they were freed from the heavy chignon. He wanted to see her tresses against her pale skin, enveloping the curve of her breasts and hips. He wanted to lay her down upon his bed and mould the shape of her to his so that she would never forget him, marked and branded.

The racing beat of her heart belied the bravado she was showing him as he undid the small mother-of-pearl buttons that held the last of her bodice together.

He had done this before, in this very room three years ago, unlaced Lucinda and understood the beauty beneath the cloth, but this time was different. This time she was his wife, promised to him, bound in law and troth and honour.

Marriage. His parents had never venerated the spirit of such a union, but to him... He stopped.

Not empty words after all. The wedding ring he wore glinted in the light, catching gold.

'Only for an heir...?' She phrased this in a question, running her tongue around the dryness of her lips as her head tilted back.

Asking for more.

He pulled the cloth away and her breasts fell out into his gaze, then his hands lay across them, the fullness firm and pale.

Lust ruled now, heating blood, shallowing breath, raising skin. His mouth came around one rose-hued peak and he sucked, hard, the burn of want and need, the ache of completion, the trembling primeval blaze.

She groaned and he kneaded the other nipple, the thread between them snaking into hardness, snaring desire.

'Now.'

Her voice, and no longer a question. Raising his head, he simply picked her up, her bodice trailing downwards and the skirt she wore pulled up across his arms, the dainty beauty of her ankles and shins on show.

She did not fight him, but lay still as he placed her on his bed. No resistance. His hands came beneath her skirt, into the silk of her petticoats, under the thin nothingness of her drawers. Until only skin remained, thick and swollen and soft feminine skin, wet with her wanting.

'It may hurt, my love.' He had to warn her as he unbuttoned his trousers. She did not look at his nakedness, for her eyes were closed now, the quiet blush of need on her cheeks, the trembling, too, of something unknown. He wished he could find the words that she wanted him to give her, but the truth was more important.

'I need you, Lucinda. I need all of you.'

At that she opened her eyes, acquiescence and knowledge now in the blue as one arm reached out to caress the planes of his stomach before falling lower. An elemental virgin-siren, the release of her breath heard in the quietness, a thin line of beaded sweat on the top of her lips.

Kicking off his boots and trousers, he lifted her

skirt and opened her legs, the searing flesh of his manhood stilling as his fingers parted heat—balanced, waiting, poised on that moment of change that comes to every new bride.

Slipping inwards, driving hard, breaking flesh as she arched up to him, slick in the coupling. Her hands tried to push him away, her nails digging into his back, the terror of it written into one single keening cry. And then stillness as he waited, engorged, filling her, tightening, the deep pain of loving changing into a different consciousness.

Her breath came quick now, the dead weight of him pinning her down, unmoving.

'Wait, sweetheart.' It was all he could say. Wait until we become accustomed to each other. Wait until your body answers. Wait until the waves of response begin.

And then they did. A slight quiver of flesh, an easing, a softening, the first call of her body as she moved and allowed him a different access. Slowly. Out and in again. Deeper. Faster. Wider. Harder. Again. And again. He prayed that the pain was lessening and changing into some life-filled thrall that was indescribable and heightened. He knew that he had her when her hands came around his back and she held him to her as if she might never let him go.

She could neither breathe nor think. Every part of her was centred in the place between her legs where he was in her, joined by flesh, the hurt leaving now, not as ragged, and another pain building. A different pain. One that held her stiff and breathless, reaching for what was promised.

One that made her shake and groan and stretch as his movements quickened, needing the beauty of it, feeling the togetherness of what brought a man and a woman into a single person, nothing between them save the knowledge of each other. His breath against her throat, the movements faster now, reaching up and racing against hope and heat and desperate need.

And then a release, a melting ache of absolution quivering through the stiffness, widening and deepening, rolling across her stomach inside everything. She shouted out, her voice heard far away, the beaching waves unlike anything she had ever felt or known.

Lost in sensation. Adrift. Satisfied. Crying. Her tears hot on her cheeks and brushed away softly by a husband who had astonished her.

She heard the thundering of her heart inside her head, a languid lethargy in her limbs, the weight of Taylen and the heat of him drawing energy away.

Still joined. She could feel him twitch, the thick engorgement inside. Sweat ran through all the places between them.

'Thank you.' His words, caught between deep breaths.

Smiling, she closed her eyes, unable to say more, tears drying tight against her cheeks. She wanted to stay here just like this in the silence, wrapped inside each other's skin, the sun slanting across the room in a yellow curtain of light.

Heaven.

'I always wondered why my brothers were so… happy being married. Does everyone feel this?' She had to know, had to understand.

'No. My parents hated each other with a passion.'

'So they sent you away?' She watched him, his body bare in the light, the edges of the marks on his back creeping round on to his ribs. One finger traced a scar in wordless question.

'On occasion. And when I was here they ignored me,' he said, watching the ceiling, and Lucinda knew from the tone in his voice that the things he was thinking had been stored inside him for a long, long time.

'Lady Shields's maid said that you were in hospital in France?'

'In Rouen. My grandmother hurt me when we were on holiday there. I had asked one of her friends if I could live with them, you see, and she found out and was furious. But it was only after my uncle came to pick me up a good month later that I understood the true meaning of…brutality.'

He whispered the word, softly, anger leaving him stiff and motionless. 'My mother's brother decided I needed lessons in…obeying him and took such tutorship to heart.' He looked at her then full in the eyes, the torment of memory bright and fierce.

'I was twelve years old and my parents had both

died the previous summer. Twelve is no age to fight back, you see…and I couldn't. He…he…'

Shaking her head, she placed her fingers on his lips as if to stop what he might say next. 'I love you, Taylen. I love you because the things you have been through have made you who you now are. Strong. Certain. I think I must have always loved you, even then, when we first met, even without the memory of it.'

A single tear traced its way down the side of her face and he kissed it away before covering her lips and taking all that she said inside of him. Again.

Tay watched her as she fell asleep, lost safe in the arms of dreaming. Her lashes were long and curled, the tips dipped in lightness and even in slumber her dimples were still apparent. Three years of waiting for her and he had ruined it with his stupid truthfulness.

He slipped away from her body and sat on the bed, the blood of sacrifice easily seen on the top of his thighs.

How could she love him after the things he had told her? How could she find it in herself to do that? Maybe now it was possible in the first flush of passion, but tomorrow when the truth settled? What might happen then?

Every confessed word had been wrong and heavy and he swallowed twice, guilt rising with anger as he fumbled with the drawer to one side of his bed and extracted a hundred pounds.

Hers for the bargain.

He placed the notes carefully upon the counterpane and did not look back again as he stood to collect his garments and leave the room.

In the morning he rode to the home of Lance Montcrieff's wife a good five miles from Alderworth. He had installed Lance's widow in one of his smaller estates since his friend's death when she had been ousted from her home by the heir and had visited her a number of times since returning to England a month and a half ago. He knew that Elizabeth Montcrieff wanted more from him than he could give and part of the reason he needed to see her this morning was to put an end to the hopes of any type of relationship between them.

Lance had loved his wife, well and truly, and Tay knew that his friend would have wanted his family to be settled and secure. Without any other relatives to help her, he felt she was his responsibility.

The butler took him straight through into the library and he was greeted almost immediately by Elizabeth.

'I did not know you were coming this morning, Duke.' The velvet in her voice was smooth. On her lips was the lightest of colour. The heavy perfume she favoured filled the air between them.

'There is a chance of leasing a town house in London, Elizabeth. It is central and there is a school just around the corner suitable for the girls. I think you would be happy there with the chance of more society and a wider group of people to talk to.'

She watched him intently. 'I hear that your wife has arrived at Alderworth. It is the only topic of conversation one hears at the moment around here.'

Her brown eyes were resigned, her smile calm. She was not a woman given to histrionics and she was sensible enough to understand he did not wish for tears.

'I am sorry if I have given you any cause to think there could have been something more between us…'

'You have not, Duke. You have been most circumspect and generous.'

'It was Lance's final wish as he died. He made me promise to look after you, but life has changed and my wife is…' He stopped. What was Lucinda to him? A mother for his child? Or much, much more?

Her hand came down across his own. 'I understand. You have helped me with a home and a living, Duke, and for that I shall be for ever grateful. You have done your duty ten times over.' Unshed tears banked in her eyes. 'I could not have wished for a more thoughtful man in the face of my own loss and loneliness. I hope her Grace knows what a treasure she has in you.'

He smiled at her words. 'My lawyer says that you have not touched the money I deposited into your account.'

'I have not needed to. Everything has been provided for me here. But now…' She hesitated. 'Now I think I will repair to London and see what that town has to offer us. You have been more than generous and I will always be grateful.'

'Nay. It was Lance's share.'

She shook her head. 'I know the real money did not come in until after his death when you diversified into other areas. I am certain that you know that, too.'

Elizabeth Montcrieff had never looked so beautiful to him, a woman of honour and integrity. He hoped that she would find what it was she needed from London and that somewhere in the future he might bring Lucinda to meet her.

'There is one more thing,' he said as he turned to leave. Reaching into his pocket, he extracted the ring Lance had worn in Georgia and handed it to her. 'This should be yours.'

He laid the gold in her palm. *LM.* The initials of his first real friend. But now he had another. The thought came from nowhere, but the truth of it was undeniable.

Lucinda.

Suddenly exhaustion overtook everything. He wanted to be away from this house and out in the open again, feeling the wide space of freedom over his head and the chance of redemption in his heart. He couldn't go home, not just yet. He needed the hope of Lucinda's words for a while longer, unspoilt by the consideration that must blossom when she had time to think about all that he had told her.

Saying goodbye to Elizabeth, he rode for the village to buy a drink.

Chapter Fourteen

'His Grace has been called away to one of his other properties, your Grace.'

Mrs Berwick gave her the information as Lucinda came down to the dining room for breakfast.

'Did he say when he would return?' Lucinda kept her voice even and controlled, though her hand shook as she helped herself to bacon and eggs.

'No. He did not. Sometimes it is a few days before he is back, but this time…?' The housekeeper left the question unanswered.

'I see.'

And she did.

Taylen Ellesmere had run from Alderworth as fast as he had been able to even with her ill-given exclamation of love. It was the blood. Her blood. Her virgin blood of pure deceit. He had been trapped into a marriage, beaten by her brothers and forced into years in a far-off land with no hope of return and all because of lies. She knew that now, the proof of it on the bed sheets and in the soreness between her legs. He had never touched her there.

It was her husband who had held her neck still after the accident and made certain that the damage was not worse. She remembered that, too, the paleness of his face above her as he had strained to keep her immobile, the cold rain streaming down upon him and shattered glass in all of the broken and damaged lines of his skin.

Every single thing he had told her family had been true about the lack of relationship between them and she had sacrificed him because of it.

Only an heir. She understood the words now as she had not before. An heir from the only wife he was ever likely to have and all because of her lies. The notes on her bed when she awakened came to mind, spread out beside her. It looked a lot when counted in falsehoods.

But other thoughts also surfaced. The secrets that he had shared with her last night were not easy or small truths, the gift of confidence surprising and humbling. He had laid his soul at her feet even as anger had marked his eyes, brittle, shameful fury stained in green and he had not turned away when she said that she loved him.

One hand strayed to her stomach. *Please let his seed take. Please, please let a child grow.*

She prayed for that with all her heart.

She wanted him back. She wanted to tell him that

her lie had been sorely mistaken and that she was sorry. She wanted to hold him against the hurt of his youth, in her arms away from the loss of an innocence that should have been safeguarded.

But he would not come and the only companion left to her was the unkempt dog who followed her back to her room.

'I am not certain if you are allowed in here,' she said in the lowest of voices, for she had already seen the animal being shooed out a number of times today. Kneeling, she offered her hand to him and he sidled over, his tail fixed as it always was between his legs.

'Are you hurting?' The query had her placing her fingers upon the matted hoary coat and wondering what other care the animal had missed out on. Perhaps he was more like his master than she had originally thought, tossed out from home and beaten.

She reached for one of her brushes and began to try to untangle the knots. Surprisingly a coat that was both lighter and longer began to emerge, the dog looking more and more presentable with each stroke.

'Like a swan,' she said to him and laughed as he lay down, his body comforting against her own. 'If you were mine, I should call you Swan.'

The sudden and unexpected sounds of feet moving along the corridor outside made her stiffen as the door-handle turned. Her husband appeared, dressed in his riding cape with a hat in hand.

His eyes went to the dog, a frown lingering as he called to the animal. It stood instantly and walked across to stand beside him, the bony ridge of its back prominent.

'He followed me in here.' It was all that Lucinda could say, banal and hackneyed, she knew, but her tongue was tied and she could not decide how to greet him, a stranger who had been a lover and was now back in the guise of a man who looked…unknown.

Confusion and ire surfaced and as he came closer she scrambled upright. A strong perfume was evident on his clothes.

'Thank you for last night, Lucinda.'

Another flush of red crawled up into her face. If he would not castigate her over her mistake, then surely it behoved her to mention it.

'My memory was faulty after the accident in the carriage. I believed that you had…enjoyed more than I wanted to offer.'

'And now?'

'Now in the light of yesterday I can see that I was mistaken in my accusations.' She made herself hold his glance. 'It cannot have been easy to have had your reputation so unkindly maligned and for that I apologise.'

He smiled, his skin creasing at the corner of his eyes, an outdoor man, a man who did not bother too much with the fripperies of fashion. 'My reputation was maligned a long time before you added to it. What do you remember?'

'Running into your room. You were reading and

naked. I remember that clearly. Machiavelli in Italian? I thought you had kissed me?'

'I did.'

'I also think you might have touched me.' She raised a hand and placed it across her breast. 'Here.'

'That, too.' His right hand joined hers, cold from the morning outside. She shivered and his other fingers drew a line down her cheek. 'I touched you like this,' he offered, 'and like this,' he added, cupping the flesh under her bosom. Even through the material of her gown her blood began to pump.

'And I wanted you to?'

He nodded.

'You must have hated me then, after my brothers told you I had said that you ruined me?'

Only for an heir. Only for an heir.

'I do not hate you.'

'But the payment you left on the bed. Is that only what this is?'

He stopped her questions simply by holding her against him, tightly bound, his jacket sprinkled with rain and wet.

'Last night…the things I told you…' He stopped, holding her close with the dog around their feet. She could not see his eyes or his face, but she could hear the beat of his heart against her ear.

When he did not speak she began to. 'Everyone has their secrets, Taylen. I ran away with a man when I was seventeen. Emerald, my brother's wife, stopped me before I boarded a ship and married him. It would have been a huge scandal if anyone else had known.'

'But they did not?'

'My brothers hushed it up and nothing else was ever said. I saw him again about five years later and thanked the Lord that I had been caught.'

'That bad?'

'He became a dandy, a man who enjoyed puce waistcoats and powdered hair. I doubt he thought of anything else at all. Then when I was twenty-two I fancied myself in love with another swain who turned out to be married already and just wanted a… dalliance. He was Italian, you see, and had not mentioned his family circumstances.'

'How did you find out?'

'My brothers never liked him and they sent a runner to Rome. I cried for a week until I understood that it was my fault really that any of these things had happened. After that, until I met you, I was quite circumspect. And when you left after our wedding I was virtually a recluse.'

'I wrote to you three times from Georgia, but you never replied. Did Cristo not give you my letters?'

'He did, Duke, but all you talked about in them were the environs where you now found yourself and a duty message was not what I wanted at all. So I decided that it was in my best interests never to think of you again.'

'You did not think I would come back to you?'

Lucinda breathed out. Every day she had hoped

it. Every day she had held her breath and wondered would it be this day that Taylen Ellesmere might come home. To her.

The knock at her door had them both turning, however, as the butler appeared in the doorway.

'Mrs Moncrieff is here, your Grace, and it seems that one of her daughters has gone missing. I have placed her in the blue salon.'

'Thank you. I will come down.' Anxiety covered Taylen's words as he accompanied his servant from the room. Not knowing whether to follow or to stay, Lucinda hesitated and her husband was gone from her sight even as she tarried.

Montcrieff. Was that not the name of Taylen's partner in the gold mine in Georgia? Shutting the door behind her, she made her way down the stairs after them.

In the blue salon she found a beautiful woman weeping in her husband's arms, her head against his breast.

'Emily has not returned from the Partridges and I sent a servant for her but there was no sign at all. When you came to me, Duke, I think she overheard that we might be leaving Tillings and going to London and she has made friends here and did not wish to go.'

She burst into noisy sobs and Lucinda could only stand and watch the spectacle like an outsider. The same perfume that had hung heavily on her husband's clothes was in this room as well.

She could see both the lines of guilt on his fore-head and the familiar way the woman curled into his strength. Elizabeth Montcrieff wore his ring, too, she noticed, on the third finger of her left hand, the gold engraving glittering in the light.

Betrayal? Every part of her body wanted to deny what she was seeing, but she could not. Turning back to her room, she raced up the stairs as if a ghost was on her tail.

'I do not hate you.' He had said those very words not ten minutes before, but he did not love her, either. Not enough. For all his fine words, perhaps he was a cheat. A man with as many mistresses as he had years still to live; so many, in fact, that here was one straying into their very home, a demi-wife with his ring on her finger to prove the commitment.

She was glad for the key Taylen Ellesmere had given her and, locking her door against any intrusion, she tried to think of just exactly what she would do next.

Elizabeth held him as she might once have held her husband and as Tay tried to disengage her grip he saw a quick flash of a dark dress.

Had Lucinda come down the stairs behind him? Had she seen Elizabeth entwined about him and sobbing? Lord, if she had, she might imagine other things, too.

With a real effort he moved away from Lance's widow and poured her a brandy.

'Drink this. It will help.'

Thankfully she did swallow the draught without question and the tormented and hysterical crying stopped.

'If I have lost her, too…'

'You won't have. Emily will have gone to one of her friends' place to hide or to wait and see what you do as a result of it.'

Hope flared in dark eyes. 'You think she might have?'

'I do.'

The sobbing began again, quieter though now. 'She has been difficult since her father's death and I have not been as strong as I have needed to be.'

'Then take a lesson and begin in London, Elizabeth. The school there is a good one and the girls will have all the care and direction they require. A new start is exactly what you all need.'

'Could you come back to Tillings with me now and talk to her, when we have found her? She listens to you just as she used to listen to her father.'

Tay's heart sank. He knew that it would be dark before he could return home to Alderworth. He was also worried about Lucinda, but with a carriage waiting outside and an anxious mother inside he had no time to go upstairs and explain everything to her.

Tomorrow he would take his wife out riding and show her the estate. Perhaps if she was willing he could also take her back to his bedchamber and find the same magic that they had discovered last night.

* * *

It was already morning. Lucinda had fallen asleep fully dressed under the cover of a thick blanket that lay at the bottom of her small bed after waiting nearly half the night to see whether Taylen would return.

But he had not come home. He had gone with the beautiful dark-haired woman and as the hours had tumbled one across the other she knew that he would not be back. She felt sick with the implications of what that might mean.

Had he left again, this time with the full intent never to return? My God, her brothers had been right. Exactly right. She should have heeded their word and refused to accompany him to his estate. Once a snake, always a snake. Yet he hadn't been that at all. He had been honest and honourable. It had been her memory at fault and he was the one who had suffered.

A knock on the door had her sitting up, running the back of her hand quickly against her eyes and trying to place a smile where anguish had just been.

'May I come in? I have your breakfast tray.'

Scrambling up, Lucinda unlocked the door and a maid came bustling in with freshly baked rolls and a pot of tea.

'Mrs Berwick said I was to tell you that the master will be a-riding home this morning from the direction of the local village, your Grace. She said that the groom could find you a mount should you wish to venture out and meet him.'

The idea appealed. A ride might blow away the cobwebs Lucinda felt building and give her freedom to think. The added bonus was that meeting him out in the open would allow them to talk in private.

If she got one of the stable hands to show her the way she would not get lost and the weather outside looked finer than it had in weeks. When the dog came through the door she decided to take him, too, reasoning that the exercise would be good for the hound.

The horses standing in the stables were by and large older hacks, though one smaller filly caught her attention.

'What of that one?' she asked the stable boy. 'The roan mare at the end?'

'Her name is Venus. She's a mite skittish in temperament, though, for she came with his Grace's black as a pair and when Hades is gone she's apt to fret.'

The perfect ride, then. If she had any chance of meeting up with the returning Duke, the odds had just got better.

'Who usually takes her out?'

Silence told her that nobody did.

'I can saddle up a more docile horse if you would rather, your Grace.'

'No. This one will be fine.' Lucinda liked the lines of Venus and she felt desperate for a good long stretch. None of the other horses here looked as if they would give her any more than a slow canter.

With anticipation she mounted and was surprised by the docile way the horse allowed her a seat. The day was blue and it had been a while since she had sat on the back of a horse in the countryside and raced across the land, feeling the wind in her hair and liberty in her veins.

After all that had happened she needed to simply feel. The wonderment in such an unexpected loving still left every fibre in her body alive with promise and had her heart racing.

She had lain there when she had awoken and felt…different. A woman who understood exactly what it was that others spoke of in the hushed tones on the far side of rooms. Yet now with Taylen's absence everything had returned to only bewilderment.

Veering left at the main gate as the stable boy had directed, she allowed Venus her head, racing across the line of fence and bush with the sun on her shoulders. The silence of the place was absolute, the birdsong long since diminished and the day shaping up into a glorious one. The dog loped at her side in an easy gait.

At the top of the incline the lands of Alderworth spread out around her as a tableau and Lucinda wished she had brought her drawing things to capture such a view. Her eyes searched out the paths coming in from all directions, but there was nothing. Perhaps Tay had stayed on longer, lying entwined in the arms of the beautiful widow, and regretting the confidence he had allowed in his marriage bed.

A brace of loud shots had her turning as a group of men burst from the trees a good five hundred yards away.

Hunters. Lucinda felt the quiver of her horse's fright even before she bolted, whipping the reins from her hands and tearing off in the opposite direction from where they had appeared.

She could only hang on, her fingers entwined in the hair of the mane and her feet solid in the stirrups. A hundred yards and then two, the hilly terrain giving way to a long valley and trees. The branches whipped her face as she tried to stop, shouting at her horse to slow as hooves beat faster against the muddy ground. Then she was off, flying through the air with the rush of landscape beside her and down on to the slope of a gully. She might well have stopped if there had not been a disused well at the bottom, the slopes rolling into the mouth of it and over into darkness.

A good six feet down she clung to the roots of a tree and tried to force her body into the space between earth and wood. Already she felt sick, disorientated, dizzy. Pain brought her back to the moment and the last thing she remembered was the dog looking down before turning away from the gap in the sky, the sound of his panicked barking disappearing on the wind.

One of the lads came out to meet him as Taylen cantered in to the stables. He had left the village as early as he could and made excellent time back to

Alderworth. Looking at his timepiece, he saw it to be twenty minutes short of twelve. Emily had been reunited with her mother after a number of hours of searching and was suitably apologetic, though with a night behind him in the local inn Tay was glad to leave and head for home.

A sort of panic had gnawed at him for hours, the idea that something was not quite right pervading all his thoughts.

'Will you be joining her Grace out riding, your Grace?' The young stable hand's face was tinged with worry.

'The Duchess has taken out one of the horses?'

'Venus, your Grace.' A full frown now lingered on his forehead.

'You let her take Venus?'

'I offered her the choice, but she was most insistent. The stray dog went with her, your Grace, and I had the impression she hoped to meet you on the way.'

Tay scanned the hills behind Alderworth and the pathways to the front.

'What time did she leave?'

'Two hours ago, your Grace.'

'Saddle Exeter for me then, and see to Hades. I will be back in fifteen minutes ready to leave.' Dismounting, he took his leather satchel and hurried inside.

Mrs Berwick was in the kitchen when he found her and up to her elbows in flour.

Tay tried to temper his worry so as not to disturb his housekeeper, but he could hear it in his voice nevertheless as he asked his question.

'Did the Duchess tell you where she was going riding today, Mrs Berwick?'

'Towards the village,' the other answered quickly. 'I gave her the directions for the pathway you would take home and she rode out to meet you.'

A whining at the door stopped him and the dog came in, panting from its exertion. Relief budded for the stable hand had said Lucinda had left with this animal, so perhaps she had already returned. The arrival of the same lad a second later put paid to such a hope.

'Her Grace is still not back, your Grace. The dog came a few minutes ago and I thought she would follow. But nothing...'

Mrs Berwick was now wiping her hands off, a look of alarm spreading across her face. 'The weather is changing, your Grace. I think it will rain soon.'

'What was my wife wearing?'

'Her riding jacket and skirt. They looked both serviceable and warm.'

Almost three hours since anyone had seen Lucinda after she had left. Kneeling down, Tay lifted the front paws of the dog and saw the telltale red dirt of the hills to the east on his feet. He had not crossed a river then or the silt would have been washed away. The choices narrowed.

Venus was not an easy mount and the terrain became hillier past the track into the village. Other more sinister thoughts followed. Had Lucinda fallen and knocked her head? He distractedly swiped away his hair. The Wellingham physician had been most explicit about the consequences of such a mishap.

Half an hour later Tay rode across the land to the east calling Lucinda's name. Six Alderworth servants fanned out on horses all around him doing the same and at every pathway that dissected the main trail he sent a man off to see if she might have branched off. Forty minutes and then fifty went past, with not a stirring of anything untoward.

His hands gripped the leather reins as the thought of not finding her consumed him. He seldom panicked, yet here he was allowing ideas to come that took him to the edge of it.

If she had hit her head somehow... The warnings that Posy Tompkins had spoken of in the park had been specific. Even a little knock might do it...

His wife's soft honesty, her smell, the way she smiled at him and stood by him. The colour of her hair falling across his body, pale against the dark, a perfect match. He could not have just found her to lose her again. The dog ran next to him, easily stretching to the pace of his horse, as one by one the miles were swallowed up.

She was shivering and even that small movement dislodged dirt from the spaces between the timber, hurling them down the steep sides of the hole where they fell into water.

Fifteen feet, she reasoned.

Two hours at least since she had been here, the sky above darkened with rain. Her head ached with the fall.

'Please, God, don't let it end like this,' she prayed and then found herself shouting Taylen's name, as loud as she could manage again and again into the silence.

A spider startled her as it jumped on to her riding jacket. She had always hated insects, but as this one with its tiny spiky legs tiptoed up her sleeve, she felt strangely aligned with it, both of them down a hole in the cold and far from safety. She watched as it crossed to a leaf further away towards the light.

'Go well,' she whispered and watched as it spun a web and swung up to another twig and then another. If only she might do the same, she thought, but her hand could not reach the branch above and the lip of the well on the other side was just too far away with skirts to hinder her.

Her throat was scratchy from shouting and her only hope of rescue lay in Dog. *Please let him have gone back to Alderworth,* she prayed. *Please let him bring help.* Her husband would come, she knew he would, and surely at the house the alarm must have already been raised.

But what if he did not come by dark? The thought crept into panic, stuck down here amongst what was left of the old tree roots. What would crawl out when the sun set and the moon rose and the cold of the night became apparent?

Again she shook away such thoughts. She was a Wellingham and she was strong. A little dark and cold could not hurt her and spiders did not bite.

She would sing, that is what she would do. She would sing and sing until they came, with her rusty voice and her lack of tune and her spirits would be raised. Sound would echo from the hollow stone and if Taylen was somewhere nearby he must surely hear it.

A sea shanty he remembered on the ship back from the Americas rang out around the small glade that Tay had followed Dog down to and he tilted his head to ascertain the exact direction.

Oh Blow the man down bullies, blow the man down,
Way, hey, blow the man down…

Lucinda. She was alive. He did not question the pure ache of relief as he dismounted and ran to an old disused well on the side of a hill.

Not wishing to scare her by suddenly appearing, he chanted the next line of the words back to her loudly.

A pretty young damsel I chanced for to meet…

The only sound then was that of sobbing, heart-broken wailing that had him lying across the edge of the opening.

When he looked down fear caught in his throat.

His wife was positioned precariously and the only thing allowing her any purchase was an old rotten tree that had fallen over, creating a makeshift ledge.

Nothing looked stable or safe.

'I think the bough beneath me will break if you come down here,' she said, her voice strained and hoarse as she tried to contain her crying. Even as she said it more dirt dribbled down the wall to be lost in the darkness of the bottom. A splash told Tay that water lay below. 'There are spiders here, too. At first I did not mind them, but now...' She stopped, giving the impression she had made herself do so.

'Stay very still, then. Don't move at all.' He glanced around for something to tie a rope to and found it in the trunk of another tree.

'No. If you fall...'

'Then we both go,' he replied, and across the rain and the dirt and in the space of eight feet their eyes caught, saying things to each other that they had not been brave enough to voice as yet.

'Is she your mistress?' Her quiet words were lost in worry.

'Who?'

'The woman I saw you with in the downstairs parlour?'

'Elizabeth Montcrieff. She was Lance's wife, my

partner in the gold mine in Georgia. I have been helping her financially.'

'But the ring you were wearing was on her wedding finger?'

'Because it once belonged to her husband and I gave it back to her. That was all.' Her chin wobbled and he saw her swallow, but another falling piece of the ledge brought them back to the present danger. 'Don't move while I get the rope and push yourself to the very back so that I can come down to you.' The dog ran in circles around the top of the well, barking wildly.

A moment later he had the lifeline fastened and started to climb down the side of the drop. When he reached Lucinda he simply laid his arms about her and held her close. She was cold, her teeth were chattering and her hair was plastered to her head with the rain. It felt so good to hold her and cast away all the nightmare thoughts he had had on the ride here.

'It will be all right, sweetheart. Here, grab the rope and I will push you up.'

He took both her hands and guided them about the thick plait of jute. 'Don't look down. As I push you need to pull as hard as you can and try to scramble up on the rope. When you get to the top, find the tufts of grass and heave yourself over. Do you understand?'

She nodded.

'Are you ready?'

She nodded again.

Making a stirrup with his hands, he got her to

place her boot upon it before bringing it up as far as he could go. 'Can you see the edge?'

He felt her flurry of movement though he could not look up, his face jammed against the earth and his breathing heavy. Then the weight was gone, her boots disappearing as she levered herself across the mouth of the hole, a few errant stones coming down upon him and stinging his back.

She was safe. Lucinda was safe. He thanked the Lord for her deliverance just as the ledge crumbled away completely and he disappeared into the blackness of space.

Chapter Fifteen

Taylen was gone. The rumble of earth had taken him to the bottom, the tree he was jammed in against disappeared with him, leaving only emptiness where a second before he had stood.

There was no reality to it, no recognition of the horror of it all, only an aching searing loss that had Lucinda lying down on the grass and screaming out his name.

She could just make him out at the bottom of the hole, partly buried beneath a pile of rocks and dirt, his head turned downwards. Thankfully the width of the old tree had missed landing on him and lay at an angle to one side. Grabbing the rope, she measured the full length of it and determined it finished a few yards from the bottom. Could she get down there or would she dislodge more of the crumbling walls and damage him further? The rain solved the question completely as she saw the water running in a steady stream. He would drown if she waited too long.

Removing her stockings and boots, she tied hooped knots all the way along the stem of the rope in the way her brothers had shown her how to do so many times in her youth. Coiling the rest of the line, she then threw it over the edge, watching as it swung heavily against the side of the well. Would it hold? The tree Taylen had fastened it around had not moved at all and the anchor looked well fashioned. Fear made her sweat, the close cloying air in the hole would be even worse at the bottom and she could not see how she might be able to climb out carrying him. She would be stuck there again until help came.

Swallowing away panic, she took a deep breath before making two good tight fists and levering herself over the side, the knots and their hoops allowing both her fingers and toes a good grip as she descended.

It was easier than she thought and within a few moments she was at the bottom of her lifeline. It was a few feet short and, letting it slip from her hands, she dropped the rest of the way to land on her feet to one side of Taylen, the mud slithering between her toes and the water icy cold.

He was still alive when she touched him, still breathing as she sat to take his head carefully upon her lap, away from the water.

'Please, please be safe,' she whispered, the echo of it hollow in the depth of the earth. Blood dribbled down his face from a cut on his brow and there was a large swelling at the crown of his head. Reaching for the hem of her riding skirt, she wiped at his cheeks, the red and brown of blood and mud strangely mixed, and his skin pale beneath their hues.

Her brothers had bought her a gift of inestimable value, a man she could respect and admire and adore—a man who had risked his life to save hers and who now lay unconscious as payment for his valour.

Already the sun had fallen, daylight leached from dusk, the long shadow of night upon them. Holding him closer, she tried to impart some of her warmth into his cold, her fingers tracing the shape of him in the darkness.

He was hers and she would protect him. At Alderworth now the alarm would surely have been raised and help would be coming.

The sounds of others came quietly at first and then more loudly, the length of rope trailing above twitching and raised. She could see nothing now, the black complete.

Then there were more voices, men's voices. She recognised some of the tones of the Alderworth servants as another line dropped down beside her. A thicker rope this time and longer.

When a figure came from out of the gloom she could only watch, scared to move in case she hurt Taylen further.

A tinder flared and then there was light, a face outlined by the flame. He pulled three times on the rope and another one dropped, a man she did not recognise at all on the end of it. In his hands was a long roll of heavy calico, the ends tied to folded poles of wood.

'Briggs, your Grace. The dog led us here. Has he woken at all?'

She shook her head in answer.

'The doctor has been summoned and will be at the house by the time we are back with him.'

Laying the fabric of the stretcher to one side, they pulled the contraption into a narrow bed. The mud and water had soaked through the canvas even before they lifted Taylen slowly on to it. The pain must have leaked into his unconscious mind for he groaned, the ache in his voice making Lucinda grimace.

'Be careful,' she pleaded as the stretcher was hoisted, one foot up from the ground and then two, both men steadying an end each as they all rose, the eerie shadows of the torches showing up broken patches of the sheer earthen walls.

She was the only one left down here now, and she got to her feet unsteadily after such a long time sitting, the stretcher disappearing over the top of the lip in a calm and easy way.

Safety. Lucinda could almost taste the relief of it. The dog was barking and more lights above took away the gloom. She could make out the flares against the black sky as another figure descended.

Briggs again and holding the rope she had fashioned into foot and finger holds out to her.

'I will come up beside you, your Grace. Just hold on and they will pull you up.'

A moment later jostling hands helped her over the top and she was once again standing in open air, the huge blackness of sky above her, a few stars twinkling through the gaps in the clouds.

Taylen lay motionless, his cheeks pale and the dark runnels of dried blood powdered on his temple. He barely seemed alive, though when Lucinda laid her hand against his he tried to turn and say something. His green eyes were lost in the swollen bruising.

'You are safe now,' she said. 'There will be no more pain, I promise.' As if he understood his eyes closed of their own accord and he breathed out, heavily.

The blankets covering him were thick and warm and Lucinda felt someone place another one across her shoulders. When a cart was drawn into place a few yards away she watched as more blankets were laid down on the floor as a cushion to transport her husband back to Alderworth.

Swan the dog crawled in beside him.

'The Duke will need complete rest and quiet,' the doctor proclaimed as he regarded Taylen a few hours later. 'He has had a nasty knock to his head and concussion has resulted. From my experience with similar cases it may be a week or so until he comes to his senses, for Briggs told me it was at least twelve feet to the bottom of the well.'

The Ellesmere physician stood to one side of the bed as he stated his findings, a passionless man with little in the way of a comforting bedside manner.

'But he will recover?' Lucinda asked the question with trepidation, for Taylen was looking worse and worse as the hours marched on.

'The brain has its own peculiar timings and reasons to stay inactive; some people come back to consciousness very quickly, others languish on the netherworld for weeks or months or even years. Some stay there for ever. It is God's will. Talk to him. Tell him all the news of the house. There is a new school of thought gaining traction that says those in a deep coma are none the less aware of things about them if they have a constant source of translation from a loved one.'

A loved one? Did she qualify as that or would any interaction between them make him even worse?

'If you need me in what is left of the night, send a messenger. Otherwise I will return tomorrow afternoon to see how my patient is progressing.'

Then he was gone, Taylen lying still and Mrs Berwick fussing about with the sheets at his side.

'Are you certain you do not wish me to stay, your Grace?'

Lucinda shook her head, not trusting herself to speak and when the woman finally took her leave she sat on a chair beside her husband and reached for his hand. The nail on his right thumb had been pulled off and there were cuts across the fingers. 'If I could heal you, my darling, I would,' she murmured, tucking the blanket in further and dousing the candles so that only one still blazed, protected by a glass cover as a precaution against fire.

She watched him as the sun appeared above the hills that she held no name for, the horizon aglow with pink and yellow. She watched the rise and fall of his breath, too, and the pulse in his throat where the stubble of a twelve-hour growth darkened his skin.

His chest was bare and she could just make out the tail end of the scars by his neck where the marks had curved around from his back and licked at the sensitive folds of his throat.

Hurt by life and by his family, and then censured by society and tossed out of England all because of her lies. And all the time he had stood up to her brothers with the knowledge of what he had not done. Halsey, too. The broken ribs and the ruined face. Nobody had ever believed in him and loved him as they should have.

Nobody until now. Her grip tightened.

'I love you, Taylen. I love you so much that it hurts.' She hated the tears that were gathering in her eyes. 'If you die I don't know what I will do because there is nobody else who understands me, who makes me feel…perfect.'

Not flawed, not foolish, not merely pretty, but beautiful and strong and completely herself. Finally after all these years she knew what she had been missing, a friend, a lover, a man who might sacrifice his life to save her own.

Anger came next and she shook his hand before holding it to her lips. 'Don't you dare leave me, Taylen, because if you do I will kill you, I swear that I will...'

'Water?' The voice came croaky and deep as dark-green eyes found hers, dazed with the strong painkillers. She could not quite believe that he was conscious.

'You can hear me?'

He nodded. 'You were...threatening me.'

'And loving you.' She had to say it, had to make him understand.

'That, too.' The creases around his eyes deepened.

'For ever. I will love you for ever.' She did not try to stop the tears now as they fell in runnels down her cheeks.

Tipping his head, she offered him a drink of boiled water from a jug, careful to give only small sips in the way that the doctor had directed.

Pain scrawled deep lines into his face and he grimaced as he tried to move.

'You have a bad bump to the head and your ankle is sprained. The doctor says you are to stay very still. He will be pleased to know you have woken.'

'How...long?'

'Just a few hours. It is five o'clock in the morning and they brought you to Alderworth last night after eleven.'

Reaching for her hand, he held on.

'Don't go.'

Before she could even answer he had fallen back to sleep.

Everything hurt. His head and his eyes and his neck. He had a tight bandage wound around the top of his forehead and a flickering light had been left beside him.

Lucinda—his last moments of seeing her safe, climbing up the rope from the well at the bottom of the Thompson's Ranges. She had spoken to him some time later in the cold and the mud and then again somewhere else.

Here. His bedroom. A small hand entwined in his own. Warmth and hope and safety, her breathing even and deep beside him and the moon waning towards the dawn. Home. With his wife. Closing his eyes again, he fell asleep.

Asher Wellingham was there when he next woke up, stretched out on a chair, his long legs before him. Lucinda had gone. He felt around for her with the hand that she had held and found the bed empty.

It was almost noon because the sun was high and the shadows at the window folded down on to one another. The blue openness of sky through the drawn curtains hurt his eyes with its brightness.

'You saved Lucy and put your own life at risk. I want to thank you for that. If you had not come when you did…' He stopped, regrouping emotion before beginning again.

Seeing him awake, Asher spoke, as if his message was urgent. 'Lucinda has told us that she was mistaken about her allegations of intimacy with you at Alderworth three years ago. We had you thrown out of England on a lie, Alderworth, and you would have good reason to hate us.'

All these words at once, Tay thought, tumbling into the air around him. Where was his wife? He wanted her back.

'Lucinda?'

'She has slept beside you for the past three nights since the accident. We all thought it was time she looked after herself and took a break, though I should imagine she will be back before the clock strikes the next part of the hour. It seems she cannot stay away.'

Exhaustion hammered at Tay like a mallet and he let his eyes close.

The next time he awoke it was night and Lucinda was there, watching him.

'Welcome back.' Her smile was shy and her hair was loose, dancing in pale waves across her shoulders and down her back.

'Beautiful.' And she was, in every single way that he might imagine.

'Thank you for saving me, Taylen.' Her fingers traced the lines of a scratch across the back of his hand as though measuring the hurt. 'If you had not come…'

He stopped her. 'But I did.'

Tonight the world was sharper, less hazy. He could even lift his head from the pillow and it did not ache.

'How many days?'

'Four.'

He brought up his free hand to feel the bandage.

Memories. After Rouen. A small child without a hope in hell of protecting himself.

Lucinda knew everything hidden and still loved him?

A bunch of wildflowers sat in a vase opposite the bed, and for the first time ever the bile did not rise up in Tay's throat as he thought of his uncle. It was over, finished, and there was all of the future to look forward to. The peace of it made him smile as he spoke. 'You look happy.'

'I am. With you here next to me and a whole night of just us. Ashe also sat with you each time that I did not. Taris came, too, and Cristo. They all hope you can forgive them.'

This time he laughed. 'Forgive them for forcing you upon me? Forgive them for making my life… whole?'

Catching her hand, he brought it to his lips and

noticed an injury on the top of her knuckles from the fall. Further up on her wrist an older scar from the carriage accident lingered. He wanted to wrap her in his arms and keep her close.

When she lay down beside him to sleep he knew that he would never be lonely again.

They were all in the Alderworth dining room at the end of dinner, celebrating the first time that Taylen had been able to come downstairs unaided.

A week since he had fallen down the well. Lucinda thought it seemed like a lifetime ago.

Everyone was present, her brothers and their wives and Posy.

Cristo made certain that a comfortable chair was angled in the best way for Tay to sit in and Asher got him a drink. It was strange to see her brothers fussing over a man they had hated not so very long ago.

When Taris raised his glass he gave a toast. 'Here is to you, Taylen, and a warm welcome to our family. The beginning may not have been exactly comfortable, but we have many years now to make up for it.'

Tay smiled and took Lucinda's hand. 'Without your…help—' he gave the word the inflection of a question and everybody laughed '—I may not have found my wife.' He raised his own glass now and looked directly at her. 'To you, Lucinda, and to family.'

His green eyes brimmed with a happiness that softened the lines in his face. To Lucinda he looked the most beautiful man in the world, her man, and a husband who made her feel strong and real.

Intrinsically flawed? No, she felt far, far from that.

'To life and to laughter,' she toasted in return and looked around the table at the smiling faces as she held up her glass.

Happiness was a feeling that was almost physical. Emerald's jade talisman was warm in her palm and she knew for certain that she would ask Emerald if she could give it to Posy, who sat next to her with a look on her face that she thought might have been her own a few months back.

An observer of life, but wanting so much more.

'Has your memory returned fully yet, Lucy?' Beatrice asked the question.

'It hasn't. But there are new memories now which have replaced those old ones.'

'Then let us drink to that.' Cristo stood and poured fresh brandy into all the glasses. 'But be warned, Duke, once a Wellingham, always a Wellingham. Eight of us now and that is not counting any of the children.'

Lucinda's eyes met her husband's. Children. How she hoped that the time would come when she held the heir of Ellesmere safely in her arms.

Chapter Sixteen

London—three months later.

Tay had always hated these big society events for all of the falseness and the inherent censure within them. As the Duke of Alderworth he had been invited because of his title, but the *ton* had tiptoed around him, feared him, he supposed, and worried about what he might do or say next, every new and over-exaggerated myth that had built up around him adding to their trepidation.

An outsider. A Duke asked because it was harder to leave him out, such a slight a reminder of how far the Alderworth star had indeed fallen. Oh, granted, there were those amongst the *ton* who would gravitate to him, but they were often men he felt no true communion with or else young bucks satisfying their first urges to kick the traces and to irritate their more-than-disapproving families.

But tonight with the lights of the chandeliers full upon him and a dozen of the Wellinghams around him it was different. Every eye in the place might be turned towards their party, but the usual alarm that prickled inside him on entering such a salon was missing.

Safety. Belonging. The feel of his wife's hand tucked through the crook of his arm and her oldest brother beside him.

'A smile might persuade those who are here to criticise you to do otherwise, Tay.'

'You think it that easy?' Months of getting to know Asher Wellingham had brought them together as friends.

'The *ton* revolves around a large measure of deceit. Surely you have learned at least that?'

Such an answer did make it easy to smile, to simply laugh at all the implied deceit and make use of it. Taylen saw Taris smile, too, his wife, Beatrice-Maude, beside him in the company of Cristo, Emerald and Eleanor. Asher's friend, Jack Henshaw, also lingered amongst them, Posy Tompkins on his arm and dressed in the most absurdly expensive gown, the diamonds on the cloth glittering in the light. The plain jade pendant she had around her throat seemed very out of place in the ensemble and Tay remembered seeing the piece around Lucinda's neck and wondered.

Altogether they made up a high-ranking and prominent group and although the power of money and title was behind them, it was something much more than that again that made Tay's heart swell with pride.

Respect was something he was not used to, but it came tonight in waves from those who watched them, the consequence, he supposed, of the years of good works and care of others the Wellinghams had been involved in. And he belonged, not in the game room amongst the card sharps and the drunken care-for-nothings, but here in the bosom of the protective custody of the Carisbrooks. One of them. For ever.

His hand tightened on his wife's. 'Can I reserve every single dance, sweetheart?'

'I have already pencilled you in, Tay.'

In a light gold dress Lucinda looked unmatchable, her hair wound into curls and the *décolletage* on her dress showing off the creamy skin of her breasts.

'Should your bodice be quite so revealing?'

She simply laughed. 'This from a man who insists I come naked to bed every night?'

'There it is only us, but here...' He looked around. A good percentage of the men in the room had their eyes fastened upon his wife and he knew exactly why. It was the joy that seemed to well up in Lucinda like a fountain, spilling around her as laughter and honesty and delight. And there was something else that only he was privy to, a wild and wonderful se-cret that had not yet been told to anyone, save him.

They would have a child in less than six months,

and there had been no payment except for love involved in its conception.

His whole being filled with a feeling that almost frightened him with its intensity and yet when he looked at Taris and Ashe and Cristo he saw the same desperation in their eyes, too. Men made whole by their women and astonished by the fact over and over again.

'How many hours until we can be back in our bedchamber?' he whispered and saw the flush of pleasure stain her cheeks. God, he loved her puritanical bent because it was so much fun dismantling it every single night.

'Five waltzes at least, Duke,' she replied, knowing how he enjoyed holding her close to feel the slight swell of her stomach between them. Three months along. The newest Ellesmere. Another Wellingham. A cousin for all the numerous children who ran and laughed in the great estates of Falder and Beaconsfield and Graveson. Another belonging. More protection. A tight circle of safe-keeping.

Like an onion, he thought, and Lucinda was his very centre.

A soulmate. He had never expected one, never believed that after all he had been through he might find such paradise.

Tripping as he walked, he clutched at the stick he needed to use now, a reminder not of his infirmity, but of their survival.

Asher's arm came out and steadied him. 'If you get tired, we can go home.'

Tay knew Asher hated these large gatherings and smiled at the hope in his voice. 'I have promised your sister that I will dance with her.'

'You feel up to it?'

'My balance is getting better with each passing week. Doctor Cameron said that soon there will be only a little of the vertigo left.'

'A lucky escape. It could have been so much worse.'

'Lucinda could have fallen instead of me.' Taylen had relived this horror during so many nights that the dread of it was like a familiar stranger walking with him.

'No, I meant for you, Tay. You could have died.' Amber eyes looked grave.

'But instead I found everything I was looking for.' He gestured to Lucinda and to the Wellingham family all about him.

'And as Cris said, once we claim someone we keep them for ever.' Taris added this from behind, and laughter accompanied the group as they walked on to the overcrowded dance floor.

A few hours later Lucinda and Tay lay in bed with moonbeams across their bodies and the winds off Hyde Park making the trees sway as shadows on their walls. Swan the dog lay in his own bed of fur by the window, tucked into sleep. He accompanied them everywhere now, his fearful demeanour changed to one of contentment.

'I love you,' Lucinda said softly to her husband, her fingers moving across the skin of his chest and feeling his heartbeat strong and even.

'And I love you back,' he replied, the smile in his voice bringing her in further. It was colder tonight and he always felt so very warm. 'When I found you at the Croxleys' ball and offered you money for a legitimate Ellesmere heir, I did not realise that it was my heart I was giving away instead.' He stilled her hand. 'You have it all, Lucinda, every piece of my love and if anything was to happen to you...'

'It won't.' She turned over and lay across him, his face within the veil of her hair and his worry vanished to be replaced by a look that simply took her breath away.

'That first time when you came to my room at Alderworth I thought...' He stopped and swallowed. 'I thought that you might be the one to save me and I was right, sweetheart.'

'We saved each other, Taylen, and this child shall be the beginning of a whole new dynasty of Ellesmeres.'

Turning her beneath him, his lips came down across her own, all the magic that she had felt from the very first second of meeting him beginning over again.

* * * * *